THE
DEAD
KEY

THE
DEAD
KEY

D. M. PULLEY

fTHOMAS & MERCER

MYSTERY
PAL

This is a work of fiction. Names, characters, organizations, places, events, and incidents are either products of the author's imagination or are used fictitiously.

Published by Thomas & Mercer, Seattle

www.apub.com

Amazon, the Amazon logo, and Thomas & Mercer are trademarks of Amazon.com, Inc., or its affiliates.

ISBN-13: 9781477820872
ISBN-10: 1477820876

Library of Congress Control Number: 2014946857

Printed in the United States of America.

Thank you, Irv, for holding my hand
every step of the way. You said it best:

*Our love is an endless course
And I am the runner, euphoric.*

PROLOGUE

Midnight fell at the First Bank of Cleveland with the lonely clang of the great clock in the lobby. Its dull ring wandered past the heavy doors and empty chairs of the banking floor, down the hallway to the dark room where she hid. It was the first sound she'd heard in an hour besides the whisper of her own breath. It was her cue.

She eased the door to the ladies' room open and peered out into the darkness. Down the gloomy corridor and into the banking room, long shadows slashed across the floor, making familiar daytime objects sinister. Someone was watching—the night guard, her boss, someone—she was sure of it. There was always someone watching at the bank. She stood frozen in the doorway, knowing what would happen if she was caught. She would be arrested. She would be fired. She would lose everything. But then again she didn't have much to lose. *That's probably how he talked me into this mess,* she thought, shaking her head. She couldn't believe she'd agreed to go through with it. But she had. After a full minute, she stepped out of her hiding place and let the door swing shut behind her.

Her tiny footsteps clacked on the stone slabs of the banking floor, rippling through the silence. Wincing, she tiptoed past the teller booths and into the lobby. The large clock ticked out the seconds as she crept by the revolving doors and floor-to-ceiling windows that separated her from the dark night outside. The headlights of a large sedan caught her through the glass as it turned down Euclid Avenue from East Ninth Street. Frozen, she didn't breathe until the car had passed. When it finally did, a low whimper escaped her throat. She wanted to run back to the bathroom and hide there until morning, but she kept going. He was waiting for her.

The watchful portrait of the bank president, old Alistair Mercer, glared at her as she slipped under him and down the corridor to the left. There was no sign of the security guard at the elevator desk. It was just as he promised.

The street lights streaming through the lobby windows faded as she made her way around the corner and down the winding stairs into the darkness below. Somewhere down there he was waiting. With each step, she gripped the brass key tighter, until it felt lodged in her fist. She had stolen it from the safe the day before, hoping no one would notice. No one did.

No one had noticed when she hadn't left with the others at five o'clock. The guard had snapped off the light in the ladies' room without even checking the stalls. He had been right about everything so far.

The still air seemed thicker when she reached the bottom of the stairs. The red carpet had disappeared in the blackness, but she could tell by the cushion beneath her feet it was still there. She pictured the door to the vault and made her way silently across the floor. Her heart pounded in her ears as she strained to hear the sound of a flashlight clicking on, a ring of keys rattling, or the dull thud of heavy footsteps. There was nothing. Slowly adjusting to the dark, she could just make out the clerk's desk in the corner. It was a black barricade guarding the entrance to the vault. She hurried over to it, crouched down behind the counter, and waited.

When nothing happened, she slipped open the drawer to the left of the chair and blindly felt the objects inside until she found the one she wanted. It was another key. As she straightened up, a hulking shadow loomed over her. She opened her mouth to scream. A large hand clamped down.

"Shh!"

The leathery palm crushed her lips, smothering her voice. Her flailing arms and fists were bound up in the shadow's grip. She was caught.

"Hey, it's me! It's all right. It's all right. Sorry I scared you. You okay?"

Her straining muscles went limp at the sound of his voice. She nodded and nearly crumpled to the ground. His hand was still over her mouth.

"Did you get it?" he asked.

She nodded again.

"Good." He released his hand so she could breathe. "Come with me."

He grabbed her wrist and led her through the round doorway and into the vault. She couldn't see a thing, but she could tell by the sound of their footsteps on hard metal exactly where they were.

"Okay." He flipped on a small flashlight and scanned hundreds of tiny metal doors lining the steel walls. "We're looking for Box 545."

The wall of boxes was a dim blur. Her heart still racing, she stepped toward them with a key in each hand. Gothic script labeled the metal doors with rising and falling numbers in an overwhelming array, until the one that read "545" finally emerged. She slipped each key into the door and waited a beat. Any minute she expected to see a security guard or police officer appear with gun drawn.

He pressed his barrel chest against her back, circling an arm around her waist. She closed her eyes and leaned against him, wishing they were back at her place or the hotel or anywhere but the vault. His breath was hot against her neck.

"Come on, baby. Let's see what we got."

The little door swung open, revealing the long metal box inside.

Bile rose up in her throat. This was breaking and entering, grand larceny, fifteen to twenty years at least. In her whole life, she'd never even stolen a pack of gum. Breaking into the vault had always been the plan. He had explained it to her many times. But now that she was actually doing it . . . Oh Lord, she was going to throw up.

He pushed past her, oblivious to the stricken look on her face, and pulled the safe deposit box out of its vault and set it onto the floor with a loud clunk.

She flinched.

"Relax, babe. Charlie's taking a break. He won't be back for at least an hour. Got him a date with a friend of mine."

He chuckled under his breath as he flipped open the lid. Stacks of hundred-dollar bills lined the top of the box. Beneath the cash lay a large diamond necklace. He reached up and smacked her on the ass triumphantly.

"Ha! Didn't I tell ya? Jackpot!"

Her eyes widened at the sight of the enormous stones. *It doesn't belong to anybody anymore*; she silently repeated the words he had said many times. *No one will ever miss it. No one even knows it's here.* Kneeling down, she reached out a shaking hand to touch a diamond.

He snatched the necklace away and pulled a velvet bag from his coat pocket. "Grab that box," he ordered. "I bet it's a ring, but don't get any ideas, eh?"

"Ideas?" she whispered, only understanding his meaning after the word left her lips and she had opened the tiny box. Inside it lay an enormous diamond engagement ring.

"Hey, that's nothing compared to the one I'll get you someday, gorgeous." He brushed the side of her face and winked. The metal of his wedding band left a cold trail down her cheek.

He grabbed the box from her and stuffed it into the bag and began counting the cash. The laugh lines around his eyes deepened as the total grew higher and higher. They had never discussed how much was enough.

She tore her eyes back to the molested box on the floor. An old black-and-white photograph was hidden beneath the cash and jewelry. It glowed yellow in the faint light. It was a tintype of a beautiful young woman in a floor-length dress wearing the diamond necklace. It could have been a wedding picture, she realized, and then she noticed the other items—a lace handkerchief, a few folded letters. Love letters, she mused, and wondered for the first time about the person who had placed them there. From the look of the parchment and the photo, it might have been fifty years ago. She reached in to pick one up.

"Hey! Are you daydreaming over there? We don't have all day." With that, he snapped the lid to the box closed and hauled it back up and into its place.

The sound of the metal door closing brought her back to her feet. She obediently turned each key, relocking Box 545. Pausing at the door, she felt she should say a prayer or something. It was like a burial. *Would anyone ever find the photo of the woman again? Or her love letters?* According to the records, the box hadn't been opened in years. The number stared back at her.

"Okay! On to Box 547."

"Right. 547." Her voice sounded far away. It was all a strange and terrible dream. This wasn't a vault, it was a mausoleum. And they were grave robbers.

The keys found and unlocked 547 as if they had a mind of their own. He deposited the looted treasure into the empty box and closed up the hole in the steel wall that now hid their terrible secret. She removed the keys. They were heavy in her hand.

He grabbed her by her narrow shoulders and planted a huge kiss on her lips. "Just you wait, baby! We're going to be set for life. A few more months of this, and we'll never have another care in the world." He kissed her again and squeezed her ass, before pushing it gently out the door.

He didn't notice her staring down at the swell in her belly as he led her out of the vault. It would be impossible to hide it much longer. But in a few more months they would be together, she told herself. Set for life. Just like he promised.

She paused at the entrance. Box 545 was still somewhere back there in the dark. She whispered to no one, not even herself, "I'm sorry."

Then the heavy round door swung shut.

CHAPTER 1

Saturday, August 8, 1998

Iris Latch sat up with a jolt. The clock was beeping frantically. It was 8:45 a.m., and she was supposed to be downtown in fifteen minutes. *Shit.* The alarm had been sounding off for a half hour straight. It was practically rattling the rickety walls of her apartment, but somehow she'd managed to sleep through it. She untangled herself from the sheets and rushed to the bathroom.

No time for a shower. Instead, she splashed cold water on her face and scraped the taste of dirty ashtray out of her mouth with a toothbrush. Her stringy brown hair didn't even get brushed before being yanked through a rubber band. She threw on a T-shirt and jeans and ran out the door. On a good day, Iris looked fair to attractive, with her lanky, tall frame and long hair, especially if she remembered not to slouch, but this was not a good day.

The morning sun shined in her eyes like an interrogation light. Yes, she'd been drinking last night, Officer. Yes, her head hurt. No, she was not the most responsible twenty-three-year-old under the blinding sun. In her defense, it was completely messed up to have to work on a Saturday. No one should be out of bed at this hour on a weekend. Unfortunately, she had volunteered for this shit.

Earlier that week, Mr. Wheeler had called her into his office. He was the head of her department, a lead partner in the firm, and could fire her on the spot. It was like being sent to the principal.

"Iris, how are you liking your work so far here at WRE?"

"Um, it's okay," she'd said, trying not to sound as ill at ease as she felt. "I've been learning a lot," she'd added in her job interview voice.

She hated her job at Wheeler Reese Elliot Architects but couldn't very well say that to him. All she did day after day was mark up blueprints with a red pen. Hundreds of sheets of paper showing each little piece of rebar in every concrete beam, and she had to check them all. It was mind-numbing, soul-crushing work, especially since she was qualified to do so much more. She had graduated summa cum laude from Case Western Reserve University. She'd been promised "cutting-edge" structural design projects, but three months into her big engineering career, she'd been reduced to a paper-marking monkey. She'd said as much to her assigned mentor, Brad, that Monday in a fit of desperation. A day later she was sitting in the hot seat across from Mr. Wheeler. Brad had ratted her out. Was she going to get fired? Hysterical butterflies swarmed her stomach.

"Well, Brad thinks you have a good head on your shoulders. Perhaps you're ready for a little change of pace." Mr. Wheeler smiled a corporate smile.

"Uh, what do you mean?"

"We've just landed a very unusual project. The partners think you might be a good fit for it. It involves fieldwork."

Fieldwork would mean leaving her dreaded cubicle. "Really? That sounds interesting."

"Wonderful. Brad will bring you up to speed on the details. This project is of a rather sensitive nature. Our client is relying on us to keep it confidential. I really appreciate the two of you being willing to put in the overtime. It won't go unnoticed."

Mr. Wheeler had clapped her on the back and shut the door to his corner office. Her smile had dropped at the corners. There was a catch. Brad later explained they would be working over the weekend. For free.

It was total bullshit, Iris thought, gritting her teeth as she threw herself behind the wheel and gunned her rusted-out beige Mazda down the street. At the stoplight she fished a half-empty bottle of Diet Coke from the littered floorboards and lit a cigarette. But what was she supposed to do? Say no?

As the car neared downtown, Iris realized she had no idea where the heck she was actually going. She rifled through her purse to find the address she had scribbled down. Cigarettes, lighter, lipstick, receipts—she tossed the contents of her bag onto the passenger seat with one eye on the road.

A horn blasted. She looked up just in time to swerve and avoid hitting an oncoming garbage truck. Slamming the brakes, she squealed to a stop.

"Shit!"

The pile of garbage on the passenger seat flew to the floor. The missing scrap of paper landed on top. Snatching it up, she read:

1010 Euclid Avenue
First Bank of Cleveland
Park in the back

At East Twelfth Street and Euclid, the clock on the dash blinked 9:15 a.m. Brad would be standing at the door, tapping his foot, checking his Seiko and wishing he hadn't recommended the flaky new girl for this field assignment. She stuffed everything back into her purse while the red light took an eternity to change.

The building at 1010 Euclid Avenue flashed by her window in a blur of stone and glass. *Shit*. Her car sped through a really yellow light left onto East Ninth Street and then hooked around onto Huron Street. It should have been the back of the building, but the only signs read "No Parking." Iris began to panic. Huron would take her all the way back to East Fourteenth Street before she could turn around. There was no time for that. She was already way late for her first assignment out of the office.

She pulled into a narrow driveway that dead-ended into a closed garage door. It was identical to the other blank receiving doors lining the street. Both sides of the sidewalk were empty, and the street was dead quiet. Most of Cleveland was a ghost town on weekends. Overhead, a fifteen-story, soot-stained office tower stretched into the sky. Rotted boards covered half the windows, and the endless rows of brick blurred together. Was this the building? Craning her head up made it feel like it might slide off her neck. Hangovers sometimes take a while to really set in. She squeezed her eyes shut and blew out a slow breath. She had to stop drinking like every night was a frat party. College was over.

Images of the night before flipped by like a broken filmstrip. She had gone to a work happy hour down at some new bar in the Flats. With each tequila shot, the evening had gotten blurrier. Nick had been there. He was the cute interior designer she'd been flirting with at work for weeks. He liked to swing by her desk and chat. For Iris, it was a welcome break from marking up shop drawings with a red pen like a glorified secretary. Who knew what it was for him. She would laugh at his jokes and blush a lot—that was the extent of her skills in the "come-hither" department.

Nick had bought some of the shots. His arm draped over her shoulder, he'd whispered something in her ear she couldn't quite understand over the throbbing music. Next thing she knew, he was driving her car back to her place. He'd kissed her, and the whole world had spun out of control. All she remembered after that was him dragging her up the stairs to bed and telling her to get some rest. She supposed she should be grateful he acted like a gentleman by not taking advantage of her. But, Jesus. Was she that bad of a kisser?

Something creaked loudly. Iris's eyes popped open at the sound, and her car lurched. She stomped on the brake to keep from slamming into the receiving door in front of her as it rolled open. Brad stepped out and waved.

"Good morning, Iris!"

"Brad! Hi." Her voice was muffled by the window. *Idiot.* She rolled it down and said again, "Hi! How'd you get in there?"

"I have my ways," he said, arching an eyebrow. "Nah! The security guard showed me where to go."

Brad was a model engineer, in his crisp J. C. Penney shirt and freshly ironed slacks. He looked like he'd already gone to the gym, had a shower, and eaten a four-course breakfast. Iris, by comparison, looked like she'd been pulled out of a shower drain.

"Can we park here?"

"Yep, come on in."

Iris's car followed Brad into a dungeon-like room, which turned out to be a loading dock. There were two grimy truck bays and a broken concrete slab big enough for three parking stalls. Iris pulled her sputtering car next to an immaculate Honda that could only be Brad's. A sign posted on the wall said "Short-Term Parking, Deliveries Only." The loading dock grew dark as the small garage door rolled closed behind her. A horrible smell like rotting meat and vomit crawled up her nose and nearly sent her running to a corner to puke. There was a large rusted-out dumpster in the corner.

"Smells great, huh?" Brad joked. He pointed to a red button on the wall by an abandoned security office. "Make sure you close the garage door when you come in."

"Sure. But how do I get in without you?" she asked, covering her mouth and nose.

"There's a squawk box next to the garage door outside. Ramone will let you in."

Iris nodded and glanced around for this Ramone, but he was nowhere to be found.

"Okay. Let's get started." Brad pulled a huge field bag out of the spotless trunk of his Accord.

It occurred to her that she hadn't remembered to bring a field bag or so much as a clipboard with her. That figured. She grabbed her oversized handbag out of her car and threw it over her shoulder, making as if it had more than lipstick and cigarettes inside it. "Okay."

Brad led Iris through a long service corridor and into a dark hallway. They followed the faint glow of daylight ahead past bronze elevator doors until they reached the main lobby of the First Bank of Cleveland.

Iris gawked at the coffered ceiling soaring fifteen feet overhead. Everything from the inlaid wood panels to the bronze window casements to the giant old clock over the entrance looked hand-crafted. The tiles on the floor were tiny and hand laid to form an art deco mosaic with a round rosette set in the center. Two antique, bronze revolving doors faced Euclid Avenue. They seemed insulted by the rusted chains and padlocks hanging from them. Gleaming letters spelled out "First Bank of Cleveland Est. 1903" on the wall over two solid metal doors with swirling cast-bronze handles that led to some other room. The doors were closed.

"What year was all this built?" Iris studied the gilded clock over her head. Its scrolled hands had ground to a halt years ago.

"Sometime before the Great Depression. You never see this type of craftsmanship in postwar buildings."

"When did it become vacant?" Iris asked.

"I'm not too sure. I think the county ledger said something."
Brad rifled through a file he pulled from his workbag and read
aloud, "First Bank of Cleveland closed December 29, 1978."

"I wonder why," Iris thought out loud.

A cheap placard on the wall contained tiny rows of black velvet, where loose or missing plastic white letters spelled out the
names and office numbers for at least twenty men. On the opposite
wall hung the portrait of a severe old man, who glowered at her
with red-rimmed eyes as she silently read the name engraved on
the frame, "Alistair Mercer, President."

"Lots of things went belly-up when the city defaulted.
Businesses shut down, nobody could find a job. Lucky for us, we
have a lot of work to do."

She gazed up at the coffered ceiling and its hundreds of tiny
murals and gilded filigree. It was a shame. Whatever had gone
wrong at the bank all those years ago had locked it away for nearly
twenty years.

A warm breeze whistled through the bronze revolving doors.
She could almost picture men in tweed suits and secretaries in
high heels filing into the lobby one by one. Hundreds of people
must have walked through each day. She wondered if any of them
ever bothered to look up.

CHAPTER 2

Thursday, November 2, 1978

Beatrice Baker froze just inside the First Bank of Cleveland building and gaped at the enormous ceiling like it might fall down on her head. She'd never seen anything so grand and intimidating in her whole little life. The sight of it nearly sent her reeling back out onto the sidewalk. A man in a three-piece suit and heavy sideburns gave her a polite nod before heading out the revolving doors. He thought she belonged there, she realized, and she tried to smile back.

Up on the ninth floor, Mr. Thompson scanned her job application, then tossed it onto his desk. "So tell me a little about yourself, Miss Baker." He leaned back in his leather chair and lifted his thick, graying eyebrows at her.

Beatrice was perched on the edge of her seat with her legs crossed at the ankles just as she'd been taught. "I graduated from Cleveland Heights High School last spring. Since then I've been working as a clerk at the Murray Hill Convenience Store."

It was the script she and her Aunt Doris had been rehearsing for weeks. She spoke clearly, slowly enunciating each word. She tucked a lock of ironed blond hair behind her ear.

"What sort of work are you doing at a convenience store that qualifies you to be a secretary here at the First Bank of Cleveland exactly?"

"Well, let me see . . ." Beatrice paused to keep her voice from wavering or falling to a whisper. Her aunt had told her to speak up and be confident. "Answering phones, placing orders, and balancing the register each day."

"Do you type?"

"Eighty-five words per minute!" This part of her résumé was actually true. She had practiced on Doris's old Remington for months.

Mr. Thompson looked her sternly in the eyes. She tried not to fidget as he sized her up. "Don't look uncomfortable or defiant," Doris had warned her. "Just be an honest girl with nothing to hide."

Beatrice was tiny, blond, blue-eyed, neat, pretty—everything Doris said she needed to be. Her tweed skirt and knit blouse were ill-fitting. Her shoes were cheap. Her accent was faint, but her aunt assured her the hint of Appalachia only added to her charm. At sixteen, she was far too young for the job, but she'd lied on the application about that and many other things.

His eyes paused on her blouse, which was unbuttoned just enough to flash a little cleavage. What Mr. Thompson didn't know was that her aunt had stuffed tissues into her bra to make her look older.

She squirmed uncomfortably and tried to direct his gaze back to her face. "I appreciate your consideration. Working for the First Bank of Cleveland would be a real honor."

"Really? Why is that?"

Doris had lectured her the night before. "These banker types don't want to know your life story. They just want to know if you can type and look cute doing it."

Beatrice had gaped at her aunt's comment. "What are you saying? All that matters is if I'm pretty enough?"

"Pretty enough, young enough, fresh enough. Nobody wants to hire someone with a past." Doris had slumped on the couch and taken another drink. "Poor girls like us without rich daddies, without fancy schooling, without a husband, we have so few cards to play. You got your good looks and your good name. That's it. You can't afford to squander 'em. If you play the hand wrong, little girl, you'll end up slinging hash in some dive just like me."

Beatrice had studied Doris's ruddy cheeks and rough hands. "What happened, Aunt Doris? Why don't you work at some bank?"

"Don't you go worrying about that now. It's in the past. So what are you gonna say when he asks why you'd be honored to work at the bank?" Doris had prompted her.

"The First Bank of Cleveland wrote the mortgage on my parents' house twenty years ago, and we've been loyal customers ever since." She smiled as she lied to Mr. Thompson, feeling like her face might just crack under the pressure.

He folded his arms across his chest skeptically. He could see right through her—she was sure of it. She struggled to hold his piercing gaze without flinching. His eyes wandered back to her chest.

"Well, we like to think of ourselves as a family business around here. Although I must say, hiring a young girl like you does concern me a bit. We lose so many, you know. All that time spent training the girls, and then they up and leave. They run off and get married." He tapped his fountain pen on his desk blotter. "We may be a family business, but we have to keep our eye on the bottom line. How do I know you'll be a good investment, Beatrice?"

"Um . . ." She cleared her throat. "I don't have any plans to get married, Mr. Thompson. I . . . I want a career."

"That's what they all say."

"But I mean it!" She took a breath to regain her demure composure. "I don't want to cook and clean house all day."

"What about children?"

The color drained from her face. "Children?"

"Yes, children. Do you plan to have any?"

Her eyes began to water, and she quickly dropped them to her lap. She dug her fingernails into her palm. She couldn't believe he was asking her such a personal, awful question. "No."

"Really? Pretty girl like you? I find that hard to believe." He set his pen down onto the desk blotter.

She wasn't going to get the job. After all those months of preparing and all of Doris's advice, she wasn't going to get it. She had to say something if she was going to have any chance in the world.

"I grew up taking care of five brothers and four sisters, sir, and I can say with absolute certainty that I have no interest in having a baby. I am not spending one more minute knee-deep in diapers! No, sir! I want something better, and you have no idea what I've gone through to get it. I want this job!" She nearly shouted the words, and then recoiled at the sound of her own voice.

He laughed out loud. "Well, well, Miss Baker. Aren't you just full of surprises? That's exactly the kind of dedication we're looking for. You're hired."

She blinked the fire from her eyes. "Really?"

"Be here at 9:00 a.m. sharp Monday morning. Report to Linda in Human Resources on the third floor."

She strained to hear the instructions through the adrenaline buzzing in her ears. Something about a Linda on Monday.

"Thank you, Mr. Thompson. You won't regret it."

The room spun with his impertinent questions and her own audacity as she followed him across the shiny floor of his corner office, past the mahogany bookshelves and crystal wall sconces. Five brothers and four sisters—where did she come up with that? So many preparations, and it all came down to whether or not she was going to get pregnant. She didn't know whether to laugh or cry.

At the door to his office, she stopped and waited for him to extend a hand to shake. Doris had taught her what to do if anyone made the gesture.

He patted her on the shoulder instead. "That'll be all, Miss Baker."

CHAPTER 3

Saturday, August 8, 1998

"What are we doing here exactly?" Iris asked, turning away from the chained doors of the old bank.

"WRE was selected to perform a renovation feasibility study for this place. I hear the county is thinking about buying it." Brad pulled out his tape measure and clipboard.

"A renovation feasibility study," Iris repeated as if she knew exactly what that meant.

"Yep. It's going to take longer than usual. There are no legible blueprints from its original construction because the Building Department had been keeping the archives under some leaking pipes. Everything was water damaged." Brad shook his head at the ineptitude of government workers. He pulled open the tape measure and handed her the dumb end. "We're going to have to reconstruct the plans to show the adaptive reuse options for the building."

Iris stared at him for a moment, debating whether or not she could go on pretending she was following along. She took the loose end of the tape measure and walked with it to the other side of the room. "Okay. I give. What does that mean exactly?"

"We've been hired by the current owner, Cleveland Real Estate Holdings Corp., to whip up some floor plans showing the potential here for new offices and retail. I guess they figure they can finally get a better deal than the tax write-off they've been taking all these years." He made a note of the measurement and motioned her and the tape measure end to the opposite wall.

"Tax write-off?"

"Rust Belt cities have been a tax haven for years. You buy a building at a deep discount and let it sit vacant, taking a huge loss. It helps a company's balance sheet come tax time, especially if they're making a killing elsewhere."

Iris studied the tile mosaic on the floor to hide the confusion on her face. "Now they want to sell it? Is that why Mr. Wheeler said something about all this being confidential?"

Brad made a few more notes and snapped the tape measure closed. "The county has been looking to relocate its headquarters downtown, and our design plans are supposed to help sell this place to them. This building owner is competing with several others, and the county hasn't gone public with their plans."

Iris nodded and glanced at the graph paper he was marking up. Brad had already sketched a rough outline of the first floor and was neatly filling in the measurements.

"If you want my opinion, they should just tear this place down. With all the asbestos and lead buried in here"—Brad waved his hand at the gorgeous ceiling—"it'll cost a fortune to do anything else."

Iris couldn't argue as he led her from the front lobby through the heavy bronze doors. The banking area on the other side was enormous by modern standards and consisted of two high marble counters in the middle of the cavernous room, flanked on either side by identical rows of teller stations. The bank tellers had stood in little booths behind tight bronze prison bars with only a mail slot–sized opening to pass paper through.

Iris peered inside one of the tiny stalls. There was a small counter and an antiquated adding machine, and barely enough room to turn around. It was utterly claustrophobic, and she felt bad for the woman who used to stand there. Iris turned and tried to imagine the room the teller saw from behind the tight bars.

Mosaic tiles, mahogany, and bronze—everything was shrouded in dust. The ceilings soared up fifteen feet at least, holding nothing but stale air and the faded echoes of hard-soled shoes and clacking keys. The whole place was a lost black-and-white photograph.

Iris was overwhelmed by a strange melancholy, knowing it would all be torn down if Brad had his way. *They'd probably turn it into a parking lot*, she thought, trying to shake the feeling she was standing in a buried tomb.

"So what's the plan for today?" she asked, hoping for a larger role than just holding the tape measure at Brad's command.

"First, we need to lay out the basic column grid and get some overall dimensions. We'll leave the site survey to the civil engineer. Then we'll develop the floor plans and typical wall sections."

It was the closest thing to actual structural engineering she'd been asked to do since she was hired. The building was a fifteen-story tower with a footprint that was easily 100 by 150 feet. It took the better part of the morning just to lay out the first-floor grid. The rest of the first floor contained the loading dock, restrooms, and two sets of stairs. Iris passed by the grand staircase, adorned with long marble slabs and wrought-iron railings that wrapped around the elevator housings, and headed toward the second set of stairs hidden off the loading dock. A burned-out "Exit" sign hung over the door. Inside, the cold concrete treads and cinder-block walls rose up from the glow of the emergency flood lamps. The air was thick with what smelled like sour urine. Iris took quick measurements and slammed the door shut.

The lunch hour came and went. Iris grew light-headed as her blood sugar plummeted. By one o'clock she was certain she was going to faint.

She let the dumb end of the tape measure droop. "I'm getting pretty hungry."

"Yeah, me too. Let's stop and take a break." Brad was so engrossed in his graph paper he'd hardly talked all morning.

"Where do you want to go to grab some lunch?" she asked, stretching her cramped hands.

"Oh, I brought mine."

Of course he brought his lunch, she thought irritably. *A Boy Scout is always prepared.*

"Shoot! I guess I didn't think to do that. I'm going to have to run out. Do you want me to pick anything up for you? Soda?"

"No, I'm good," Brad said as he pulled out a brown paper bag. "I'll grab a quick bite and keep at it here. Come find me when you're done."

"Sounds good!" Iris said brightly, as though his work habits weren't completely annoying. It was a Saturday, for sobbing out loud, and he couldn't be bothered to stop for lunch? She grumbled to herself as she found her way down the front stairs, through the main lobby, through the service corridor, and back to the loading dock.

When she returned thirty minutes later, she pulled her car in front of the blank garage door. She pressed the button on the black speaker box and waited. Nothing happened. She pressed it again and scanned the empty street and sidewalk. A bead of sweat ran down her back. She toyed with the idea of just going home, but the squawk box crackled to life, and the door rolled open.

Inside the filthy loading dock, Ramone was nowhere to be found, but he must have been there somewhere to open the door. Weird. She took one last puff off her cigarette and dragged her butt out of the car. As much as she hated the idea, the back stairs up to the second floor seemed like the fastest way to get back to Brad. She'd already slacked off enough that day.

She scrambled up two flights of emergency egress stairs, trying not to breathe the fetid air. It still reeked like an outhouse. When she got to the door marked "Level 2," the handle was locked. *Shit.* She pounded the door. "Brad! Brad, I'm locked out! Hello?"

Now what? The spiral of concrete stairs led in both directions, and she debated whether to go up or down. The treads wound up and up for what seemed like miles. It was so mesmerizing as she leaned over the rail, she almost forgot the smell.

The sound of boots scuffing on concrete came from several flights up.

"Hello? . . . Brad? . . . Ramone?" her voice echoed in the tower.

A door slammed way up near the top, and then there was silence.

"Hey!" she shouted after it. "What the . . . ?"

The door behind her swung open. It was Brad. "Were you the one making all that noise?"

"Yeah. Say, have you been in there the whole time?" Iris scowled and looked up again at the stairs above her.

"Down the hall." He shrugged and held open the door.

Iris left the stair tower, telling herself the other person in the stairwell must have been Ramone. Maybe he was hard of hearing. "What'd I miss?"

"Not much. I'm glad you're back. This place is giving me the willies!"

Me too, she thought. They were in a large lunchroom area populated by orange plastic chairs and empty tables. Some of the tables still had napkin dispensers sitting on them, filled with yellowed napkins.

"I see you found a good place to eat lunch." She motioned to the tables. "It's kinda weird that all of this stuff is still here, isn't it?"

"Tell me about it. This isn't the strangest part either."

Iris raised her eyebrows and followed Brad to an alcove that contained three vending machines. The machines were still lit and buzzing. They advertised five-cent coffee, Mars bars, and cans of Tab.

"Are you kidding me?"

"Wait. There's more."

Brad pulled a nickel out of his pocket and put it in the coffee machine. Iris's jaw dropped when it spit out a Styrofoam cup and began to fill it with a black liquid that must have been sitting inside the machine for years.

"Want some coffee?"

"Oh, I'm good!"

Iris backed away. Her eyes darted from the tables to the cup dispensers to the half-full trash cans. "It's like a nuclear holocaust came through here and left all of the furniture." She peered down at the red and green floor tiles and saw her footprints in the dust. They were the only sign of life past the year 1978 in the whole room.

CHAPTER 4

It was 5:00 p.m. when Brad finally packed up the tape measure. "I think we'll call it a night."

"Sounds good." Iris nearly took off running for the loading dock. They'd only managed to finish laying out the floor plans for two levels, but she couldn't care less.

"I'll meet you back here tomorrow bright and early."

Iris nearly tripped over her feet. She hadn't agreed to work Sunday too. *Damn it.* "Uh, okay. What time?"

"Oh, nothing crazy. Let's say 9:00 a.m. again. Okay?"

"Sure," she said through gritted teeth. Brad sucked.

On the way home, Iris decided she needed a drink. It was a Saturday night after all, and she'd earned it. Just one drink. There was nothing waiting for her at home but dirty laundry and dirty dishes anyway.

The red walls and stained ceiling of her favorite bar, Club Illusion, were just as she'd left them two nights before. Ellie was still behind the bar, as if she'd slept there. With her dyed-black hair, nose ring, and tattoos, she couldn't have been more different than

Iris, but Ellie was the closest thing she had to a best friend, even though they rarely saw each other outside the bar. They had met at Club I two years earlier when Iris applied for a weekend job.

Besides beer and cigarettes, they didn't have much else in common. It was kind of sad when Iris stopped to think about it, which she didn't like to do. She didn't have many girl friends. Any, really. The other women in engineering school were few and far between and tended to be high-strung or painfully quiet or both. Worse, they were boring. They came from nice families. They had nice manners. They were nice girls. They didn't swear or smoke or spit. As much as she hated to admit it, Iris was just another one of them. She attended every class, turned in every assignment, and did exactly what she was supposed to do.

Iris plopped down on her usual bar stool. Ellie poured two whiskey sours and grabbed an ashtray. The regulars hadn't trickled in yet, and the frat boys were still on summer vacation. They had the place to themselves.

"How goes life in the salt mines?"

Ellie must have thought it was hilarious that Iris had to sit in an office every day. She didn't give a shit what the world thought she was supposed to do. Ellie was a sixth-year art student with no plans of graduating. Pleasing the parents or the teachers wasn't even a thought. She was free. At least, that was the way it seemed.

Iris forced a smile and took a huge swig of whiskey. "Just peachy. How's tips?"

"Shitty. If things don't pick up, I'm going to have to get a real job."

Ellie would never get a real job.

"Nice tattoo. Is that new?"

The new addition to the intricate mural running down her left arm was a black-and-white image of two dice sitting in a skeleton hand.

"Yes, ma'am. Just took the bandage off this morning. It comes from this Nietzsche quote I read once. 'The devotion of the greatest is to encounter risk and danger and play dice for death.'"

"Wow." Iris nodded, trying not to stare at the angry red skin surrounding the bones. She'd never had the guts to write something on herself she couldn't erase. It looked like it hurt.

"So what's new with you?" Ellie asked.

Iris was thrilled to have something fun to say for once. She often wondered if Ellie found her remotely interesting, or if she was merely tolerating the engineering nerd who kept coming around. "You won't believe where I was today. I spent the whole day surveying this weird bombed-out building downtown. It was fucking crazy in there."

Iris filled her in on the post-apocalyptic scene in the cafeteria.

"Tell me you drank that coffee," Ellie said, laughing. "Which building was it?"

"First Bank of Cleveland. It closed down in the '70s. Ever heard of it?"

"Nope."

"I guess it closed down around the time the city went bankrupt. How does a city go bankrupt anyway?" Iris polished off her drink in one large gulp.

"Eh. Everyone's got their theories on that one. My old man thinks it was some conspiracy down at city hall. Of course, he thinks the river catching fire was a conspiracy too."

Iris nodded. In the five years she'd lived there, she'd heard her share of Cleveland underdog conspiracy theories.

"Want another one?"

Iris could see the whole night play out as she stared into the bottom of her glass. She and Ellie would tie on a buzz. The bar would fill up. Some random guy would sit down next to Iris and strike up a conversation. For a few fleeting hours, Iris would be the most fascinating woman he'd ever met. He would laugh at all of her jokes and hang on her every word. They'd be the closest of friends until the end of the night, when she'd mutter some excuse and stagger home alone. She never let them take her home. She sighed, thinking of Nick.

"Not tonight. I have to work tomorrow, if you can believe that shit."

"What's up with that?" Ellie went ahead and poured herself another cocktail.

"They asked me to take on this weird assignment at that bank I was telling you about. It's after-hours."

"And you said yes?"

Iris shook her head. "I didn't really have a choice. The head of the department asked me to do it."

"What, was he going to fire you or something if you said no?"

"I don't know. Probably not. But it's supposed to be this great opportunity to show my worth and maybe get better assignments."

"Your worth? Christ, Iris! Never look to a job for that, okay? You can't trust these corporate types. They'll chew you up and spit you out without a second thought if it makes them more money. Fuck 'em! Do what you want."

Iris nodded in agreement as she stood up to leave.

CHAPTER 5

The evening sun hung over the east side of town like an orange heat lamp. As Iris climbed back into her car, Ellie's words still stung. She couldn't just tell her boss to take her job and shove it. She lived in the real world, where people went to work and didn't just sit in a bar all day picking out new tattoos. *"Play dice for death." What the hell does that even mean?*

Her father would agree. She could almost hear him say the words. Iris lit a cigarette in protest. She didn't want to grow up to be like her parents, whittling away the time, eating bran cereal and watching *Wheel of Fortune*. She didn't want to be her mother, reading her grocery-store romance novels, pan-frying steaks for a husband who ignored her, and muttering her opinions into the clothes dryer. She didn't know what she wanted, but it sure as shit wasn't that. It all seemed so damned pointless.

Iris took the back roads home from Club Illusion to her run-down apartment in Little Italy. Up Mayfield Road, the tiny shops were playing Frank Sinatra and Dean Martin at full volume. She turned down her block. Her street sign read "Random Road," and it was fitting. It had been hilarious in college; now it was just sad. The rent was cheap, and that's all that mattered when she was scraping by on $500 a month in school. Now that she was gainfully employed with a salary of $33,000 a year, she could do better.

Iris parked her car on the street and headed up the driveway, where three crumbling houses were stacked one behind the other on a narrow lot. Each shoddy house had been converted into shoddier apartments. Her neighbor was camped out on her front porch, guarding the sidewalk as usual.

"Hi, Mrs. Capretta," Iris said cheerfully as she hurried past. It was a lame attempt to avoid the inevitable. The old woman's face puckered no matter what she said. The nose pads of her thick glasses had sunk into her puffy skin decades earlier, and Iris secretly speculated whether Mrs. Capretta could even lift them off her face anymore.

"Pharmacist tried to cheat me today," she growled. "Don't go shop down the street. They'll rob you blind!"

"I'll be careful. Thanks!" After three years living behind Mrs. Capretta, Iris knew better than to argue or ask questions.

Iris didn't know the names of her other neighbors. There were a couple grad students in the house in the rear, and an Indian family of four lived in the apartment below hers. They didn't speak much English, but they smiled and gave her a little bow whenever they met in the driveway.

She grabbed the mail and climbed the crooked stairs up to the second floor of the collapsing house that she called home. She was greeted by a small puddle on the floor just inside her front door. The roof was leaking again. She stepped over it and made a mental note to call her slumlord in the morning.

The light blinked on her dusty answering machine.

"Iris? Iris, are you there? This is your mother. Give me a call, okay? It's been too long, honey. I'm starting to get worried. Love you! Bye."

It had only been a week since they'd last talked. Iris sighed and picked up the phone.

"Hello?"

"Hi, Mom."

"Honey! It's so nice to hear your voice. How are you doing?"

"Just fine. I'm kind of tired." Iris was already tapping her foot. Her mother had no life of her own. She'd been a stay-at-home mom, and ever since Iris had moved away, she didn't know what to do with herself.

"How's the job going?"

"Pretty busy. I just got a special assignment, so that's good." Iris shuffled through the mail—junk, junk, student loan bill.

"How exciting! Well, it's about time they took some notice of you, honey! You're so brilliant. I was just telling your father the other day that it's high time someone put you to good use. All this paperwork they've got you doing is ridiculous—"

"Mom! Stop. I'm being put to good use, okay? My job is not ridiculous."

Iris tried to ignore the thinly veiled insult. Both of her parents were mildly disappointed in her chosen career. Her father felt civil engineering was reserved for the duller students, who couldn't handle organic chemistry. In truth, Iris had no problem with any of her classes. Science, math, and finding the correct answers to complicated equations came easily to her. The problem was the questions were so painfully pointless. She didn't really care about the diffusion rate of this gas through that liquid or whatever. Determining whether or not a building would fall down, on the other hand, actually seemed meaningful. Iris had tried to argue that constructing bridges and dams was a hell of a lot more important than working for some chemical company developing new house-paint formulations. It wasn't enough that she had taken his advice and majored in engineering. He expected more.

"Of course, sweetie. It's just that when someone graduates valedictorian around here, people want to know what they're up to. I ran into Mrs. Johnson just the other day. She was convinced you'd become a brain surgeon."

"Mrs. Johnson taught Home Ec, Mom." Iris rolled her eyes. She tore open the loan bill that stated $574.73 was due every month for the next fifteen years. It was a prison sentence. "Everything's fine. Listen, I have to go. I worked all day, and I'm beat."

"Okay, honey. Thanks for calling. I just need to hear your voice every once in a while."

"I know. Give my love to Dad, okay?"

"Okay, I love you, honey. Bye-bye."

The line went dead.

"Who gives a shit what Mrs. Johnson thinks, Mom? Jesus!" Iris yelled at the dead receiver.

Sweatpants, a couple slices of cold pizza, and a beer later, she plopped down onto her secondhand couch. The VCR blinked 8:30 p.m. She chewed a fingernail. Her eyes scanned her tiny apartment for something to do. A bookshelf stuffed with college textbooks was wedged in one corner. On the other side of the room, a blank canvas was sitting on a dusty easel. It had been sitting there, along with her paints and brushes, ever since she moved in and decided that corner would be her art studio. That was three years ago.

Iris stood up and walked over to it. She poked the canvas with a finger and surveyed her neglected tools. They looked ridiculous to her now. Who was she kidding? She was no artist. While she was in school, she never had time to paint. But now she did. She didn't have homework. She didn't work nights. Outside of drinking with Ellie, she didn't even have a social life. Most of her college friends had left town after graduation. Some went back home, and the others had gone on to bigger and better cities for bigger and better jobs.

Iris grabbed her lighter off of the coffee table and lit a cigarette. Why hadn't she left too? She blew out the smoke and glanced back at the blank canvas. She didn't have a good answer.

It's temporary, she told herself. She might go to grad school next year. In a few years, she might send a résumé to a top-rate engineering firm in New York. She was being smart, taking it slow, and working in the industry for a few years before making any sudden moves. It was what her adviser had suggested when she confessed she wasn't sure what she wanted to do after graduation. It had made sense at the time, especially since she didn't have the guts to say out loud what she'd secretly suspected for over a year— she didn't want to be an engineer at all.

The thought was ridiculous. Five years of school, and now she just wanted to give up? It had only been three months. How could she possibly know if she liked it yet? Iris grabbed another beer from the fridge. It would take time. She had to give it a chance. It was her father talking in her head now. Besides, that student loan bill wasn't going to pay itself.

Sometime around midnight she dragged herself to bed.

CHAPTER 6

Iris was still half-asleep when she pulled up to the rolling garage door behind the old bank. She was ten minutes late, but she was too tired to care. Brad could kiss her grits if he decided to give her any grief. No sane person works on Sunday. It didn't help that she kept hearing Ellie say "Fuck 'em" in the back of her head.

"You feeling okay?" he asked as she slumped out of her car.

"I'm fine." Iris forced a smile. This was a big career opportunity, she reminded herself. Brad recommended her for the job; she should act excited. It could lead to bigger and better things, but the only emotion she could muster was mild annoyance.

She grabbed her duffel bag from the backseat. At least she had managed to cobble together a field bag. She even had her own tape measure.

"Thanks for coming early. I just got news we're fast-tracking the project, starting Monday."

"Oh? Were we slow-tracking it before?" Iris asked with mild sarcasm.

"Not exactly. Mr. Wheeler wants schematics of the founda-
tions by the end of the day. Then we need to give them at least a
floor a day to keep up with the design development team."

Brad led her up the loading dock and through the service corridor behind the elevator shaft. They passed the entrance to the
main lobby and continued down a hallway that was beige from top
to bottom. Fluorescent bulbs hummed overhead.

It had taken them eight hours to finish one and a half floors on
Saturday. Iris did some quick math in her head. If they were going
to continue working their normal shift at the office and then do the
survey work after-hours, she'd be working around the clock.

"So, are we supposed to work until 2:00 a.m. every night?" Iris
demanded in a voice much harsher than she intended. *Shit.* She
had just breached the unspoken professional credo—thou shalt
not bitch and moan. She sweetened her voice. "I mean, I don't see
how we can do that without help."

Brad turned to look at her with deadpan eyes. "You want to
keep this job, right?"

The color drained from her face. "Of . . . of course I do!" She
couldn't afford to lose her job after three months. It would ruin her
résumé. Was he threatening to report her to Mr. Wheeler? Wait,
was he laughing?

"I'm just messing with you, Iris!" He chuckled. "Mr. Wheeler
wants you working on this building full-time, starting tomorrow."

Iris wanted to hit him on the head with her bag for teasing her,
until the second thing he said registered. "You mean I get to work
here instead of the office?"

"Yeah. Ha! I really had you going!"

"Yes, you did, you bastard! Who knew you were such a
prankster?"

"Well, you should never underestimate the quiet guy." He
grinned and opened the door at the end of the hall. She followed
him through it and down a dark stairwell.

The heavy door thunked closed behind her. The stairwell was almost completely black, and a cold draft wafted up from wherever they were heading.

"Will you be working here too?"

"Not too much." He clicked on a small flashlight. "I'm supposed to supervise you and keep up with the other work at the office."

Iris was being furloughed from the office fishbowl. Her days would be spent unsupervised, in sneakers and jeans. She smiled in the darkness at the thought, until something crawled across her hand. She let out a squeak and shook it violently. There were cobwebs clinging to the handrail. She yanked her hand back and told herself that the tickling on her neck couldn't possibly be a spider. The winking beam of the flashlight streaked the cinder-block walls with shadows as they climbed down deeper into the bowels of the building.

After two flights of stairs, the flickering light finally stopped moving. When she caught up to Brad, he was struggling to open a heavy steel door. He gave it a solid kick, and it swung open, crashing loudly into the adjacent wall. The stairway landed in a narrow corridor that led to a large room with two enormous round doors.

"Holy shit!"

She stared at one of them. Cursing was not professional, but the one door must have been eight feet in diameter. There was a giant wheel spiked with handles in the center of the door that reminded Iris of a pirate ship's helm. She reached out and spun it. It wasn't locked. The door was twelve-inch-thick solid steel with locking bolts the size of soup cans lining the perimeter.

Brad walked the vault door open and laughed. "Hey, who wants to rob a bank?"

"Whoa."

Iris stepped inside. It was a long, narrow room not more than five feet wide but at least twenty feet deep. The ceiling was polished bronze. The two side walls were lined from top to bottom and end to end with hundreds of little doors lined up in rows like apartment mailboxes.

"What the heck are these? This isn't where they keep the money, is it?"

"Nope. That vault is over there." Brad motioned across the marble corridor to the second, larger vault door on the opposite wall. That one was so huge, the floor stepped down in front of it so it could swing open. Iris could see from where she was standing that the larger vault was full of empty metal shelves.

"So what is this?"

Each little door lining the walls was identical, except for the numbers engraved in Gothic script. Each door had two keyholes. Iris reached out and touched one.

"This is the vault with the safe deposit boxes. It's the place where people lock away their most precious possessions. Or, you know, stuff they don't want anyone to find."

Iris scanned all the little metal doors and saw that one of them hung open. She walked over to it and peered inside. The door concealed a steel-lined cubbyhole. It was empty. Iris reached in past her elbow. The walls were smooth and cold. She pulled her hand out and closed the door. It swung freely back open.

"I guess you need a key to lock it," she said to no one.

Her footsteps echoed off the bronze floor as she headed back out of the vault. Round corkscrews of shaved metal crunched under her feet. She bent down to pick one up and came face-to-face with a safe deposit door that was riddled with holes.

"What the heck happened here?"

"They drilled it open," a gravelly voice said behind them. It belonged to an older black man in a blue collared shirt that said "Security." An ID tag hung around his neck, and a giant ring of keys dangled from his belt.

"Oh, hi." Iris straightened up. "You must be Ramone."

"That's me." He was tall, thin, and slightly crooked. Looking at his short gray hair and tired eyes, Iris guessed he was at least fifty years old. His dark brown skin looked as dry and dusty as the vault floor.

"I'm Iris. I think you're going to be stuck with me for a few weeks."

He walked over to her, his black sneakers silent on the vault floor, and shook her hand. It was a gentle handshake, but his hand felt like sandpaper.

"It's nice to meet you. Do I need to get another set of keys for this young lady?" he asked Brad.

"No, I'll just give her mine," Brad said.

Ramone seemed satisfied to get the business settled. He glanced at one of the safe deposit boxes, then turned to Iris. "Is this your first time down here?"

"Yeah. It's like being inside a coffin!" Brad answered for her. He kicked the outside walls and walked around the corner. "You know, these vaults are solid steel. The walls are like a foot thick. They don't build 'em like this anymore."

Iris nodded in agreement. When Brad had wandered down the hall with his tape measure, she dropped her voice and asked, "What do you mean, they drilled it open?"

"The box," Ramone said in a three-pack-a-day baritone. "Whenever someone wants to claim their stuff, they have to drill 'em open. You know, after they submit a formal request to the State of Ohio and get a warrant."

"I don't understand. Aren't there keys?"

"Yeah, I guess there are somewhere, but I don't think anybody knows where."

"What do you mean? Don't the people who put their stuff in here have a key?"

"Not always. Sometimes people die and no one ever finds the key. But that ain't the problem." He grinned like it was an inside joke.

"What's the problem?"

"Problem is, the bank fired everybody so fast when they shut down, they lost track of the master keys!"

"The master keys?"

"Yeah." Ramone pointed to a door. "You see, you need two keys to open the box: the key they give to the person who rented the box, and the master key for the box."

Iris stared at the two keyholes and noticed one hole was larger than the other. She looked at the box and then back at Ramone. He seemed to know an awful lot about it.

Ramone pointed to Box 1143. "I got to watch them drill this one. It took 'em forever to find the sweet spot. That little old man was pissed. Said it took him two years to get all his paperwork approved." He laughed a raspy belly laugh like it was yesterday.

"How long ago was that?"

"Must've been ten or fifteen years ago. No one's been down here in ages."

There were rows and rows of locked doors inside the vault. Her eyes widened as she processed what he had said. "Do you mean there's still stuff in these boxes?"

"Yeah, a few of 'em. Hard to say how many. At least, for the time being anyway." He tapped on a door.

"What do you mean?" Iris asked.

"Well, the owner's going to gut it and sell the place, last I heard. I don't know what they're going to do with all of this stuff, but time is running out." He waved his hands at the walls as if he'd be glad to be rid of them. From the looks of his hands and crooked back, he had been stuck in the building for decades.

"But don't the people want their stuff back?"

"Beats me." Ramone shrugged. "Lot of 'em are probably long gone. Dead or moved away. After all the years I spent working in this place, I keep my money in a coffee can."

Iris looked again at the doors that had been forced open. There were ten. She quickly scanned the rows and columns of doors. They were stacked twenty high and over thirty deep on each side. That was at least twelve hundred boxes, she calculated, and only ten had been drilled open. That left hundreds of boxes that might still contain God knows what.

Brad emerged from around the corner, holding his tape measure. "Hey, let's see if we can't get this basement laid out today."

Iris heard a note of irritation in his voice. She jumped to attention and grabbed her clipboard. A few steps down the hall, she glanced back. Ramone was still standing in the vault, studying the boxes.

CHAPTER 7

Monday, November 6, 1978

The head of Human Resources led Beatrice up the elevator to the ninth floor, down a hall, and into a large room. There were eight desks paired into four rows. The desks were surrounded on three sides by a ring of closed office doors. There were no windows to the outside. The room was lit only by buzzing fluorescent bulbs and the occasional green desk lamp.

"Ms. Cunningham will be in charge of you," the woman in the polyester suit explained.

"Oh, I thought I was working for Mr. Thompson." Beatrice scanned the seven women corralled in the room, each at her own desk.

"Honey, all of these ladies work for Mr. Thompson. He's the head of the department." The HR lady rolled her eyes. "Ah, here's Ms. Cunningham now."

A powder keg of a woman barreled toward them. She was short and round, and her stockings rubbed together loudly as she went. She had an exasperated look in her eyes and a worn-down pencil in her hair.

"Is this the new girl?"

"Yes, this is Miss Baker." She turned to Beatrice. "Ms. Cunningham will show you the ropes around here. Let me know if you have any problems."

Ms. Cunningham nodded in agreement and marched back toward her office. Beatrice had to run to catch up.

She pointed Beatrice to the chair and slid her large girth behind the desk. "Where are you from, Miss Baker?"

"I'm from Marietta originally." Beatrice crossed her fingers that that would be the end of the inquiries regarding her past.

"What brings you to Cleveland?"

"I came to stay with my aunt in Cleveland Heights two years ago."

"Interesting."

Ms. Cunningham examined Beatrice intently. The woman must have been at least sixty, but there was nothing grandmotherly about her. It became clear to Beatrice that this was going to be the real interview for the job.

"Why did you leave home, Miss Baker?"

"My father died and my mother . . ." Beatrice took a moment and let her voice break. "My mother became very . . . um . . . ill." She lowered her eyes to the floor as if shamed by her mother's mental health. "I had nowhere else to go."

Aunt Doris had insisted that her story had to reveal something terrible, humiliating even, to satisfy her interrogator. When Beatrice glanced up, she could see that Ms. Cunningham's eyes had softened.

"Can you type?" she asked.

"Eighty-five words per minute."

"Excellent. Let me give you one word of advice, Miss Baker. I take everything that happens in my department personally. If you have any concerns or observe anything that doesn't meet our standard of excellence here at the bank, I need you to report it to me immediately." She looked Beatrice hard in the eye, and then smiled. "Let's get you started."

An hour later, Beatrice sat at a small metal desk in the third row of the secretarial pool, staring at her shiny, new electric typewriter. *It must have cost a fortune,* she thought, as she turned the switch on and off, fascinated by the low hum of the motor as it whirred to life. She ran a finger over the soft button keys. They felt like the control panel of a spaceship compared to the long claws of Doris's old Remington.

Standard-issue stapler, tape dispenser, steno pads, pencils, pens, paper clips, binder clips, and scissors all gleamed in their wrappers under the fluorescent lights. She hadn't received any assignments from Ms. Cunningham yet, so Beatrice slowly unwrapped and studied each one. She opened the drawers of her desk one by one, inspecting the insides before carefully placing every item in its proper place.

Years earlier, organizing her dollhouse had given her the same giddy satisfaction. Even though every little chair and bedside table she'd collected was mismatched and came to her dirty or broken, Beatrice meticulously cleaned each one and positioned it perfectly in its proper place. Her mother would mock her for caring more about the insides of that little three-foot box than her own house. But the house she grew up in wasn't really hers. She was just a guest in it—that's what her mother would say. It turned out the dollhouse wasn't really hers either. One day when she was thirteen, she came home from school and it was gone.

Beatrice was lining her pencils up in a tight row when the polished black phone on her desk rang. The sound made her jump, and for a moment she just stared dumbly at it. No one had taught her the correct procedure for answering outside calls. It was her first test in her new position. She straightened herself in her seat and picked up the phone. Summoning her most formal voice, she said, "Good morning, First Bank of Cleveland."

"You need to relax. You're making me nervous," a woman's voice whispered into the phone.

Beatrice blinked at the rotary dial on her desk for a moment. "Wha—? What do you mean?"

"It's just your first day. Take it easy. Your obsessive organizing is making the rest of us look bad."

Beatrice realized it must be another secretary in the room. She lifted the phone away from her ear slightly and glanced at the desk next to hers. The older woman sitting beside her was swiftly typing. Francine was her name. When they were introduced, Francine had glanced up from her work with only the slightest nod. With her horn-rimmed glasses and pursed lips, she reminded Beatrice of an old schoolmarm. It certainly wasn't her on the phone.

Beatrice glanced furtively at the women seated in front of her. In the next row, two overweight motherly types were seated side by side, quietly filing. An almost elderly woman sat at a desk two rows up, separating a pile of papers into neat stacks while speaking tersely into her phone: "No, I don't have the C-3 form. I sent you a C-44, and that should have been sufficient . . ."

Next to the angry grandmother sat a pretty young woman who couldn't have been more than twenty years old. She was struggling with her typewriter, trying to force several pages through the roller. Beatrice heard her softly curse when one of them tore. None of the women in front of her had called.

Beatrice had no choice but to turn around to find the voice on the phone. She cautiously scanned the ring of closed doors surrounding the work area. Muffled voices were coming from behind several of them. Mr. Rothstein was on the phone. A tall silhouette moved across the frosted-glass panels of Mr. Halloran's office. She only knew their names from the little signs on their doors. The coast was clear, so she slowly turned in her seat and looked behind her.

There were two women seated in the last row. One had her head down, typing. The other was holding a phone. Beatrice heard her whisper "Bingo!" in her ear. "Meet me in the ladies' room in five minutes." She hung up before Beatrice had a chance to answer.

Beatrice snapped her head back around, having barely glimpsed the mystery woman's brassy blond hair and red lipstick. Ms. Cunningham hadn't specifically said that chitchatting in the secretarial pool was frowned upon, but she hadn't heard any friendly conversation so far. Speaking aloud seemed to be reserved for business purposes only.

Five minutes ticked by one at a time on the big clock hanging over the front of the room. Beatrice finally stood up at her desk and looked around. Ms. Cunningham hadn't so much as cracked her door since showing her to her chair. The surrounding office doors were still shut tight, and the other secretaries' heads were down in their own business. Beatrice was unsure if she needed to ask permission to use the bathroom but was too embarrassed to ask. She tiptoed out of the secretarial pen toward the ladies' room. Her small feet padded silently on the olive-green carpeting until she reached the hall, where her shoes clacked loudly on the linoleum tiles. The racket sent her scurrying like a startled cat into the restroom.

"Good Lord! Why are you so high-strung?"

Beatrice spun around and was face-to-face with the mystery woman. She was a knockout, like a movie star. Her smoky blue eyes were lined with false lashes and charcoal. Her blond hair was set in a French twist with a crown of tight curls. The blouse was low cut, and the skirt was an inch shorter than it should be, making the woman look almost garish.

"Um, I guess I'm a little nervous." Beatrice let her eyes wander around the ladies' room, trying not to seem so anxious. She leaned against a sink for effect.

The stranger sauntered to the window and lifted a piece of marble from the sill. She retrieved a pack of cigarettes and a lighter from underneath. She was clearly amused at Beatrice's confusion. She lit a cigarette and explained, "Old Cunningham banned smoking in the secretarial pool last year. Said it was a fire hazard. So, what's your name?"

"Beatrice."

"I'm Maxine, but you can call me Max. Don't worry so much. Cunningham may be a bulldog, but she's okay. She's certainly not going to fire you on your first day or anything." Max paused to blow smoke out a cracked window and look Beatrice up and down. "How the hell did you get this job? You can't be more than sixteen."

Beatrice stiffened at the accuracy of Max's assessment. She focused on the perfect red lip-stains at the end of her Virginia Slim to keep from fidgeting. "I'm eighteen, actually. I applied for the job."

"Did Bill interview you?" Max asked with an arched eyebrow.

"Bill?"

"You know, Mr. Thompson."

"Yes, Mr. Thompson interviewed me." Beatrice began to wonder what the heck she was doing in a bathroom watching Max smoke when she should be at her desk. "What do you care?"

"I don't, but it just figures. Mr. Thompson has a weakness for the young girls, if you know what I mean."

Beatrice's mouth fell open.

"Oh, keep your girdle on! I don't mean he molests Girl Scouts or anything." Max smirked, seeming amused at how easy it was to shock Beatrice. "I'm just saying he likes hiring young girls. He hired me a few years ago. Catch my drift? Just be happy you got to meet with Bill instead of that goat Rothstein. He handpicked Cunningham and the other bloated old maids in the room. Rothstein would have sent you back home to your mama!" Max chuckled.

Beatrice changed the subject. "Are we allowed to go to the restroom without telling someone?"

"Sure, but if you're gone longer than five minutes, you better have a damned good excuse. The poor girl that had your job last kept running to the toilet and got fired. It was probably for the best, though."

"Why's that?"

"She had family problems, if you know what I mean."

Beatrice shook her head.

"You know." Max pointed to her belly.

"They fired her for that?" Beatrice's eyes widened. She paused and looked at the open bathroom stall and pictured a poor girl sick on her knees. The tiles looked cold and hard.

"Of course! First Bank of Cleveland is a family business. Kind of ironic, right? Just keep your head down and your ears open, and you'll get the hang of things around here. Besides, now you have a friend to show you the ropes."

"Uh, thanks!" Beatrice was beginning to wonder how Max, with her cleavage and long lashes, fit into the family business.

Max ground out her cigarette on the windowsill. "Listen, meet me in the front lobby at 5:00 p.m. I'll buy you a drink and tell you all about it."

Before Beatrice could answer one way or another, Max was out the door and clicking down the hall.

CHAPTER 8

At 5:01 p.m. Beatrice met Max in the lobby and followed her out the heavy revolving doors. She wanted to call her aunt to tell her that she would be late, but she couldn't risk being scolded like a child in front of Max, who was pulling her by the arm down the street.

The wet, cold wind bit at their legs as they made their way from 1010 Euclid Avenue up East Ninth Street. The street was clogged with Buicks and Lincolns and the occasional bus. Men in long coats with perfectly coiffed hair crowded the sidewalks. Most kept their heads down as they rushed past the "For Lease" signs dotting the storefronts. No one smiled as they brushed shoulders, each one trying to get ahead of the next guy. Jobs were getting harder to come by; that's what Aunt Doris had said.

After a few blocks, Max turned a corner onto a side street and led Beatrice down three steps and through a door that read "Theatrical Grille." The bar was dark, dank, and nearly deserted on a Monday evening.

A stout man with a thick, black mustache and bushy lamb chops stepped out from behind the bar with his arms open wide. "Ah, Maxie! *Bella!* How are you this evening?" He picked up her manicured hand and gave it a ceremonial kiss. "Who's your beautiful friend?"

"Oh, stop flirting, Carmichael!" Max swatted at him. "This is Beatrice."

"Beatrice, welcome to my pub. What can I get you lovely ladies? Your first round is on me." His merry eyes and rosy cheeks made Beatrice grin back at him as if he were a long-lost uncle.

"I'll have a stinger. How about you?" Max looked over at Beatrice.

"Me?" Beatrice squeaked. She had never been in a bar before. "Uh, a stinger sounds great."

To her relief, Carmichael didn't ask for proof of her age; he just bowed deeply and disappeared back to the bar.

"So, what did you think of your first day?" Max slid into a booth and lit a cigarette.

"It was great."

"Great? Oh, come on now."

"Okay. It was pretty dull." Nothing had happened all day. Ms. Cunningham seemed to have forgotten about her, and none of the men in the offices asked for her help. "I guess I don't know what I'm supposed to be doing yet."

"Old Cunny will have to assign you to one of the middle men if you want to get busy and keep this job."

Beatrice flushed at the unflattering nickname Max gave their boss. The mention of losing her job helped maintain her composure.

"The middle men?"

"Yeah, the little guys that work for Bill. The ones in all the offices. No one really knows what they do. They sit in their offices and take calls, and every once in a while they want you to type something. If you want to stay at the bank, you need to find one that likes you and stick with him."

"Who do you work for?"

"Well, seven years ago when I started, I was working for this mouse of a man named Miner. He would scamper around and stare at me with these little beady eyes. But he got the ax four years ago." She paused as Carmichael brought over the drinks. The tall fluted glasses were filled to the brim with something pink and fizzy, and each was topped with a cherry. "Come to mama." Max grinned as she sipped off the top of the glass and popped the cherry in her mouth.

"Thank you," Beatrice said to Carmichael, and waited until he left to turn back to Max. "So what happened after Miner left?"

"Well, old Cunny tried to get rid of me, but Bill convinced her to keep me on a special assignment, and I've been working for Bill ever since."

"A special assignment?"

"I can't really discuss it." Max waved her hand.

"Does he let you call him Bill?" Beatrice debated whether to ask about the assignment. Maxine seemed nice enough, but she couldn't help but wonder about the cleavage falling out of her tight blouse.

"Oh God, no!" Max laughed. "But what he don't know can't hurt him, right?"

Maxine took a deep drag off her cigarette and began to fill Beatrice in on the office gossip. The stern librarian, Francine, was Mr. Thompson's cousin, and a spinster. One of the heavy ladies was a divorcée. The other was a widow. "The Sisters Grim," as Max called them, were always together. "They eat together, work together, go to the bathroom together—it's a little queer, if you ask me," Max said with a smirk and a wink.

Beatrice nearly spit out her drink. "But I thought you said this was a family business!"

THE DEAD KEY 51

"Well, sure, but what family doesn't have its secrets?" Max's eyes twinkled. "So what about you, kid? What's your story?"

Beatrice turned her eyes to her glass and drank the sweet fizz slowly as she stalled for time. She didn't know how much she could trust this new friend who loved to gossip. Her glass was suddenly empty, and she was still struggling with what to say.

"Garçon! Another round!" Max called to the bar, and turned her giant, probing eyes back to Beatrice. "So, where are you from?"

"Marietta." That was an easy one.

"How long have you been in Cleveland?"

"About two years. I came to live with my aunt." She was careful not to mention Doris's name, and Max didn't ask. The lies were becoming so natural to her that Beatrice almost believed them.

Apparently, that was enough information for Max to piece a few things together. She nodded as if she understood what could happen to a girl in a small town that might make her leave.

The next round of drinks came. Max stirred hers and began to chew on the little red straw. Beatrice took a long drink of the sweet stuff and felt her head begin to lighten and drift.

"I've lived in Cleveland all my life. I grew up on the west side. My dad was a cop." Max took another sip and changed the subject. "I think you might do well working for Randy Halloran. The girl that had your job last used to do everything for him, and now he's a bit lost."

"You mean the one that had . . . ?" Beatrice pointed to her stomach.

"Yep. I'll find a way to introduce you. But watch out, kid. That man's a shark."

"A shark?"

"Just keep an eye on his hands, especially after long lunches. He's a bit of a lush."

"Like a drunk? But won't he get fired for drinking on the job?"

"Of course not. His father is the vice president of the bank!"
Max laughed. "He's got a job for life."

"That doesn't seem fair."

"What's fair about anything?" Max's eyes flickered. "These rich
bastards grow up in their east-side mansions, go to their private
schools, and never do a hard day's work in their little privileged
lives! The important thing is that if he likes you, your job is safe."

By the time they left the bar, Beatrice was more than a little
dizzy. The cold wind felt good on her warm cheeks. The streets
of Cleveland were empty at 8:00 p.m. Not even a taxicab could be
found. The two of them made their way to the corner bus stop and
sat down on the bench. An empty paper bag blew by and landed in
the dirty snow in front of the shelter.

Max lit another cigarette. She gazed down at the bag and then
surveyed the empty street. "Man, this town is dead! I would love to
live in a real city, like New York or Chicago."

"Why don't you?" As far as Beatrice could tell, Max could do
anything.

"Oh, someday I'll leave this dump." Max stared up at the factory soot in the streetlights.

She waited until Beatrice was safely on the bus. "Are you going
to be okay by yourself?" Beatrice asked, looking at her beautiful
new friend and then around at the empty sidewalks.

"I told you. I've lived here all my life." Max smiled and sauntered away toward Terminal Tower.

CHAPTER 9

"Beatrice? Can you take a memo?" Mr. Halloran poked his head out of his office after lunch. Max had made good on her offer, and Beatrice had been working for Mr. Halloran on a regular basis for almost two weeks. He met her at the door and led her toward the desk with his hand on the small of her back. It was getting more and more difficult to overlook the way his hands and eyes lingered on her body.

"Something's different," he said with a half smile. There was vodka on his breath.

"Hmm? Oh, I have a new blouse."

Max had taken her shopping the week before. "I'm not looking at your sad, flea-bitten wardrobe for one more minute!" Max had cackled, and swiped Beatrice's paycheck out of her hand. "We're going shopping!"

"Shopping? But . . ." Beatrice frowned at her oversized plaid skirt and the run in her panty hose she'd tried so hard to hide. Standing next to Max's sleek, flared pants and skintight blouse, she looked utterly ridiculous.

"What's the matter? Doesn't your aunt let you out of the house?"

Beatrice shrugged. She had been ducking out of work a few minutes early each day to avoid going out again with Max. Her aunt had been furious when she'd come home drunk two weeks before.

"Come on, Bea! You're a grown woman. You can't let your aunt run your life."

"But I don't have any money for shopping."

Max had waved the paycheck in her face.

"Yeah, but I don't even have a bank account."

"Well, that's easy to fix!"

Max had grabbed Beatrice by the hand and pulled her back through the main lobby of the building to the banking floor. The tellers were just closing up for the day. Max dragged Beatrice over to one of the barred windows.

"What am I going to tell my aunt? She told me to bring my paycheck home to her."

"Are you friggin' kidding me?" Max demanded. "How long are you supposed to be her meal ticket?"

"Oh, I don't think she'd steal it. She just doesn't want me to go spending it all. That's what she says. She wants me to save up so I can afford a place of my own someday."

"Well, that's nice. But you can't just put your whole life on hold, waiting for someday to get here. What if it never does, and then what do you got?"

"What am I going to tell her?"

"Tell her . . . tell her the bank has requested that all of its employees open savings accounts to 'improve investor confidence.'"

Max was a genius. It was as if Mr. Halloran or some executive were talking. That settled it.

Beatrice smoothed the lapel of her new knit top. It was covered in little paisleys and hugged her ribs.

"I like it." Mr. Halloran grinned. After an uncomfortable pause, he seemed to remember himself and turned toward his desk. "Have a seat. I need you to take a letter."

Beatrice obediently opened her steno pad. After practicing nearly every day with her Gregg shorthand manual on the bus to and from work, she had mastered a sloppy sort of shorthand. She was beginning to feel like a real professional.

"Attention: Mr. Bruce Paxton, Federal Reserve Board." He gazed out his window at the Cleveland skyline. "I understand your interest in our recent trading activity; however, I must remind you that the Gold Reserve Act of 1934 has been repealed . . ." Beatrice took notes while he lectured the addressee. She lost all track of the content of his words as she jotted them down in little swishing lines. She was almost able to keep up. He closed the letter with, "President Nixon may have abandoned the country to inflation, but we are banking on gold. We intend to fight this investigation all the way to the Supreme Court."

Her eyes widened as she jotted down the words. "Is someone investigating the bank, sir?"

"Hmm?" he replied as if he had forgotten she was there. "Uh, no, Beatrice. This is just a formality. Just tag it with my usual closing and type it up."

"Yes, sir." She stood to leave.

"Wait, Beatrice. There is another matter I'd like to discuss with you."

She sank back down to her seat. "Yes?"

"What I am about to tell you can't leave this room, do you understand? Can you keep a secret?"

She swallowed. "Um. Yes, sir."

"We have reason to believe that there is a mole working here at First Bank of Cleveland, someone who is trying to sabotage the company from within."

"A mole?"

"A spy." His eyes simmered darkly.

Beatrice waited for him to say more. According to the letter he had just dictated, the Federal Reserve was investigating the bank, and she wondered if that had anything to do with it. After a long pause, she had to ask, "What does this have to do with me?"

"You're friends with Maxine McDonnell, aren't you?"

"Yes, of course."

"I need you to find out what special projects she's working on with Mr. Thompson."

"You don't think Max has anything to do with this, do you?" Her stomach sank.

"Her? No," he said, waving his hand dismissively. "I just need to know what Mr. Thompson and his team are up to."

"And you think Max will tell me?"

"She'll feel more comfortable talking with you. Girl talk. You know." He winked at her. "Of course, I'm going to need you to keep this conversation strictly between us. Maxine can't know you're working for me."

He walked over to her chair and took her hand. As he gazed down at her, his smile deepened. His eyes darkened. "Can I count on you, Beatrice? Your loyalty will not go unnoticed."

The way he was standing over her, she panicked he would lean down and crush her with a kiss. She rose from her seat awkwardly and took a step toward the door. "Of course, Mr. Halloran."

"Randy," he said, leaning closer. He was still holding her hand.

She shook it firmly just as she'd been taught and then wrenched her hand free, making as if her notes needed sorting. "Of course, Randy. I'll see what I can find out."

"Wonderful. I'll expect a report sometime in the next two weeks."

She nodded and scurried to the door. "Okay, happy Thanksgiving!"

"Happy Thanksgiving to you too, Beatrice."

Back at her desk, Beatrice shuddered at the thought of what might have happened if she hadn't escaped when she did. Max had said, "The man's a shark." And now the shark wanted her to get information out of her one and only friend.

They had even shaken hands on the whole deal. It was self-defense, she protested, but now she was trapped. Her very job might depend on getting Randy what he wanted. But Max would know something was fishy if she started asking about secret projects.

"Hey!"

Beatrice let out a small squeak. Max had appeared next to her desk, as if on cue. She shook her head a little and tried to laugh casually. "Oh goodness, you snuck up on me." She wasn't fit to be a spy.

"You look nuts. I think we need a drink!" With that, Max grabbed her elbow and led her out of the office and down the street to the Theatrical Grille. "Say, what are you doing for the holiday tomorrow night?"

"Oh, I think my aunt has to work. She's always working the holidays." Beatrice remembered Doris complaining the week before about the drunks who would wander into the diner late at night on Thanksgiving to avoid spending time with their relatives.

"So are you going back home to Marietta?"

"No, my mother and I don't . . ." Beatrice trailed off, at a loss for words.

Max's penciled brows were raised, but her eyes were soft. "Why don't you forget your silly family and come home with me tomorrow?"

"Are you sure it would be all right with your family if I came with you?" Beatrice was overwhelmed by the generous offer, especially considering what a horrible friend she was turning out to be.

"Are you kidding? I come from an Irish Catholic family. I doubt they'll even know you're there."

Max pushed her way into the Theatrical.

Carmichael waved from the bar and rushed to their side. "*Bellas!* What can I get you today?"

Max kissed him on the cheek. "How 'bout a couple of screw-drivers? We're working girls after all—we need all the tools we can get!"

CHAPTER 10

Thanksgiving morning, Beatrice woke up to an empty apartment. Aunt Doris had come in late the night before and left early. Beatrice was getting worried that she hadn't really seen or talked to her aunt in days. She was relieved she didn't have to lie about working late when Max insisted on having a drink at the Theatrical or about opening her own bank account, but it wasn't like Doris to come and go in the dark.

Beatrice peered over the arm of the couch at her aunt's room. The door was wide open, and the bed was made. Beatrice never went into her aunt's bedroom. It had been off-limits since she moved in. Even when Doris was gone, Beatrice always respected her aunt's wishes.

"You can live here as long as you follow two rules—keep your space clean, and stay out of mine," she'd said with a grin and a smack on the back. Beatrice suspected that taking in her troubled niece was a stretch for Doris. She'd always lived alone, as far as Beatrice knew, and didn't care much for family. At least, the family didn't care much for Doris. Her mother wouldn't even speak her name.

Beatrice sat up on the couch and stretched. The lumpy cushions always left her feeling bruised. She pulled her hand-knit slippers onto her size 6 feet and padded across the cold floor to the tiny brown refrigerator. She filled a coffee cup with OJ and foraged for breakfast. The fridge always contained at least a six-pack of beer and a leftover pizza, but that morning it was nearly empty. One beer and a few slices of cheese. When she closed the refrigerator door, she noticed a small note on the Formica counter.

"Dear Beatrice, I have to work late tonight. Swing by the diner and wish your old auntie a happy Thanksgiving. Love, Doris."

Happy Thanksgiving, Beatrice thought, and looked around the empty room. She reminded herself to be thankful, but a familiar loneliness sank into her gut. It had been so long since the holidays were happy. Memories of turkey and bacon wafting out of her mother's shotgun kitchen had nearly faded away, but not quite. There was a time when her father would tickle her under her chin, and her mother would laugh. She was a little girl then. She felt her throat tighten. This year was supposed to be different. She gripped her mug of juice until the tears dried in her eyes.

Beatrice neatly folded her thin, flowered bedsheet and stashed it with her pillow in the hall closet as she did every morning. She returned to the sofa and peeked again into Doris's bedroom.

The room was tiny, barely big enough to hold the queen-sized bed and its painted iron headboard. The bed's lattice crown was twisted with iron flowers and vines, but the paint was cracked and peeling. A ratty patchwork quilt covered the mattress. The bed was shoved against the far wall next to a crooked window, and Beatrice could see the brick driveway through the yellowed sheers that hung from a rusted curtain rod. She inched her way inside.

A small dresser flanked the wall next to the door, leaving just a thin strip of worn wood flooring between it and the bed. The path led to a narrow closet door. It was slightly open, and the sleeve of Doris's flannel robe waved at her. Dusty knickknacks crowded the top of the dresser. In the corner, several necklaces strangled a porcelain cat. Beatrice couldn't remember seeing her aunt wear jewelry of any kind, ever. She stepped into the room and ran a finger over the gold chains and beads.

In the other corner, two young women smiled up at her from a black-and-white photograph. The girls looked strangely familiar. They couldn't have been more than eighteen years old with their happy, wide-eyed, and optimistic faces. It was the image of her own mother, Ilene, that Beatrice first recognized from a few buried photographs she'd seen growing up. The other woman must be Doris. She snatched up the photograph in disbelief. Doris looked beautiful. This younger version of her aunt was nothing like the stout, worn-out woman she had come to know. Her hair was neatly curled in a bob. She was wearing high heels and a dress.

Despite how unsettling it was to see Doris in a dress, eventually Beatrice found herself staring into her mother's eyes. Ilene smiled innocently up at her from the picture frame. It didn't seem possible that the girl in the photograph could also be the woman who raised her. Tears made the picture a blur. She carefully placed the photograph back in its dusty home.

Beatrice crept toward the closet. As she touched the door, cold fear inched up her spine, and she couldn't help but look over her shoulder. She had no idea what Doris would do if she caught her snooping. Wincing from the hard slap she could feel coming, she swung the closet door open.

A tightly packed pile of clothing threatened to collapse on top of her. It was as though twenty years' worth had been shoved inside.

Coats, suits, dresses, blouses, linen bags—all were crammed onto the three-foot rod. Wire hangers were stacked one on top of the other. The floor and shelf above the rack were packed with shoe boxes.

Beatrice could not remember Doris wearing one thread of clothing in the lot. Her fingers itched to pull out an item and take a closer look, but she was certain she would never be able to fit it back into the mess. A glimpse of a mink coat teased her from the back of the closet. Knee-high leather go-go boots with three-inch heels leaned toward the front.

The Doris she knew wore the thick-soled leather lace-ups favored by nurses and cashiers. Her aunt's daily wardrobe consisted of polyester pants and white button-down shirts. Beatrice couldn't remember her wearing anything else. There was no sign of Aunt Doris in the whole closet, except for the robe hanging on the inside of the door from a nail.

Beatrice carefully closed the closet and approached the dresser. She didn't know why she was being so quiet. Doris wouldn't be home for hours, but she found herself holding her breath as she opened the top drawer.

Granny underwear and socks were folded in straight piles. Beatrice averted her eyes and shut the drawer. She nearly lost her nerve and checked the door. There was no one there. The middle drawer was next. She found five pairs of polyester slacks and seven button-down shirts. This was the Doris she knew and loved—or tried to anyway. That left the bottom drawer. She pulled on it, but it resisted. The drawer facing was plain pine and had a little carved flower in the middle. Beatrice scowled at the dainty rose as she struggled to wrench the drawer free, pulling again and again. It finally flung open, and she fell back on her rump.

Paper—reams and reams of yellowing paper were strewn about in the drawer. Beatrice lifted a page from the top of the three-inch pile. It was on letterhead that read "First Bank of Cleveland." It was a notice to a customer regarding their safe deposit box. Beatrice scowled and looked at it more carefully. It was a carbon copy. She could tell by the feathered ink around the edges of the typeface. The letter was signed "William S. Thompson, Director of Audits." Under his name were the initials of the typist, "DED." Doris? Had Doris typed the memo? Beatrice sat back, stunned, with the paper in her hand. Had she worked at the bank too?

Beatrice laid the letter back down in the drawer. Doris hated answering questions about the past. She never explained why she had left Marietta all those years ago, or why she and her sister, Ilene, hated each other. She certainly never mentioned working at the bank.

Beatrice thumbed through more pages, looking for some sort of explanation. Underneath sheets and sheets of bank letters, she noticed a different type of paper toward the drawer bottom. It was beige and soft, like cloth. She carefully lifted the stack of bank letters at a higher angle so she could get a better look at the parchment below. It was covered in beautiful cursive ink. She read upside down.

My Dearest Doris,

The nights without you are killing me. I must see you again. Forget this terrible business, forget my wife, forget everything but our love. Every time I . . .

She couldn't make out any more of the letter without pulling it out of the drawer. She didn't dare try. Doris would notice if her things had been shuffled around. She closed the drawer, careful not to disturb any of the papers, and tiptoed out of her aunt's bedroom.

Beatrice sat on the couch, bewildered. Aunt Doris had been in love, or rather someone had been in love with her. That someone had a wife. Her head spun with the possibilities. Did the affair happen while Doris worked at the bank? Was the man some shark, like

Mr. Halloran? Did she lose her job because of it? Beatrice glanced back at her bedroom.

Doris had secrets; she had a closet full of fancy clothes that she never wore and a drawer of letters. On top of the dresser, the black-and-white photograph sat in its frame, and her aunt was young and smiling.

CHAPTER 11

Monday, August 10, 1998

That Monday, Iris didn't roll out of bed at 7:50 a.m. It didn't matter if she was a few minutes late; there was no one to check up on her in an abandoned building. No makeup or awkward business casual clothes were required. In her old T-shirt, jeans, and baseball hat, she left for work feeling like herself instead of her stilted impression of a grown-up engineer. It was almost like not going to work at all.

Her beater car pulled in front of the rolling garage door behind the old bank at 8:41 a.m. Iris got out and stretched leisurely. A block away, a young woman was rushing down the sidewalk in a suit, balancing a coffee and a briefcase. Iris smiled to herself and pressed the white button by the loading dock entrance. Somewhere inside, Ramone heard the call and opened the door. She parked across all three spots in the loading dock and finished her cigarette, downed her coffee, and set out for another day of wandering the deserted hallways of the First Bank of Cleveland with her tape measure.

Clipboard in hand, she spent the morning tracing her steps down the hallways that circulated around the dead elevators on the third floor of the old bank, drawing a rough sketch of the floor plan. She stopped at a door that read "Human Resources" and pushed it open. It was another drab 1970s room with low drop ceilings, bad carpet, and avocado furniture. The broken windows were boarded up, so she flipped on the lights. She walked through the sitting area and behind the receptionist's desk. The drawers had been pulled open, and papers were strewn everywhere. A name plaque lay facedown in a file drawer. Iris picked it up and read "Suzanne Peplinski." She placed the name plaque back on top of the desk, as if Suzanne might be coming back soon. The center drawer of the desk still had a handful of paper clips and an unopened box of pens sitting inside it.

"What happened, Suzanne? You leave in a hurry?" she joked, and pushed the drawer closed. It was more creepy than funny.

Iris's shoes thumped past the desk and into the office behind it. The door read "Director of Human Resources Linda Halloran." The desk in the middle of the room was empty. Iris opened the drawers and saw that they were empty too. The bookshelf behind the desk was barren. There were no traces of Linda anywhere. Iris broke out her tape measure and plopped her clipboard on the desk with a thunk. It took five minutes to measure the room and mark up her sketch. When she picked her notes back up, her fingers left claw marks in the thick dust coating the desk. She wrote "Wash Me" next to her fingerprints, then brushed her hand against her jeans.

Iris left Linda's office and wandered over to a narrow file room. Eight feet by fifteen feet she measured, and marked the graph paper. There were ten filing cabinets lining one wall. Yellowed labels were still taped above each handle. Iris scowled at them. She set her clipboard down and pulled out a drawer. It was still full of manila folders. She pried one open and found a hand-typed pay stub.

"What the fuck?" she said under her breath.

The bank had shut down and left its records behind. Looking down the row of cabinets, she realized they probably contained detailed information on every person who worked at the bank. Iris glanced over her shoulder at Linda's empty office and pulled out another drawer. Haas, Haber, Hall, Hallock—there were no files for Halloran. Iris looked again but found nothing. Maybe Linda left long before the bank shut down.

"What about you, Suzanne? Are you in here?"

Miss Peplinski's file was right between Peples and Peplowski, where it was supposed to be. Iris yanked it out of the drawer and opened the folder. A small, yellowed photograph of a woman in her late forties smiled up at her with slightly crooked teeth. The attached form listed Suzanne's birth date, her address, and her social security number. Iris flipped back to the picture. Suzanne would have been sort of pretty if it weren't for the checkered blouse with the built-in bow tie and the frizzed-out hairdo. Maybe it was the flickering fluorescent lights, but she began to feel like the woman in the photo was looking back at her. She flipped the file closed.

Poor Suzanne, Iris thought. *One day you're sitting at your typewriter minding your own business, and the next day you're fired.* Suzanne probably showed up on time to work every day, like a good worker bee. *And look what it got her.* Maybe her bartender friend, Ellie, was right. The bank owners just chewed her up and spit her out when it suited them.

Iris left the file room and plopped herself down at Suzanne's desk. The chair was padded but not comfortable. Iris spun the paper Rolodex wheel. A flurry of dust scattered across the strewn papers that covered the fake wood desktop.

A coffee mug sat on the opposite corner of the desk next to an ashtray. *At least Suzanne was allowed to smoke at her desk*, Iris thought, and pulled her own cigarettes out of her field bag. She checked the ceiling for an active smoke alarm before lighting one. It was a tiny rebellion, smoking on the job, but Iris couldn't shake the feeling she was going to get caught. It wasn't professional.

"Fuck 'em," Iris muttered, and took another drag but kept a watchful eye on the door.

The box of ballpoint pens in the center drawer caught her eye. She could always use more pens. It wasn't like Suzanne needed them. Iris picked up the box and gave it a gentle shake. Something hit the bottom of the metal drawer with a clink. It was a small bronze key.

"What the . . . ?" She picked it up. There was "547" engraved on one side. Surrounding the number were tiny letters that read in a circular arc "First Bank of Cleveland."

Iris sucked on her cigarette, turning the key over in her hand. The longer she studied it, the more she suspected that it was for one of the safe deposit boxes in the basement vault. It was too small to be a door key, and then there was the number. She ground out the cigarette in the ashtray and pulled the drawer open wider. Ramone had said all of the vault keys went missing when the bank was sold. Maybe they'd been right there in Suzanne's desk all along.

She shoved aside the paper clips and highlighters in the center drawer and found nothing. She pulled open the other drawers one by one and shuffled through papers and hanging files. If she found all of the keys, she figured, someone would be overjoyed—Mr. Wheeler, the client, somebody. A twenty-year-old mystery solved by a lowly engineer just doing her job, going above and beyond the call. Maybe they would even let her open one of the boxes. They would track down its rightful owner, who would surely be some sweet little old lady down on her luck.

Before Iris had a chance to fully plan the hero parade through the streets of Cleveland, her hunt came up empty. She slumped back in the chair with the one key in her hand. Not ready to give up, she told herself there could still be more keys lying around in the building. Besides, she couldn't just put Key 547 back in the drawer and walk away. What about the little old lady? Maybe that little old lady was Suzanne Peplinski. The key was in her desk after all.

Her eyes darted around the abandoned office. It wouldn't really be stealing if she took it, she argued. She wasn't taking it for herself. With that, Iris slipped the key into her back pocket.

CHAPTER 12

Iris left the old bank late that evening with the key still in her pocket. She needed a drink. Outside the loading dock, the sweltering heat of August was waiting, but at least the air wasn't full of dust. She lit a cigarette and hiked up East Ninth Street, past the office building where WRE occupied the ninth floor. There wasn't a bar in sight. East Ninth was a no-man's-land for blocks. She didn't want to walk all the way down to the bar district known as the Flats. Not by herself. She was about to turn back when she saw a small lit sign for Ella's Pub on Vincent Avenue.

Dank, smoky air greeted her at the door. The pub's shotgun layout included a long bar on one side of the aisle and seven vinyl booths on the other. The place was deserted except for the barkeep and another man, slumped at the far end on a bar stool. She shoved her heavy bag into one of the empty booths and slid in beside it. Her back and fingers ached from walking all day, clutching a clipboard in one hand and a pen in the other. No amount of stretching seemed to help, but she tried again, lit a cigarette, and closed her eyes.

"Hard day?" a voice asked next to her. The little old man from behind the counter looked like he'd been living under the bar for fifty years. He was wrinkled and smoke stained from head to toe. His bushy eyebrows were raised in a smile.

"Hard enough." Iris couldn't help but grin at him and his rosy, bulbous nose and impossibly large ears. One of Santa's naughty elves had apparently been banished to Cleveland. She tried not to stare at his earlobes as they hung like mud flaps nearly down to his collar.

"What can I get for you?"

"Guinness. Do you serve food?"

"Ah, I wish we still did. We have some snacks at the bar. Do you like peanuts?"

"Sure, thanks."

"It's my pleasure, and please . . . call me Carmichael." He bowed a little and went to fetch her beer and nuts.

Iris took the key out of her pocket and turned it over again, thinking about the desk where she'd found it. Suzanne was older but not that old in her company photo. She was probably still alive. She'd be at least sixty, but that was hardly dead and buried.

Out of the corner of her eye, she noticed Carmichael coming back with her order and palmed the key. He set down her drink and a bowl of nuts with the flourish of a five-star waiter.

"Thank you, Carmichael."

"You let me know if you need anything else." He winked and went back to his perch behind the beer taps. A small black-and-white TV was playing a baseball game in the corner. Carmichael and the guy at the end of the bar stared at it without speaking.

Iris took a gulp of beer and opened her hand to look at the key again. She had technically stolen it. But only to give it back to its rightful owner, she argued. Who was that exactly? There was Suzanne, who may or may not be alive. Then there was the owner of the building, which was some real estate holding company that bought it for a song, from what Brad had told her. They didn't care about the building; it was just a tax write-off. First Bank of Cleveland shut down twenty years ago and left its files and furniture behind. They weren't exactly abandoned to vandals, Iris reminded herself. The doors were chained, and the building was guarded. Still, would the owners even care about Suzanne's desk, or would they just pitch everything into a dumpster when they sold the building? Suzanne, she decided, was the only person who might know who owned the key.

The beer went down too easy as she crunched the peanuts and perused the bar. It was frozen in time, just like the old bank. All of the beer signs and music posters were at least fifteen years out of date.

Carmichael noticed her eyes wandering and waved. She pointed to her beer glass, and he nodded. He poured a second pint and brought it over. He was about to go back to his game when she decided to strike up a conversation.

"This is an interesting place."

"You like it?" He smiled.

She nodded. "How long have you been here?"

"Oh, I bought the place must have been thirty years ago," he said, looking up at the tin ceiling. "It was different then. We called it the Theatrical Grille. Ever heard of it?"

Iris shook her head.

"Once upon a time there was a famous jazz club right where you're sitting. It was the hottest spot in town. Ella Fitzgerald played right over there." He pointed to a corner in the back. "I was just a kid then, but it was something."

Iris raised an eyebrow and tried to picture a band packed into the tiny corner. "What happened?"

Carmichael threw up his hands. "Times change. Music changes. Even a city as old and rusty as this one changes. Short Vincent was the hottest strip in town back forty years ago. Shoot, twenty years ago. Now everyone is down in the Flats listening to that god-awful dance music. I can't stand the stuff. Makes my head hurt. Young girl like you, you probably like it, right?"

"Not so much," she lied. "Sounds like you've seen a lot over the years."

"You don't know the half of it." He chuckled and shook his head.

Iris glanced around at the dated décor and decided to risk a more personal topic. "Do you remember the First Bank of Cleveland?"

He frowned and ran his fingers through his thinning hair. "Of course! It was only a few blocks away. Used to get all sorts coming in here after five o'clock." He moved to the other side of the booth to sit down. "You don't mind if I sit, do you? I have a terrible back."

"No, please." Iris took a swig from her pint glass. "Do you know why the bank closed?"

"I heard they sold it, but I can't be sure. It was the strangest thing. One day it was there, and the next day it was gone. Chains on the door, boards on the windows. They even took the sign off the front of the building in the middle of the night." Carmichael's forehead creased into a road map as he frowned.

"You're kidding."

"It was terrible. All of those people went to work one morning and found out they'd lost their jobs. The way I heard it, most of them didn't know until they tried to open the door. Some people lost a lot of money in the deal." Carmichael's eyes darkened and his shoulders seemed heavy. "Some of those people came in here that day. It was a mess . . ."

Iris nodded. If she'd been fired like that, she'd go to the nearest pub too. Talking about it seemed to deflate Carmichael.

"Ah, well." He waved his hand at the past and turned his attention to Iris. "What is a young girl like you doing asking about the old bank? That must have been at least fifteen years ago!"

"It was twenty years ago actually." She took another big drink. "I'm working in the old bank right now, if you can believe that."

Carmichael's smile dropped a little. "I don't believe that. What do you mean?"

Crap. Iris was supposed to keep the work at the bank confidential. That's what Mr. Wheeler had said. The county didn't want anyone knowing their plans for the building. "Oh, you know. The owner is doing a . . . routine inspection. I'm working for the architect." Iris congratulated herself on thinking fast and took another drink. Hell, what would a bartender care about the county plans anyway? "I have to survey the building, and I'm telling you, it's weird!"

She described the cafeteria with its empty tables and ancient vending machines. She told him about the conference rooms that still had notes scribbled on the chalkboards. She stopped herself from saying more. The personnel files, the safe deposit boxes, the fact that she was working alone in a huge building seemed like information best kept to herself. Besides, Carmichael's intense stare was starting to weird her out.

"You mean no one has been in there for all these years? Amazing!" He slapped the tabletop, grinning, but his eyes still seemed way too focused. He pointed to her beer. "Let me get you another."

The two beers on an empty stomach were hitting her hard, and the place was starting to give her the creeps. She shook her head. "No, I should be going, but thanks!"

The old man nodded and tore a handwritten bill for seven dollars off of his notepad. As Iris waited for change, she scanned the sketch on her clipboard. The graph paper read, "Wheeler Reese Elliot Architects, LLC" at the top. Next to the crisp logo, her sloppy writing looked like a third grader's. She sighed as she scanned her messy drawing. She would have to clean it up before handing it in for review. As she studied the sheet, something else began to bug her. She rifled through her file until she found the plan for the second floor. She compared the sketches of the second and third floors and discovered that they didn't match. Somehow she'd missed a full column bay on the third. Her drawing was ten feet short. She smacked herself in the head. She examined the two drawings side by side, trying to reconcile the discrepancy. She threw up her hands and stuffed the drawings back in her bag. She would have to go back to the third floor and see what she'd missed. It would only take fifteen minutes, she decided, and tamped out her cigarette. She had to go back to the building to get her car anyway.

Carmichael handed her the change. "It was very nice to meet you, miss."

Iris stood up from the booth and extended her hand to shake his. "I'm Iris. It was nice meeting you too, Carmichael."

She headed out the door but stopped short.

Carmichael was behind the bar, rinsing out her glass. He raised his bushy eyebrows. "Did you forget something?"

"Yeah, sort of. I meant to ask when we were talking about the old bank. Did you ever know a woman named Suzanne Peplinski? I think she used to work there."

"I can't say that I did. Was she a friend of yours?"

"No. I just think I found something that might belong to her." Iris shrugged and waved good-bye.

His voice stopped her. "You found something?"

Iris didn't answer.

"There's a saying where I come from, *bella*. Never steal from a graveyard. You might disturb the ghosts."

CHAPTER 13

Behind the old bank, Iris pressed the worn white button on the squawk box and waited. It was nearly dark outside, and the streets were deserted. The words "you might disturb the ghosts" echoed in her ears, and she pressed the button again. She stared into the black, recessed lines of the speaker box as if it were a video camera and Ramone was watching. But he wasn't.

She pressed the button again. Her car was trapped behind the metal door. After a solid two minutes had passed, she kicked the garage door and stomped to the front of the building to search the windows for signs of life.

The streetlights filled Euclid Avenue with a yellow haze. She pressed her nose to the glass next to a revolving door and peered into the main lobby. It was murky with shadows, and there was no sign of Ramone inside. She banged on the glass anyway.

"Shit!" she hissed.

She took a step back. The front of the building was clad with rough-hewn granite blocks. The street number 1010 was carved deep into one of the stone quoins above the sidewalk. Next to the address was a shadowy blank spot, where a large plaque had been bolted. Iris guessed that this must have been where the First Bank of Cleveland sign had been removed in the middle of the night. The hollow metal sleeves for the bolts were still embedded in the stone as if they were waiting for another sign to come along.

Iris craned her neck up. Red brick and sandstone stretched up to the chemical-orange sky. Each little window was topped with a stone crown, and all of them were dark. The roofline cornice hovered high over the sidewalk. Even in the near dark, its ornate brackets and stone flowers were majestic.

Headlights flashed three blocks down, reminding Iris it was too late at night to be walking alone on the streets of Cleveland. The traffic light at East Ninth and Euclid turned green, but no cars were at the intersection. An overweight woman was waiting in the corner bus shelter for her ride home.

"I cannot believe I'm taking the friggin' bus home tonight," Iris muttered to herself as she crossed the deserted five-lane road toward the shelter. She turned back and surveyed the old bank again. There were no lights on. "You just had to go get a beer. Great idea, Iris."

She turned toward the bus stop when a flicker caught her eye. Squinting up at the fifteenth floor, she saw the flicker again. It was a flashlight. She wanted to scream at the top of her lungs to Ramone but knew it would be a waste of breath. He wouldn't hear her, and there was no way she would be able to throw a rock far enough to hit a nearby window.

A passing car reminded Iris she was still standing in the middle of Euclid Avenue. She ran back to the rolling garage door on Huron Street. Her smoker's lungs were burning by the time she reached the call box. She pounded the white button three times. Almost instantly the door sprang to life. Iris closed her eyes in relief. *Thank God.* She could get home tonight. When she opened them, Ramone's face was just inches away.

"Oh God!" she yelped.

Ramone just glared at her. Apparently, pounding the button on a speaker box could be highly irritating.

"Ramone! You scared the shit out of me!"

"Was you expecting someone else?" he said in his smoker's growl. "Don't ever bang on the button like that again, okay?"

"Sorry. I've just . . . How did you get down here so fast?"

"I was just around the corner."

"No. I saw you. You were up on the fifteenth floor."

"What the hell you talkin' about?" He looked at her like she was on drugs.

"You. With a flashlight. Up on fifteen. I saw the light through the windows."

His focus sharpened. "You sure about what you saw?"

"Yeah, there was definitely a flashlight moving around up there."

"You stay there," he said, motioning to her car. "I'll go check it out." He reached under his shirt to grab a humungous flashlight hanging from his belt. She caught a glimpse of a black gun in a holster next to it. That settled it. She scuttled over to her car like she was told and watched him disappear down the service corridor in her rearview mirror.

Iris locked her car doors and laid her seat back to hide. *You might disturb the ghosts,* Carmichael's voice taunted her. "Shut up, Carmichael!" she whispered.

For the first few minutes, she sat frozen, fretting about what was happening up on fifteen. Then she picked her fingernails clean. She counted the cigarette burns on the ceiling of her car until she finally broke down and lit one. She cracked the window and listened for the sound of a gunshot or a flashlight beating someone over the head. The digital clock glowed 9:01 on her dashboard. Five more minutes, and then she was getting the hell out of there.

She turned her thoughts to who the intruder might be and came up with nothing. The bank had been shuttered for twenty years. *Why the hell would anyone be skulking around now? It's probably just Ramone's girlfriend putting her pants back on.* The thought made her chuckle, but nothing about the guard's grizzled demeanor said he'd been laid in the last decade.

Her cigarette burned down to the nub. To keep from lighting another one, Iris pulled the plans for the second and third floors out of her purse and examined them again. There was the same number of columns running north to south, and the elevators were in the same location, but something was missing around the service corridor. There was no way she was going up there alone in the dark that night. The clock read 9:04. Two more minutes until she drove to the police station.

She was just about to turn the car on when Ramone came lumbering down the loading dock stairs in the rearview mirror.

"Whoever it was must've left." He looked annoyed and tired.

"But who could it have been?" She couldn't believe how nonchalant he seemed. He was a frigging security guard. Wasn't he supposed to be in riot gear or something?

"Every once in a while a homeless person finds their way into the building. They're harmless. Just looking for a place to sleep." He lit a filterless cigarette with a paper match. Ramone may not have been much of a guard, but he was hard-core.

"But how do they get in?" She hadn't noticed any broken windows or giant holes in the wall while walking around the building.

"Oh, you'd be amazed. They're like rats. They find their ways. Mechanical ducts, roof hatches, tunnels . . ."

"Tunnels?"

"The old steam tunnels. They connect a lot of buildings downtown. This building is linked up to the whole block."

"But we surveyed the whole basement. We didn't see any tunnels."

"I'll show you 'em tomorrow. You should be gettin' home."

Iris nodded in agreement and then thought to ask, "How about you? Don't you ever go home?"

"Yeah, every few weeks. I'm what you call a full-time guard. They pay me to sleep here."

"That sounds terrible," she said without thinking. She didn't mean to be judgmental, but between the dumpster and the dreary silence, she felt for the guy.

"Oh, they pay me pretty good."

"Aren't you worried? You know, about the intruder?"

"Who, me?" He seemed surprised at her concern. "Shit, I've been here thirty years. If somethin' was going to happen to me, it would've happened already."

He opened the dock entrance for her and shuffled back into the building as the door rolled shut.

CHAPTER 14

Thursday, November 23, 1978

Beatrice was about to leave the apartment and go see Doris at the diner when she heard a knock at the door. She froze. No one ever knocked on their door.

"Who . . . who's there?" Beatrice called as she backed away from the sound. Her eyes darted around the apartment until they locked onto a kitchen knife.

"It's Max."

Beatrice rushed to the peephole. Max was standing in the stairwell, tapping her foot. "Max! What are you doing here? I mean, how did you find me?"

"You're not hard to find, kid. Open the door."

"But . . ." She cut herself off and frowned. Max had never taken her home, and Beatrice had given a false address at work. She unbolted the door.

"So is the Wicked Witch of the West home?" Max pushed her way into the apartment.

"No, she's at work."

"Nice place."

"Thanks. It's not much but . . ." Beatrice looked around the tiny two-room apartment she called home at a loss for words.

"Say, is that what you're wearing?" Max asked.

Beatrice looked down at her bell-bottom jeans and the over-sized shirt knotted at her waist and shrugged. "What do you mean?"

"You're coming to Thanksgiving, remember?"

Beatrice looked at the clock. It was 12:30 p.m. "Isn't it a bit early?"

"We do Thanksgiving dinner at 1:00 p.m. at my house. If we don't start early, we never finish." Max laughed.

Beatrice hesitated, thinking about Doris, but she could always stop by the diner on the way home. "Okay. What should I wear?"

An hour later they arrived at the McDonnell home in Lakewood, a small working-class suburb just west of Cleveland. The house had a large front porch with a bench swing hanging at one end, and two rocking chairs at the other. The stone stairs were worn down from millions of footsteps. Max swung the door open, and the chatter of the crowd inside spilled out onto the porch. The tiny house was stuffed to the brim with people and the warm smell of turkey fat and baked pumpkin.

Max dragged Beatrice into the crush of people. The names and faces flew in rapid succession—Rhoda, Ricky, Mary, Timmy, Sean, Patrick. Max rattled off the introductions, and after the first ten, Beatrice gave up trying to keep track. Every new face had a smile and a nod. Small children weaved in and out of the forest of pants and panty hose that filled the long and narrow living room. Crying babies were bouncing on hips. Max pulled Beatrice deeper into the house until they reached the kitchen.

Chafing dishes and foil-wrapped pans covered the counter from end to end. A two-foot stack of paper plates sat near the sink, and two women were busy preparing the meal.

"No room for more cooks!" the older woman sang cheerfully without looking up.

"Hey, Mom. I want you to meet somebody."

Max's mother glanced up from a large pot. Her face was thin and worn, but her blue eyes were mirror images of her daughter's. Her graying hair was pulled back in the French twist that Max often wore. In her apron and pearls, she was a page from a 1950s *Better Homes and Gardens* magazine.

"You must be Beatrice. I've heard a lot about you. I'm Evelyn McDonnell."

"Pleased to meet you," Beatrice said shyly, and shook the woman's flour-covered hand.

"Hi, Beatrice! I'm Darlene." Darlene's loose shirt had several food stains, and her hair was a mess of red curls.

"Hi!" Beatrice waved back and said to them both, "Thank you for having me to dinner."

"It's our pleasure, dear!" Evelyn beamed.

Beatrice marveled at the endless array of food on the counter and Evelyn's serene smile as she stirred pots and pulled sheet pans from the oven.

"Maxine, would you please let everyone know that we'll be eating in ten minutes. And ask your father to come carve this bird."

"Stay here," Max ordered Beatrice and then pushed her way through the crowd.

Beatrice played with her hands awkwardly, standing in the corner. There was nowhere to sit in the small, square kitchen. Evelyn lifted what looked like a prehistoric bird of prey from the oven and set it on the butcher block in the center of the kitchen. It was the biggest turkey Beatrice had ever laid eyes on. It was amazing the tiny woman could lift the thing.

"Is there anything I can do to help?" Beatrice asked, feeling awkward and useless.

"Not a thing! You're a guest in our house. I'm just so glad to finally meet a friend of Maxine's."

"Yeah, she usually only hangs out with old men," Max's sister snorted.

Evelyn narrowed her eyes. "Darlene, honey, why don't you go get some more napkins from the cellar?"

Darlene opened her mouth to argue but thought better of it. She exited the kitchen with the gait of a Mack truck.

"You'll have to forgive Darlene." Evelyn waved an oven mitt. "She's always been a little jealous of her sister."

Beatrice smiled to make light of the incident. "Max has been a wonderful friend. She's really helped me fit in over at the bank."

"Well, she's been working there for a long time," Evelyn said, laying tinfoil on top of the enormous turkey. She turned to pull the carving set from a drawer. "I just hope they get to the bottom of all those accusations. It's such a scandal!"

"Scandal?"

Evelyn nodded, sharpening the carving knife against a honing rod. "What bank doesn't keep reliable records of their deposits? The whole thing is simply mad. They'll be lucky if the police don't get involved."

Beatrice's jaw nearly dropped at the word "police."

"Is somebody talking about me?" a deep voice asked.

Beatrice turned and saw a young man waltz into the kitchen.

"Oh, Anthony. Don't be silly," Evelyn scolded him with a smile. He bent down and kissed her on the top of her head.

"Hi, Mom! Who's your friend?" He motioned to Beatrice. His broad shoulders, square jaw, and heavy brow were offset by boyish blue eyes and dimples.

"This is Beatrice," Evelyn said, wiping the carving knife with a rag. "She works with Max at the bank. We were just talking about the crazy mess they're trying to sort out over there."

"Are you harassing my friend, Tony?" Max said from the doorway.

Tony's face broke into a smile again as he spun around. "That's Detective Anthony McDonnell to you!"

"Don't mind him, Beatrice. He's been insufferable ever since he made detective last year. Mom, I can't find Dad anywhere, but the masses are growing restless."

"Oh, he's probably out smoking a cigarette in the garage. I'll go get him. Anthony, please start slicing up that beast."

Max pulled Beatrice out of the kitchen. "Come on, let's get some fresh air."

They fought their way through the packed living room to the front porch. Somewhere along the way Max had managed to grab two drinks. She handed one to Beatrice and plopped down on the porch swing to light a cigarette.

"Your mom is very nice," Beatrice began.

"Yeah, she's amazing. I have no idea how she manages to deal with all of this. I don't think I could do it. Hell, I have no desire to do it."

"Yeah." Beatrice turned to the window. A red-faced toddler was pulling at her mother's hair. "What did your mother mean about a scandal at the bank?"

Max stopped sucking on her cigarette and raised her eyebrows. "I'm not sure. What did she say?"

Beatrice recounted what Evelyn had said about the deposits and the police, trying not to sound as though Mr. Halloran had given her an assignment to spy on her friend.

"Oh God!" Max shook her head, clearly irritated. She downed her cocktail and hit her cigarette again. "My mother is an idiot!

There is no fraud or police investigation. The bank lost some records, and I'm helping to reconstruct them."

"Is that the special project you've been working on with Mr. Thompson?"

Max paused, studying Beatrice's face. "Yeah. I took an irate phone call from a customer a few years back. Seems like the bank lost her safe deposit box. I went to Mr. Thompson, and he asked me to work on the problem. The whole project had been sort of hush-hush because Bill didn't want a bunch of rumors flying around the office."

Beatrice nodded, even though what Max had said made no sense to her. For one thing, why would Mr. Halloran care about an audit of the safe deposits? And why did Max's mother know so much if the whole thing was hush-hush?

Max saw her scowling and sighed. "My mother was worried I was having some sort of affair, since I was working so many late nights at the office. I had to tell her something so she wouldn't cart me off to the nunnery. I could kill her for being such a loudmouth. Can you keep this a secret? Bill might fire me if he thinks I'm blabbing this stuff all over the office. If I can get this job done for him, I might even get a promotion."

"Of course!" She couldn't look Max in the eye.

Maxine stood up and threw her cigarette into the snow piled up against the side of the porch. She linked elbows with Beatrice and said, "Great! Let's go eat. I'm starving!"

CHAPTER 15

Beatrice had never eaten so much food in her life. Three glasses of wine and four courses into the meal, she thought her stomach would burst. In the chorus of clinking glasses and silverware, Beatrice had learned about Aunt Mae's rose garden, a sister's cat, and a nephew's potty habits. Her face ached from smiling, and her neck was stiff from nodding. She whispered to Max she would be back, and hoisted herself up from the chair.

She waded past four crowded tables to the door. The air out on the front porch was blessedly cold and still. She blew out a long trail of steam. There had to be a way to leave the party gracefully. She was exhausted from all the chatter. Besides, Doris might be missing her at the diner. There were so many questions she wanted to ask her.

Max's brother Tony was slouched in the bench swing, smoking a cigar. "Nice night."

"Yeah it is."

"Do you want to sit down?"

"Oh, no, thanks. I feel like I've been sitting for hours."

"I know what you mean." He grinned. "I'm impressed you were brave enough to face the entire McDonnell clan. How are you holding up?"

"Oh, I'm having a lovely time." As she spoke, she glanced through the steamed window, looking for Max. Her chair was empty.

"Well, Maxie must really like you. She never brings friends home." He tapped his cigar on the porch rail and asked, "Do you have family near here?"

"I live with my aunt on the east side. I really should be getting back soon. My aunt is working, and I'd feel terrible if I didn't wish her a happy Thanksgiving."

"Well, you are in a pickle, aren't you?" His dimples were back. "I mean, my mom hasn't even brought out the desserts yet."

"Oh gosh. I don't want to be rude," she said, feeling a twinge of desperation. The sun was beginning to set behind the house.

"I don't know about you, but I can't eat another bite," he said, patting his perfectly flat abdomen. He stood up. "What do you say we bust out of here?"

"What do you mean?"

"Leave it to me." He opened the front door for her and whispered, "Let me do the talking."

Five minutes later, Beatrice was in Tony's unmarked Ford LTD, staring at the dull red emergency light on top of the dash. Max had protested them leaving, but no one ever seemed to argue with Tony. He had them all wrapped around his finger. Beatrice made a mental note to apologize to Max on Monday.

The CB scanner buzzed softly below the eight-track player as they drove through the snow across the crooked river.

Tony seemed amused at her fascination with the dashboard. "You ever been inside a police car?"

Beatrice shook her head.

"I'd been in plenty before I joined the force. If you can't beat 'em, join 'em, right?" The way he chuckled reminded her of Max. "Say, I hope my sister isn't getting you into too much trouble there at the bank."

"Trouble?" Beatrice frowned. "What do you mean?"

"Oh, she's such a busybody, getting into everyone's business. If I didn't know better, I'd say she should have been the detective."

"Do you mean the missing records?" She tried to seem casual.

"That and a million other little intrigues. She's always coming up with conspiracy theories about the rich families in town and their relationships with the bank. You know, First Bank of Cleveland has the highest deposits of any bank in northeast Ohio. You should be proud to work there." He rolled the car off the freeway and began making his way south toward Little Italy. "You live up Mayfield, is that right?"

She blinked and realized she hadn't told him where they were headed. "Um, yeah. Did Max tell you where I live?"

"Not exactly. Let's just say it was discussed."

"Discussed?"

"Maxie was all worked up about some mix-up at the bank on your address. You may want to look into that, by the way. Apparently, your file has an error in it. It says you live at a restaurant or something."

Beatrice gaped at him. Someone had discovered that she had lied on her employee questionnaire, and it was Max.

"I told you she's a busybody. She even had me look you up in the police records." He flashed her a reassuring grin. "Don't worry. You weren't in there."

"Is that legal? Why would she do that?" Her voice was becoming shrill.

"Well, it's all public record. I just have better access. What can I say? I'm a sucker for my little sister."

Beatrice opened her mouth to say something, but nothing came out. Tony turned toward her at a stoplight. "Don't worry so much. Max really likes you. Besides, what have you got to hide?" He patted her knee as if that settled the matter.

Beatrice smiled uneasily. "Could you drop me off at the diner up there? My aunt is working."

Tony slowed the car, and Beatrice tried to relax. Perhaps Max's snooping was truly harmless. She'd invited her to Thanksgiving after all. Maybe she really was just a busybody. Beatrice decided to change the subject.

"So, did you just say that the bank works with all of the richest families in town?"

"Yep, from Carnegie to Rockefeller, it seems like they all preferred the First Bank of Cleveland. Half of 'em actually sit on the board of directors. Brodinger, Swede, Mathias, Wackerly, Halloran . . ."

Beatrice had heard of Rockefeller, but none of the other names registered until he said Halloran.

"Some even speculate the Covelli family holds an interest at the bank."

"Who?"

"You live in Little Italy and haven't heard of the Covellis?" He raised an eyebrow.

Her expression was blank.

"They're the last family in town that's still connected to Sicily, or so we think."

Beatrice nodded, even though she wasn't sure what he was talking about. The car slowed, and he pulled to the curb in front of the diner where her aunt was pulling a double shift. Tony got out of the car and escorted her to the front door.

"It was very nice meeting you, Beatrice. If you ever need anything,"—he reached into the pocket of his wool overcoat and handed her a card—"call me."

She took the card. It read "Detective Anthony McDonnell, Cleveland Police Department." It wasn't quite clear if he was offering her police protection or flirting with her. "Thank you, Detective," she said shyly.

He chucked her chin. "Happy Thanksgiving, Beatrice."

The unmarked police car left tracks in the snow as she stood there holding the detective's card in her hand.

CHAPTER 16

Beatrice walked into the greasy heat of the diner and looked for Doris. The bright lights made everything seem more dingy. Random customers, mostly older men, were scattered around the room, sipping coffee and eating pie. The diner was running a skeleton crew from the looks of things. There was only one cook in the back and one waitress, limping around with a pot of black coffee.

Beatrice waved her down. "Hi, Gladys. Happy Thanksgiving! Is Doris here?"

"Oh dear!" The old woman set down her scorched pot on the breakfast counter. "Beatrice."

Beatrice's smile disappeared.

Gladys grabbed her hand and led her to a chair. "I had no idea how to reach you. I'm so sorry, but Doris is at the hospital."

"What? What happened?" Beatrice felt the blood drain from her face.

"Oh, honey." Gladys patted Beatrice's hand. "I'm not really sure what happened. One minute she was fine, and the next thing we knew she was on the ground. The ambulance came and took her to University Hospitals. Mick went with her. That was two hours ago."

As Gladys explained, her voice sounded farther and farther away. Beatrice sank down onto one of the stools at the lunch counter.

"Let me call you a cab so you can get to the hospital." Gladys patted her hand.

Beatrice might have nodded, she wasn't sure. She had no idea how many minutes she sat there staring at the floor until Gladys helped her into a taxi and paid the driver to take her to the emergency room. The icy air outside the diner forced her to blink.

She turned to Gladys and managed to whisper, "Thank you."

The emergency room was bedlam. Every seat was full. People were leaning against the walls. There was a baby crying somewhere. One woman clutched a wet red towel around her hand. A man sat with his head between his knees. There was a line five people deep at the registration counter. Beatrice kept her eyes on her feet as she waited to talk with the nurse.

When she finally reached the counter, the nurse was busy writing something on a clipboard. "Um, excuse me? I'm looking for Doris Davis. I think an ambulance brought her here."

"Was she admitted?" the nurse asked without looking up.

"I'm not sure. They said she was taken in an ambulance."

"You need to check with admitting. Go out those doors and walk two blocks that way," the nurse said, pointing the way with her pencil. "Next!"

Beatrice wanted to protest, but her eyes filled with water. She backed away from the counter and ran out of the waiting room. Outside, her stifled tears became sobs. She leaned against a light pole and shook with them.

"Are you okay, miss?" a voice asked.

Beatrice didn't bother to look up at whoever was talking. She waved them away and stumbled down the sidewalk, wiping her wet face with shaking hands.

Doris had been taken to the intensive care unit. The lady behind the counter directed Beatrice to a bank of elevators. She reached the fifth floor and found her way to another desk.

"M-my aunt was brought here tonight in an ambulance. She fell at work."

The night nurse looked up at Beatrice's red eyes and smeared mascara, and her face softened a little. "What's her name?"

"Doris Davis."

"Let me see what I can find out." The nurse walked away, leaving Beatrice alone in the ICU lobby. Beatrice could hear the muted whirring and beeping of machines just beyond the reception desk. The air smelled like industrial cleaner and urine. The thought of Doris spending the night there made her nauseous, and she collapsed into a chair, rocking back and forth.

Under her breath she hummed, *"Hush-a-bye . . . Don't you cry . . . Go to sleep my little baby . . . When you wake, you shall have . . . All the pretty little horses."*

It was her lullaby growing up. She couldn't recall anyone ever singing it to her, but it must have happened. She couldn't remember how old she was when she started singing it to herself.

The nurse finally returned to the lobby, carrying something. It was Doris's purse. The nurse set it down on the front desk and walked over. Beatrice stopped breathing. She was sure Doris was dead.

"Your aunt had a stroke."

The purse on the sterile desk was the end of a tunnel. Beatrice felt herself sinking.

"She's in a coma," the nurse continued. "Dr. McCafferty has gone home for the night, but he'll be back tomorrow to answer any questions you might have."

Coma. The word registered slowly. She sucked in a breath. Doris wasn't dead. "Can I see her?"

The nurse led Beatrice down a narrow corridor flanked with glass doors. They reached the last door on the right, and the nurse cracked it open. Inside, a woman lay motionless on a stark white bed. Tubes laced in and out of her nose and right arm. Beatrice hardly recognized the body on the gurney, but it was Doris. Beatrice backed away from the open door and staggered toward the lobby with her hand over her mouth. She'd almost reached the elevators when the nurse's voice stopped her.

"Wait. Don't forget her purse!" she called, and carried the brown bag over to Beatrice. "We never recommend leaving personal items like this here at the hospital. We can't be held responsible for them."

Clutching the purse, Beatrice walked the half mile home from the hospital alone. The cold wind tore through her coat as she climbed the hill, but she could barely feel a thing. When she finally reached the apartment, she let herself inside and sank onto the couch, still gripping Doris's purse. The leather was soft and worn.

Her eyes circled the room. What now? What was she going to do now? She tossed the bag onto the coffee table in front of her. It fell, spilling everything to the floor—seven dollars, a hairbrush full of gray snarls. Her aunt's pack of Kools was half-empty and wrinkled. She put the pack to her nose and smelled the cigarettes. Her eyes filled with tears again.

She tenderly picked up her aunt's key chain and cradled it in her palm as if she were cradling Doris's hand. She hadn't touched her hand in the hospital. Instead she had run away.

Beatrice gripped the keys until they hurt. She recognized the apartment key and the key to the basement laundry. There was another key that she figured must be for work. The last key was strange. It was smaller and more intricate than the others. It looked older. She turned it over and saw that it had a number on it. It read "547." She stared at it until her swollen eyes fell shut.

CHAPTER 17

Beatrice walked into the office on Monday still in a trance. The doctor had given her a long explanation involving bursting blood vessels, smoking, and bad luck, but she could barely make sense of any of it except that Doris may never wake up.

"You look awful!" Max mock scolded her. "Were you out drinking last night?"

Beatrice didn't dare speak. Tears burned the corners of her eyes. She couldn't cry at work; she couldn't afford to lose her job at a time like this. There was rent, bills, and food to pay for all by herself. Alone. A tear spilled down her cheek.

"Meet me in the bathroom. Go now," Max commanded.

Beatrice obeyed. She made her way to a stall and sat down. She couldn't remember the last time she had eaten.

Max came barreling in. "Hey, what's going on with you?"

"My aunt's in the hospital. She had a stroke. I . . . I don't want to talk about it."

"When did it happen?"

"Thanksgiving. I found out after your brother dropped me off."

"My God! I'm so sorry. Is there anything I can do?"

There was genuine concern on Max's face. The sight brought Beatrice to sobs. Max was the first person to offer her help since her aunt's stroke. The nurses were cold. The doctor talked about her aunt as if she were a broken car. She buried her head in her hands.

Max handed her toilet paper to wipe her eyes. "We need to get you out of here. Take the elevator down to the lobby. I'll meet you there in five minutes."

"But what about . . . ?"

"You let me worry about Cunningham. She can't see you like this. Just go."

Beatrice nodded. She stood on shaky legs and caught a glimpse of her red, puffy face in the mirror. Max was right. She couldn't go back to her desk this way.

Five minutes later, Max stepped out of the elevator, grinning. "Old Cunny was feeling very generous today. We both have the day off to help you cope with your family tragedy. Christ, it looked like she might cry herself. How 'bout a drink? You look like you could use one."

Beatrice didn't care where they went as long as she wouldn't be alone anymore. She followed Max out the front doors and up the street to the pub.

Carmichael was behind the bar, prepping for the day, when Max pounded on the glass door. It was locked. The Theatrical Grille didn't officially open until 11:00 a.m. *"Bellas!"* he sang out from behind the door. "What can I do for you?"

"Open up, Carmichael! We have an emergency," Max shouted.

"But you know I can't serve you until I open. The police will give me all sorts of headaches."

"My brother and father insist." Max pushed her way into the bar. "Bring us two gin rickeys."

Carmichael paused to consider the argument and eventually nodded. Max pulled Beatrice to a booth and sat her down. "Tell me everything."

Carmichael rushed over with the drinks, and Max pushed one to Beatrice. Beatrice took a long, slow sip and let out a little gasp as the liquor burned down her throat. She took another sip and the story poured out, from her car ride with Tony, to the beeping machines at the hospital. Max listened and handed her tissues from time to time.

"Then they told me to take her purse home because it wouldn't be safe there. The purse wouldn't be safe there, but I was supposed to leave a whole person. A purse is not as important as a . . . person." Beatrice sniffed. The tears were welling again.

"Of course not." Max patted her hand. She finished her drink and waved Carmichael over with another round. "So did you find anything interesting in it?"

"In what?"

"The purse." Max grinned.

Beatrice stared at her incredulously. It was a wholly inappropriate question, wicked even, but that seemed to be the point. After an hour of weeping, the shot of humor made Beatrice smile just a little.

"You know, I did find something sort of interesting." She pulled her aunt's key chain out of her handbag and set it on the table. "There's a really weird key here."

"It's a safe deposit box key."

"How do you know?" Beatrice picked it up and studied it again.

"Well, it has a number for the box, and it's from our bank. See, it says 'First Bank of Cleveland.'"

"I wonder why Aunt Doris has a safe deposit box." Beatrice squinted and reread the tiny engraving. What she really wanted to know was whether the key had anything to do with the strange letters she had found in her aunt's bottom dresser drawer.

"Oh, you'd be surprised. People put all sorts of things in them. Money, jewelry, legal stuff, you name it."

"What sort of legal stuff?" Beatrice was fairly certain her aunt did not have money or jewelry.

"I don't know. Wills. Birth certificates. Deeds. Hospital records. That kind of thing." Max shrugged. "That's what I've been working on with Bill, you know."

Beatrice shook her head. There were so many things she didn't know.

Max lit another cigarette. "Safe deposit boxes. People stop paying for them. They forget about them, or they get sick or die, and the bank is stuck holding their stuff."

"So what does the bank do with the stuff?"

"Well, they have to keep it for five years by law, but then if no one comes to claim the contents, the bank is supposed to turn everything over to the state."

"What does the state do with it?"

"They sell off the stuff and keep the cash. They supposedly keep a record in case the next of kin comes forward, but they hardly ever do. It's a racket!"

"That's horrible!" Beatrice wiped her nose with a bar napkin. "What if the people realize what happened and want their stuff back?"

"That's what happened a few years back!" Max said with big eyes. "It must have been about four years ago. This little old lady called up my line and wanted to know what had happened to her son's baby shoes and a bunch of other stuff. It took me forever to get a straight answer out of Bill. When I finally told the lady that the state probably threw it all away, she lost it. She came to the bank a few weeks later and threatened to shut the place down. She claimed the State of Ohio had never heard of her or her box. She wanted to go to the newspapers. You should have seen it! You could hear her screaming in Bill's office plain as day!"

"What happened?"

"Nothin'," Max said, stirring her drink with a little red straw. "We never saw the lady again. I got curious, you know? I decided to go look for her."

Beatrice sat waiting. Finally, she asked, "Did you find her?"

"She had died. Car accident." Max puffed on her cigarette. "You know, it didn't feel right. It happened like two days after she came into the bank. It just seemed, you know, strange. I talked to Tony about it. I tried to make him open an investigation. He thought I was nuts. Of course, he wasn't a full detective yet."

"What? You think the bank had something to do with the car accident?" Her voice had dropped to almost a whisper even though the bar was empty. Max shrugged and tugged at one of her brassy curls.

"I'd never seen the office so quiet after that lady left. There were all sorts of meetings. The vice presidents came down and spent hours in Bill's office. He looked like he'd seen a ghost at the end of the day. Tony thinks I'm just imagining things."

"Did you ever tell Bill what you thought?"

"God, no! I did ask a lot of questions. He said I showed 'initiative.' He decided to put me on a new project the next day. I've been auditing the safe deposit boxes ever since." When Beatrice looked at her blankly, she added, "You know, calling the owners, checking the records, that kind of thing."

"Why is it such a secret? That doesn't sound so unusual."

"Well, Bill says he wants to keep it under wraps so that the Deposits Office doesn't get wise they're being audited." Max paused and said in a lower voice, "Besides, every once in a while I find out that some record's gone missing."

Beatrice nodded. Max's mother had mentioned missing records at Thanksgiving. She couldn't shake the feeling that Doris was involved in all of this somehow. The letter she had found was about a safe deposit box. Then she remembered something Max's brother had said. *Max should have been the detective.* "Would it be possible for me to find out what's inside my aunt's deposit box?" Beatrice realized how it sounded and added, "I'd never steal anything from it, but maybe there's a will . . . or something she needs."

"No. Not legally. Not while she's still alive." Max paused and slowly grinned. "But rules sometimes get broken."

CHAPTER 18

Monday, August 10, 1998

Iris closed her apartment door behind her and rested her head on the wall. What a long friggin' day. She dropped her bag in the hall and shuffled into her kitchen to hunt for something to eat. It wasn't until she'd torn through a carton of leftover Chinese food that she could bring herself to look at the answering machine. She rolled her eyes and pressed the button, muttering, "What now, Mom?"

"Iris? Iris, are you feeling any better, honey? Give me a call. I'm worried about you."

Erase.

Iris sighed and pulled off her dust-covered clothes and heard something clank to the floor. It was the key she'd taken from a secretary's abandoned desk. It wasn't abandoned, she corrected herself. Suzanne Peplinski and all of her coworkers had been locked out of the building without any warning.

She picked the key up and bounced it in her hand. The long vault with over a thousand little doors flashed in her head. They were all locked. Ramone had said many of the boxes were still full because the bank had lost the master keys in the sale twenty years

ago. But how? How do you lose keys to an entire vault? Why didn't
the public demand that the boxes be drilled open? She turned the
key over and over and sank back onto the couch in her underwear. Whoever owned the key might have lost something precious
inside Box 547, some little piece of themselves forever locked away
and forgotten.

Maybe no one even remembered what was lost. *A key is worthless unless you know what it's for,* she thought, running a finger over
its teeth. It reminded her of a time years ago she'd gone snooping
through her father's top drawer and found an old leather wallet
filled with keys. Iris spent months trying to decipher them. None
of them went to the house or either car. Her father never took
them to work. Even when he spent weeks away from home on
business, the keys never left the drawer. At eight years old she'd
invented a hundred twisted scenarios filled with secret rooms and
buried treasure chests to explain them. But no matter how hard
she looked, she never found one lock the keys opened. She never
had the guts to admit to snooping and ask about them. Eventually,
she gave up and moved on to something else, but she never quite
looked at her father the same way again. He had locked something
away. Something she could never see or touch no matter how hard
she tried.

Iris spun Key 547 between her fingers. The key had a secret. No
one would just throw a safe deposit key in a drawer and forget it.
If the key wasn't important, its owner wouldn't have opened a safe
deposit box in the first place. It wasn't supposed to be left buried
in the building. In a graveyard, she corrected herself. According to
Carmichael, the building was a graveyard.

Thoughts of the wandering flashlight in the building made her
slap the key down on the coffee table and light another cigarette.
It was really none of her business anyway. She blew a wisp of hair
off her cheek. Her eye wandered from the dusty TV screen to the
blank canvas in the corner and then back to the key on the table.

"Do what you want." That was Ellie's advice.

Fuck it. She picked it back up and stomped into the kitchen to find her phone book. It was buried in the back of a cabinet under the soup pot she never used. She wrestled the tome out of the cupboard and to the ground with a thump. Suzanne Peplinski was not a ghost.

There were three Peplinskis listed—Michael, Robert, and S. She glanced at the stove clock and saw that it was almost 10:00 p.m. Her mother would be outraged, but she decided to try calling anyway.

She picked up the phone and dialed S. Peplinski first. The phone rang three times and a young woman answered.

"Hello?"

Iris cleared her throat, realizing that she hadn't planned anything to say. "Um, hello . . . Uh, you don't know me, but I'm looking for Suzanne. Suzanne Peplinski. Do you know her?"

"Yes, she's my aunt."

"Do you think you could tell me how I might reach her?" Iris asked sweetly. Her heart was racing. She had actually tracked Suzanne down. *Take that, Carmichael,* she thought. There were no ghosts.

"What is this all about?" The woman sounded annoyed.

"I think I found something of hers," Iris said, and realized she'd have to give more. "I think I found her wallet." She hated to lie, but for some reason she didn't want to divulge anything about the key to anyone but Suzanne. Perhaps because she had stolen it, she reprimanded herself. How was she going to explain that?

"Just a second." The woman set the phone down, and Iris could hear her shouting. "Aunt Susie! Did you lose your wallet? Your wallet? . . . *Your wallet!*" Apparently, Susie was hard of hearing. A moment later the exasperated voice returned. "Here, why don't you talk to her, okay?"

An older, raspy voice crackled on the line. "Hello?"

"Suzanne? Is this Suzanne Peplinski?" Iris shouted into the phone.

Iris heard a high-pitched squeal on the other end of the line. "Damn hearing aid," the woman muttered, her voice far from the receiver. Then she said, "Yes, this is Suzanne. What is this all about? You know you're calling awfully late!"

"Sorry, ma'am. I know it's late, but I think I found something of yours." She paused, searching for the words, and finally settled on, "Did you by chance used to work at the First Bank of Cleveland?"

There was a pause. "Yes . . . but how do you know that?"

"I'm sorry. I know it's none of my business, but I've been working in the old building—you know, the one at 1010 Euclid Avenue—and I found something odd." Iris stopped herself before saying, "in your desk." She guessed the woman wouldn't take too kindly to a perfect stranger going through her things.

"Something odd?" the woman said, and coughed a little. "What are you talking about?"

"I found a key, and I think it might belong to you. Did you ever rent a safe deposit box at the bank?"

"A safe deposit box? Are you kidding? I didn't even have a bank account back then. What in the world would I do with a safe deposit box?" There was a long pause, and then she muttered, "Listen, I don't know what that girl told you, but I've never had a deposit box."

Iris's eyes bulged. "Excuse me? What girl?"

"I'll tell you the same thing I told her. I would never trust my money to those crooks!" The sound of smoke blew into the phone. "And I was right, you know. Those bastards chained the doors up tight in the middle of the night. People had to petition the feds just to get their personal things out of their desks! I say that Alistair and those crooks got what was coming to 'em!"

Iris grabbed a pen from the junk drawer and started scribbling on an expired pizza coupon: "What girl? / Alistair got what was coming / Petition feds."

"Did you go back for your things too?" Iris asked, chewing on her pen.

"What for? I told you, I didn't keep anything at the bank."

So maybe the key wasn't Suzanne's after all.

"I'm sorry. Did you say you were telling someone else about this?"

"I'm not saying anything. That girl was crazy. Calling me in the middle of the night like that."

A voice was talking impatiently in the background. Iris didn't have much more time.

"Who called you in the middle of the night? Do you remember?"

"Of course I remember. I'm not crazy, you know." More smoke blew against the receiver.

"Of course not. Who was she? Did she work at the bank too?" Iris pressed.

"It was that itty-bitty thing up in the Auditing Department. Beatrice. Beatrice Baker. Don't believe a thing she says, by the way. She's a liar."

CHAPTER 19

Suzanne's voice rasped in the back of her ears all night. Maybe Suzanne didn't know anything about the key. Then again, she sounded like a paranoid nutcase the minute Iris had asked about it. Iris tossed and turned in her bed, mulling it all over in her head, until only one thought was left—who was Beatrice Baker?

Iris arrived at the back door of 1010 Euclid Avenue almost on time the next day. She pressed the button and rested her sleep-deprived head against the stone wall. In the morning light, all of the midnight drama over flashlights, keys, and lockboxes seemed ridiculous. The door, the sidewalk, the street—everything looked completely ordinary.

As usual, Ramone opened the door without showing his face. Iris parked and sat with her cigarette, debating what to do first. She wanted to run up to the fifteenth floor and see where the flashlight had been darting around the night before, but she wasn't sure she had the guts. Then there was the missing bay on the third floor. She tried to focus on that, but Ramone's comment about the basement tunnels was more intriguing. Ramone was more intriguing for that matter. She still didn't know where the security guard spent his days and nights in the empty building.

It was the voice of her father in her head that made the decision for her. No matter how interesting Ramone and the building might be, she still had a job to do. With a defeated sigh, she fished out the third-floor plan from the old gym bag she'd been using for her pathetic collection of tools and set it on her clipboard. Brad needed the schematics for the first seven floors by Monday. She marched up the loading dock stairs and down the service corridor.

Iris yanked open the door to the third floor and retraced her steps. She slowly counted the columns, starting at the east wall and working her way west. The columns matched. The window count matched.

Everything fell apart in the library. The long and narrow library that ran the length of the third floor on the west side of the building was only twenty-five feet wide. She measured the room again. To match the floor below, it should really be thirty-five feet wide. The library didn't have any windows, because the bank tower abutted the old Cleveland rotunda building to the west; it was a party wall. Iris rifled through her purse to find the second-floor plan. According to her sketch, the exterior wall for the floor below was ten feet farther west than the wall she was leaning on.

She tapped the wall with her pencil as she read the drawings; it sounded hollow. She pounded it hard with her fist. It was definitely not old lath and plaster. It sounded like drywall on studs. Her eyes traced the wall up and down the room. It was seamless. The wall was painted tan and lined with large portraits of old white men. Mr. Wackerly, Mr. Brodinger, Mr. Mathias—every ten feet there was a portrait with a name on a little gold plaque. Their eyes followed her as she went up and down the west wall. Aisle after aisle of books, and she still could not find a door, a window, or an access panel.

Iris gave up on the library and headed to the northwest corner office at the front of the building, where Linda Halloran's desk sat empty. She counted the windows and checked her plans. One window was missing. She counted again to be sure. She walked to the west wall of the office and pounded it. It sounded just like the wall in the library. It was covered in ugly wood panels, but there were no seams. There was a large bookcase in the corner. It was eight feet tall and four feet wide.

Iris walked over to it and nudged it with her foot. It barely shuddered. *Solid oak,* she thought. She peeked into the tiny gap between the bookcase and the wall panel and saw nothing but a shadow. Iris looked down at the green shag carpeting and then back up at the bookshelf. There was no way she'd be able to slide it. She inspected the empty wood shelves and did some quick mental calculations. There was the heavy wood desk and a couple leather chairs in front of the bookcase. They all looked pretty expensive. She hesitated, then walked around the desk and slid the chairs out of the way.

The huge bookcase stood bare and defenseless against the wall. *No one will miss you,* she thought. With her eyes squinted nearly shut, she reached up as high as she could reach, put one foot on the wall, and pulled. The hulking wood creaked off its bearings and began to tip. It teetered on its edge, then the monstrous piece of furniture came crashing down. Wood splintered and cracked. Iris felt the floor vibrate as the bookcase crashed into the corner of the desk and careened to the floor. She stayed crouched with her arms up in front of her face to block shrapnel. She half expected Ramone to burst in with his gun drawn. When nothing happened, she let out a nervous giggle and brushed the dust off her clothes.

She turned and saw exactly what she had hoped to find behind the bookcase. It was a door. Its dark wood matched the surrounding paneling. She tried the small bronze handle, but it was locked. She fished the skeleton key Brad had given her a few days earlier out of her pocket and slid it into the lock. It wouldn't budge. She tried again to be sure.

There had to be a key somewhere. She decided to try Linda's drawers one more time. She felt inside each drawer, corner to corner, for the key. All she found were two paper clips and a thumbtack. She slammed the drawers closed and sat back in Linda's chair, dejected. She glared at the broken shelves, then back at the desk. The wood top was scarred where the bookcase had crashed, but something else about it bothered her. It looked just like it did the day before—big, heavy, and empty. She ran her hand across the writing surface and froze as she realized what was wrong. There wasn't a speck of dust. She stared at the spot where she had written "Wash me." Her words had been completely erased. The wood was pristine. Her eyes darted around the room. The desk was the only thing in the room not caked with grime.

She jumped out of the chair. Someone else had been there. Someone had seen her words in the dust. She ran out of the office into the hallway as if the perpetrator might still be standing there with a dust rag. She stood still and listened carefully to the quiet. The wandering flashlight up on fifteen taunted her.

It was probably just Ramone, she told herself. She forced herself to inhale and exhale slowly three times. It was his job to wander around the building, and if he wanted to clean random things, it was his prerogative. Maybe he was obsessive-compulsive. Maybe he was crazy.

"Hello?" she called out into the hall. "Ramone?"

There was no response. She listened hard again for footsteps or the panting of a madman. If anyone was on the floor with her, she would hear them. The thick silence blanketed everything.

Iris turned back toward Linda's office and the hidden door. At least she'd found the missing space. She drew a blank room ten feet wide and fifty feet long on the third-floor plan and marked the location of the door and missing window behind Linda's bookcase.

The room ran the length of the library and backed up to the emergency stairs. She stared at the plan. The bookcase hiding the door made no sense. It weighed a ton even empty. She wondered if Linda had even known the door was there at all. Iris narrowed her eyes and focused on the place the secret room met up with the stairs. Maybe she'd missed something.

Ramone probably had the key to the mystery door. She also needed to ask about his dusting habits, but she had no idea how to find him. There was a phone out on Suzanne's desk. She lifted the receiver but wasn't surprised it was dead.

Iris picked up a chipped coffee mug and thought about her conversation with the woman who used to drink from it. A girl had called Suzanne in the middle of the night to ask about a safe deposit box. Her name was Beatrice Baker.

Iris sprang up from the chair and headed into the filing room. Inside the drawer marked "Ba–Br," Beatrice Baker's file was right there in black and white. Iris pulled the manila folder out and flipped it open. The first page was filled with hundreds of little handwritten ticks and swirls. It was some sort of writing but unlike any she'd ever seen before. There were pages and pages, and they all looked the same. "What the fuck?" Iris whispered. There was no 1970s headshot, no employment records, and no sign of Beatrice in the entire file.

"What are you doing in here?" a deep voice demanded.

Iris shrieked at the top of her lungs, and her arm crashed into the open drawer. She spun around to the voice, brandishing her Magnum flashlight, ready to throw it in self-defense. It was Ramone.

"Jesus, Ramone! You can't sneak up on me like that!" She tucked Beatrice's file under her arm. "What's the problem?"

"I said, what the hell are you doing up here? It sounded like you were tearing the place apart. You're liable to wake the damned dead!"

She swallowed hard when he mentioned "the dead." Then she realized he was talking about the loud crash a few minutes earlier. "Oh, I had to move a bookcase." She waved her hand as if it were a trifle. Ramone grunted, and she hurried past him, eager to change the subject. She picked up her clipboard and stuffed Beatrice's file under her notepad as if it belonged there. "I'm actually glad you're here. I need some help with a door. It's over here."

He followed her past Suzanne's desk to Linda's office and the wreckage she'd created.

"Why didn't you come and ask me for help?" He glared at the toppled bookcase and back at her.

Iris grimaced and held up her hands. "Uh, I guess I didn't think anyone would mind."

Ramone shook his head. Iris plastered an apologetic smile on her face. The important thing was Ramone wasn't going to quiz her about her snooping in the file room or the folder she'd just stolen. The name Beatrice Baker was peeking out from under her notepad. She adjusted her drawings to hide it. Her heart was still racing as she eyed the spotless desk. She couldn't ask about it now. The question would sound nuts. He probably thought she was a wack job already. Instead, she motioned to the door. "I'm dying to know what's behind this."

"Why? It's just a bathroom." Ramone fumbled with his keys.

"A bathroom?"

"All the corner offices had bathrooms back then—'executive washrooms'—so the big shots wouldn't have to wash up with the regular folks." He shook out a key from his large key ring and tried it in the knob. It wouldn't fit. He tried several more.

"But why would they put a bookcase in front of the door?"

"Who knows? Maybe it was busted and they just decided not to fix it." Ramone tried one more key and then backed away from the door. "The key doesn't match up. They must have changed the lock when they shut the bathroom down. Little things like that got lost in the shuffle, you know."

Iris reexamined the third-floor plan, frowning. She showed it to Ramone and asked, "How could all of this be a bathroom?"

"It's not," he said, pointing at the drawing. "This is the bathroom. This is the mechanical chase. This is the cold-air return." He traced the different spaces out with his fingertip.

Iris nodded, feeling completely humbled. She hadn't thought of the mechanicals. Ramone knew more about how a building was put together than she did.

"Do you want to go look at the bathroom upstairs from this one? They're probably identical."

"No, that's all right. I'm heading that way next anyway. Thanks, Ramone." Iris silently vowed to stop trying to be an amateur detective and focus on being a mediocre engineer instead. Ramone began shuffling back to wherever it was he spent his days. "Hey, Ramone?"

He turned and raised his eyebrows.

"Did you . . ." The words "clean off the desk?" stuck in her throat. It would sound too stupid, and she already felt dumb enough. "Forget it."

He shook his head and headed back down the hall. She listened carefully, memorizing the sound of every footstep, until the door to the emergency stairs swung shut with a loud creak.

Iris spent the rest of the morning drafting the fourth-floor core plan. She carefully laid out the exterior walls, the hallway, the elevators, the restrooms, the monumental stairway, and the emergency egress stairs in the southwest corner. She was determined not to make any more mistakes. She counted the columns twice. Everything matched the third floor. When she'd satisfied herself that there were no missing parts of the building, Iris stopped and stretched.

The blueprints were coming together, but it all seemed pretty futile. According to Brad, the building was probably going to be torn down, along with all the riddles hidden inside. No one would ever know what had really happened. The little old lady who was missing Box 547 was probably dead and buried.

Iris wandered down the long hall to the northwest corner, where there was an office above Linda's. The door at the end of the hall was marked "Recorder's Office." Behind it was a preserved office space similar to the Human Resources area downstairs. If it weren't for the thick layer of dust and a dead plant in the corner, it would have been just an ordinary workday before the staff arrived.

Iris paused at the receptionist's desk. There was a cup still full of pens and a family portrait all in plaid. The yellowed faces watched her from their faux-gold frame. *Don't disturb the ghosts,* Iris told herself as she opened a drawer. It was full of large rubber stamps. One read "FILE." One was an adjustable library stamp, on which the secretary would dial in the date—it was set to December 28, 1978. Iris picked up one. It was caked in dried red ink and read "RESTRICTED ACCESS" backward. She set it back down and fixed her gaze on the corner office.

A small plaque hung from the office door that read, "John Smith." Iris swung the door open and peeked inside. The shades were drawn, and the walls were dark. She tried the light switch, but the bulbs were burned out. Iris felt her way to a window and pulled open the blinds. Twenty years of debris rained down on her head. She sneezed and swatted at her clothes and found herself in a room full of filing cabinets. They lined the walls and were clustered in the center of the room. She blinked through the dust sparkling around her head at the maze of files.

"What the hell is all this?" Iris whispered.

None of the drawers were marked. She pulled one open. It was bursting with manila folders, each one only labeled with bizarre symbols. She read a few tabs—"!!@%," "!!@^," "!!@&." She pulled out a folder marked "!!#%" and opened it. The papers inside were yellowed with age and covered with accounting figures. In the upper right corner, "KLWCYR" was typed on each page. In the lower right corner, she found "!!#%."

Iris forced the file back in its drawer and slammed it shut. She had a job to do, she reminded herself. She couldn't afford to waste any more time. Iris pulled out her tape measure and sketched the room. She made her way to the back corner and was relieved that there wasn't a huge filing cabinet blocking the door to the executive washroom. She'd broken enough furniture for one day. She grabbed the small bronze handle that matched the door in Linda's HR office, and it turned.

Inside, white marble floors gleamed in the sunlight streaming in from the north window. An enormous, gilded mirror hung above the porcelain sink. Flowers and little cherub faces framed the antique looking-glass. Iris turned the hot-water handle. Nothing came out. She looked in the toilet and saw it was dry. The floor of the shower stall was rusted from a faucet leak that had dried up years ago.

Iris made her measurements of the room. It was exactly ten feet wide as it was supposed to be, but it was only ten feet long. The wall adjacent to the mechanical ducts Ramone had described was tiled, but there was a large grated panel near the floor by the toilet. She crouched down next to it and shined her light into the grate. Between the louver slats she could just make out the smooth gleam of sheet metal. It must be the cold-air return, she decided, and made a note on the plans.

As Iris closed the door to John Smith's office, she couldn't get Suzanne's voice out of her head. "Those bastards chained the doors up tight in the middle of the night."

Whoever he was, he was long gone.

CHAPTER 20

Outside, East Ninth was hot and crowded as all the other worker bees filed out of the surrounding office buildings and into the scattered diners and restaurants for lunch. Iris lit a much-deserved cigarette and walked two steaming blocks to Panini's for an overstuffed pastrami sandwich. After elbowing through the crowd at the counter and fighting for paper napkins and condiments, she found a bench near a window and dug in.

"Hey, stranger!" a voice called from across the room. It was Nick.

Iris grabbed a napkin and wiped the mustard off her chin. Her stomach flipped with his easy smile. He'd driven her home four days earlier after a work happy hour. She had been sloppy drunk, and she'd given him a sloppy kiss. He didn't seem too impressed at the time. Her cheeks flushed as he pushed his way through the crowd toward her.

"Hey, Iris. Where've you been?"

"Hi, Nick." She felt flattered he had even noticed her absence. "Mr. Wheeler decided to let me out of the office. I've been working down the street at the old bank building."

He set his tray down next to hers. With his wavy hair and rumpled khakis, he was almost annoyingly handsome. "Wow. How'd you swing that?"

"Brad volunteered me. I think he was trying to help." Iris felt herself sitting up straighter and wishing she'd worn a cuter top. *Shit. Is that a mustard stain?* She crossed her arms to hide the blemish.

"Trying to help you do what?" he smirked.

"Hmm? Oh, keep me from going crazy, I guess."

"Is it helping?" He raised his eyebrows at her with a slow grin. She could still feel his warm lips on hers.

"Uh. Sort of." She kept her eyes on her sandwich. What was really driving her crazy was not knowing why he had just dumped her at her house after kissing her.

"Hello there. Can I join you guys?" A beautiful blond walked up with a petite salad in her hand. Iris recognized her from the office.

"Hey, Amanda. Grab a seat." Nick patted the bench next to him. Amanda had on a silk blouse and white skirt that fit her perfect ass like a glove. Iris could never wear white. Within minutes of pulling on anything pristinely white, she would sit in a pool of ketchup or fall into the greasy latch of a car door. Iris could never keep up with a white skirt.

"Do you know Iris?" Nick asked.

"Of course. You're over in engineering, right?"

"That's me." Iris was certain there was a piece of spinach in her teeth.

"I've been meaning to stop over and talk with you," she said with a saccharine smile.

"Really?" Iris was confused. Amanda was an architect and in charge of parading around like a model as far as she could tell. "About what?"

"Amanda's a staff liaison," Nick said with a mouth full of roast beef.

"Liaison to who?" Iris frowned.

"Exactly. You see, Nick? The entry-level staff doesn't even know who's running this firm."

"Well, that's not . . ." Iris began.

Amanda kept right on talking: "The younger staff is the future of this company, and it's up to us to set our goals. The partners really want to see more out of us."

"More," Iris repeated, trying not to show her irritation. She had just worked the entire weekend for free. What more could they possibly want?

The "partners" were the old men who sat in their offices all day, hogging the windows. The only one Iris had ever talked to was Mr. Wheeler. She pondered that fact for a moment and then realized it wasn't quite true. She had talked to another gray-haired guy in a suit a few weeks back. He'd caught her in the hallway skulking to her desk.

"Good morning, Iris," he'd said with a creepy smile.

"Oh . . . uh, hi!" she'd replied because she didn't know his name. It didn't help that she'd been hungover and fifteen minutes late that morning.

"So . . . How are you adjusting to life here at WRE?"

It had been a reasonable question, but she couldn't help but think that he'd seemed to enjoy watching her squirm.

"Um. It's great." She forced a smile. "We've got some really interesting projects going."

"Don't we though?" His twisted grin had hinted that he knew she was full of shit. "Better get to it then, hmm?"

With that he just sauntered back behind some closed door on the other side of the office. She'd sort of blocked the whole exchange out, but on some subconscious level, she'd been avoiding any direct contact with the partners ever since.

Amanda continued yammering on about increasing work hours and opening stock options to the entire staff. Iris pretended to be interested while she tried to figure out how she was going to stuff the giant sandwich in her mouth with Nick sitting right there. There was no feminine way to do it. Besides, Iris couldn't see herself staying at WRE long enough to become fully vested in stock options anyway, so it was hardy an incentive. Nick and Amanda were talking like lifers. It was depressing. She was sure they'd be very happy together.

After lunch, the three of them headed back toward the office, Amanda chatting all the way. Iris found herself lagging behind to keep from pushing the blabbermouth into traffic. At the first opportunity, she waved her good-byes and trotted across East Ninth Street toward the bank. After listening to Amanda drone on for twenty minutes, she could really use a smoke.

"Iris, wait!" Nick called from behind her. He jogged up to her side. She shoved her cigarette pack back in her bag. No one at work knew she smoked. It was frowned upon.

"Yes?"

"I need to see inside the old bank. Can you give me a tour?" He cocked his head at her funny, or maybe the sun was in his eyes. She couldn't tell.

"Really? Why?"

"Mr. Wheeler wants to get my opinion on whether any of the historical interiors can be salvaged. WRE might advise the county to restore some of it if the sale goes through." He held up a large camera bag she hadn't noticed before.

Iris nodded. "Sure. Come with me."

Wheeler seemed to be taking a real interest in the project. Maybe her hard work would actually get noticed. *Oh shit.* He wanted to save the "interiors," and she'd just demolished a bookcase. At least she'd saved the chairs.

Iris led him into the alley behind the building. Ramone buzzed them in, and she escorted Nick past the loading dock to the main lobby. She filled the awkward silence with chatter.

"The First Bank of Cleveland closed in 1978. They chained the doors in the middle of the night, if you can believe that, and left all of this stuff behind. Furniture, coffee mugs, pictures, files. It's all perfectly preserved. I can't believe that in twenty years nobody came along sooner and stripped it clean. Somebody must really care about this place. I mean, what vacant building has an armed security guard? I guess they're worried about someone stealing it all. I don't know who would want to steal this stuff, though."

Besides me, Iris thought. She'd taken Beatrice's file that morning. Then there was Suzanne's key. It wasn't stealing, she protested. She was just trying to help some little old lady get her things back. The little steel doors in the safe deposit vault ran through her head, along with the flashlight up on the fifteenth floor.

Iris realized she'd fallen into a dead silence. "So. What specifically do you want to see?"

His warm brown eyes twinkled with amusement at her nervous stream of babble. "I need to see a typical office area to get a sense of the furnishings and the finishes."

She held his gaze a half second too long. Color rose in her cheeks. She turned away and pointed to a wall sconce. "Have you seen these fixtures?"

"They're beautiful," he said behind her.

She glanced over her shoulder, and he wasn't looking at the walls. He was looking at her. *Damn it. Why does he have to be so attractive?*

"I really need to see the upper floors."

"Okay. I haven't gotten past the fourth floor yet, but I've seen a few offices."

She led him up the monumental main stairwell instead of the emergency egress stairs. They weren't as direct but they were certainly prettier, with their marble and wrought iron. She felt herself swaying her hips more than usual as she climbed the steps in front of him.

They poked around the fourth floor for over an hour. Nick took pictures with his camera while Iris took more measurements and notes on her clipboard. The fourth floor contained mostly file rooms with doors marked "Deposits" and "Lending." She'd lost track of him for a while until she heard him yell, "What the hell is up with this?"

She followed his voice into John Smith's office of abandoned filing cabinets. "I have no idea. I guess they needed more file storage."

"Huh. These are all still full?"

"Weird, right?" She began to worry that her tour was a flop and he wasn't getting enough photos of furnishings or whatever. "Here, come check this out."

Iris led him around the file cabinets and into the fancy bathroom. "This is the 'Executive Washroom.' Can you believe this stuff?" She motioned to the gilded mirror and the marble shower stall.

He shook his head, slowly surveying the room.

"I mean, it's gorgeous but kind of messed up. Like the rich guys needed to be separated from the filthy masses or something." She was babbling again.

Nick took a couple pictures.

"Okay. I'm going to . . ." Iris paused, realizing she would have to squeeze past him to get to the door. The room was narrow, and Nick was right in the way. She took an awkward step toward him, hoping he would get the hint. "Go get back to my drawings."

He just stood at the sink, not budging. He had stopped taking pictures and was watching her with an amused grin. She would have to practically rub against him to get past. Maybe that was the idea. His eyes held hers for too long.

"Um. Are you gonna . . . ?" The word "move" got caught as his smile faded and his eyes fell to her lips. The room was suddenly quite small and hot. They were completely alone. No one even knew where they were in the empty high-rise or that they were together.

His gaze fell to her T-shirt, which now seemed too tight. Iris's pulse jumped. This was beyond flirting or joking around. *Shit*. She took a step back and nearly tumbled into the shower behind her. He caught her by the waist.

"Whoops! Thanks, I . . . I'd better go." Her voice fell to a whisper.

"I don't think so." He pulled her to his chest and kissed her squarely on the mouth. Her lips had a mind of their own and kissed him back. When they came up for air, she felt drunk and dizzy. Even the voices in her head were speechless. He kissed her again, harder, and she felt her knees buckle beneath her. *Oh God.* She wrenched herself away. Iris had strict rules. She never took guys home from the bar. She never slept with a boy on the first date, not that she ever went on dates.

"Wait. Nick. What are we doing?"

"Something I should have done the other night," he breathed, pulling her back and kissing her again. The kiss was deeper. Her blood was madly rushing everywhere but her brain. She'd never been kissed that well before.

She barely broke free. "What? But we can't."

"Sure we can. Who's going to know?" His fingertip traced her breast as he kissed her again. A tidal wave of heat rose up inside her.

"Nick. I don't . . ." But his lips found her neck, and it was all over.

Her knees and everything else rigid and principled in her entire body melted to the floor. She couldn't string two thoughts together, it all happened so fast. They were on the ground. His hands and lips stripping her defenses one by one along with her clothes. His naked skin pressed hot against hers. He was relentless, until every thought in her head shattered into a million blinding pieces.

When she came back to her senses, they were lying side by side on the ground, struggling to catch their breath. Iris pulled herself up on one elbow. Their clothes were scattered around the dusty floor like a bomb had gone off. Her thighs were still trembling. *Jesus.* Nothing like that had ever happened to her before. None of the three college boys she'd been with had done anything close to that. She was mortified. *We have to get dressed. What if someone at work finds out? What if Ramone finds us like this? What if he heard us?* She might have been screaming; she had no idea. Blood flooded her cheeks. She laughed nervously, teetering on the edge of hysterics.

"What's so funny?" Nick was lying peacefully with his eyes closed.

She had to say something. "Oh, I was just wondering if this is what the company had in mind when they said they were looking for 'synergy' in the younger staff."

"Maybe we should make a suggestion. I know I'm feeling like a real team player right now." He stretched and ran a leisurely finger down her back as she struggled with her bra. *Had this been his plan the whole time?* She swatted his hand away.

They pulled themselves to their feet and peeled their clothing off the floor. She stopped buttoning and stole a glance at him. He was at least five years older than her. He'd probably done this before. He caught her looking and tousled her mussed hair. It was something a big brother would do. She glared at him for a moment while he tucked his shirt into his jeans.

Of course he's done this before, she thought, eyeing the torn wrapper on the floor. He walked around with condoms in his wallet. He had done things to her that no one had ever done. He was a grown man. And she suddenly felt like a stupid young girl.

"What's the matter?" he asked.

"What do you mean?"

"You look pissed."

"I . . . uh . . . don't do stuff like this."

"Me neither." He winked and kissed her on the cheek.

Liar.

She went to the gilded mirror to smooth down her hair. Little gold cherubs were watching from their perches. They'd seen it all. She turned her back on them and wondered how many other women had been in the room and under what circumstances.

CHAPTER 21

Monday, November 27, 1978

It was past noon when Max and Beatrice stumbled out of the Theatrical and into the winter sun. Fresh snow sparkled blindingly between the long rows of plowed slush. Beatrice recoiled in the light.

"Let's go back to your place for a little while," Max said, leading Beatrice to the bus stop at the corner. "We'll swing back by the office later tonight and see what we can find out about your aunt's deposit box."

Beatrice was already reconsidering the idea but was too drunk to argue. As much as she wanted to know why Doris had letters from the bank and what was in Box 547, she knew it was wrong. Doris would never forgive her. She'd have to tell Max, but not now. Later.

By the time they reached Doris's one-bedroom apartment, Beatrice was dead on her feet. She dropped her bag next to the door and collapsed on the couch. She hadn't slept much since her aunt was admitted to the hospital. Alone at night in the apartment,

Beatrice jumped at every little noise. The last thing she remembered was offering Max a beer from the fridge.

Beatrice had no idea how long she'd been sleeping. The apartment was dark and quiet when she opened her eyes. The clock on the stove read 5:15 p.m. It was the sound of papers rustling that snapped her awake. She pushed herself up, becoming increasingly alarmed.

"Who's there?" she whispered into the dark room.

The front door was closed. The light in the kitchen was off. The only light was spilling out from Doris's bedroom, along with the sound of paper being pulled from a drawer.

She jumped off the couch and raced to her aunt's door. The closet door was open. The bottom drawer of Doris's dresser was empty. Max was sitting on Doris's bed, surrounded by piles of documents.

"What are you doing?" she shrieked.

Max dropped the sheet she was reading.

"Who said you could be in here?" She rushed over to her aunt's closet and slammed the door. She spun back around, eyes darting from the stacks and stacks of papers piled on the bed to the empty drawer. She would never be able to put them back the way they'd been. "How could you? How could you do this?"

"Honey, I'm sorry, I just . . . I didn't mean any harm," Max stammered. "You fell asleep and, well, I got bored."

"I'm not even allowed in this room!" Beatrice screamed. "These are her things! How could you touch her things? Get out!"

"Come on, Bea," Max argued, backing away from the bed.

"I mean it! Get out! You can't be here!"

Max hurried out of the room and grabbed her bag. She threw it over her shoulder and opened the front door. She turned back to Beatrice. "I'm sorry, kid! I really meant no harm. I had no idea that . . ." Max almost said more but seemed to change her mind. She stepped out into the cold stairwell and softly closed the door.

It took Beatrice over an hour and a long, hot shower to unclench her fists. She combed her hair until her scalp was raw. She put on her best sweater and wool pants. She had to see Doris.

Beatrice navigated the sterile hallways and elevators of the hospital without looking up from the ground all the way into Doris's tiny room. The woman lying on the bed didn't even look like her aunt anymore.

"I'm so sorry," she whispered.

She stood next to the bed and watched a machine move her aunt's chest up and down rhythmically, waiting for some change at the sound of her voice. It was the first time Beatrice had tried talking to Doris since the stroke, but nothing happened.

"I didn't know she would look through your things."

Beatrice studied Doris's face, half hoping it would twist with rage. Her cheekbones jutted from her gray face, and the orbits of her eyes were sunken and dark. Jowls pooled around her neck. Even her hair looked worn thin. It had only been five days, and the Doris she knew was already gone. She reached over and touched her aunt's hand. It felt cool and still.

"It's just that it's been so nice having a friend. I needed a friend. I used to have friends, you know. I did. Back home." Her voice broke as she stifled a sob. "I wish you were here to tell me what I should do."

She stood up from the chair and wiped her tears. Doris hated to see her cry. Beatrice struggled to control herself until she could say in a clear, strong voice, "I'll come back and see you tomorrow."

Beatrice was waiting for the elevator when a nurse at the front desk waved her over.

"You just missed your uncle!"

"My uncle?" Beatrice repeated, and was about to say she must be mistaken when the nurse interrupted.

"Yes, not five minutes ago. If you hurry, you might catch him in the lobby. We were all so relieved to see that your aunt had another visitor."

Beatrice frowned.

"It's just that you seemed so young and were always alone. I hate to admit we almost called Child Services." The nurse chuckled.

Beatrice's blood froze in her veins. Child Services. She hadn't considered until that moment that she was still technically a minor—a minor without a guardian. She swallowed hard and nodded.

"The timing couldn't have been better—with your uncle, I mean. We really needed to speak with the next of kin regarding your aunt's wishes." The woman in the white uniform glanced up at Beatrice's face. "Oh, don't worry about it, hon. You just pull yourself together, okay? Your uncle took care of everything."

"What uncle?" she wanted to shriek, but she was too terrified to stand there for one minute longer. The elevator dropped her off at the lobby, and she rushed through, half hoping and half terrified she would catch a glimpse of this "uncle." There was no one but an old woman in a wheelchair. She was crying.

Beatrice practically ran all the way back to Doris's apartment. Her aunt had never been married, at least not that she knew about. Had the hospital even asked for a marriage certificate? They had only asked that Beatrice sign the book every day. The book, she realized. Her "uncle" must have signed the book too.

When Beatrice finally made it back home from the hospital, she felt like she might need medical attention herself. Between her "uncle" and Child Services, she might just have a heart attack. She dropped her purse on the kitchen counter and pulled open the tiny fridge. She hadn't eaten in hours, maybe days. She couldn't remember. A can of beer was sitting next to an open box of baking soda. There was some ketchup, a slice of bread, and half a carton of orange juice. She grabbed the juice. What uncle?

With the sudden rush of sugar, Doris's recent late nights away from home came into focus. Maybe she was seeing someone. Maybe that someone visited her in the hospital. The light was still on in her aunt's bedroom. Piles of paper were still arranged into neat stacks on the bed. Beatrice walked over and sat where Max had been sitting and looked at them.

One stack was all typed on First Bank of Cleveland letterhead. They were carbon copies. Beatrice had struggled to type letters similar to these at work, piling sheet upon sheet with carbon paper in between. She picked up the letter that sat on top of the stack. It was dated January 5, 1962.

Dear Mrs. Howell,
    We regret to inform you that your account for Deposit Box No. 815 is delinquent. If you do not remit payment, First Bank of Cleveland will have no choice but to close your account. Unclaimed property will become the ward of the State of Ohio. You have fifteen days to comply.
Sincerely,
William S. Thompson, Director of Audits

Beatrice raised her eyebrows, looking at the letter. Max had just been talking about this over drinks. She leafed through the stack of papers. They were all similar. Beatrice counted them up and found twenty-six. She set the stack down and puzzled over them. She couldn't think of a reason why Doris would keep copies of things like this, especially after all of these years.

The typist signature read "DED" for the first several letters, but then it changed. The dates grew more recent as Beatrice sifted through the pile. The most recent letter was dated June 12, 1977. It was signed like all of the others by Bill Thompson. The typist was MRM. Beatrice scowled. *Max?*

She eyed another stack. It was a pile of steno pads, each one of them covered in pages and pages of shorthand. Beatrice squinted at the top sheet and found she could only make out every third or fourth word of her aunt's sloppy style—"sale," "locked," "gold," "Cleveland."

She set them aside and moved on to the stack of handwritten letters. A nerve twitched up her back in protest. This was trespassing into her aunt's private affairs, but her eyes got away from her.

My Dearest Doris,

Nothing is the same since you left. The charade at work and home is killing me. I want to shout my love from the rooftops and damn the consequences. I want to spend every night with you. One day soon we will be together, and all of the lying and sneaking around will be over. Just be patient, baby. Remember our plan and how much I love you. Meet me Saturday at our place.

Forever Yours,

Bill

Beatrice's eyes bulged as she read the last line. A man named Bill was having an affair with Doris. There was no doubt about it. She leafed through letter after letter, all written in the same scrawling hand, and all signed by Bill. There were at least fifty letters. Her eyes darted back to a bank letter signed by William S. Thompson. She picked it up and compared it to the love letter in her hand. The penmanship matched.

The papers fell from her hand. Doris once had an affair with Bill Thompson. The mystery man who had visited Doris in the hospital might have been Bill. Beatrice stumbled out of the room in a daze. She fished the lonely can of beer out of the fridge and cracked it open. It tasted awful.

Doris had a pile of old bank records in her bedroom and a safe deposit box. None of it made sense, but Box 547 might hold the answers. Beatrice rifled through her purse until she found her aunt's keys. She fanned the key ring out in her palm, searching for the right one. The beer can hit the ground. Key 547 was gone.

CHAPTER 22

Beatrice marched into the office Tuesday morning, spoiling for a fight. Max had simply gone too far. She tried to convince herself that Max had stolen the key to help Beatrice access the box, but her stomach didn't buy the explanation. How could she just take it like that?

Of course, Max was nowhere to be found on a Tuesday morning. She always came in late. While that had never bothered her before, suddenly Beatrice was enraged by the inequity. She looked up at the Sisters Grim, the old crone, the mousy girl in the corner, and Francine clacking on her typewriter next to her. They all worked hard. They kept their heads down. They didn't sneak off to the bathroom to smoke, and they certainly never came to work two hours late.

As if on cue, Francine nodded a terse greeting.

"Good morning, Francine," Beatrice muttered.

Beatrice tried to busy herself with some filing Mr. Rothstein had given her, but she found herself looking over her shoulder for Max all morning. When the lunch hour came and went with no sign of Max, she became even more infuriated. Was Max avoiding her? Did she call in sick? She tapped her foot against the floor. Francine glared at her, clearly annoyed. Beatrice stopped and got up, exasperated.

In the restroom, she checked her hair and makeup in the mirror and paused. Maybe her aunt's illness had aged her, because the woman staring back at her in the mirror looked much older than the girl she remembered. Her blond hair was swept up, and she'd taken to wearing red lipstick, just like Max. She grabbed a paper towel and scrubbed her lips until they were pink again.

She was just sitting back down at her desk when Mr. Halloran opened his door and motioned her to his office. Her stomach sank a little as she grabbed her notepad. He always crowded the door so she had to brush against him to get by.

"So Beatrice, how is your special assignment working out?" he asked, staring at her legs.

She kept her knees and ankles pressed together tightly. "I'm sorry?"

"What are you finding out about Mr. Thompson's project?" His long, manicured fingers softly traced the edge of his leather blotter. His eyes traced the line of her neck. From the droop of his eye, she could tell he'd been drinking again.

She cleared her throat and shifted in the chair uncomfortably. After a moment's hesitation, she decided that she didn't owe Max her loyalty any longer. Max was a thief. "Well, apparently Mr. Thompson has been performing a secret audit of the safe deposit boxes. Maxine McDonnell says she's been following up on the records and calling customers."

Mr. Halloran stopped gazing at her neck. "Is that it?"

"Yes . . . Well, except that some of the records are missing altogether."

"Missing?" He raised his eyebrows.

Beatrice knotted her hands, wishing she hadn't said so much, but it was too late. "All I know is that a few years ago a customer claimed the State of Ohio had no record of repossessing her safe deposit box . . . That's when the audit started."

A wide smile spread across Randy's face. "Well done, Beatrice. I'll be sure to let Ms. Cunningham know what a valuable asset you're turning out to be. I'm going to be giving you all of my assignments from now on."

Beatrice didn't know whether to smile or frown and did neither. For better or worse, she was working for Randy. If anything Max had said could be trusted, Beatrice's job at the bank was safe.

He stood up and grabbed a large stack of files. "These records are restricted access and quite sensitive. I need them sorted according to the footnotes and refiled. Can you get them back to me by the end of the day?"

The heavy files made her list to one side as he dropped them in her arms. "Of course, Mr. Halloran."

He led her to the door. "Please, Beatrice, call me Randy."

Back at her desk, Beatrice opened the first file and puzzled over the typed sheet of paper. It was all numbers—rows and rows of dollar amounts and dates. The header read "STHM" and the footer read "%$%." She began making piles of the sheets according to the symbols at the bottom of each page as Mr. Halloran had commanded. Within minutes her desk was covered with the stacks of paper, and she realized she was drawing attention to herself and the sensitive documents. She gathered them up and began stuffing the pages into blank manila folders in her file drawer.

An hour later she carried the stack back to Mr. Halloran's office and softly knocked on his door. When there was no response, she turned the handle and peered inside. Mr. Halloran's desk was empty. Relieved there wouldn't be another awkward encounter, she set the stack of files on the edge of his desk. A narrow wood door behind his desk stood open. She'd never noticed it before. There was a glimmer of white tile.

Beatrice craned her neck to get a better look inside the mysterious room. There was a large stone sink and a shower. She took a few steps forward for a better look.

"It's pretty old-fashioned, isn't it?" Mr. Halloran's hot breath fell on her neck. She hadn't heard him walk in.

Beatrice jumped. "Oh, I'm so sorry, Mr. Halloran, I was just leaving the files . . ."

"Randy," he corrected her, smiling slyly as he stepped toward her.

She instinctively stepped back. "I'm so sorry, Randy. I was just leaving you the files and noticed the door open. It was incredibly rude of me."

He was uncomfortably close. She took another step back.

"The whole point of these rooms is privacy. Privacy is very important, don't you agree?" he said, and ran a finger down the length of her arm.

Panic swelled inside her. She had backed into his private washroom. His office door was shut. He lifted her chin, tilting her face up to his. Her mind raced through her options as he studied her lips. Kicking and screaming her way out of the bathroom would get her fired. His eyes twinkled as she squirmed. *He really is a shark,* she thought, and in a flash the answer came to her. *What would Max do?*

She leaned toward him, pressing her hips dangerously close to his. In her most seductive voice, she murmured, "Randy, we don't really have time for this, do we?"

It caught him off guard. Before he could react, she eased out from the corner. One foot in front of the other, she sauntered out of the bathroom all the way back to her desk, too terrified to look back.

She sat down, knees shaking. One row behind her, Max's desk was still empty.

CHAPTER 23

By the time Friday morning came around with no sign of Max, Beatrice was worried. It was as if she'd disappeared into thin air. Beatrice had expected a phone call, a note, something from Max to say she was sorry or at least ask how Aunt Doris was doing. Nothing came. Day after day her desk sat empty.

Beatrice kept busy filing for Mr. Halloran and avoiding going into his office. She'd taken to using the mailboxes outside Ms. Cunningham's door to leave her work for him. He was hardly ever at his desk anyway, she noticed. The lunches had grown longer, and some days he didn't come back to the office at all. That was fine with her.

She couldn't stand not knowing what happened to Max any longer. After lunch, she walked over to Ms. Cunningham's closed door.

A muffled voice behind the door said, "I need more time, Dale! You can't expect me to trace thirty accounts overnight . . . I know we have time constraints. She missed the meeting . . . Well,

I can't take her statement if I can't find her . . . Yes, the deposits are still there . . ."

Beatrice tapped on the door. She heard the dull thud of heavy footsteps on carpet, and then the door opened. Old Cunny stood blocking the doorway. "Can I help you?"

"I'm sorry, Ms. Cunningham, but I was wondering . . ." She bit her lip.

"Yes? What?" Her boss's terse voice, along with the strange conversation she'd just overheard, almost made Beatrice forget.

"Umm. Do you know where Maxine McDonnell is?" Beatrice asked, and then felt like she needed to add some legitimacy to her question. "Mr. Halloran had a question about one of her assignments." It wasn't a complete lie, she reasoned.

"I'm sorry to tell you that Maxine resigned Tuesday morning."

Beatrice's mouth fell open. Max quit. But she had been hoping for a promotion after she finished Mr. Thompson's secret audit. It didn't make sense.

"Is that all, dear? I really need to get back to my work."

"Okay. Thanks." Beatrice couldn't believe it. Max was gone. She hadn't even said good-bye. And she still had her aunt's key.

"You know, now that I think of it," Ms. Cunningham said, "you should go check with Mr. Thompson to see if he needs any more help. Maxine leaving has left him shorthanded."

With that, Ms. Cunningham closed her door.

Beatrice glanced down the hall toward Mr. Thompson's office. She hadn't seen him since he'd hired her. Now that she'd read his love letters to Aunt Doris, she didn't know if she could look him in the eye.

His door was closed. She knocked softly, to no reply. Maybe he had left the office, she hoped. She knocked harder and waited. Just as she was turning to head back to her desk, the door swung open and she was face-to-face with "Bill," as he was known to the women in her life.

"Can I help you, Bethany?"

Beatrice paused but didn't correct him. "Ms. Cunningham wanted me to stop by and see if you needed any additional assistance."

"Well, that was very kind of both of you. I'm doing just fine, but if I need some assistance I'll let you know." He started to close the door when something occurred to him. "Actually, could you please deliver something to Ms. Cunningham for me?"

He left the door open, and she followed him in. His office looked just as she remembered it. There was a photograph of a pretty woman and two smiling girls sitting on the bookshelf. Beatrice felt ill at the sight of his family, knowing he'd promised Doris he'd leave them.

He handed her a stack of files. "Thank you, Bethany. You have a good weekend."

"Thank you, sir." She couldn't put into words what she really wanted to say. Looking at him, she never would have guessed he was the sort of man who would lure a woman into an affair. Mr. Thompson was paunchy with salt-and-pepper hair, and his kind eyes and warm smile were almost grandfatherly. She might have believed he really cared about her weekend by the way he talked to her, but he didn't even know her name.

CHAPTER 24

Beatrice passed Max's old seat on the way back to her desk. She stopped. Looking at the stapler still sitting there, Beatrice realized that Max may have left more things behind. Maybe Doris's key was in the desk. Maybe Max had left a note or some sort of explanation.

Max did whatever she wanted, and no one ever said a word about it. Maybe it was time that she stopped worrying so much, Beatrice told herself. Her boss didn't even know her name. Ms. Cunningham, despite her warning to Beatrice that she took everything at the office personally, barely stuck her nose outside her office door. The other secretaries ignored her. No one really cared who Beatrice was or what she did now that Max was gone. Maybe it was time to do what she wanted to do. At that moment, Beatrice wanted Doris's key back.

At 5:00 p.m. Beatrice put her purse on her shoulder and followed the other women to the coatrack in the hall. She put on her coat, her hat, and her gloves alongside the other secretaries and walked to the elevator lobby. Just as everyone was climbing into an elevator car to go home, she stepped away as if it were an after-thought and headed into the ladies' room. No one noticed.

The lavatory was empty and dark. The overhead bulb was off. Beatrice squinted in the faint light streaming through the window where Max would blow smoke. She stepped into a stall and sat down to wait.

For over an hour she sat still and quiet. She had to be sure that everyone was gone. It was a Friday, and even the managers who liked to stay late would surely be going home on time. The holidays were upon them. There was Christmas shopping to do and family to see. She had noticed all week how eager everyone was to leave work. The streets downtown seemed to empty early each night as she sat in the shelter waiting for the 82 bus to take her home.

Beatrice had no one to see and nothing to do but go to the hospital and watch machines move air in and out of her aunt's wither-ing body. Beatrice caught a glimpse of herself sitting in the stall in the dim bathroom mirror. Gaunt and pale, she looked like a ghost of herself.

The street noises outside grew quiet. She waited until it had been a full ten minutes since she'd heard the whir of the elevator in the hall and slowly crept out of the bathroom. The clicking of her boots on the tiles echoed off the walls. She slipped them off by the bathroom door and silently padded down the hall in her stocking feet.

No one was chattering on the phone or rustling through files. The floor was deserted. It was so quiet, she was certain that some-one would hear her heart pounding against her rib cage. The hall-way floodlights were still lit, but the big fluorescents that hung over the rows of desks had been shut off. The doors that surrounded her workspace were all dark. Only dim yellow lights from the street below filtered through the frosted glass.

The faint light from the hall was bright enough to see by as she sat down at Max's desk and pulled open the center drawer.

Instead of pens, paper clips, and other office supplies, it was filled with nothing but paper loosely scattered across the drawer. She felt around the piles for Doris's key and found nothing but more paper. Beatrice pulled out a sheet and struggled to read it in the faint light. It was covered in scribbled shorthand. Beatrice squinted at the notes and finally gave up and switched on the small desk lamp in the corner. Max's shorthand was not as neat as her own, but she could just make out the words among the ticks and curlicues on the page.

> Box 304—payment delayed, notified 6/7/78, Taylor Cummings, repossessed 6/19/78; Box 305—delinquent, contacted 6/6/78, Marion Delaney, no forwarding address, repossessed 6/19/78

It was a record of Max's audit. It seemed odd that it was written in shorthand. The notes were brief already, and they didn't appear to be dictated by anyone but Max. Mr. Thompson, or anyone else outside the secretarial pool for that matter, wouldn't be able to read them. It was almost as if Max had left them just for her. Her eyes wandered down the page, and her eyebrows raised as she read,

> State of Ohio Treasurer's Office contacted 6/25/78, no record of repossessions. Contents unaccounted for.

Max had called the state to verify the repossessions. There were pages and pages of records for the safe deposit box audits, and each page concluded that the state had no record of taking possession of the box contents. She leafed through sheet after sheet until it really hit her. The contents of over a hundred safe deposit boxes were officially missing. Max was verifying the missing accounts and keeping records in shorthand so that no one else could read them.

Doris had kept records of safe deposit boxes too. Beatrice carefully gathered all of the notes into a neat stack. She opened one of the larger file drawers, looking for a manila folder, and heard something clank at the bottom. It was a half-drunk pint of whiskey. She fished the little bottle of Old Grand-Dad out and shook her head at Max.

As angry as she was, holding the bottle made her feel nostalgic. Work would not be the same without her friend. She unscrewed the cap and took a little sip in honor of Max. It burned rolling down. She put the bottle back and poked around in the large drawer until she was satisfied her aunt's key wasn't inside. She grabbed an empty folder for Max's odd notes and slid the drawer shut.

She opened the smaller drawer above it and found a hairbrush and a small makeup bag. Whiskey was one thing, but leaving makeup behind seemed stranger. The small satin bag was heavy. It jingled like a pile of coins. She hesitated a second and then shrugged. Max had no qualms going through her aunt's purse. She opened the bag and felt inside.

A door closed down the hall behind her.

Beatrice's heart stopped at the sound. She zipped the makeup bag shut as footsteps approached her from behind. She turned. A tall security uniform came into view. She considered running down the hall, but that would just make her look guilty. There was a gun hanging in a holster on the guard's hip. Her only hope was to seem like she belonged there.

She tried to relax her shoulders and smiled. "Good evening!"

"What are you doing on the floor this late, ma'am?"

It wasn't an accusation really. Not yet.

"Oh, I forgot my makeup bag," she said, holding up the little zippered case for the man to see. "I'm such a clod!"

She stood up, putting the bag in her purse, and gathered the folder of Max's notes from the desk. The name stitched on his uniform read "Ramone." She stared at the letters to avoid his eyes.

"The floor's closed. It's time to go home."

He led her to the elevator lobby, and she followed far behind him, praying he wouldn't notice that she wasn't wearing shoes. Her boots were still sitting by the bathroom door. She couldn't walk out into the snow in her stockings.

"Shoot. I'm sorry. I've got to use the powder room. Excuse me for a moment."

She dashed to the restroom before he turned around. Closing the door behind her, she threw on her boots and stuffed the file of Max's notes into her purse. She pulled out the makeup bag again and searched for Aunt Doris's key. It wasn't there. Just a pile of hairpins and loose change. Max's desk had one more drawer she hadn't searched yet. There might still be time, she told herself, and she may not get this chance again.

She walked into the bathroom stall where she had hid earlier that evening and flushed the toilet for the benefit of the guard waiting outside. Gazing at the window as water ran in the sink, she could almost picture Max standing there. She would have taken a cigarette out from under the loose stone where she stashed them and smirked at Beatrice for being nervous. It gave her an idea.

Beatrice turned off the tap and walked over to the windowsill. She lifted the loose piece of marble at the corner where Max hid her cigarettes. Underneath was a hollow clay tile. Beatrice reached inside. Something hard and metal brushed against her fingertips.

It was a huge ring of keys. Beatrice pulled them from the hiding spot and fanned them out. There must have been thirty of them of all shapes and sizes. The large steel ones looked like they were for office doors. A smaller key ring was attached to the large one. It held thirteen small brass keys. Her heart quickened as she picked one out. It read "D" on one side, with the words "First Bank of Cleveland" etched around its outer edge, just like her aunt's key. She flipped through the others. Each had a letter. None were Key 547.

There was a knock on the door. Beatrice jumped.

"Time to go," the security guard barked.

Beatrice threw the ring of keys into her bag and carefully placed the loose stone back where it belonged. When she returned to the hall, Ramone was visibly irritated. He motioned her toward an open elevator door.

Beatrice knew she was pushing her luck, but she still needed to find her aunt's key. "Darn it! I forgot something else. I'm supposed to bring some notes home to look at over the weekend. I'm such an airhead. I'll be right back."

He grumbled behind her as she ran back to Max's desk. She held up a one-minute finger and pulled open the last file drawer. It was crammed full of files. She pushed them aside and felt the bottom of the drawer for the key. She came up with nothing but a handful of pencil shavings. She randomly grabbed one of the files to make her story to Ramone plausible and slammed the drawer shut.

"You find everything you need all right?" Ramone's deep voice asked from just over her shoulder.

Beatrice stifled a shriek. She hadn't heard him following her. "Um, yes, thank you."

"It's time to be going now, Miss—?"

He was going to report her. She was standing at Max's desk pretending it was hers, and he wanted her name. She decided to play deaf. "Yes?"

"What's your name, miss?"

"Oh," she gulped. "Maxine. Maxine McDonnell . . . I really should be going." With that, she rushed over to the elevators as fast as she could without running. A car was waiting, and she stepped inside and pressed the button for the lobby.

Thankfully, the guard didn't follow her. He didn't leave Max's desk. He just stood there staring at it, seeming lost in thought. He finally looked up at Beatrice, standing there in the elevator.

"Have a good night, miss," he said with a grim face, and the elevator doors closed.

CHAPTER 25

Saturday, August 15, 1998

Iris berated herself the rest of the week for being an incorrigible slut. How could she have just crumpled onto the floor after a few kisses? It was beyond her control, she argued. It wasn't her fault he was a mind-scrambling kisser. It wasn't her fault that the scant sex in her life up until Nick had been lukewarm at best. They had kissed once before. They had flirted. It wasn't the same as dating but it was something, she reasoned. Besides, adult women could have sex with men they liked without being branded or punished.

But she was being punished. He didn't call.

By noon that Saturday, there was no doubt about it. She was just a piece of ass to Nick. He would never take her seriously now. The sweaty walls of her apartment were closing in on her. She had to get out.

It was even hotter outside. She trudged past Mrs. Capretta's rocking chair without even looking up.

"Well, how do you like that? People don't even say hello to their neighbors anymore. I expected it from the Orientals upstairs, but not from you, Iris."

"Sorry, Mrs. Capretta. How are you today?" Iris sighed, avoiding eye contact.

"Better than you from the looks of it . . . What's the matter? Boy trouble?" Mrs. Capretta rocked in her chair in her moth-eaten housecoat.

"Sort of."

"You career girls got your heads all screwed up. In my day we knew how to keep a man. You want my advice?"

Not really.

"Learn to cook, and keep your legs shut! That's how you land a husband."

Iris rolled her eyes.

"You think you're too good for marriage? Sure, you say that now when you're twenty-three. Just wait till you're thirty-three, then forty-three. Come talk to me about how great your career is then. Ha!"

"Okay. Thanks." That was just the pep talk she needed, she thought wryly.

Mrs. Capretta squawked after her, "That's what happened to my Betsy, you know. Wasted all her good chances, and now she's alone . . ."

That settled it. Iris was moving. She clomped down the street to Calabria's, her favorite coffee shop. She grabbed copies of the *Free Times* and *Around Town Magazine*, along with her coffee, and found an air-conditioned corner. Her eyes skimmed the east-side rentals, until she compulsively began reading the listings for Tremont, where Nick lived. He had just bought a condo near Lincoln Park and had been flashing pictures around the office for weeks. It wouldn't exactly make her a stalker if she found a place nearby.

She rolled up the papers with a sigh. Maybe Mrs. Capretta was right. She should have kept her legs shut. As she munched her bagel, the cover of *Around Town* caught her eye. She unrolled the paper and read, "Dennis! And the Default of 1978 . . ." It was the year that made her stop and unfold the paper. First Bank of Cleveland closed around that time. Iris had seen the "Dennis!" yard signs all over town. There was an election coming up in the fall.

From the story lead-in, Congressman Kucinich was running against a Republican intent on dredging up the incumbent's sordid past. According to the article, Dennis Kucinich had been mayor of Cleveland at the ripe age of thirty-two, when the city defaulted on several bank loans. It was a low point in the history of the city, right up there with the burning of the Cuyahoga River. Cleveland was the laughingstock of the country and the poster child for Rust Belt decay. A once-great metropolis became "the mistake on the lake." She'd heard pieces of the story before, but she had never really understood the details. She kept reading.

The city had run up a huge debt as politicians promised "no new taxes" while increasing their budget spending. The city's debt was financed by loans from several local banks because its bond rating was so low. The article listed the financiers, and Iris's eyes widened when she read that First Bank of Cleveland was the largest local bondholder of the city's debt.

Kucinich's administration of young-gun advisers had alienated the old business establishment by refusing to let them privatize the electric utilities. On December 15, 1978, when the bonds came due, the local banks refused to work with the mayor's office to renegotiate the terms. First Bank of Cleveland was one of six banks to refuse to roll over the debt. The bank's board of directors were the most influential businessmen in Cleveland. The elite aristocracy included Theodore Halloran, Samuel Wackerly, Alistair Mercer, and many more, the story read.

Images of the portraits hanging in the library of the old bank loomed in Iris's mind. She'd seen at least twelve old white men glowering at the books. She scoured the article for more information on the bank and its board of directors and found none. The story went on to describe Kucinich's voting record in Congress. His opponent, James Stone, reportedly claimed that the ex-mayor's failure to the City of Cleveland spelled failure for the country if Dennis was to be reelected. Iris folded the paper and stuffed it into her purse.

She walked home in the heat of the day. There had to be more to the bank closure than business as usual. The abandoned files, the full desks, the dead plants—it all looked like evidence at a crime scene. Besides, why would a perfectly good fifteen-story building just sit frozen in time for twenty years? She'd seen abandoned buildings in downtown Cleveland before. She drove past them every day. They were shuttered and gutted, picked clean of anything valuable. Looking through their broken windows, she could see there was nothing left. Why was 1010 Euclid Avenue a perfectly preserved time capsule with an armed guard? Her thoughts kept returning to the vault.

She pushed through the door of her sweltering apartment and saw the light on her answering machine blinking. She threw her purse in the corner and ran to the little black box of hope. Maybe Nick had decided she was worth a phone call. But it was her mother. Again.

"Iris? Iris, I'm starting to get worried. You need to call home."

"Okay, okay." It had been a few days longer than she intended. She picked up the phone and dialed home without even looking at the keypad. The phone number hadn't changed in twenty-three years. "Hi, Mom."

"Iris! Well, it's about time you called. I've been worried! Are you all right?"

"I'm sorry, Mom." She hadn't meant to worry the poor woman. "I've just been really busy with work."

"Well, you could have called to let me know. I am still your mother even if you are all grown up now." Her mother sighed on the other end of the line. "So. How's the new assignment going? Are you liking it?"

"Yeah! I'm working in the field now on this old building. It's fascinating! The head of the company, Mr. Wheeler, chose me out of everyone to take the lead on the survey." Iris found herself bragging even though she suspected Mr. Wheeler had only picked her because she was the cheapest employee.

"Oh, honey! That's wonderful! I'm so glad you're having a good time."

Iris smiled. "How's Dad?"

"Hmm? Oh, he's fine." She paused. "I think he's making the adjustment just fine."

"Adjustment?"

"Oh, didn't I tell you? His company just went through a downsizing. You know they're doing it everywhere. He'll be just fine, don't you worry. He's really enjoying having more time to work out in the shed."

Her dad had been fired. Her mother straining to be sunny and bright about it just made it seem worse. "Mom! When did this happen?"

"Last week."

"Is he all right?" Iris asked, even though she knew she wouldn't get a straight answer.

"He's doing great! He was really tired of the job, you know. He'd gone as far as he could. Now it's on to the next thing." Her enthusiasm was grating Iris's nerves.

"Can I talk to him?"

"Not now, honey, he's sleeping. Do you want me to have him call you?"

"Yeah. Thanks, Mom." She knew her father would never call her. He hated talking on the phone, or at least that's what he said the one time Iris had risked complaining about it. She tried not to take it personally, and to take the rejection like a man or someone her father might respect. "Well, I've got to go."

"Whatcha gonna do today?" Every phone call had to end on a positive note.

"I have to go find a new apartment."

"Oh, that's exciting! I can't wait to see it. Let me know if you want me to come down and help you move in."

"Sounds good. Thanks, Mom."

"I love you!"

"I love you too . . . Mom?"

"Yes, honey?"

Iris paused as a foreign emotion overwhelmed her—she was feeling protective of her parents. She didn't know if they had any savings. She didn't know if her father had a severance package. As a rule, her parents never discussed money. "Call me if you need anything, okay?"

"Oh, don't worry about us, honey. We'll be fine."

CHAPTER 26

Iris's dad had spent the last twenty-five years of his life working more than fifty hours a week as a floor manager for the automotive supply company that had just laid him off. He was a good worker. He showed up early and stayed late. He'd missed every one of her soccer games working overtime shifts. And for what? He had lectured her for hours on the virtues of engineering and how it would lead to a secure and steady career. Now he was unemployed, and Iris couldn't find her goddamned lighter. She eventually just lit a smoke off the stove.

They'd chewed him up and spit him out, just like Ellie said. Five cigarettes later, she was tired of pacing. The apartment was a hotbox. She hated it. She'd lived there for three straight years with the curry smell, stray cockroaches, and Mrs. Capretta's insanity. Iris stomped down the driveway with the apartment listings under her arm. Mrs. Capretta's sink was running as Iris ducked under her window.

The streets of Tremont were lined with run-down houses next to recent renovations. She did her best to sort through them, making a point of not wandering too close to Nick's condo while she tracked down apartment listings. Every thirty minutes or so she rang a buzzer and got a tour.

By 4:00 p.m. she had seen all of the ant traps and caked-on counter crud she could stomach in one day. There was one more place on her list, and that would be it. She turned down a one-way street and pulled up to a small house. It was newly renovated. The appliances were cheap but had never been used. Wall-to-wall Berber carpet had just been installed, and there wasn't an ant trap in sight. *Done.* She signed the papers that afternoon.

A celebration was in order. She walked a half block from her new front door and into the Lava Lounge at the corner. Glossy portraits of martinis hung on the purple walls. Green olives danced in the glasses, swinging from toothpick poles like little round strippers. Iris plopped herself down at the empty bar and ordered her first vodka martini. *Here's to new beginnings,* she thought, holding up the delicate glass. The drink scorched her throat on the way down, and she resisted a shudder.

"Drink okay?" The bartender was easily in his forties and gave Iris the creepy once-over.

She pulled the newspaper out of her bag to send the guy packing to the other end of the bar. The classifieds were covered with her scribbling from the day of house hunting. She flipped back to the front page and reread the headline: "Dennis! And the Default of 1978." She sipped the vodka and read the story again. The city defaulted on December 15, 1978. She stared at the date. It was just two weeks before the First Bank of Cleveland closed.

Before she knew it, her vodka was gone and her head felt too loose on her neck. She had to get out of there or she wouldn't be able to drive home. Stepping back out into the oppressive heat reminded her that her new apartment had central air-conditioning. Iris had never lived in the complete luxury of climate control. She was moving up in the world. The liquor buzz was still building as she sauntered over to her car. The urge to celebrate her good news with somebody besides her mother became overwhelming, and she couldn't help but think of Nick. She had just leased an apartment three blocks away from his townhouse. They were practically neighbors. Even if they did just have casual sex in an abandoned building, they were still friends. Right?

That settled it. The key found the ignition on the second try, and her car navigated itself through the narrow streets until she'd found the front door she'd seen in a framed photo on Nick's desk. At least she was pretty sure it was the right one. She waltzed up the front steps ready to shout, "Hi, neighbor!" and throw her arms around him. That was the vodka-fueled plan.

She was just about to knock when she heard peals of laughter coming from inside. It was a woman's voice. Not just any woman; it was Miss Staff Liaison Amanda's voice.

"So, show me how this spackling stuff works. I've only read about these things, you know."

Iris could hear Nick saying something back, but she couldn't quite hear what.

"That son of a bitch!" she hissed under her breath as she stumbled back down the stairs to her car. Nick, the office Casanova with all of his easy smiles and arms around her shoulder, had moved on to the next girl. She smacked herself hard in the forehead. He didn't care about her. She ripped the door open to her car. He just plucked some low-hanging fruit. He plucked the hell out of it. She slammed the door shut.

Iris careened her way across town and back into her second-floor sauna. What had she expected? She slammed through the front door. He was a twenty-eight-year-old man who had no use for a dumb girl like her—at least not anymore.

Iris lit a cigarette and flopped on the couch. The answering machine was blinking. It wasn't Nick. She no longer harbored any hope it was Nick. It blinked at her for a solid minute before she stomped over and hit the button.

"Hello? This is Suzanne Peplinski. You asked me to call if I could remember anything else. Well"—the hushed voice on the recording dropped down to almost a whisper—"maybe you should come by and see me."

Iris played the message again. She pulled the key to Box 547 out of her change purse and looked at it. Someone had left it in the secretary's desk. Some girl named Beatrice had called Suzanne in the middle of the night to ask about a safe deposit box twenty years ago.

"Who fucking cares? Enough already!" Iris muttered, and grabbed a beer from the fridge. That little old lady or whoever it was who lost Key 547 should have gone looking for it herself.

Iris took a long shower and climbed into bed half-drunk. Echoes of Nick's and Amanda's laughter made her put a pillow over her head. They were perfect for each other, with their perfect bodies, perfect clothes, and perfect lives.

All Iris had was her shitty job surveying a creepy building by herself. She wasn't even that good at it, missing bays on the plans and getting sidetracked. Mr. Wheeler had only picked her for the field assignment because she was just dumb enough to do what she was told and not ask questions.

The thought made her sit up in bed. The old building was filled to the rafters with questions that begged to be asked. Beatrice Baker's personnel file was full of weird notes. The bank shut down fourteen days after the city of Cleveland went bankrupt. People didn't even get a chance to clean out their desks. Keys were lost. Safe deposit boxes were abandoned, and the building had been kept under lock and key for twenty years. Maybe there was a reason Mr. Wheeler had chosen the youngest staff member to survey the building by herself. He didn't want anyone asking questions.

She shook her head, and the room sloshed back and forth from all the beer and vodka she'd drunk. It was a ridiculous notion. Mr. Wheeler was just trying to save a buck by sending her into the building alone. Still, the flashlight up on the fifteenth floor wandered back into her spinning head. Someone had been up there looking for something.

The clock read 11:30 p.m. It was too late to call Suzanne back.

CHAPTER 27

Sunday morning Iris woke up on the couch with a vodka headache.

"Ouch!" she groaned. Her hands wrapped around her skull in a futile effort to keep the invisible hammer from pounding it to bits. She lay there until the second wave of nausea passed.

Suzanne's key was missing. She'd passed out holding it. She could tell from the red mark on her hand. Iris forced herself up. It wasn't on the coffee table or the couch. She searched under the couch, the rug, and the cushions.

"Damn it." Iris lit a cigarette and slumped back. *A key doesn't just disappear.* She crossed her arms angrily and felt something poking at her chest. *Darned underwire,* she thought, and unhooked her slept-in bra. Something fell out and hit the floor. It was the key.

"There you are." Iris picked it up and looked hard at the number 547 etched into its face. "Who do you belong to?"

The key didn't answer, but she wished it could. She lay back down.

When Iris had managed to keep an entire cup of coffee in her hungover stomach, she picked up the phone and dialed Suzanne's number.

"Hello," a raspy voice answered.

"Suzanne?"

"Yes."

"This is Iris. You called me last night."

"Of course. Iris. You should come and see me this morning. My niece is at church until noon."

"Can you tell me what this is about?"

"If you want to talk, come to 13321 Juniper Drive in Lakewood. I'll be waiting." The woman coughed, then hung up.

"Okay, crazy lady. I'll be right there," Iris said into the dead line, and set the phone down. It was nuts, she told herself, but she had taken the key to find its rightful owner. Regardless of whatever drunken theories she'd conjured up the night before, it was her responsibility now. Iris rehooked her bra and slipped the key into her back pocket.

Juniper Drive was a long, crowded street in Lakewood one hundred blocks west of Tremont. Iris navigated her way through the tight grid of bungalows until she found the right one. It was a small brick box with aluminum awnings and a screened-in front porch. An old woman was sitting in a rocker behind the rusted screen.

Iris squinted into the porch. "Are you Suzanne?"

"You must be Iris. Come in. Come in. We don't have much time before my niece gets back from Mass." Suzanne waved her through the splintered side door. The tiny porch was wall-to-wall green plastic carpeting, a wicker sofa, and Suzanne's rocker.

"Hi." Iris eased herself down onto the creaky couch. "Um, thanks for inviting me over."

Suzanne's face was so brown and shriveled she must have spent the last twenty years smoking in a tanning bed. The only thing that vaguely resembled her personnel portrait was her teeth.

"Well, after you called I started thinking . . ." She pulled an extralong menthol out of a red leather cigarette purse and lit it with a shiny, gold fashion lighter. "About the bank. I didn't mention it before on the phone, but you know there were investigations. Police investigations before the bank closed."

"Really? Why?"

"I'm not sure. The police questioned all of us. They asked me all sorts of strange questions about the files. I didn't know a damn thing of course. But I talked to one of my friends, Jean—you know, in private—to find out what the heck was going on. She said that strange things had been happening."

"What sorts of things?"

"Files were disappearing from the Deposits Office. And keys . . ."

"Keys for what?"

"The safe deposit boxes, among others," Suzanne said through a cloud of smoke. "You see, the story to the customers was the keys got lost when the bank was sold to Columbus Trust and they chained the doors, but they were lost a couple weeks before that. It was a witch hunt through all the departments right up until the day they chained the doors."

"Did your friend tell that to the police?" Iris leaned forward on the couch and stared into Suzanne's leathery face. The woman's pale blue eyes were trained on her cigarette.

"Well, no. She didn't."

"Why not?"

"There were threats." Suzanne said it flatly, as if it were common knowledge.

Iris waited for more information, but Suzanne seemed lost in thought. She tapped a two-inch ash into the crystal tray balanced on her knee. Thick blue veins ran the length of her skinny calves.

Iris couldn't help but wonder if the old bat was just making it all up. She seemed to like the attention.

Finally Iris had to ask, "What sort of threats?"

"I got a call in the middle of the night the week before the bank closed." Suzanne gazed out the ratty screen at the brown grass dotting the front lawn. "The man said I would do well not to mention any odd goings-on at the bank. Said I should cooperate with police but keep my mouth shut."

"Or what would happen?"

"Didn't say really, but I had a good idea. A few people disappeared around that time."

"Disappeared? Who?"

"That girl, Beatrice, for one thing. I got that phone call from her late one night about some safe deposit box. I didn't think much of it at the time. But you know it kinda got to me. I couldn't stop thinking about it. So I went to see her. I went all the way up to the ninth floor to find her a few days later. She wasn't there. No one knew where she was, and the way I heard it, she never came back."

"What do you think happened to her?"

"I couldn't say." Suzanne stamped out her cigarette.

"Why did you say she was a liar?"

"Some girl I never met called me up thinking I had some deposit box at the bank. That was a lie! Lord knows who else she blabbed that nonsense to. You can't be too careful. At least, I can't."

Suzanne had been scared. Iris supposed she would be too if some man called in the middle of the night with threats. None of this had anything to do with why she'd driven all the way to Lakewood. She pulled the key out of her pocket and showed it to the old woman.

"Is this yours?"

Suzanne's eyes narrowed. She lit another cigarette and blew out an angry stream of smoke. "I told you. I ain't never had a safe deposit box."

"Do you know who it might belong to?" Iris pressed, not wanting to admit she'd taken it directly from Suzanne's desk. "Maybe this Beatrice person."

"I really couldn't say."

Damn it. Iris shoved the key back in her pocket. "So . . . whatever happened with the police investigation?"

"Nothin'. That was the thing. One day they were calling everybody, and the next day nothin'."

"So, then, what did you mean when you said the other day that some people got what was coming?" Iris asked.

"A couple rich families went bankrupt. It was all over the news. The Hallorans. The Wackerlys. Old Man Mercer died. They said it was a car crash." Suzanne shrugged. "Maybe it was."

The name Halloran was familiar for some reason. Iris puzzled over it until she remembered Linda up on the third floor. Her last name was Halloran. Iris shook her head, trying to knock loose the connections between Linda, Suzanne, Beatrice, and the bank. Suzanne's story didn't add up. Then again, she probably had a screw loose.

"You better be careful who you go asking about the First Bank of Cleveland," Suzanne said, pointing a bony, brown finger at Iris. "There's a reason that building hasn't been bothered all these years."

"Is that why you called me? To tell me to be careful?"

"Well, I wasn't going to say nothin', but you seemed like a nice enough girl on the phone. I didn't want to have you on my conscience." She lit another cigarette.

"Thanks, I guess, but what do you think is going to happen exactly? I mean, who really cares about the old bank at this point?" Iris eyed the smoke and debated lighting one herself.

"You'd be surprised how many of those fat-cat bankers is still around." Suzanne looked Iris dead in the eye. "The last person that called me at home asking about safe deposit boxes disappeared. I just thought you should know that."

Something on Suzanne's wrist flashed in the sun. It sparkled like diamonds. Iris squinted at the hint of a bracelet. She opened her mouth to ask about it, but the roar of a station wagon pulling into the driveway stopped her. A pretty young woman got out of the car and retrieved a little girl from the backseat.

"Sheryl!" Suzanne waved the young woman over. "Come meet Irma. She's telling me all about these neat encyclopedias we could buy."

"What?" Iris glared at Suzanne in protest.

"Christ." Sheryl sighed under her breath. "Miss, don't pay any attention to my aunt. She doesn't really want what you're selling. She just likes to talk. You should really be going now." She set her daughter down inside the front door and motioned Iris to the driveway.

"But . . ." Iris still had questions, but it seemed her time was up. She stood and played along. "Thank you for your time, Ms. Peplinski. You know how to reach me if you change your mind about the books."

Iris headed down the driveway to her car. She scanned the street, lined with rusted American cars, trying to make sense of what Suzanne had told her. The crazy old woman claimed she didn't know the owner of the key. Beatrice Baker had called Suzanne about a safe deposit box, and then she disappeared. The old lady was worried it would happen again.

"What a nutcase," Iris whispered, but an uneasy feeling settled into her gut. Someone had hired Ramone to guard the building with its abandoned files and whatever was still locked in the vault.

Back on the porch, Suzanne was still in her rocker, smoking. She waved as Iris pulled away.

CHAPTER 28

Friday, December 1, 1978

The late bus dropped Beatrice at the end of Doris's street. Her bag was heavy with Max's files and keys. *Who's the thief now?* It was a small comfort to know she had something to trade for her aunt's key. That is, if she ever saw Max again.

Beatrice climbed the crooked stairs toward her aunt's door with her eyes at her feet. It wasn't until she reached the top steps that she realized the door wasn't shut. A sliver of light was gleaming at her. She froze. She knew she hadn't forgotten to lock it, and she always turned out the light. She dropped to her knees with a hand over her mouth. The walls were paper thin, and the apartment was tiny. She held her breath and listened. Her heart pounded out the seconds as she watched the doorway for moving shadows.

After several minutes had passed, she crawled up the last three steps on her hands and knees and pushed the door open wider. Inside, the room where she slept had been torn apart. The cushions of the couch were flung onto the floor. The three drawers in the kitchenette were pulled out and dumped on the ground. The refrigerator door was standing open. Paper, pots, pans, and silver-ware covered the ground.

She shot up in alarm. All of her clothes had been violently ripped from the hangers and were piled on the ground next to the radiator. The bed in Doris's room was thrown up against a wall, and the worn quilt and sheets had been torn from the mattress. Dresser drawers were smashed around the room. Doris's trampled underwear covered the floor. The closet door had been thrown open and all of its contents tossed out. The mink, the tweed suits, the hatboxes, the go-go boots all were in a knee-deep pile next to the bed.

Beatrice snatched up the fur coat protectively. A burglar would have taken the mink. It didn't make sense. She picked up the photograph of young Doris and Ilene off the floor. The glass was cracked. She cradled the picture frame and fur coat, sinking to her knees.

An empty dresser drawer lay smashed on the ground next to her. Beatrice stared at it until she couldn't see anything but her own tears. *Who would do this? Why?* Then something occurred to her. Her aunt's letters and bank files were gone. She looked behind the mattress leaning against the wall and around the floor. They were nowhere to be found, and yet she had left them all on the bed in plain sight.

Beatrice backed out of her aunt's room. The kitchen drawers, the cushions, the medicine cabinet in the bathroom—they'd all been emptied and tossed on the ground. Someone had been look-ing for something. Her aunt's purse was splayed out on the couch frame. The lining had been ripped out; the seams had been cut. Even her cigarette pack had been pulled apart. Then Beatrice real-ized her aunt's key ring was gone. An image of the safe deposit key, the key Max had stolen, flashed in the back of her mind.

She couldn't stay there. Someone had Doris's keys. They might be back. They might have noticed that Doris didn't live alone.

Beatrice grabbed her old suitcase off the floor. She stuffed all of the clothes and toiletries she could fit in the bag. She fought it closed and dragged it to the open door. The frigid air outside had begun to fill the room, but Beatrice couldn't feel a thing. She yanked the full suitcase thumping down the stairs and into the snow. She ran back up to the open door and scanned the ruined insides of the apartment once more before slamming it shut.

The bag left a trail in the snow behind her, until she reached the end of the street. Calabria's Diner, where her aunt had worked, was still open. There was nowhere else she could think to go. She picked up the heavy suitcase and tried to walk with some composure the half a block to the restaurant.

Beatrice pushed the door to the diner open and was greeted by a warm blast of air and the sizzle of the fryer in the back. The restaurant was half-full. Beatrice dragged herself over to a booth and shoved her overstuffed luggage under the table. She collapsed onto the vinyl seat and put her head down on the coffee-stained Formica.

A few minutes later, a pair of orthopedic shoes walked up beside her. It was Gladys.

"Beatrice, honey. How are you doing? How's your aunt holding up?"

Beatrice lifted her head and forced a weak smile.

The old woman nodded and put a hand on her shoulder. "Can I get you something, hon? It's on the house."

"Soup?"

"Coming right up." Gladys squeezed her shoulder and walked away.

The room around her was distorted with overwhelming smells and sounds and buzzing yellow light. She might throw up, she realized, and buried her head in her hands. She couldn't call the police. What would she tell them? She'd been robbed, but the burglar only took some old love letters and keys. She didn't even have proof she lived there—she wasn't on the lease. Worse yet, it wasn't legal for her to be living on her own at all. She was still technically a minor. The police might drag her away to a foster home or worse. She dug the palms of her hands into her eyes to plug the tears.

The smell of food forced them back open. Gladys had brought a bowl of soup, a plate of fried chicken, a salad, and a Coke. It was a feast.

"You just let us know if we can do anything to help, okay, honey?" The sweet old woman patted her hand.

Beatrice nodded, afraid to speak.

As she ate, the wheels slowly began to turn in her mind. She had to do something. She couldn't call her mother. She wouldn't call Max. Then a light clicked on in between her dark thoughts. She reached into her coat pocket and pulled out a business card. It read "Detective Anthony McDonnell." Tony had written a second phone number on the back. The clock that hung over the lunch counter read 8:16 p.m.

"Do you need anything else, honey?" Gladys asked, waddling toward her.

"Do you have a pay phone?"

CHAPTER 29

Max's brother Tony answered the phone after six rings. "Hello?"

"Detective McDonnell? This is Beatrice . . . Max's friend."

"Right. Beatrice." She could hear him smiling. "Is everything all right?"

"Well, no." Her voice cracked a little. "Can you meet me at Calabria's Diner?"

"I'll be there in twenty minutes. Can you wait?"

"Yes. I'll be here." She was relieved that he didn't ask questions. She wasn't quite sure what to tell him.

Beatrice returned to her chicken and soup and ate until she couldn't stomach any more. She picked at the salad and tried to figure out what to tell Tony. She needed help. She didn't have anyone else to call, but she wasn't sure she should trust Max's brother. Max had stolen her aunt's key.

Beatrice glanced down at her handbag, still heavy with the things she'd taken from Max that evening. The huge ring of keys lay at the bottom. Then there was the file of notes hidden in shorthand, and another file she'd pulled out of Max's desk at the last minute while the security guard tapped his foot.

She pulled the mystery folder out and examined the label. It read, "Box 447." Inside she found a typed form on First Bank of Cleveland letterhead. It was addressed to the State of Ohio. The title read "Custody Transfer." The form listed the box owner as "Beverly Lerner." It gave her last known address and social security number. The date of repossession was listed as June 16, 1973. A catalog of contents was provided. Beatrice scanned the list and saw that Box 447 contained birth certificates, a will, and fourteen diamonds. Her eyes locked on the word "diamonds." The karat size was given for all fourteen, and each diamond was bigger than the last, with the largest being estimated at six karats. Box 447 had once contained a fortune.

She pulled out the folder of Max's handwritten notes and searched until she found it. Box 447. Max had tried to reach Beverly on June 1 and couldn't find her. The phone had been disconnected. Max's note at the bottom of the page read in shorthand, "State has no record of repossession."

She turned her eyes back to the bank form letter. In smaller print there was a paragraph full of lawyerly words turning over custody of the box contents to the state for "holding or auction." The letter was signed by "William S. Thompson, Auditing Department." She traced the signature with her finger and realized it had been stamped onto the form letter as was done with so much other standard correspondence. She searched the bottom of the sheet for the processor's initials and found them in the lower left corner. They read "DED." *Doris?*

Behind the custody form, Beatrice found a single sheet of paper labeled "Note to File." It was a typed record of Max's phone call to Beverly. The final note read, "Customer nonresponsive." The initials at the bottom of the page read "MRM." Max had typed the record.

Beatrice sat back in her booth and chewed on her straw. Max had been given the assignment to audit the safe deposit boxes by Mr. Thompson after an irate customer claimed that her box had been repossessed unfairly. Max proceeded to call customers, presumably ones who were no longer paying their fees or whose boxes had been reclaimed, to verify their whereabouts and the validity of a repossession. Max had a drawer full of organized files documenting repossessions. After an irate customer came forward demanding her possessions, Max had been convinced something was not right at the bank. She had even asked Tony to open an investigation. Max followed up on the notices herself and found out that the state had no record of any transfers. Fortunes had vanished. Now Max was gone. Max had taken her aunt's key while Beatrice was sleeping and then up and quit her job the next day.

"You look deep in thought," a husky voice said from across the table. Tony slid into the seat across from her.

"Oh. Hi." Beatrice hadn't realized how much time had passed. She'd planned to put everything away before he arrived.

"What is all this?" he asked, looking at the piles of papers.

"Oh, it's just work stuff." She shook her head and gathered up the papers as if they were of little interest. "I sort of fell behind at the office. My aunt's been ill."

She hated using Aunt Doris as an excuse. Sympathy wouldn't help. She didn't check to see whether his eyes softened on her behalf. She just shoved the papers back into her bag as quickly as she could manage. When she looked up, he was waving Gladys and her coffeepot over.

"I'm sorry to hear about your aunt."

"Thanks. She's over at University Hospitals. I don't think she's going to make it." Beatrice bit the inside of her lip. It was the first time she'd said it out loud. Tears pooled at the corners of her eyes.

Tony slid his hand across the table to hers and gave it a gentle pat. "I'm so sorry."

An uncomfortable silence settled over the table. His hand was nearly twice the size of hers. He pulled it away when the coffee arrived and went to work doctoring his mug with cream and sugar—three heaping spoons of sugar. Beatrice cracked a small smile.

"What can I say? I guess I like things sweet." He winked at her. "So, what can I do for you, Beatrice?"

She knew the question was coming. She still didn't know what to say about the missing key or the bank letters, so she began slowly. "Someone broke into my aunt's house."

The good humor drained from his face. "Are you all right? Were you home?"

"No, I was at work."

Maybe his concern for her safety would keep him from asking too many questions. Tony took out a small pad of paper and a pen. Maybe not.

"What's the address?"

She told him.

"Your aunt's name?"

"Doris Davis."

"Was anything missing?"

"I . . . I don't think so." She swallowed hard. She didn't want to tell him about the love letters and the files from the bank. She should have never snooped and found the papers in the first place.

"Did your aunt have any valuables you may not have been aware of? Cash? Jewelry?"

Beatrice immediately thought of the safe deposit box key. If her aunt did have any valuables, they were undoubtedly hidden away in a vault at the First Bank of Cleveland. The only other person besides her aunt who knew about the key was Max. "I don't think so. There was a mink coat, a TV . . ."

"Were they taken?"

"No." Her tiny frame was dwarfed by the height of the table, and she could feel herself shrinking in the detective's eyes. She couldn't afford to look like a lost twelve-year-old, and sat up taller. She forced out a stronger voice. "It doesn't make sense, does it?"

"No," Tony said, making small notes on his pad. "It doesn't."

"That's why I thought to call you. It just doesn't seem like a normal robbery."

He studied her carefully. Being Max's friend, she prayed he would trust her. She batted her eyes just a little. Flirting couldn't hurt. It seemed to work to her advantage, as the focus of his eyes softened.

She released the breath she'd been holding. "I really appreciate you meeting me here, Tony. How's Max doing?"

He flipped his notepad closed at the change of topic and sipped his mug of sugared coffee.

"I haven't talked to her for a few days. She's on vacation," he said, and then paused. "I thought you knew that. Aren't you two pretty good friends?"

"Vacation?" She frowned. "No, I didn't know that. Where did she go?"

"Cancún." He looked at her sharply. "Did you two have a fight or something?"

"No. Well, sort of. I guess we did," Beatrice said, stumbling. "Where is Cancún?"

"Mexico. She'll be gone a couple weeks. Said something about needing to get away for a while. Now that I think of it, she wanted me to give you this if I saw you." He reached into his wallet and pulled out a small key.

Beatrice's eyes swelled at the sight of it. It was labeled "547." He dropped it into her palm.

"What's that for anyway?"

Beatrice wiped the astonished look off her face. "Oh, this? . . . It's for my locker at work. I thought I had lost it!"

"I have no idea why she thought I might see you. I told her she was nuts. But you know Max. She's gonna get what she wants one way or another."

In some fit of remorse, Max had given her Doris's key back. Maybe Max was a friend after all. Maybe Beatrice was the one who shouldn't be trusted. She had snooped in Max's things and stolen an entire ring of keys. Worse, Beatrice had betrayed Max's project to Mr. Halloran.

"Listen, I'll check into your aunt's break-in, but without anything missing it's gonna be hard to get anyone to do much. Cleveland's a big town with big problems. Most B and Es don't go very far."

"Do you think it's safe for me to go back tonight?"

"I wouldn't. Besides, if the burglar knows you and your aunt are away, they may try to go back and even squat there. Drug addicts love a free place to stay. It may be our best chance at catching the perp. I'll swing by there a few times in the next week or so. I'll let you know what I find out. Do you have another place to stay?" he asked, raising an eyebrow like he suspected she was only sixteen.

"Me? Sure! Of course. I'll just go stay with my cousin for a few days." Beatrice panicked as she nodded. She didn't know why she said it. The words just came out, and she couldn't take them back. Lies were becoming second nature.

The matter was closed. "Where can I reach you?"

"Uh, you can call me at the bank. I practically live there anyway." She gave him her extension.

He paused and studied her face one last time as if he was trying to decide something. This was the moment where he would call her bluff and haul her off to juvenile detention. Instead, he simply nodded and stood to leave.

"You take care of yourself, Beatrice."

CHAPTER 30

Beatrice dragged her heavy suitcase through the snow all the way to the hospital. She'd seen families sleeping in the waiting rooms as she'd come and gone after work. She decided it was her best chance at shelter for the night. She made her way up to the intensive care unit, where her aunt had been lying for over a week. It seemed like years. The nurse didn't look up as she pulled the bag behind her and into her aunt's room. Beatrice found the small closet in the corner reserved for patients' personal items. She stuffed her suitcase inside and forced the door closed. It would have to do for the night.

She collapsed into the stiff vinyl chair next to her aunt's pillow and put her head on the edge of the bed.

"Someone broke into your apartment," she whispered in the dark.

She confessed it all to Doris, hoping the shock of it might wake her up. The apartment, the letters, the key, the missing fortunes, Max fleeing to Mexico—Beatrice told her aunt everything. The woman didn't move.

Sometime after 1:00 a.m. a loud beeping sound woke Beatrice
up. She startled at the alarm and grabbed Doris's hand. Air was
still rattling in and out of the tube in her mouth. Her sunken chest
was still moving up and down. A nurse floated into the room. She
turned off the alarm and changed the bag of saline hanging from a
hook over her aunt's shoulder.

"Miss, I'm sorry. Visiting hours are over," the nurse said in the
scolding voice Beatrice had grown accustomed to at the hospital.

Beatrice took the elevator down to the main lobby, where an
old man was snoring in a chair. She curled up on a hard bench,
using her purse as a pillow. She laid with one eye open for most of
the night. Some point after 5:00 a.m. she abandoned her vigil and
drifted off to sleep, until the doctors and nurses changed shifts two
hours later.

Beatrice spent the weekend lurking in the hospital. She ate in
the cafeteria, washed up in the public restrooms, and slept where
she could. It was a blur of fluorescent lights and hushed voices.
She spent most of her time sitting with Doris, trying to figure out
what to do next. Eventually, she'd fall asleep in the chair, simply too
exhausted to string her thoughts together.

Sunday afternoon she awoke to an older man with a white coat
tapping her on the shoulder. "Miss? Miss? Are you okay?"

"Hmm?" Beatrice replied sleepily.

"I'm Dr. McCafferty. I've been attending to your aunt. Some of
the staff are concerned that you've been . . . spending so much time
here. Do you have any other family?"

"Family?" Beatrice straightened in her seat. The nurse's comment about contacting Child Services rang in her ears. "Uh, yes.
My uncle. I believe you met him?"

"Yes, but is he here with you now?"

"No. He . . . he works weekends sometimes. He asked me to
keep Doris company."

"I see," the doctor said, nodding. He checked the chart at the end of Doris's bed and then turned to leave. Beatrice was grateful the two questions were the extent of the doctor's concerns. She decided to risk a question of her own.

"Is she . . . is she going to be all right?"

"We're doing all we can. I suggest you speak with your uncle about that, miss."

Once the doctor left, she leapt to her feet and grabbed the chart from the end of the bed. She scanned the sheet, desperate for some clue of her aunt's condition. She couldn't make sense of all of the numbers and initials and check marks. Only one thing stood out. Big letters were scrawled across the bottom of the page in angry red ink. They read "DNR." She read the letters again and again, not knowing what they might mean.

CHAPTER 31

Monday, August 17, 1998

Iris barely made her Monday deadline. Brad showed up in the loading dock at 8:00 a.m. sharp, expecting a full set of drawings for the first seven floors. She had yanked herself out of bed at 4:00 a.m. to put the finishing touches on her survey. Her roll around the bathroom floor with Nick the Tuesday before had cost her a couple of precious hours and most of her dignity, but she'd be damned if it cost her her job too.

She met Brad at the dock and slapped the fully annotated plans into his hands. He looked them over and put them into a manila folder. "These look pretty good. There's been a slight change of plans. We need someone here for a few weeks drafting the plans directly."

"Drafting directly," she repeated, trying to keep the question mark floating in her head out of her voice. She had no idea what he was talking about but nodded in total agreement.

"They'll be bringing over a workstation for you to use. Do you feel comfortable working in AutoCAD?"

"Yeah." Iris had used the drafting software in school.

"I brought a copy of the style manual," he said, producing a binder from his bag. "The most important thing is that you draw to scale and use the proper layers."

It was beginning to make sense to Iris. They wanted her to draft the plans on a computer at the building rather than making hand drawings for another person to transcribe.

"Are my sketches too messy for them to follow?"

Brad chuckled. "No, it's not that. The scope just expanded, and the schedule's tight. Mr. Wheeler doesn't want us wasting any time running back and forth from the office."

"The scope expanded?"

"Yep, we're going whole hog on this one. It seems as though someone down at the county is determined to buy this old pile of bricks. We've made the short list. It's between 1010 Euclid and the old Higbee Building. They want full floor plans with structural, mechanical, electrical, plumbing, you name it. I think they're crazy!"

They were going to save the building and its marble stairs and cathedral ceilings after all. More importantly, she would be working far away from the office doldrums for weeks, maybe even months. Iris couldn't help but smile. Mr. Wheeler and Brad were trusting her with a really big job.

"You'll be the primary drafter for the structure," Brad continued. "We'll bring in the mech-Es and double-Es next week."

"Will you be here too?" She tried not to visibly cringe at the thought. That would be the end to her freewheeling jeans and T-shirt workdays—let alone her hours fornicating with coworkers on bathroom floors. Brad was all business, from his parted brown hair to his polished leather toes.

"Nope." He was obviously a little disappointed. "I'm too expensive to be on-site full-time drafting. There are perks to being young and cheap."

She forced a small smile and tried to tell herself it wasn't an insult or any sort of reference to her personal life.

Iris and Brad discussed the logistics of her assignment for the rest of the morning as she gave him a guided tour of the floor plans she'd drawn. He took a few measurements at random to verify her work. They paused in Linda's HR office, and Iris stood in front of the smashed bookcase to block the view. Fortunately, Brad was less concerned about the furniture and more interested in the space hidden behind the locked door.

"Did you confirm this space here marked 'bathroom,' 'cold-air return,' and 'mechanicals'?"

"Well, I couldn't get any access," she said apologetically. "The door is locked, and Ramone doesn't have the key."

"But how did you determine what the spaces are?"

"Ramone told me . . . and they match the fourth floor."

"We'll need to remove the door and probe some of the walls to confirm it," Brad said, making notes on the plan. He looked up at her scowling face and added, "Don't worry. You couldn't have done more without some equipment. In two weeks we'll have a contractor cut some holes."

Iris nodded, but the perfectionist straight-A student inside her deflated a bit. Brad's review was the closest thing to an evaluation she'd received since starting the job, and she'd just been given a B. She tried not to sulk as she followed him back down the stairs to the loading dock.

"All right. I guess I'll leave you to it. I'll check in Friday on your progress. They'll deliver the workstation at the end of the week."

Brad walked out the overhead door, and she was alone again in the dock. Ramone was nowhere to be seen as usual. She paused, looking around the dimly lit cavern, and shivered in the dank, putrid air. Suzanne's words echoed in her mind. "There's a reason that building hasn't been bothered all these years."

The reason the building hadn't been bothered was that nobody wanted to buy it until now, she argued. Downtown was full of vacant buildings. A real estate investment firm bought it as a tax write-off. They bought it to just let it sit—that was the point. If they were planning to sell it to the county, there couldn't be some deep, dark secret buried inside. She had to stop running around talking to crazy old women.

Iris climbed the dock stairs up to the service elevator door just beyond the loading platform. She was hoping the elevator still worked but hadn't tried it yet. She pressed the button and was surprised when it actually opened. Inside, she hit the button for the sixth floor and stood there waiting. She hit it again. Nothing happened. *Shit.* She had to find Ramone.

Ramone's office couldn't be far, but she hadn't seen any sign of it yet. Her first day in the building with Brad, they had been down in the basement vaults when Ramone had appeared out of nowhere. Maybe it was down there.

Iris walked the long service corridor to the third set of stairs, hidden in the back of the building. She flipped on her Magnum flashlight and pulled the heavy door to the basement stairwell open. The white beam poured down the dark well. The sound of water dripping echoed up from the cold stone floor. She gripped the flashlight like a weapon as she crept down the concrete steps toward the basement.

At the bottom of the stairs, the clang of something metal hitting the ground on the other side of the door stopped her in her tracks. She recognized the muffled sound of Ramone's gravelly voice. He was cursing. She eased the door open a crack and caught a glimpse of Ramone. His back was to the door, and he was crouching inside the vault. Steel tools glinted in the light on the floor next to him.

He threw one to the ground with a loud "Fuck!" He turned toward her and leaned his head back against the wall of safe deposit doors. He might have been trying to pick a lock, she realized.

He lit a cigarette and studied a long, thin awl with disgust. Then he lifted his eyes in her direction. She ducked behind the door and it slammed shut. *Shit.*

Thinking fast, she began twisting and pulling at the handle and kicking the door, making a terrible racket. "Damn door!" she shouted, pounding on the steel. "Ramone? Ramone, are you in there? I need help with this stupid thing."

She slammed her shoulder against it and nearly fell to the ground when Ramone swung the door open.

"What the hell you doin'?" he barked. A flicker of rage lit his bloodshot eyes.

She decided to go with her act and prayed he bought it. "That damned door nearly slammed on my hand! This place is a death trap, I swear!"

Ramone shook his head. His expression softened to mere annoyance. "This isn't a good time. I can't show you the tunnels today."

Iris blinked. She'd forgotten all about the tunnels. "Actually, I need your help with the elevators. I can't get them to work." She held up her hands like a helpless girl.

"You need a key," he grumbled, not amused by her act. He pulled out his large ring of keys and handed one to her. It was marked "E."

His set of tools was gone from the vault floor. From his tired eyes, it didn't look like he'd ever had any luck with them, but it did explain why he might be willing to live in the dusty tomb of a building. Maybe he figured he was sleeping next to his retirement fund.

"Thanks!" Iris turned to go back up the stairs.

"The elevator's over there." Ramone pointed her around the corner, past the vaults.

"Oh! Thanks! I guess that would be faster. I hate those stairs!" she yammered as she skirted past him and out of sight.

Once she was around the corner, she breathed easier. She found the elevator and pressed the call button. An unmarked door stood open just a few feet away from where she was waiting. She glanced over her shoulder and then tiptoed over to it.

The room was no bigger than a closet. Wedged inside there was an army cot, a chair, a small TV, and a TV tray table. It couldn't be more dreary, with its beige walls and a bare lightbulb. *So this is where Ramone lives,* she thought. *No one should have to live this way.* She found herself sort of hoping he would succeed in opening a box or two. Time was running out.

There was a framed black-and-white photograph of a beautiful dark-skinned woman in a white hat on the TV tray next to his cot. *His mother?* Tucked in the corner of the frame was a more recent color photograph. It was a small headshot of a beautiful blond young woman. Staring at it, she felt someone's eyes watching behind her. She snapped her head around, but no one was there.

She turned back and studied the color photo one more time. The girl wore a high-collared blouse and bright red lipstick. Her hair was up in a twist. Iris couldn't linger in the room. Ramone wasn't far. She tore her eyes away and hurried to the elevator.

CHAPTER 32

Inside the elevator, Iris stared at the numbered buttons. She was pretty sure she was supposed to draw up the eighth floor next, but she had to get her clipboard out of her bag to check. As she fumbled through it, three files fell out, scattering papers all over the elevator floor.

"Damn it."

The elevator doors slid shut. She shoved the papers three at a time back in her files, until something caught her eye. It was a sheet full of hand-drawn swirls and tick marks. Iris picked it up and studied the odd markings again. They'd come from Beatrice's personnel file. She picked them up one by one, skimming through the nonsense until a number jumped off one of the pages—547.

It was the same number as Suzanne's key. She rifled through more pages and saw it again. Then again. "547" was written all over the notes left by Beatrice Baker. *It couldn't just be a coincidence,* she thought. Beatrice had called Suzanne about a deposit box. Key 547 was in Suzanne's desk, and now the number was all over the

strange notes hidden in a personnel file. Maybe the key really did
belong to Beatrice.

Iris stood up and lifted her finger to push the button marked
"8," and hesitated. Beatrice Baker had worked on the ninth floor—
that's what Suzanne had said. There wouldn't be any harm in taking a look. Besides, there was no rule that said she had to survey
the floors in order. She pressed "9," and the elevator car carried her
up the tower.

A long, narrow hallway led from the service elevator to the
northwest corner of the ninth floor, where a set of double doors
were wedged open. The gold letters on the wood read, "Auditing
Department." *This is it,* Iris thought, as she pushed her way in.

Through the doors was a large room with eight typing stations
packed tightly together. A ring of office doors surrounded the type-
writers on three sides. Iris walked the perimeter of the work area,
reading the nameplates next to the doors. The third was marked
"Randall Halloran." Iris paused. Suzanne had said the Hallorans
went bankrupt after the bank closed. Iris swung the door open
to Mr. Halloran's office. It looked similar to the others she'd seen
already. The wood was a little darker. The desk was a little bigger.
There was a tufted chair with a tall back pushed behind it.

Iris sat down behind an enormous desk blotter. She pulled
open the center drawer. It was empty. She opened another drawer
and another, trying to find some clue as to who Mr. Halloran was
and why he went bankrupt. A silver letter opener and a dried-up
fountain pen were the only items left behind. Like Linda in Human
Resources, Mr. Halloran had cleaned out his desk. Behind her, the
bookshelves were also bare. She peeked into the washroom, trying
not to think of Nick. An old bottle of aftershave sat next to the
gilded mirror. It smelled terrible.

Beatrice was probably a secretary, Iris thought as she exited
Mr. Halloran's office. Suzanne had called her a "young girl," and
something told her that a receptionist like Suzanne wouldn't just

casually go looking for someone with an office and a door. Iris certainly wouldn't. She didn't feel comfortable speaking to any of the bigwigs at WRE. They would pass her in the hall and nod, but she was fairly certain none of them even knew her name. Except maybe Mr. Wheeler.

None of the eight secretarial stations in the center of the room had nameplates. They were anonymous. "Where are you, Beatrice?" she whispered.

Iris plopped down at the closest desk. She thumbed through random files in the largest drawer. Scraps of paper, typewriter ribbon, binder clips—she found nothing of interest in the drawers and nothing that said "Beatrice."

There was a clank as she pushed the drawer shut. Iris raised her eyebrows and opened it again. A glass pint bottle under the files was sloshing about. The label read "Old Grand-Dad." She glanced around the empty room, then cracked it open. It just smelled like whiskey. Whiskey didn't go bad, did it? She took a tiny sip. It was sour and burned holes in her throat all the way down.

"Ugh! You do not improve with age, Grand-Dad," she said, grimacing.

There was nothing but office supplies and congealed cough drops in the next several desks. Iris plopped herself down at the last dusty workstation.

The view from the typewriter was oppressive. A drop ceiling hung low overhead. It was probably some 1960s renovation to cover up the gorgeous hand-painted ceiling and keep the ladies' eyes on their work. The school clock hanging on the far wall had burned out years ago, but sitting there Iris could almost hear it ticking. Some poor woman had spent eight long hours a day in that chair facing that clock. She knew exactly how it felt. The desk wasn't that different from Iris's tiny workstation at WRE. No windows and surrounded by the watchful eyes of men. It was depressing how similar her working conditions really were to that of a secretary, despite her fancy degree.

Iris pulled open each drawer, finding nothing until she reached the last one. Inside, rows of green card-stock folders hung empty from little metal hooks. She ran a fingernail over them as if ruffling a deck of cards. As she closed the drawer, something in the bottom caught her eye. She shoved the hanging files aside. It was a small book with a gray binding. Iris picked it up and read the cover: *A Guide to Simplified Gregg Shorthand*. She opened to the middle and immediately recognized the strange writing. It looked exactly like the notes she'd found in Beatrice's personnel file.

An inscription on the first page read, "Dear Beatrice, Practice makes perfect. Love, Aunt Doris." This was Beatrice's desk. Iris turned the pages of the manual one by one as if they might contain the answers to all of her questions about the bank. She found nothing but instructions on how to write in shorthand. On the last page she found another note. It read, "Practice on your own time, kid. Love, Max."

Iris read the words "Love, Max" again and gazed up at the circle of offices. There wasn't a Max on any of the doorplates. Were they lovers? she wondered, turning the book over. Maybe Max was one of Beatrice's bosses. Sexual harassment wasn't even a crime back then. She could picture the young secretary sitting there, keeping her head down at her desk. Trying not to be noticed. It struck Iris as incredibly odd that a secretary without a nameplate on her desk would disappear when the bank closed. Beatrice was a nameless, faceless employee. Why her?

Iris flipped the handbook closed. After a moment's hesitation, she put it in her field bag. It wouldn't be missed, she told herself. Besides, deciphering the bizarre notes Beatrice had left in her personnel file would be far more entertaining than watching TV reruns that night. More importantly, it might help her figure out what the hell to do with Key 547.

It was almost noon. She had wasted over an hour looking for Beatrice. With only five days to sketch eight more floors, she had to get to work. She pulled her tape measure and clipboard out of her bag and set them on Beatrice's desk.

CHAPTER 33

Within thirty minutes, Iris had the conference rooms, the bathrooms, and the storage closets mapped using the fourth floor as a template. She returned to the Auditing Department and began to sketch the layout. She opened one office door after another, marking the windows and partitions. By the time she reached "Joseph Rothstein," her hand was aching from holding the clipboard. She set it down on his desk and stretched.

Mr. Rothstein's old office was a mess. His desk was piled high with files and books, his shelves were crammed full of binders, and there were stacks of reference manuals on the floor. Rothstein didn't have his own bathroom or that big of an office, but he worked really hard, or at least spent his time trying to look like he did.

Volumes of books sat on the shelf with titles like *Full Reserve Banking*, *Macroeconomics Volume I*, and *The Gold Standard*. There wasn't even room for her to write on the desk. She shoved a stack of spiral-bound notebooks aside. Mr. Rothstein's calendar for December 1978 was buried underneath them.

Iris scanned the appointments and notes etched in blurred ink on yellowed paper. They were mostly illegible. She moved another notebook so she could see the most important date of all. On December 29, the day the bank closed, it looked like Joseph was on vacation. The word "Bermuda" was circled—at least she thought that's what it said. Poor Mr. Rothstein went to spend the holidays in the tropics and came home to find out he'd lost his job.

Iris suddenly felt like she was trespassing. She didn't need to know the intimate details of the man's life. She started to cover the calendar back up when small red letters caught her eye. "Det. McD---- --6.555.----" They'd been smeared in a coffee stain, but the letters directly below them still read "FBI" clear as day.

Did bankers often call the FBI? she wondered, staring up from the blotter. Opposite the desk an enormous bulletin board hung from the wall, covered in charts and graphs and financial gobble-dygook. Then she spotted what was looming large in her own mind. It was a question mark. "Cleveland Real Estate Holdings Corp.?" was written on a little slip of paper. She'd seen the name before somewhere but couldn't quite place it. There were other little notes tacked up on the board scattered between the graphs—"Cleveland Urban Growth Foundation?," "New Cleveland League?," "Cuyahoga Coalition?"

There had to be more to it. She searched each little day on Rothstein's calendar for another clue, but between the smears and bad penmanship it was hopeless. The ink was all blurry shades of black and blue—all of it but the note about the FBI and some-thing peeking out from the upper corner in red ink. She pulled the paper out of the black leather corner of the blotter. "Where is the money?" was written in blazing red. She read it again and still couldn't make any sense of it.

Her watch reminded her she was actually supposed to be working. With an exasperated sigh, she grabbed her tape measure and took the room's dimensions. Iris stepped out of Rothstein's office and assessed the number of rooms she had left to measure. Even though it was a thousand times better than sitting at her desk back in the office, the survey work was getting monotonous. What she really wanted to do was to sit down and read Beatrice Baker's notes.

Iris headed down the dusty green carpet to the next office. It looked wrong. Iris slowed her pace. The room had been turned upside down. Sheets of paper were strewn all over the floor as if someone had torn open a feather pillow. The drawers had been pulled out of the desk and upended. Most of the books had been thrown from the built-in mahogany shelves. Paper, books, pens, paper clips, and a few broken picture frames covered the marble floor tiles. Dust covered everything, and the papers had yellowed in the sunlight coming through the skewed blinds.

Iris bent down and picked up a shattered photograph. It was a family portrait. A stout middle-aged man grinned at her with his rail-thin wife and two pimple-faced daughters. Everyone was in printed polyester. The man reminded her of one of her father's golf buddies. Whoever he was, he never got a chance to clean out his desk. Looking at the mess, she could almost hear the racket of slamming drawers and falling books. Someone had been pissed.

Iris waded through the wreckage to take her measurements. On her way out, she nearly rolled her ankle on a cracked coffee mug. It said "Best Dad on Earth," with a little green alien giving a thumbs-up sign. She kicked it out of her way, sending it crashing against a bookcase.

The bronze plate on the door read "William S. Thompson, Director of Audits." Iris felt a nagging twinge in the back of her head as though someone was watching her. It was becoming a familiar feeling, walking around by herself in the empty building, but every now and then she felt the urge to run as if someone were chasing her. Her imagination was getting the better of her. There was no one there.

Iris had wasted enough time. She marched back to Beatrice's desk for her things. Her feet slowed to a crawl as she got closer. The contents of her field bag had been emptied onto the desk. Beatrice's book was open.

She hadn't left the things that way; she was sure of it. She spun around, certain someone was standing behind her. There was no one. But between her sitting at the desk and leaving Thompson's office, someone else had been there and gone through her stuff. She barely breathed as she listened for footsteps, trying to remember what Ramone's had sounded like. She heard nothing.

"Hello?" Iris called out loudly into the empty room. "Is somebody there? Ramone?"

No one answered. Maybe it was the intruder with a flashlight on the fifteenth floor. Ramone had said it was probably a homeless person. She scanned her pens, calculator, cigarettes, screwdriver, and box cutter. It was all there. Maybe she was going fucking crazy. She would have heard if someone were there, she told herself, but grabbed the box cutter anyway.

Beatrice's book was lying open to the page where a man named Max had left a note. Iris snatched the book off the desk and threw it back into her bag with everything else—everything except the box cutter.

Brandishing the razor, she slowly stepped out into the hallway. There was no one there. All she could see were footprints in the dust. She grabbed the flashlight out of her bag and shined the light on them. All of the footprints looked like hers. Iris clicked off the flashlight. She must be fucking crazy. She must have emptied her own bag, too obsessed with Beatrice Baker and Mr. Rothstein to remember. She snapped the box cutter closed.

By the time Iris walked through her own front door, her nerves were fried. Every sound made her jump. She turned on all the lights before collapsing onto the couch. The hairs on the back of her neck didn't settle down until she'd finished an entire beer

and two cigarettes. Even then, the feeling that someone was following her kept twitching. She stood and double-locked the front
door for good measure.

Anxious for a distraction, Iris pulled Beatrice's stolen file from
her field bag. She glanced over the weird writing again, then fished
out the shorthand manual. She skimmed through a few pages of
chapter one, but the instructions blurred together. There was no
easy decoding chart. It was going to take some time to learn.

She set Beatrice's personnel file down next to the manual. Each
swirl looked like the next. The system seemed to depend on how
they were arranged together. After twenty straight minutes, all she
had was, "Fuck, city, bribes." That couldn't be right. *Shit.* Maybe
she wasn't cut out for all this decoding crap. She closed the book
and tossed it onto the cluttered coffee table.

The image of her field bag emptied out on the desk kept
creeping back into her head. Had she emptied the bag herself
somehow? If not, what the hell had Ramone or whoever it was
been looking for?

All of the items she had taken from the building looked up
accusingly at her from the coffee table—the shorthand manual,
Beatrice's file, and Key 547. No one could possibly know she had
taken them, and the odds were that no one would even care. She
was going crazy. It was that simple. All of Suzanne's loony talk
about threats and investigations had wormed its way into her
brain. Talking with that old bartender the other day certainly
hadn't helped either.

"There's a saying where I come from," Iris said in her best
Italian accent, and lit a cigarette. "Never steal from a graveyard.
You might disturb the ghosts."

It wasn't funny.

CHAPTER 34

Monday, December 4, 1978

Daylight pounded through Beatrice's eyelids as the main lobby of University Hospitals began filling up with the sounds of people. Doctors were on their way to work. Patients in faded gowns were pushing their IV stands toward the cafeteria. She stretched painfully and blinked in the harsh sun. It was Monday. She bolted upright and searched the walls for a clock. It was only 7:00 a.m. She still had plenty of time to get to work.

The elevator dropped her off at the front desk of the intensive care unit. The desk sat empty. It was the morning shift change. Beatrice stepped up to the clipboard and signed herself in as usual. Then she remembered that her "uncle" must have signed in at some point as well. She flipped through the book and was dismayed that the records from the previous days had been removed. She flipped back to the page she'd signed and skimmed the list of visitors. The names of strangers who had been on the floor in the last twenty-four hours ticked by without a glimmer of Mr. Thompson or anyone from her family tree, until a name jumped off the page. "R. T. Halloran" had signed in after 9:00 p.m.

The name of the patient R. T. Halloran visited was left blank. There were twenty rooms in the ICU. She had walked past them many evenings stretching her legs. R. T. could have been there for any one of them. R. T. might not even be Randy anyway, she rationalized. She still couldn't shake the uneasy feeling in her gut. She'd been asleep in the chair next to Doris when R. T. Halloran had been on the floor. She shivered at the thought of Randy watching her sleep.

Beatrice backed away from the list. The hiding place for her bag of clothes suddenly seemed less secure. She rushed down the hall to her aunt's room and barely cast a glance at Doris before ripping open the closet door.

When her suitcase came crashing out and onto her foot, she let the breath she'd been holding out in a grunt. The shooting pain in her foot was a relief. At least she still had her clothes. She pulled the heavy bag off of her shoe. She couldn't keep living like this.

By the time Beatrice had washed up in a public restroom, changed clothes, and arrived downtown, it was only 8:15 a.m. The bank didn't officially open until 9:00 a.m., and the main lobby was empty except for a lone security guard. It was a stroke of luck. The overstuffed suitcase she was dragging behind her wouldn't draw too much attention. She couldn't leave it in the hospital closet again. It contained everything she owned in the world, along with Max's odd files and her aunt's key.

The security guard at the desk was the same one that caught her rifling through Max's desk three nights before. She nodded at him and read the name "Ramone" off his shirt as she shuttled her bag through the lobby. Thankfully, he didn't ask her any questions as she scurried quickly out of his line of sight to the elevator bank.

As she waited for an elevator, she looked down at the worn, brown leather suitcase. It was far too big to fit under her desk.

There was nowhere to hide it in the coat closet she shared with seven other secretaries and three accountants. There must be someplace to stow it in a fifteen-story building. Watching the floor numbers light one by one as the elevator made its way down to the lobby, she remembered something Max had told her. The offices on floors eleven through fourteen were vacant. The previous tenants had moved out years ago when the East Ninth Street corridor was expanded.

Beatrice stepped into the elevator and tentatively pressed "12" on the control panel. It refused to light. She tried again and then started pushing all of the buttons from "10" to "15." None of them would light. She pressed "9" and frowned at the other numbers as the elevator doors slid closed. There was a small keyhole in the control panel. She touched it with the tip of her finger. Could a key lock and unlock entire floors? The keyhole was smaller than a door key. She studied it and then rummaged through her suitcase until she came up with the key ring she'd found in Max's hiding spot.

The elevator doors pushed open at the ninth floor as she was sifting through the keys. She quickly pressed "2," and they closed again. She needed more time. One after the other, she searched. Small letters and numbers were etched in the faces—"11S," "TR," "WC." She stopped at a smaller one. It was labeled "E."

"Elevator?" she whispered.

She slid the key into the elevator control panel. It fit. She turned it just as the door opened outside the cafeteria on the second floor. Beatrice could see the kitchen staff milling around, unloading a delivery. She shrunk against the side of the elevator so no one would see her and pressed "12." The number lit up, and the doors closed again.

The twelfth floor was gutted. Bare steel columns were spaced around the room like a sparse forest, and fluorescent light bars hung from naked wires. Bare windows flooded the space with daylight. There was no place to hide her bag. A security guard could easily stumble on it and throw it away or figure out it was hers. The dust on the floor made it seem like no one had set foot on the linoleum in years, but she couldn't risk it. She stepped back in the elevator and pressed "11."

The eleventh floor looked like it hadn't been touched since the previous tenant moved out. Gold letters still read "Goldstein & Stack Attorneys at Law" on the door at the far end of the elevator lobby. Beatrice stepped off the elevator and tried the door. It was unlocked.

The office was almost identical to the one where she worked, but the furniture was gone. There were the public restrooms in the hall, the coat closet, the open area for support staff, where she could see shadows of the missing desks in the green carpeting, and a ring of private offices. All of the doors were open, and the offices were empty.

Office to office she wandered, looking for a good hiding place, until she reached the largest one in the corner. It was twice the size of Randy's, and the sight of it made her stop and gape. Rich wood paneling and thick shag carpet stretched from wall to wall. The ceiling was adorned with gilded carvings and a large mural of a half-naked Grecian goddess in the center. She tiptoed across the soft carpet and into the executive's private washroom. A thin layer of dust coated every surface. The large porcelain sink had two antique bronze faucet handles—one for hot water and one for cold. She turned one knob out of curiosity. Brown water sputtered out of the faucet and then ran clear. The wheels in her head turned as she eyed the toilet and the shower. She hadn't had a shower in days.

From the dust, it must have been months since a maid or security guard had been in the room. The elevator behind her whirred to life. People would begin crowding the lobby below her any minute. She was out of time.

She ran back to her suitcase in the elevator lobby. There was a utility closet just down the hall. She dragged her bag over and shoved it inside. Max's heavy ring of keys jingled in her purse as she ran to the elevator. She pressed the button. It occurred to her too late that she would have some serious explaining to do if the elevator doors opened and some executive found her standing there. She was still debating whether to run and hide when a set of doors slid open. Thankfully, there was no one inside.

Eight hours later, Beatrice was back in the dark ninth-floor restroom, waiting for everyone to go home. Walking through the five-o'clock rush in the lobby with her suitcase would raise too many eyebrows. Besides, she couldn't even get back to the eleventh floor unnoticed until the office was empty. So she waited. The prospect of going back to the hospital for another sleepless night was unthinkable. She'd rather sleep right there in the toilet stall. At least it would be quiet.

When the glowing border around the bathroom door went black, she knew the lights had been shut off. Another ten minutes passed before she crept cautiously into the elevator lobby and looked around. Everyone was gone. She pressed the elevator call button and waited.

The eleventh floor was dark and deserted. Beatrice felt her way to the utility closet and pulled out her suitcase. It was just where she'd left it. She dragged it across the empty office to the huge corner room, with its luxurious, albeit dusty, bathroom. The orange night sky streamed in through one small window, giving her just enough light to see the ghostly outline of the white porcelain sink.

The shadow of her suitcase was hulking black against the soft white carpet in the other room. She reached down and touched the deep-pile rug. The cushy carpet would certainly be more comfortable than a wood bench. It would probably be safer too. It would only be for a few days, she told herself, just until she could find a place of her own.

She closed and locked the heavy wood door to the corner office and said a little prayer she wasn't making a terrible mistake. It was too dark in the room to see. She decided to risk turning on the lights. No one in the building would know, and no one on the street would care, she told herself.

The overhead light clicked on brightly, making Beatrice squint. The carpet was dusty, but there were no signs of bugs or rodents. The windows still had their wooden blinds. She walked over and pulled them all shut.

She closed the blinds in the bathroom as well, then flipped on the light over the sink. The face in the mirror nearly made her jump in fright. Her eyes were ringed in red. The makeup around them was smudged, making them look sunken into her head. Her hair was dull and stringy. Her face was thin and gaunt. She'd forgotten to eat dinner again. She would have to plan better tomorrow.

The faucet handle in the shower stall was a little rusted but eventually turned. The water poured out brown and red like dried blood. The sight was sickening against the muted white marble. Beatrice shut her eyes until she was certain that clean, hot water had reached the eleventh floor, and the room was filled with steam.

After the shower, Beatrice felt like a semblance of herself again. She put on her pajamas and laid her winter coat out on the thick carpet like a tiny sleeping bag. She rolled up a sweater for a pillow and curled up on the floor. Within minutes she was out.

CHAPTER 35

The wail of a police siren out on the street below woke Beatrice at dawn. She quickly got dressed and made up for work. The night of sleep had done her some good, but she was starving. She cleaned every trace of her night in the office from the room and returned her suitcase to the broom closet just in case some security person came looking.

As she rode the elevator down to the cafeteria for breakfast, she wondered how long she'd be able to get away with sleeping in the building. She wouldn't be able to visit her Aunt Doris if she spent her evenings in the ladies' room waiting for everyone to go home. She wouldn't be able to get back into the building late at night. They locked the front doors at 7:00 p.m. and didn't reopen them until 7:00 a.m. the next day.

She thought about her predicament all morning. She grabbed extra food from the corner deli during her lunch break and hid a ham sandwich and fruit cup in her purse.

The Westerly Arms apartment tower caught her eye as she walked back up East Twelfth Street, and she stopped. The lobby

of the apartment building was small but clean. She rang the bell at
the desk and waited until a short old man appeared. He had thick
tortoiseshell glasses perched at the end of his long hooked nose.
"Can I help you, miss?"

"Um. I'd like to rent an apartment."

The man looked at her skeptically over the enormous frames
of his glasses as he grabbed some forms from behind the counter.
"Are you planning to live alone?"

"Yes."

"This is downtown Cleveland, you know. It's not very safe for a
young lady . . . You sure you can afford it?"

"I think so. What are the rates?"

"Three hundred per month for a studio," he said flatly.
"Bedrooms are more."

She nodded. It was only a third of her monthly salary, so she
should be able to afford it just fine.

"You'll need to fill these out. I'm going to need two references
verifying your employment. We'll need a copy of a driver's license
or birth certificate. It will take two weeks to process." He handed
her the forms.

Her heart plummeted as he spoke. Social security number, former address, work information . . . She skimmed through the lines,
realizing how many blanks she'd struggle to fill in. She thanked the
man and walked out of the lobby and back to her office. Her aunt
had helped her fake a job application, but Doris couldn't help her
now. Worse still, Beatrice didn't have a driver's license or a copy of
the birth certificate Doris had forged for the bank. Beatrice had no
proof of who she was pretending to be. She'd never even seen her
own birth certificate.

She returned to her desk and tried to focus on her typing. Mr.
Halloran had been out for days, but the other middlemen were
keeping her busy typing up accounting summaries. She found the

endless clacking of the typewriter hypnotic and struggled to stay awake.

The telephone on her desk rang.

"Good afternoon, Auditing Department."

"Beatrice? Is that you?"

"Tony?"

"I need to see you. Can we meet tonight?" His voice sounded worn out.

"Is everything all right?" she asked, sitting up in her seat. Had he caught her burglar? she wondered hopefully. Could she go home?

"Not on the phone. Can I see you tonight?"

"I . . . I can't tonight." She couldn't explain that she would be spending her evening hiding in a bathroom and then sleeping in an empty office. "How about lunch tomorrow?"

"The Theatrical Grille. Be there at eleven thirty."

At the end of the day, Beatrice went through the same routine as the night before. She waited patiently in the ladies' room for the floor to empty. She ate her dinner of ham and fruit in the dark and watched the muted light from the window slowly fade. When the room was nearly pitch black, she scurried to the elevator and up to the eleventh floor. As she settled down on the soft carpet for the night, she pulled Aunt Doris's key out of her pocket and turned it over in her hand. She still didn't know why Doris had a safe deposit box. She set the key on top of Max's files and fell asleep.

Beatrice heard voices. At first she thought she was dreaming and rolled over onto her side. Then an alarm went off in her head as the voices grew louder. She sat up with a jolt. From the corner office where she hid, she could hear two voices in the hall not twenty feet away. She had locked the door and turned off the lights, but she still sat frozen, holding her breath, certain she'd be discovered. She searched the room for a place to hide but soon realized the men weren't looking for her. They were arguing.

Straining to hear what the angry voices were saying, she crawled silently toward the door. She became more and more certain, as she listened, that neither voice sounded familiar.

"It's gone too far," one voice said. "I don't care what the board says. This can't go on much longer. The feds are already asking questions."

"The leak is contained," a deeper voice said. "The feds don't have a thing on us. Don't tell me you've lost your nerve."

"If the feds aren't a problem, then why the hell are we meeting here again?"

"You can never be too careful."

"This is exactly what I'm talking about."

"Even if they are listening, the feds don't have a thing on us. Where's your backbone, Jim? Aren't you the one who taught me making money is a dirty business?"

"All I'm saying is we can't afford to draw the ire of city hall. All the political favors we've counted on will dry up the second we let the city default!"

"You're afraid of the boy mayor and his band of merry men? Do you think anyone will listen to him once he's driven this city into the ground? He's nothing! He's nobody! This bank, our board, we run this damn town! They'll run that stupid son of a bitch out of town!"

"You think they'll stop there? Ever study history, Teddy? Bankers like us don't fare too well when they start lighting the torches. Someone's gonna burn for this. The feds will be the least of our problems if there's a shake-up in the city council. Our friends in high places are going to scramble to save their own asses. All of the bribes in the world won't keep CPD from banging down our door."

"You've gone soft. Anyone that tries to come through here won't find a damn thing but a paper trail that leads nowhere. I don't care how mad people get. This is a matter of principle. Fuck the mayor!" Teddy shouted.

"Fuck the mayor? That's your plan?"

Beatrice bit her fingernail and strained to hear more. Cigar smoke was finding its way under the door as she pressed her ear to the jamb.

"Ah, the mayor fucked himself when he refused to play ball. No one is going to take him seriously."

"I'm not so sure about that. I think you're forgetting about our other little problem."

"Bill? He's harmless. Besides, we've got all the leverage we'll ever need on him."

"What if he decides to make a plea? A federal witness can certainly beat jail time. Shit, he may even get off scot-free."

"We're watching him. Besides, he knows his little scam is over the second the bank goes belly-up. He won't shoot the golden goose." Teddy chuckled. A long pause followed, and then he added, "He'll make a fantastic patsy when the time comes, don't you think?"

"I'm just not convinced he's that stupid."

"Ha! Have lunch with him. It'll set your mind at ease. Are you done with that goddamned thing?"

The voices grew fainter, then disappeared altogether.

Beatrice stared into the dark long after the men left the floor. The bank was being investigated by the feds, just as Mr. Halloran had suggested. The men had spoken of bribes. They had friends on the city council. They were arguing over something to do with the mayor. She'd learned far too much, but she had no idea who they were or what they were actually doing. Her thoughts kept returning to Bill—Bill, who was running some sort of scam. She at least had a suspicion of who that might be.

Eventually, the morning light trickled in from under the blinds.

CHAPTER 36

The hands of the clock moved at a glacial pace that morning. Beatrice sat at her desk trying to busy herself with her filing. In between pages, she decided to make some notes about the midnight meeting. She pulled out her steno pad and began to jot down a few details. She looked at the four words she had written in her girlish penmanship and paused. After the break-in at her aunt's house, she couldn't afford to be so careless. She crumpled the notes and shoved them into the bottom of her purse. Looking at her steno pad again, she thought of Max.

Beatrice scribbled her notes in shorthand. Over three pages filled up fast as she described the conversation she had overheard in little ticks and swirls indecipherable to anyone outside the secretarial pool.

The clock finally struck 11:20 a.m. It was time to meet Tony. Beatrice stood up quietly and hurried to the elevator with her overstuffed purse hanging at her side.

The Theatrical Grille was empty for lunch. The jukebox was playing the blues as Beatrice walked through the door into the dark room. It took a moment for her eyes to adjust. Carmichael was sitting behind the bar, reading the paper.

He perked up at the sound of the door and leapt off his stool to greet her. "Welcome! *Bella!* How are you today?"

"I'm fine." Then she thought to ask, "Say, Carmichael, have you seen Max around?"

"Maxie? No. It's been too long! You are meeting her here?" He raised his eyebrows hopefully.

"Actually, I'm meeting someone else." She looked down the empty bar and then the row of red booths. There was no sign of the detective. She checked the Old Style clock on the wall and saw that she was five minutes late. "Was there a man here waiting for someone?"

Carmichael raised his eyebrows. "A man? No, but no man would leave if they were waiting for you." He winked at her. "He'll be here soon. I guarantee it. Can I get you something to drink in the meantime?"

"Coffee?"

Carmichael looked disappointed but nodded and headed behind the bar to start a pot. Beatrice picked a booth in the middle and faced the door. A few long minutes later, Carmichael brought a mug over to her. "So where's Maxie been lately? It's not like her to stay away so long."

Beatrice wasn't sure what to say and sipped her coffee to buy time. It tasted like tar, but she forced a smile. "Still on vacation, I guess."

"Tell my sweet Maxie I said hello, all right?"

Beatrice was just about to give up and leave when Tony plowed through the door. "I'm sorry I'm running late," he said, shoving himself into the seat across from her.

Carmichael immediately poured another cup of coffee and brought the mug and a full bowl of sugar to their table. Apparently, Carmichael and Tony had been introduced. The detective began dumping spoonfuls of sugar into his cup, and Beatrice waited patiently for some sort of explanation.

When he finally looked up from the mug, she was startled by his face. He hadn't slept in days from the looks of it. The boyish crinkle around his eyes had been replaced by the heavy bags of an older man. His jaw was peppered with stubble.

"Max is missing." He glared at Beatrice as if she might know where his sister had gone.

"What?" Beatrice gasped. "I thought she went on a vacation."

"So did I. I went to her room at Mom and Dad's, looking for something she'd borrowed, and something just didn't seem right. She had packed hardly any clothes, and all of her summer stuff was still in boxes. So I did some checking at the airport. She wasn't on any flight to Mexico that I could find. We haven't heard from her in over a week."

"They said she quit her job at the office," Beatrice blurted out.

"What?" His eyes flashed angrily. "When?"

"Last Tuesday." Beatrice lowered her eyes. "I'm sorry I didn't say anything before. I didn't want to get Max in trouble."

Tony stared at her sharply until his focus dulled into a pained frown.

"It was all so sudden. She didn't clean out her desk or anything. Her things were still there."

The minute she said it she regretted it. Now she'd have to explain how she knew that, and possibly more. She bit her tongue and looked at the table, unsure of what to do next. There was so much more to tell. The conversation she'd overheard the previous night replayed in her head. Teddy had said something about a leak being contained. Her heart stopped beating for a moment as she considered what that could mean. Max was gone.

"Beatrice," Tony said in a carefully controlled voice. "I need you to tell me everything." The thin line of his lips pressed together.

The cop in him was keeping him focused, but she could see the protective older brother raging in his eyes.

Beatrice still wasn't sure she could trust him, but at this point she really didn't have a choice. "Something is happening at the bank. Something illegal, and I think Max is somehow involved."

Tony nodded grimly, then took out his notepad and began jotting things down. She told him about the safe deposits that had gone missing, Max's special assignment, and the conversation she'd overheard. She altered a few details, like the fact that she'd overheard the conversation in the middle of the night while she was sleeping on an office floor. She also left out that she now had a full ring of keys that seemed to unlock every door at the First Bank of Cleveland, and that she'd stolen those keys from Max's hiding spot in the ladies' room. She did admit to having found Max's files and reading them.

When she had finished telling her version of the truth, he looked at her with those detective eyes, and she knew it wasn't going to be that easy. "What did your Aunt Doris have to do with all of this?"

Beatrice hadn't said a word about her aunt, the key, or the love letters. Her eyes widened in alarm. "Wha— . . . what do you mean?"

"Well, the burglary to your aunt's apartment just didn't fit the profile of a B and E, so I did some checking around. Doris Davis worked at the First Bank of Cleveland a while back, didn't she?"

Beatrice paused and then nodded miserably. She hadn't wanted to drag her poor aunt into this sordid business.

"Beatrice, I need you to be up front with me about all of this. I know more than you think."

He looked at her long and hard with that last statement, and she realized the jig was up. He had checked up on her. She wasn't sure just how much he had found out, but she couldn't afford to not have Tony on her side.

"Aunt Doris worked at the bank years ago—I'm not sure how many. When she had her stroke"—Beatrice's eyes watered, and she worked hard to keep her bottom lip from quivering—"I looked through some of her things and found some letters. I think she'd had an affair with Bill Thompson. I found his love letters. She also had some records—letters about the safe deposit boxes. Max found the letters and read them when I was sleeping. Then she stole a safe deposit box key I'd found in Doris's purse. That was the last time I saw her."

"When was that?"

"Last week." Beatrice wiped a tear. "She never came back to work after that."

"What did the burglar take from your aunt's apartment?"

"The letters. I think they were looking for something else too."

"I think you're right. I've been in the apartment, and I've been watching it for a few days now," he said, making a few more notes on his pad. "Any idea what else they were looking for?"

"I'm not sure. Maybe the key, but no one else knew about it, and Max had already taken it." It wasn't until that moment that Beatrice admitted out loud that Max was a suspect for the break-in—at least in her own mind.

Tony rubbed his forehead and looked over his notes. "Max came to me a few years ago with this crazy story. Someone was robbing the safe deposit boxes. She said it was a big conspiracy. She'd been snooping around and 'gathering evidence.'" He paused, and Beatrice could see the guilt wrenching his face.

"She came to me last week and said she had finally found 'undeniable proof' about her theory. She was all fired up. I told her what I'd told her over and over before. No one at the department is interested in investigating the First Bank of Cleveland. I tried to open a case when that woman claimed her safe deposit box had been repossessed illegally—Rhonda Whitmore. That was her name. I took her statement after Max told me the story. Rhonda claimed she'd been keeping up with her payments, and one day she went into the bank to change her will and was told the box had been repossessed and to take her complaint up with the state. She did call the state. They had never heard of her or her deposits. They just disappeared into thin air, along with fifty thousand dollars in bond certificates. We were really getting somewhere, you know?"

Beatrice remembered hearing the story from Max. "What happened?"

"Nothing. My chief told me we had nothing but supposition. He refused to insult a businessman like William Thompson without proof. He wouldn't even let me bring him in for questioning." He ran a hand over his three-day beard. "Then the poor woman got hit by a car. It was filed as a hit-and-run. Max told me I had no backbone. That I should have investigated anyway. That case nearly got me fired. I couldn't bring up the bank back at the station after that."

"Do you think that there really are some bribes going on?" she asked quietly.

Tony frowned and stirred his coffee. "I want to say it's impossible, but times are tough right now. A lot of guys I'm workin' with have two mortgages to pay . . . I don't know."

"Those men, they mentioned that the feds were asking questions. They also talked about how a leak had been 'contained.'"

"You think they were talking about Max."

"Do you think Max would have gone to the feds?"

"I wouldn't put it past her. If she is working with the FBI, they may have her under wraps right now. I'll have to see what I can find out." He stopped talking and looked at her like he was unable to decide what to do with her. "You need to be careful, Beatrice. Where have you been staying?"

"What do you mean?" She tried not to look alarmed. Maybe he'd been following her.

"I haven't been able to track you down outside of work lately."

He had been following her.

She swallowed hard. "I've been working late."

"So have I."

He didn't believe her, she could tell. If he'd been following her, he knew she had slept at the hospital. She squeezed her hands together under the table, waiting for him to announce he was taking her into custody.

After an agonizing pause, he finally said, "You still work at the bank. Do you think you can poke around and find out who this Ted and Jim really are?"

"I . . . I think so," she said, even though she wasn't nearly that sure. Teddy and Jim could work anywhere in the building. An image of the personnel office sprung to mind. There had to be a directory in there somewhere.

"I hate asking, but all of my sources have dried up over there. Meet me here next week and we'll see what we've found out. Contact me immediately if you hear from Max or if you need anything." He stood to leave. His eyes held hers, and she could see a hint of tenderness inside them. "Beatrice?"

"Yes?" she said, shrinking in the booth.

"The minute things get too scary, I want you out of there."

CHAPTER 37

Tuesday, August 18, 1998

Iris woke up Tuesday morning stiff and sore on the couch. An enthusiastic housewife was holding up her trash like a trophy on the buzzing TV screen. Click.

Piles of Beatrice's papers covered the coffee table. Somewhere underneath the piles, a key and a manual were hiding. Iris buried her head back in a pillow. Ten minutes later, she hauled her ass up and gathered all the evidence of how stupid and crazy she was, thinking she could solve some twenty-year-old missing-person case with a shorthand manual. She shoved the mess into the kitchen junk drawer. She was late for work. Again.

When she pulled up to the old bank, she was shocked to see Nick standing outside the rolling garage door. He held a camera and clipboard in his hands and was apparently waiting for her. She stopped her car short. She considered running him over and splattering his sleazy carcass across her windshield. Instead, she put her car in park and stepped out.

"What are you doing here?" she demanded.

"I'm here to work." He held up his clipboard, and a wicked smile spread across his face. "So don't get any wild ideas."

That's right, she remembered. He had no idea she'd caught him with Amanda. Her eyes narrowed angrily. "You have nothing to worry about, believe me."

She pushed past him and pressed the call button to open the door, then climbed back into her car. She rolled into the loading dock, leaving him in the dust.

"Hey, what's your problem?" he asked once he caught up with her on the loading dock stairs.

"Problem? Why should I have a problem? I'm here to do a job."

She pressed the elevator button and waited, glaring at the door.

"I don't know what I did to piss you off . . . But you're kinda cute when you're angry."

That's it. She turned to him, eyes blazing. "Save your bullshit flirting for some other sucker, okay? You got what you wanted, right?"

She stepped onto the elevator and turned the key for the eleventh floor. She let the elevator doors close in his scowling face. He could find his own damn way, she thought to herself as the elevator whisked her up the tower.

Iris had pressed the button for the wrong floor but didn't care. She began her usual routine, laying out her schematics. She refused to let Nick steal one more second of her time. Angry hard lines filled up her graph paper. He wasn't worth it. The sex wasn't even that good. That was a lie, but it made her feel better.

The glass doors down the hallway read, "Goldstein & Stack Attorneys at Law." They must have rented the space from the bank. Column, wall, hall—she scratched them out in red ink. She walked the perimeter and came to a corner office. The door was closed. She kicked it open. *Fuck Nick and his long, slow kisses.*

She staggered back. Sitting on the thick shag carpet was a bedsheet and some rags piled together in the middle of the room.

Empty food wrappers and debris surrounded the pile. The room reeked like a garbage can. She covered her nose and mouth with her hand. A door in the far corner stood open. Iris knew it led to a bathroom. Terror stabbed at her gut as it occurred to her that the person who slept on the floor might be lurking in there. Holding her breath, she listened for the sound of footsteps, rustling wrappers, or a switchblade snapping open.

"Hello?" she whispered into the room.

There was no response. She tentatively stepped onto the thick carpet, giving the pile of garbage in the middle a wide berth. As she edged closer to the bathroom door, her legs readied themselves to run the other way. She could see more wrappers in front of the toilet. She could just make out a muddy footprint on the tile in front of the shower stall.

A hand fell onto her shoulder.

Iris shrieked. She spun around, swinging her field bag as hard as she could. Five pounds of equipment went careening into her assailant's head. The figure stumbled behind her as she scrambled out of the room, screaming. She ran to the service elevator and pounded the call button. The car was down at the basement. She couldn't afford to wait for it. She ran down the hall to the emergency stairs. She threw her shoulder into the door and was about to fly down all eleven flights when she heard a voice coming from the hallway.

"Iris . . . Iris! It's me, you friggin' psycho!"

It was Nick. She had clocked Nick in the head. She turned and grimaced. His hand covered half his face.

"Nick?" She approached him cautiously. "Shit, are you okay? Come into the light so I can get a look at you."

She led him back into the office clearing, where she could assess the damage. He wasn't bleeding—she was relieved to see that—but she was pretty sure he was going to have a black eye.

"What the hell is the matter with you?"

"I'm sorry. You snuck up and scared the living shit out of me," she tried to explain. "You don't do that in an abandoned building, okay! It's spooky as hell around here! And there was a bed. There's some . . . person sleeping up here . . . Here, come look at this."

She dragged him by the arm back to the room where she'd found the bed on the floor.

"It looks like the building has a squatter."

"Yeah, I guess I thought you were him." She examined his bruised face and looked away sheepishly. He had called her a friggin' psycho. He was probably right.

"Hey." He lifted her chin with his finger. His eyes were soft. They seemed to be saying he was sorry for not calling. Maybe he was and just couldn't find a way to tell her. She held his gaze and found herself searching for a reason to forgive him.

She snapped her chin away and turned to leave. She was not giving in that easy. Not again.

"What the hell are you doing up here anyway?"

"I came looking for you." He grabbed her arm. "Hey, what's your problem?"

"Just leave me alone." Iris yanked her arm back.

She marched toward the emergency stairs to pick up her field bag. He grabbed her wrist. She spun, ready to give him another black eye to match the first. He caught her other wrist and held them both firmly while he searched her face.

"Iris, you're going to have to tell me what the hell is going on."

"You know what's going on! We had our fling. You don't call. You're with Amanda . . ." She trapped her tongue between her teeth to keep it from saying more.

"Amanda," he said flatly. "What do you mean, I'm with Amanda?"

"Don't give me that. I was in Tremont house hunting. I swung by. I saw her there with you." She wrenched her hands free and stepped away from him.

THE DEAD KEY 215

"Amanda's just a friend."

"Bullshit! Just how many girls at the office are you screwing exactly?"

"She came by. We had a beer. I sent her home. I went to bed . . . I would have much rather seen you." He smiled slyly and took a step toward her.

She recognized the carnal look and stepped back. "Well, then, why the hell didn't you call me?"

He shrugged. "You never gave me your number. Besides, I thought I'd catch up with you today."

"Well, I didn't know that!" she yelled, feeling more and more foolish. She hadn't given him her number. She'd been waiting by the phone, and he didn't even have her number.

"Well, now you do. Jeez, Iris. I had no idea how much you cared." His eyes fell to her lips and he leaned toward her.

Her stomach flipped. Iris ducked away before he could plant one on her. She knew what his kisses could do. "Not so fast."

"Okay." He chuckled. "Not so fast. How about dinner Friday night?"

Iris nodded in agreement and decided to flee before he managed to get her into another compromising position or noticed the big, stupid smile on her face. She scurried down the hall to get back to work.

"I've got a big deadline. Mr. Wheeler wants schematics for all fifteen floors by Friday. I'll catch up with you later," she called over her shoulder.

Nick stood in the empty hallway, holding a hand over his eye.

CHAPTER 38

Iris woke up with a start. She didn't know where she was, but she wasn't home. She was on a mattress on a strange floor. Her head was being crushed by a vise, and the whole room was pulsing. She blinked at the boxes and the blank walls and finally remembered. She was in her new apartment.

The previous night came pouring back. After Iris had slogged through the ninth and tenth floors at the old bank, Ellie and her boyfriend had helped her move off Random Road. They had celebrated with too many martinis at the Lava Lounge down the street. Iris could barely recall stumbling home. She lay back down on the floor to make the room stop spinning. It didn't work. She pulled the blanket over her head and tried to fall back to sleep. Snippets of conversations from the last twelve hours replayed at warped volumes in her ears as her brain throbbed.

"Good-bye, Mrs. Capretta!" Iris had waved from the back of a pickup truck next to her ratty sofa.

"So you really think movin' out of here's gonna be better, huh? Just remember, Iris, no matter how many times you move or how big and fancy your house gets, you're still stuck with yourself. You got me? You can't buy your way outta that one, not with all the money in all . . ." The old woman's voice trailed off as the truck pulled away.

Thanks for the parting wisdom, she had thought as she left Mrs. Capretta behind.

Later at the bar, Iris had blathered on about Nick. "He didn't call all that time because I forgot to give him my number! I'm such an ass!"

Ellie had raised a newly pierced eyebrow. "What, this guy never heard of calling Information? He sounds like the ass to me."

Iris wanted to protest, but she had nothing. Her friend was right. It wouldn't have been that hard for Nick to find her number. She sucked down the cocktail in her hand and waved the notion away. "We're going out Friday! Like a real date."

Iris rolled over and grabbed the sides of her head. Acid was rising in her throat, but she fought it back down. Ellie's harsh observation still bothered her. She strained to remember the rest of the conversation, but it was scattered.

After another drink or two or three, she finally admitted to having sex on the bathroom floor with him. This little tidbit piqued everyone's interest.

"I know! I'm such a slu-ut!" She had cackled, and almost fell off her bar stool. A few drinks later, she was staring at the table, muttering on and on about Beatrice Baker's ghost. "It's haunting me. In that building, it's following me. I just know it. Strange things keep happening. The desk, the file, my bag . . . I never should have taken . . . that key . . ."

"Let's get you home." Ellie's voice had sounded far away.

Iris cringed and rolled onto her side. She hated herself for saying stupid shit, getting sloppy drunk, and being such an idiot. She had a job, for fuck's sake. She was supposed to be a grown-up now.

"Uh, make it stop," she whimpered into her pillow.

It was late morning when she woke up again. She had no concept of time, but the sunlight was beating through her naked windows. She managed to sit up without getting dizzy. She rubbed her eyes; then a panic tore through her. She was late—really late. It was Thursday, and she had a ton of work to finish before the next morning. Brad was expecting results.

Iris was still in her clothes from the day before and didn't care. She staggered out the door after finding her keys and purse and got in the car. She didn't bother to brush her teeth or her hair. She didn't have time. The clock on the dashboard glared "11:15."

She sped toward Euclid Avenue like she'd just robbed a liquor store. Halfway downtown, she decided that passing out from dehydration wasn't going to help her meet the deadline. She stopped to grab french fries and Hi-C in a drive-through and shoved the food in her mouth at traffic lights. She almost felt human as she pulled up to the garage door that led into the bank.

The elevator jostled her mercilessly up all eleven floors to where she'd clocked Nick in the head two days earlier. Her stomach slammed into the top of her rib cage and threatened to spill out all over the floor as the elevator slowed to a stop. She felt her way out of the sadistic metal box and took several shaky breaths before looking around. The homeless pile was still sitting in the corner office. She had to get started and finish as quickly as possible.

She unloaded her equipment and hobbled straight to where she'd seen evidence of some vagrant living in the building. It didn't look any different than it had Tuesday. Ramone had probably chased the squatter out ages ago. He must do patrols, she reasoned. Still, she took the room dimensions as fast as she could. She stepped over the makeshift bed and held her breath as she worked. She stepped into the bathroom, holding her nose. The toilet was relatively clean, but there was a man's razor on the ledge of the sink. She snapped two dimensions with her measuring tape and got the hell out of there.

Her hands were clammy as she hurried out of the room. It was ludicrous she was all by herself on this assignment—maybe even dangerous. If she were in any kind of shape to go talk to Ramone, she probably would have. Cold sweat beaded up on her forehead. The hangover was going to be an all-day affair, she could tell. She caught a glimpse of herself in a hall mirror. Her face looked green. It was a good thing there wasn't a chaperone with her—she might've gotten fired. She could hear Ellie in the back of her head asking, "So, you'd rather be hacked to bits instead?"

She wasn't going to get hacked to bits, she argued. Brad seemed to think she could handle it by herself. She moved on to the next office. She didn't want to prove him wrong. She couldn't run screaming from the building like a girl. A hungover girl at that.

The rest of the eleventh floor was unremarkable. She came to a blank door near the elevators. She knew from her work on the lower floors what was probably behind it. A slop sink, cleaning supplies, and possibly a *Playboy* pinup for the janitorial staff to enjoy. Yep, it was a closet.

She quickly measured the room and clicked off the light. She was turning to close the door when her boot clunked into something on the floor. Clicking the light back on, she saw a brown leather suitcase leaning against the wall. It was covered in dust and cobwebs. The handle was worn smooth.

"What are you doing in there?" she asked it.

Iris pulled it out of the closet and laid it on the hall floor. It was filled with clothes. Women's clothes, but much smaller than what Iris could wear. She was a tall size 8, and these were petite size 4. She held up a blouse, and it looked like it might fit a twelve-year-old. Whoever owned the suitcase was tiny. She thought of Beatrice. Suzanne had called her an "itty-bitty thing." Iris laid the blouse down next to a pencil skirt and could almost picture the young woman wearing them. Iris turned back to the broom closet and frowned. The suitcase had been hiding there for years. Alone.

Underneath the clothes there were two paper files. One was filled with the same chicken-scratch hieroglyphics she'd found in Beatrice's personnel file. The other held a pile of letters written on First Bank of Cleveland letterhead.

Iris picked one up. It was a notice that the bank planned to turn the contents of a safe deposit box over to the state.

Iris tried to force the image of a young woman hiding in the closet from her mind. Something terrible must have happened. No one leaves their suitcase behind. Maybe she had packed up her clothes and those files and tried to run away. Maybe someone had stopped her. According to Suzanne, Beatrice had just up and disappeared one day.

It was none of her business, Iris told herself. That was twenty years ago, and Beatrice, or whoever the suitcase belonged to, was long gone by now. Her eyes wandered back to the blouse. It was covered in little paisleys. It was probably her favorite.

"Beatrice," she whispered. "Why were you running?"

Judging from the conservative cut of the clothes, she'd been the quiet type. *Did she live alone like me?* Iris wondered. *Did anyone even come looking for her?* The suitcase hadn't been disturbed since Beatrice or whoever she was left it behind.

Iris grabbed the folders and shoved them in her field bag. She couldn't just lock all traces of this woman back in the closet. She might be dead, and whatever was in those files might explain why. Maybe nobody cared now. Maybe nobody cared then, but it still mattered. She zipped the suitcase shut and shoved it back where she found it.

As she gazed down at the bag in the closet, a morbid thought played in the back of Iris's mind. If she were to disappear one day, who would come looking for her?

CHAPTER 39

There was no time to think about the lost suitcase after being so late to work. There was no time for dinner even. Iris had to keep going if she was going to finish the survey by morning. She climbed the stairs to the twelfth floor and found herself in an empty cavern. Each footstep echoed off the bare concrete. There was nothing but exposed columns; even the drop ceiling was gone. Air ducts, wiring, and the crumbling plaster of a 1918 ceiling hung precariously overhead. It was an engineering autopsy. The floor was gutted.

The steel columns were studded with big, round rivets the size of half dollars. She reached out and touched one. It felt like painted bone. She excitedly pulled out her clipboard and began to sketch extensive notes about the structure and even drew diagrams of the column splice plates just to be thorough. Brad would have been proud.

An hour later she peered out one of the rotting wood windows. The city street below was clogged with pedestrians and cars. The workday was winding down for everyone else, but she still had a long way to go.

The sun was low in the sky, and long shadows stretched across the concrete by the time she headed back to the emergency stairs. She realized as she climbed the steps to the next floor the door was labeled "14" and not "13." She checked her notes and counted her plans, then climbed back down to the landing below and confirmed it. There was no 13. Bizarre.

Fortunately, the fourteenth floor was identical to the one below it, and she zipped through it in fifteen minutes.

When she reached the very top of the tower, her stomach tightened. The fifteenth floor was where she'd spotted a rogue flashlight from the street below the week before. She considered turning back. The number "15" was stenciled onto the beige metal fire door. Sweat dripped down her top lip. It must have been over one hundred degrees at the top of the stairwell.

She sighted down the deep spiral of stairs to the very bottom. The railings and steps curled down, down, down, until she felt like she might fall. She grabbed the railing and breathed. The stairwell was a chimney drawing cool air up from the basement to the lower floors and sending brain-frying heat to the top.

The suffocating temperature finally trumped her fear. Iris slowly opened the door. It was too dark to see. The sun had gone down, and the glow of the streetlights hovered too far below to reach the top floor. She pulled out her police-grade Magnum flashlight and clutched it like a club.

The dust on the linoleum floor had been recently scuffed up at her feet. She could see muddled footprints, but nothing clear. The intruder might have been standing right there. She shuddered.

Stepping out of the stairwell, she let the door close quietly behind her. She inched her way down the hall, following the beam of the flashlight. It led her past the freight elevator toward the lobby. There was no relief from the heat away from the stair tower, and soon her shirt was drenched with sweat. When she finally reached the entrance lobby, she was greeted by a giant portrait of

President Alistair Mercer. Large bronze letters spelled out "First Bank of Cleveland Executive Offices" over his head.

The letters were bolted to a huge slab of marble that stretched floor to ceiling. Behind it she found a large reception desk and waiting room. An enormous crystal chandelier hung overhead, but the bulbs were burned out. Iris tried two different wall panels, and all the lights were dead. Crystal and brass twinkled in the flashlight beam as she continued across the floor.

The heavy French doors adorned with inlaid brass and ebony had no nameplate, but she figured the office must belong to the president of the bank—either that or the Wizard of Oz. Behind them she found an office as big as entire departments on the lower levels. The sheer size of the room swallowed the beam of her flashlight as she concentrated on not tripping over glass end tables and bronze floor lamps. Her eyes got away from her and wandered from the handwoven rugs to the soaring painted murals of the heavens on the ceiling. She banged her shin on an antique coffee table and stumbled into a long leather sofa. Her flashlight rolled under it. *Shit.*

Down on her knees, she spotted the light behind some wadded-up papers. As she pulled it back out from under the couch, she could see that they weren't papers. They were wrappers. Food wrappers and crumpled cigarette packs and other garbage. She leapt off the ground and trained the flashlight at the sofa. There was a makeshift rag pillow at one end. Her hand flew up to cover her mouth. Someone had slept there.

Between the heat and her heart pounding double time, spots began to float in front of her. She was going to faint.

Far away from the sofa she found a seat at a desk the size of a large bed. Her flashlight darted around the room until she was certain she was still alone—at least for the moment. She looked back at the couch with its pillow. A few more wrappers and what looked like a shirt were strewn on the coffee table. Fear churned in her stomach.

That was it. She was getting the hell out of there and going home for the night. Wandering around in the dark with a homeless person loose somewhere in the building was not part of the job description. Brad would just have to understand.

She stood up and waded back through the giant office toward the service elevator. She paused behind the marble-slab wall and listened for footsteps in the hallway. It was silent.

As she stepped out into the hall, the sound of a door clicking shut made her freeze. It was coming from the direction of the emergency stairs. And her way out.

The sound of approaching footsteps roused her into action. She dropped to her knees and fumbled with the flashlight until it clicked off. The footsteps were getting closer. She crawled blindly across the marble tiles, scrambling between pieces of furniture until she came to a wall. She followed it away from the footsteps and into the first open door she found.

Feeling her way across the office floor over couch cushions, loose pillow stuffing, and a rolled-up rug, she realized the room had been trashed. She crawled over what felt like a large picture frame. Her hands fell through a rip in what must have been a huge painting. Through the door behind her, she could see the beam of a flashlight moving on the other side of the reception room. There had to be a place to hide. She could barely see two feet in front of her as she picked her way over the debris. The desk had been overturned. One of its curvy legs lay splintered on the ground. She squinted into the dark until she found what she was looking for— the shadow of another door. She climbed around a fallen chair and into the executive washroom.

Broken glass scraped across the floor under her hands as she slipped into the room. She squeaked in surprise and pulled herself to her feet. The flashlight behind her was moving farther away. She silently swung the bathroom door closed and backed away from it. The room went black.

Trembling in the dark, she struggled not to hyperventilate. She had abandoned her field bag and flashlight and car keys and everything out by the reception desk.

Shit. Fuck. Damn it. She grimaced and carefully felt her hands for broken glass and blood. She strained to hear the footsteps of whoever it was out there in the office. Maybe they didn't know she was there. Maybe whoever it was just wanted to go back to sleep on the cushy sofa in Alistair's office. If she waited long enough, she should be able to sneak out.

The orange halo that hung over Cleveland at night seeped in through the bathroom window as her eyes adjusted to the dark. She could just make out the sink and the shower. The hot air moved in and out of her lungs like sludge. There was no oxygen in the room. Purple spots danced in her eyes. She collapsed onto the toilet and put her head between her knees.

You're going to be fine, Iris, she told herself. *Just breathe.*

A cool wisp of air fell on her arm. Iris put her hand up toward it. She felt it again. There was a breeze. She stretched out her hand until she felt where it was coming from. There was a large vent grate on the wall next to the toilet. *The cold-air return,* she thought to herself. *The air shaft must lead up to the roof.* She pressed her face to the grille and strained to see a piece of the night sky. There was nothing but black. Still, the fresh air was a godsend, and she rested the side of her sweat-soaked head against the grate.

She strained to hear the intruder on the other side of the door. With all the debris on the floor outside, she'd surely hear it if anyone was coming closer. Maybe the vagrant had passed out and she could make a run for it. *Fuck the field bag and the plans.* She just wanted to get home in one piece. She listened again.

She heard breathing.

She held her own breath but could still hear it. She lifted her head off the vent. The breathing sounded louder. It was coming from the vent itself. She jumped off the toilet, recoiling from the sound. Broken glass tinkled under her feet.

A voice whispered from behind the grate.

Her heart seized.

Then she heard it again. "Iris . . ."

Screaming, Iris crashed through the bathroom door and went careening across the room. She tripped and fell hard but scrambled back up. She flew blindly out of the office and down the corridor.

All she could hear was the whispering voice saying her name over and over. It wasn't until she'd almost reached the elevators that it registered in her head that Ramone was calling her. She stopped.

"Iris!" he bellowed again.

"Ramone?" she whimpered.

"What the hell you doin'?" A flashlight came barreling toward her, and behind it was Ramone.

"Was that you? The whole time with the flashlight? Was that you?"

"Who else would it be? You gone crazy?"

"I . . . I don't . . ." Her face crumpled into tears. "I don't know. Maybe I'm crazy! I must be going fucking crazy!"

"Hey, hey. Take it easy now. It's all right." Ramone took her under his arm and led her back down the hall.

A giant lump had swelled up on her knee where she fell. He sat her down in the receptionist's chair, then picked her field bag off the ground and handed it to her.

"Thanks," she managed, and wiped her tear-soaked face on her shirt. Her head swayed on her neck.

"Sorry I snuck up on you. I saw your car down in the dock, and I got worried."

"Sorry. I guess I should have checked in with you. I'm trying to make my deadline tomorrow, so I'm working late."

"Maybe you should let me know next time," he said with tired eyes.

"Yeah. I just thought I could squeeze in one more floor, but then it was hot, and the lights didn't work, and then I found that bed . . ."

"Bed?"

"Not a bed bed, but someone's been sleeping on the couch in the big office." Iris pointed toward it from the reception desk. "Then I heard footsteps and—I don't know—I guess I freaked out."

"Don't be too hard on yourself. This place can get under your skin. Believe me, I know." His asphalt voice was soothing.

Still, she knew she'd really sound like a freak if she mentioned hearing voices in the air shaft. Her imagination had probably conjured the whole thing anyway. It was just the heat . . . and the hangover.

He pointed his light toward the hall. "Let's get you home, huh?"

"Yeah. Just give me a minute to make sure I've got everything." She decided to make small talk to cover up her hysterics. "Say, what happened in that office down the hall?"

"What do you mean?"

"That office that's all messed up." She stood up and put her bag on her shoulder. "Here, let me show you."

She led him down the hall to the office where she'd been hiding, hoping that seeing the place again in the light might erase the whisper from her head. She clicked on her flashlight and pointed it into the room.

It was worse than William S. Thompson's office down on the ninth floor. Every stick of furniture had been destroyed. A steel wall-safe stood open on the far wall. The outline of a picture frame was sunburned into the wallpaper. The safe was empty. Her flashlight fell on the bathroom door and stayed there. She listened for more whispers.

"Damned junkies!" Ramone muttered behind her. "They come up here sometimes looking for stuff they can sell, you know. I guess somebody got frustrated."

"I guess so," Iris murmured, not really listening through the pounding in her ears as she inched closer to the bathroom door.

Iris stepped through it and brandished her light at who, or whatever, might still be in there. The bathroom was empty. She checked again and exhaled the breath she'd been holding. There was no one. She stepped inside and shined the beam into the vent grate where she had heard someone breathing. All she could see were the sides of a dull sheet-metal box that stretched beyond the reach of her light. There was a shadow pattern on the far wall. It looked like a ladder.

"You lookin' for something?" Ramone's voice rasped behind her.

"Is there a way for . . . ?" Iris searched for words that didn't sound insane. "For a person to get in there?"

"I'm not sure. Why?"

"It's just that . . . wouldn't maintenance personnel need to get in there for, I don't know, maintenance?"

"Maybe. But not since I've been here. Say, it's getting late, and I don't know 'bout you, but I'm tired."

Iris nodded and followed Ramone out into the hall. She stopped and made a note of the name on the door of the ransacked office. She had to trot to catch back up to Ramone.

"Uh, thanks for finding me. So what do you do at night around here?"

"I read," he said, and pressed the call button for the service elevator.

It was not as interesting of an answer as she'd hoped. She wanted to ask about him trying to pick locks in the vault the other day, but instead she decided to play it safe. They stepped into the elevator car, and she stared at the buttons.

"Hey, why isn't there a thirteenth floor in the building?"

"I asked that same thing years ago. Know what they told me?"

"What?"

"It's bad luck. Thirteen's bad luck. I've heard that there's a mess of buildings around town without a thirteenth floor. Ain't that somethin'? Don't know if it ever really helped this place, though."

"Huh. I'm as superstitious as the next person, but erasing an entire floor seems a bit crazy."

"It ain't half as crazy as the stuff I've seen."

Iris was pretty sure her little performance that evening had made it onto the crazy list.

"I've seen some weird stuff too," she said. "Say, Ramone?"

"Yeah?"

"I found something strange on the eleventh floor today. It was a suitcase. Someone had left it in a broom closet. Do you know anything about it?"

A small light flickered in his eyes, then went out. "I've learned not to go lookin' in closets around here. You'd do best to leave that stuff alone."

It was a strange warning that didn't really answer her question. She opened her mouth to ask again but thought better of it.

Five minutes later, Iris collapsed into her front seat and lit a cigarette. After three long drags, she glanced back at her clipboard and then cranked the ignition.

The words scrawled in the corner in her shaky hand read "R. Theodore Halloran, Vice President of Finance."

CHAPTER 40

Thursday, December 7, 1978

"Ramone, what the hell we doin' up here? The floor's empty."

A light snapped on in the hall. It leaked around the doorframe into the abandoned office where Beatrice slept. She sat up with a jolt. She had just settled into her makeshift bed for the night. Footsteps grew louder as they neared the door. It was locked, but the approaching security guards had keys. She could hear them jingling.

"Elevators have been acting real funny lately," a deep voice replied.

It sounded closer than the first. Cigarette smoke seeped under the door. Beatrice scrambled back from her bed away from the voices and into the dark bathroom. She could still hear them talking as she eased the door shut.

"What do you mean, 'funny'?"

"What do you think I mean? Cars been comin' up here the past few days all hours of the night."

"So? They probably just busted. Come on, man. Everything in this dump acts funny. Wasn't you just sayin' yesterday that those security cameras are constantly on the fritz? Let's get back to the poker game."

"What does my shirt say? Does it say 'Card Dealer'?" the rusty voice growled. "No, it don't. It says 'Security.' I'm here to do a job."

"You goin' for employee of the month or somethin'? Nobody's here, Ramone."

The footsteps grew fainter. Beatrice heard several doors open and close on the other side of the office. She didn't start breathing again until she heard the elevator bell ring and the voices disappear.

Beatrice clicked on the bathroom light and splashed cold water on her face. She gripped the sink with white knuckles. They had noticed her using the elevators. She would have to be more careful. Scanning the bathroom in the light, she realized there would have been no hiding place to keep her from being discovered, especially not if the guards had found her things on the floor in the other room. As she turned out the light, she glanced at the large grate for the vent next to the toilet, then shivered as the room went dark.

From that moment on, the journey from the ladies' room on the ninth floor up the emergency stairs to her bed was a heart-stopping ordeal. At every turn she was certain Ramone or his friend would jump out at her from a dark corner. She didn't dare set foot outside her secret bedroom at night.

To make matters worse, she hadn't had any luck tracking down a Jim or Ted in the office. Their voices continued to haunt her after their midnight conference outside her door, but she hadn't heard them outside her own head since. Tony still needed her to find out their names somehow. Time was running out until their next meeting.

"The minute things get too scary, I want you out of there." She repeated the detective's words every time she thought she heard footsteps behind her in the dark. It was a nice idea, but there was nowhere else to go. She'd filled out the forms for the apartment down the street, but she couldn't submit them. She didn't have

the proper documentation. Besides, Tony needed her help finding Max and reopening his investigation into the bank. She would
have to find a way, scary or not.

Early Saturday morning the building felt still. Beatrice gazed
down at Euclid Avenue through the dusty blinds. The road was
deserted. The sun bounced brightly off of the high-rise windows
across the street, making the abandoned room feel even gloomier.
She hadn't seen the sun in days. Even during her lunch hours it was
buried behind thick winter clouds.

She should have left the night before but couldn't face another
weekend wandering the hospital halls. The name R. T. Halloran,
written on the ICU register, still loomed in her mind.

One hundred feet below her, a man in a dark coat and hat
crossed Euclid and walked to the front doors of the bank. She
frowned as she watched him. Several minutes later the elevators
whirred to life out in the hallway. The building wasn't empty, not
even on a Saturday.

The sky went dark before she finally worked up the nerve to creep
down to the third-floor personnel office to look for files on Ted
and Jim. The emergency stair tower was lit by weak flood lamps
that hovered over the doors to each floor. An endless swirl of railings and steps led from the eleventh floor to the third. She stared
down the dark chasm and almost turned back. The thought of Max
stopped her. Max was missing, and Ted and Jim might know why.
She grabbed the rail and began climbing down the steps in her
stocking feet.

When she finally reached a beige door marked "3," she pressed
her ear to the cold metal and listened for voices. After several minutes, she was satisfied that the hall was empty and gently pulled
the door open. The squeak of the hinges was painful. She squeezed
through and silently eased it closed.

Beatrice crouched and waited in a dark corner for several heartbeats just to be sure before inching her way down the hall. The personnel office was across the elevator lobby on the other side of the floor. She hadn't been there since her first day on the job but could still picture it. She kept her back to the wall all the way to the HR department. The door was locked.

Max's heavy key ring was in her pocket. Beatrice searched the keys, trying one after another, until she found a match. The door swung open. She slipped inside the office and clicked the door softly shut behind her. Three steps into the dark room, she banged her stocking foot against a trash can with a dull clank. Sparks of pain flew from her toes and she whispered, "Aaaaah! Ouch! Ow! Ow!"

As she hobbled past the chairs and coffee table to the reception desk, it dawned on her that she had no real direction. She was in the personnel office investigating two strangers—Teddy and Jim. Her stomach sank. She hadn't planned the burglary very well. It wasn't as though a personnel chart would be just lying on the receptionist's desk. She was too scared to even turn on the light.

The faint sound of footsteps came tapping down the hall. Beatrice froze. They grew louder, until she could make out voices.

"Bill, stop it! You're terrible!" a woman giggled.

Beatrice backed away from the sound. Her eyes flew around the dark office, searching for a place to hide.

"Not out here, someone might see," the woman said, short of breath.

A key slid into the lock Beatrice had just opened, and she could see a large shadow through the frosted glass. She ran to the nearest open door and closed it behind her just as the door to the personnel office was flung open.

More footsteps, a trash can being kicked, a door slamming, and the rumble of a desk being bumped into drowned out Beatrice's shallow breathing in the next room. Muffled voices muddled together just outside her hiding place. She strained to hear them, until the sound of wet kisses and heavy breathing sent Beatrice reeling back to the farthest corner she could find.

Five steps backward, she bumped against something hard and metal. It was a filing cabinet. Her hands blindly traced its edges until she found another and another. She was in a filing room. She tried to keep her mind off of the grunting and squeaking metal on the other side of the door by counting the file cabinets. There were ten.

She decided to risk opening one in the dark. It slid open with a faint click, and she ran her hands over the files. The drawer was packed full with papers. Beatrice itched to turn on the lights and read them, but the light would leak out from the seams of the door, and she'd be caught.

Beatrice let out a small sigh as the grunting and groaning in the next room continued. The pitch black of the filing room became suffocating as the man's grunting got louder and louder, until it sounded as though he might be in the room with her, panting in the dark. She shrank into a ball with her head buried in her knees and her hands over her ears. Finally, she heard him cry out and it stopped.

"Bill! You're an animal!" the woman gasped.

The man chuckled under his sweaty breath. Beatrice heard a faint smack. "I don't know what I'd do without you, Susie . . ."

"Oh, honey." The sound of sloppy kisses filled the air again. "And I can't believe this ring! You didn't have to get me anything!"

"I thought of you when I saw it. The sapphires match your eyes."

Beatrice heard the woman's voice coo faintly.

"Just don't show it to anybody, okay? It's got to be our little secret."

"Oh, I'm so tired of all of the secrets!" she grumbled.

"You think I'm not? I want to shout my love from the rooftops. I hate all this sneaking around."

They were the same words from her aunt's love letter. It was Aunt Doris's Bill talking. Beatrice strained to hear his voice. It sounded like her boss, Bill Thompson, but she didn't dare open the door to confirm it.

"I love you too." She sighed. "Well, it's absolutely beautiful! Is it real?"

"What do I look like, some kind of cheapskate? Of course it's real." There was a pause, and Bill cleared his throat. "Say, did you get that paperwork I sent down Friday?"

"Hmm? Oh, yeah. I think it's here somewhere." The sound of drawers being opened and shut filled the now-awkward silence. "I hate meeting here, you know. Why can't we ever go someplace nice? My desk is as hard as rock."

Beatrice heard Bill chuckle and the woman squeal, "Bill, you're insatiable! Stop it!"

"I can't!"

Papers rustled. "Here they are. I still don't understand what this is all about."

"Consider it our retirement plan. I'm putting together a deal, and I can't use my name. I need a beautiful partner like you. This is going to set us up for life, Susie. In a few years we're going to leave this godforsaken town. We'll get a little hideaway somewhere on the beach. Margaritas." More kisses. "No more hiding."

"What about your wife?" Susie asked softly.

"She and her daddy can kiss my ass! All these years under his thumb. I swear, if it weren't for you, I would have blown my brains out months ago. But it's almost over. Trust me."

"Okay. But next time, can we go to a hotel like we used to?"

"Sure, baby. Whatever you want."

Another kiss, and then the fumbling sounds of clothes and feet worked their way across the floor. Wisps of cigarette smoke filtered through the door.

"Do you have to smoke that thing? You know how I hate those." Bill's voice was growing fainter, and the door closed.

The sound of footsteps faded away.

Beatrice stood up and shuddered in disgust. She waited for several minutes before daring to turn on the light in the filing room. There was nothing in there but the filing cabinets and a fluorescent light. She pulled open a drawer. It was filled with personnel files arranged alphabetically by last name. Beatrice smacked herself in the forehead. It would be impossible to find a Jim or Teddy in the drawers and drawers of paper. There were two Jameses in that one drawer alone. She didn't know their last names. That was the whole point. The entire trip was a failure, and worse, she'd had to witness Bill and Susie's office-desk romance. It was all she could do not to kick a filing cabinet.

Determined to accomplish something, she stomped over to the drawer marked "Da–Dr" to find Doris. It was a long shot but worth a try. Unfortunately, there was no trace of a Doris Davis to be found.

Then Beatrice went looking for Max's file. At this point, she figured she had a right to know everything. It was exactly where it was supposed to be. Beatrice pulled out the folder and flipped it open. Maxine Rae McDonnell, born on August 22, 1952, started working at the bank in 1971.

She turned to the second page and saw a handwritten note: "Dismissed for Cause, Arrest on sight for trespassing." A date was stamped next to it—November 28, 1978. That was the day after her friend had stolen Doris's key. Beatrice tucked the folder under her arm and closed the drawer.

Beatrice cracked open the door to the filing room with one eye shut. To her relief, the desk looked unmolested, despite what she'd just witnessed. She stared at it in the pool of light from the filing room. The nameplate on the corner of the desk read "Suzanne Peplinski." Bill had called her Susie.

Beatrice shut off the light.

CHAPTER 41

Bill and Susie's conversation replayed itself all the way up eight flights of stairs and for the rest of the night. Beatrice no longer had any doubt that Bill was stealing money from the safe deposit boxes. What she couldn't understand was why he needed Susie's help.

Poor Susie, with her secret jewelry, had no idea the ring on her finger was probably stolen. Had Bill told her aunt the same story about margaritas on the beach? She wondered how many years in the smoky diner Doris had clung to Bill's empty promises.

Beatrice pulled out her aunt's key and looked at it again. Safe deposit box number 547 must hold the answers. There had to be a way to open it.

Beatrice tossed and turned on her growing pile of laundry but couldn't shake the sound of Bill's piggish grunts from her head. She finally gave up on sleeping altogether and slipped back down the hall to the stairs. Only two flights of steps down, the ninth floor was dark, except for a few scattered security lights. She darted from shadow to shadow past the elevator lobby and through the secretary pool to Mr. Thompson's office.

The door was open, and the room was black. She felt her way along the wood-paneled wall toward the desk in the center of the room. Her hands wandered over the leather blotter and pen set until she felt the small lamp in the corner. The room lit up in a yellow glow. The small crystal clock on the desk read 2:00 a.m. The blotter was scattered with papers, but nothing of interest.

The top drawer contained pens, a letter opener, a cigarette case, and a lighter. The large file drawer was locked. She tried it twice, but it wouldn't budge. Her finger circled the keyhole in the side of the desk by her knee. She pulled Max's key ring from her pocket and tried to find a match. No such luck. Max didn't have that key.

Beatrice sat back in Mr. Thompson's enormous chair. The books on the bookcase looked like they'd never been read. The photograph of Mr. Thompson's wife and two daughters was still on the shelf. Apparently, they made Bill want to blow his brains out. Beatrice smiled at them sadly.

There was a crystal ashtray on the shelf next to his wife. It didn't look used. It was covered in a thin layer of dust, and a silver label was still stuck to the side. Mr. Thompson didn't smoke. "Do you have to smoke that thing?" Bill had asked Susie earlier that night. As she stared at the ashtray, she remembered something she'd seen in the desk.

Beatrice pulled open the smaller drawer again. The silver cigarette case was still sitting there. She picked it up, and it rattled in her hand. She pried it open and found a silver key sitting inside. She grinned. It was the desk key. It slipped into the lock and the file drawer slid open easily. Beatrice trained the desk lamp to look inside.

It was filled with rows of hanging files, and each file listed a name—Marilyn Cunningham, Francine Carter, Beatrice Baker. She was startled to see her own name in the drawer and pulled out the folder. It was her performance review file. Her résumé was inside, along with several forms that listed her salary and the date of her next review. There were a few comments scrawled in the margins such as "punctual" and "cooperative." She paused at a small note that read, "Assisting Randy Halloran. A welcome distraction." She raised her eyebrows at "distraction." It was insulting but the only shred of impropriety in the lot.

She stuffed the file back in the drawer and flipped through the others with her fingertips. Then froze. A file labeled "Doris Davis" was stuffed in the back of the cabinet. She yanked it out and flipped it open. Instead of performance records, there was an application for a safe deposit box signed by Doris dated 1962. Box Number 547. Beatrice pulled her aunt's key from her pocket even though she knew the number matched. Behind the application there were several repossession notices. Beatrice recognized some of the letters from the copies in her aunt's apartment.

There were more names of women filed away in the back of Bill's drawer. She grabbed the file for Sheryl Murphy. There was another safe deposit box application behind her name. The file for Diana Brubaker had one too. There were eight women, all with safe deposit boxes. Including Max.

Beatrice swallowed hard before picking up the one that read "Maxine McDonnell." She cracked it open, hoping to find nothing but a performance review. Maxine's safe deposit box number was 544. The repossessions listed in the letters behind her name included a diamond necklace, an engagement ring, and over $100,000 in cash.

Blinking back tears, Beatrice stuffed Doris's and Max's files back in the drawer and slammed it shut as if doing so would erase what she'd learned. She returned the key to the cigarette case and snapped off Bill's light. Sitting there in the dark, she wished she hadn't seen any of it.

She rushed back to the stairwell, hugging herself. Max and Doris both had safe deposit boxes, presumably filled with all of the items listed in those folders. Doris had been in love with Bill. He had seduced her with promises of a life together. He'd just made those same promises to Suzanne.

Beatrice closed and locked the door behind her and curled into a tight ball on the floor. Thoughts of Bill and Doris, Bill and Susie, and Bill's heavy breathing tormented her for the rest of the night. She finally fell asleep with her hands over her ears.

CHAPTER 42

Monday morning, Beatrice stared blankly at her desk. She'd spent the entire day Sunday penned up in her stolen room, pacing the floor. She had watched the street from her windows with one thought circling her head: Max was still missing.

Max had learned something at Aunt Doris's apartment while Beatrice was sleeping. Max had found something in her aunt's safe deposit box and then disappeared. It couldn't just be a coincidence. Beatrice felt the key in her pocket and wondered if Max had really managed to unlock the box.

If Max could open it, surely Beatrice had to try. She was Doris's next of kin after all. She had rights, or at least she would if Doris died. Thoughts of Doris's death filled her with guilt. She hadn't gone to see her aunt in days. She would go tonight, she decided. She'd sleep in the lobby of the hospital again if that's what it took.

Having finally come to a decision, she attempted to focus on the stack of papers on her desk. She scanned the memo in her hand, trying to remember what her instructions had been. The page was just another meaningless accounting summary in an endless pile, until she saw the signature. "R. Theodore Halloran" was typed at the bottom of the page, but the scribbled signature read "Teddy." She reread the name, and her heart jumped. Teddy was the vice president of Finance. She stared at the last name, "Halloran." Max had said Randy's father was a vice president at the bank. He was the reason Randy had a job for life.

The memo Teddy had signed advised the board of directors to reject the mayor's request to refinance the city's debt. It was a more formal version of the fuck-the-mayor comment she'd overheard in the middle of the night. There was no doubt she'd found her man. She searched the stack of papers for any other clues as to what Teddy and Jim were up to. All she found was a detailed accounting of the bank's investment practices over the last four weeks. She paused at the summary of the City of Cleveland bond holdings. Her eyes widened. First Bank of Cleveland held over $20 million of the city's debt.

At the bottom of the pile she found a piece of parchment with the official letterhead of the City of Cleveland. The letter read,

If financing cannot be renegotiated by December 15, 1978, the City of Cleveland may default. All unpaid debts will be turned over to the State of Ohio for settlement. As you know, gentlemen, recovering lost revenue may take years. Please reconsider the impact to your balance sheet.

The letter was signed by the deputy mayor.

Beatrice struggled to understand. She flipped back to the memo signed by Teddy that reassured investors "impacts to the short-term revenue stream will be absorbed by strong deposits." The memo concluded with

The mayor's inability to support the business community's investments in real estate development and the betterment of Cleveland leaves us no choice but to make this gesture of no confidence.

Beatrice couldn't wrap her brain around it all, but it seemed as though the First Bank of Cleveland was playing a game of chicken with the city. She'd seen those races down long country roads, with reckless boys and screaming girls and cars driving at full speed on a collision course. One car always ended up in a ditch. She looked at the deputy mayor's letter again. December 15 was only four days away.

Beatrice pulled out her steno pad and transcribed parts of the letters in shorthand. Then she finished her filing. At the end of the day, she left the building with the other secretaries. She stepped out into the gray, slushy street and realized it had been a week since she'd breathed in the fresh evening air.

The bus brought her back down Mayfield Road toward the hospital. Once inside, she rushed to the elevator that serviced the intensive care unit, where she'd left her aunt a week earlier. The terrible thought occurred to her before the elevator's doors slid open that her aunt might have died while she was away. Her chest tightened.

The usual nurse was at the front desk and looked up at Beatrice with a smile. "We thought you'd left town."

"Oh gosh. I'm sorry. I've been busy at work," Beatrice said sheepishly. The shame of neglecting someone in the hospital washed over her again, but the nurse's easy smile told her what she needed to know. Doris was still alive.

"Oh, don't worry, honey. We all need a break sometimes. Besides, your sister has been here a few times."

"Excuse me?"

"Your sister. She was here earlier today."

Beatrice didn't have any sisters, much to her chagrin as a young girl growing up in a dark and lonely house. "Uh, I have two. Could you tell me which one?"

"Let's see." The nurse leafed through the visitor's log. "Sandra? I think this is her. Pretty girl. She was just here yesterday. She said she was looking for you."

Beatrice's hands clenched inside her coat sleeves as she nodded at the nurse. When she reached the door to her aunt's room, she opened it cautiously. Her mysterious "sister" might be waiting for her. The room was empty. Even Doris looked like a sterile piece of furniture. She was sunken and gray and hadn't moved in the eight days Beatrice had been gone. She was growing thinner. Beatrice touched her aunt's cheek. It was still warm.

She sank into the chair next to Doris and put her head on the edge of the bed. She longed to feel her aunt's hand pat her hair, to hear her gruff laugh, to smell her cigarette smoke. She was an orphan waiting in a graveyard. She closed her eyes as a hopeless tear slid down her cheek.

"Beatrice," a soft voice whispered in her ear. "Beatrice!"

"Huh?" Beatrice muttered sleepily. She must have dozed off. Her head was still on her aunt's bed, but someone was shaking her shoulder. The tip of a high-heeled leather boot and the hem of a long wool coat grazed the floor next to her.

It was Max.

"Beatrice, I've been looking all over for you!" she said in a low voice.

"Max! Wha—? What are you doing here? You're missing!" Beatrice gasped.

"Well, not exactly." She glanced anxiously at the clock. "I don't have much time."

"Are you my sister 'Sandra'?"

"For the next ten minutes. They've been watching the room. I can't stay long."

Max looked agitated. Actually, she looked terrible. Heavy bags hung below her blue eyes, and her pale, unmade lips looked dry. Her brassy blond hair was dyed black, making her skin look ghostly.

"Your brother is looking for you, Max. What's going on?"

"I know. I don't have time to explain. Don't tell him you saw me here. This thing is way over his head. It's better if he thinks I'm gone." She reached into her pocket. "Here. Take this. Don't tell anyone you have it. I'll find you when this is all over."

"What is it?" Beatrice looked down as Max handed her a key.

Max pressed her lips together and looked pained. "It's nothing. Don't go looking for answers, Beatrice. You don't want to get involved in this."

"I'm already involved." She motioned to Doris. "What did you find in my aunt's deposit box? Diamonds? Gold? More love letters from Bill Thompson?"

"Shh! You don't want them to hear you." She pulled Beatrice out of the room and down the hall to a vacant ICU room. They froze in a shadow as a nurse walked by. When the hall was empty, Max said under her breath, "Bill is just a small-time crook. This thing is bigger than him."

"Did you know what he's been doing?" Beatrice hissed. "Did you sleep with him too?"

"I found out, okay? It's not like the old bastard's a criminal mastermind. I found out, and I've been trying to find a way out of this mess ever since."

"What do you mean?"

"He was smart enough to cover his tracks. He put everything in my name, including the damn deposit inquiries. The son of a bitch had me doing his research for him, sniffing out dead boxes and calling it an audit. It all points to me. If I go to the cops—shit, even if I go to my brother—they're going to think I'm in on it."

"Tony would believe you, wouldn't he?"

"I haven't always been an angel, Bea." Max threw up her hands. "I grew up in a rough neighborhood. I got into some trouble. All of this would just confirm what everyone already thinks about me."

Beatrice could hear the tears in Max's voice but couldn't see her eyes in the dark room.

"I believe you, Max. I really do. I heard Bill with Suzanne Peplinski the other night. He has her on the hook too." Beatrice dropped her voice and added, "Right along with Doris."

"Doris was different," Max whispered. "She had her key."

"I don't understand."

"Don't try. It'll only make things worse. Listen, I have to go. Just keep the key somewhere safe. Don't let anyone find it."

"But where will you go?"

"It doesn't matter. When I think it's safe, I'll come find you."

Max kissed the top of Beatrice's head before rushing out the door.

CHAPTER 43

Friday, August 21, 1998

Iris couldn't sleep. Every time she closed her eyes, she swore she could hear someone else breathing. Someone had been in the mechanical chase on the fifteenth floor. Someone had whispered her name. She rolled over and tried to convince herself she'd imagined the whole thing. It had been sweltering hot, and her hangover had warped her mind. Besides, she'd been terrified that some homeless man was going to slice her up with a broken bottle, but it was just Ramone doing his job. The breathing sound was just the wind whistling out of the rooftop duct. The whisper was nothing, and there was no such thing as ghosts.

A paisley blouse and pencil skirt drifted through her mind. Beatrice. The files she'd taken from the abandoned suitcase were still sitting in her field bag, but they would have to wait. The clock read 2:00 a.m. She needed sleep. Iris flipped onto her stomach and swore she could hear someone else breathing. Before she knew it, daylight was bleeding in through her windows.

Iris pulled into the back of the abandoned bank at 7:00 a.m. and downed her coffee and smoke. It was as though she'd never left. She sleepwalked over to the button. Brad was standing inside the loading dock, punctual as always.

"Good morning, sunshine!"

Iris glared at him through the bags under her eyes. He was dressed and pressed as usual. He must get up at 4:00 a.m. every day to do his ironing.

"Good morning," she grumbled. "I finished. It took me half the night, but I'm done with the schematics."

"Great! I'll let you give me a guided tour." Brad watched her pull herself out of the car and added, "I hate to be the one to tell you this, but we need the base drawings drafted by Monday."

Her jaw dropped. He shrugged a weak apology. Iris should have expected it by now, but the thought of working the weekend again still made her want to scream. She waved her middle finger in the air at him while his back was turned.

A loud banging rattled the garage door. Iris dropped her hand as Brad spun around and jogged over to the manual override button next to the dock. The door rolled open, and there stood a nerdy little man holding a humungous box.

"Where do you want this thing?" the guy yelped under the crushing weight.

"Hey, let me give you a hand with that." Brad trotted over. "Iris, where do you want to set up?"

"Hmm?" Her brain was gummed up with sleepy pudding.

"Is there a vacant office where we can put the workstation?"

"Oh, the third floor. Follow me."

Iris led them to the elevator and up to the third floor. Finding her way was second nature. The building was becoming a regular home away from home. She led her entourage to the old HR office, past Suzanne's desk, and into Linda's office. Fragments of the shattered bookcase were still strewn on the floor.

"Here, I'll just clear this stuff out of the way while you set up," she said before anyone could comment on the wreckage.

She shoved what was left of the bookcase against the wall. Besides a few deep scratches, the desk was clear. She gave the top of it a quick wipe with her shirtsleeve for good measure. As she was running her hand across the wood, she remembered it was already clean. She recoiled. They were going to set up her computer in the office where some lunatic liked to do his dusting. Not some lunatic, she corrected herself, Ramone. He was the one up on the fifteenth floor last night. He wiped off the desk. Probably. She had to stop drinking and get some sleep. It was getting hard to separate her memories from her delusions.

The two men had already dragged the computer inside.

"Thanks, Arnie." Brad set the box on the floor. "Why don't you get Iris set up here while she and I finish our walk-through?"

The scrawny guy agreed and began meticulously removing the tape from the top of the box, being careful not to tear the cardboard.

Iris spent the rest of the morning touring the building with Brad and his red pen. When they reached the stripped structure on the twelfth floor, she asked, "Did you know this was all here?"

"I did a quick walk-through about a month ago but didn't spend much time on the upper floors. Too hot and dark. They cut the power up here years ago."

"I wondered about that. Why are there still lights on the lower floors?"

"You know, I asked about that when we started. Usually when they mothball a building they shut it all down. They don't usually have live-in security either."

"So what did you find out?"

"Not much. Cleveland Real Estate Holdings Corp. bought the building around the time the bank assets were sold and the offices were vacated. They used to own several other buildings around town, but now it's just this one."

A flare gun went off in her head. She had seen or heard the name somewhere before. Brad walked on ahead of her. As she trotted after him, a yellow slip of paper on a bulletin board came to mind. *Joseph Rothstein,* she thought. She'd seen the name in his office.

Brad snapped a few measurements, not fully trusting Iris's notes, and kept talking. "Maybe they saw redevelopment potential from the start. Maybe they have a poor insurance rating and couldn't pull a policy without full-time security. You know, there were a lot of insurance fraud cases involving arson back in the 1980s in Cleveland. Who knows?"

Brad packed in the tape measure and headed back toward the stair tower, with Iris trailing behind. As they climbed the last two flights up to the fifteenth-floor inferno, she remembered she hadn't technically managed to complete the survey. She'd faked the layout at home from what she could remember, and now Brad was dragging her back up to verify it all. *Shit.*

Fortunately, he only made a quick loop around the service hallway and reception room. "So this is it?"

"I think so," Iris said, thumbing through her notes. "Everything but that locked room on the third floor. I think the mechanical chase stretches from the third floor to the roof. There are access doors and large grates in the bathrooms. I could almost see in one of them."

"Cold-air returns. Anything else?"

"I don't think so . . ." Iris frowned. *Just the ghost of a lost secretary locked up in a suitcase and a madman breathing in the air shaft,* she thought. The unbearable heat of the fifteenth floor was making her dizzy.

As if he read her mind, Brad headed toward the service elevator.

Once her ears had popped halfway down the tower, she remembered. "Oh! And the tunnels."

"Tunnels?" Brad lifted an eyebrow.

"Yeah, Ramone says there are tunnels in the basement that lead to other buildings, like old steam tunnels."

"Awesome! Let's go check it out!"

"Do you think they need to be included in the schematics?"

"Nope, but don't you want to see if we can find Jimmy Hoffa down there? Come on, it'll be fun!"

Brad wanted to do something on company time for fun. She could not have been more surprised if he had suggested they go smoke a joint in the bathroom or torn off his shirt to reveal a giant tattoo.

As they stepped off the elevator into the lower level, the slam of a door thundered down the hall. Iris turned toward the noise.

"Ramone?" she called out.

She headed past his bedroom and around the corner. The vaults were empty. The slam must have come from the door to the spider-infested stairwell that led up to the loading dock.

"Looks like he took off," Brad said behind her.

"I guess we're on our own." She managed a smile despite the nagging feeling in her gut.

"Did he say they were on this level?"

"Well, he said 'basement.' This is the basement, right?" She said it and realized the vault room looked nothing like a basement. Basements had pipes and boilers and dripping water. She glanced back at the vaults lined in bronze and marble, and it occurred to her that bank customers must have come through there from time to time to access their safe deposit boxes. Rich people with priceless valuables definitely didn't use the spooky service stairs. The service elevator wasn't fancy enough either. How did they get down there?

She pulled out her plans and compared what they had drawn for the basement with the main banking level. She and Brad had surveyed the lower level together, so she hadn't doubted its accuracy until that moment.

Sure enough, they were missing a column bay to the north underneath the main lobby. Her fingers traced the monumental staircase that flanked the east wall. The stairs stepped down from the lobby. Holding the plan like a treasure map, Iris headed east and north, until the giant vault door stopped her in her tracks. It stretched from the ceiling to the floor and was swung open against the wall.

"Brad." There was no response. "Brad?"

"Yeah?" He stepped around the corner from the service elevator.

"We're missing something on our plan. The building keeps going twenty more feet that way." She pointed at the giant metal door. Brad grabbed the plans and looked them over.

"You're right. Good catch!"

"This closes, right?" she asked, pointing to the giant steel circle blocking her way. It was the door to the larger vault where the bank had once stored its cash reserves.

"Well, it is a vault."

Iris tried not to roll her eyes in annoyance. "Let's try to close it. It's not like there's anything in the vault anyway."

She gave it a pull, but it wouldn't budge. Brad walked over and gave it his all. No luck.

"There has to be a trick to it." Brad searched the perimeter of the round door.

Iris scanned the rest of the room and located a small red button on the far wall. She walked over to it and pushed it as Brad was pulling on the door with all of his might. The door sprung free and sent Brad sprawling on the floor with an *oomph*. Iris slapped a hand over her mouth to keep from laughing.

"I see you smiling."

Brad stood up and brushed himself off. He grabbed the door and walked it closed. As the circular door swung shut to seal the cash vault, it revealed a round entryway, which led to another room.

"Clever," Brad said, walking through the portal. "They use the vault door to block access to the room when the vault is open."

Iris nodded and stepped through the round doorway. The room beyond the vaults was twenty feet wide and ran the length of the building. It was dark except for the faint light coming from the far end. Iris clicked on her flashlight. There was a small security station and a long reception desk. At the west end of the room were three small booths. Red velvet curtains were drawn to conceal a chair and a small table inside each little chamber.

"What the hell are these?" Iris asked, pulling a curtain aside.

"This must be where people went to open their deposit boxes, eh?" Brad pulled out his tape measure and set about correcting their floor plan.

While Brad busied himself, Iris walked across the soft red carpet to the far edges of the room, trying to find access to the tunnels. The walls of the lower lobby were wood and inlaid bronze, just like the main lobby above it. The faint light grew brighter as she made her way past the elevator bank and around the corner. Trapped sunlight streamed down the marble stairs from the lobby above.

Stairs were always stacked one on top of the other in a building. Maybe there were more of them. She searched the dark-wood panels cladding the triangular section of wall under the stairs until she found it. There was a door-sized panel cut into the wood beneath the upper landing. It was perfectly flush with the surrounding wall and the tight seam along its edges was barely visible. She ran her hands along the perimeter and found nothing—no handle, no hinges. When she pushed on it, a latch clicked. The panel swung open to a small service closet.

"Brad! I found something!" she called over her shoulder as she stepped into the hidden passageway and saw a metal service door marked "Utilities." She tried the handle. It was locked.

"Hey there, Sherlock! You found it!" Brad said, trotting up to her side.

"It's locked."

"You got the keys."

"Oh, right."

Iris fumbled in her field bag while Brad looked over her shoulder into her tangled mess of pens and fast-food wrappers. She could feel him smirking as she struggled to find them. The keys Brad had given her were buried in a side pocket next to her cigarettes. It took five tries, but she finally managed to wrench the door open.

"After you," he said, swinging his arm to the door with a bow. Brad was a dork.

Iris blindly felt inside the wall until she found a small light switch. A bare bulb at the bottom of the stairs clicked on. The stairs to the basement were steep, with open metal grates for treads. Iris stepped down nervously as they wobbled beneath her. A nest of spiderwebs hit her face before she reached the last step, and she struggled not to screech like a girl. At the bottom of the stairs, there was a narrow passageway. Pipes and conduit raced overhead down the narrow hallway and out of sight.

"These must be the tunnels," Brad said from behind her.

"Yeah, but how are we supposed to know where they're going?" Iris asked, peering into the dark.

"They left breadcrumbs." He pointed to a small plaque on the wall next to the stair that read "First Bank of Cleveland." He clicked on his flashlight and began heading down the tunnel. "Let's see where this takes us."

Iris nodded reluctantly and followed him down the narrow hall, ducking her head so as not to hit the tangle of pipes and wires overhead. Through puddles, falling insulation, and dangling wires, they walked for what seemed like five city blocks until they came to a larger room. The walls were old brick, and the brick ceiling vaulted over them like a Roman aqueduct.

"Wow!" Iris said, staring up at the ceiling.

"It's a junction," Brad said. "Look at all of the different paths."

Six branches headed out of the cavern. Small plaques were set over each entrance. "Terminal," "Arcade," "East 9th" the signs read.

"Where should we go?" he asked.

"I'm not sure I'm up for any more spelunking." Iris had her fill of cobwebs and dust, and she was certain she could hear mutant sewer rats scurrying in the distance. "I'm exhausted, and I still have a ton of work to do."

"Aw, where's your sense of adventure?" Brad slugged her in the arm.

"Maybe next time." She felt like a pathetic female but was too tired to care. Voices were still whispering in the back of her mind.

"I'll be right behind you. I just have to see a little more."

Iris turned and retraced her steps back to the metal staircase and the naked lightbulb and up to the lower banking level. She swatted at the cobwebs with a squeamish shudder. On her way across the carpet toward the vault, she paused at the deposit clerk's desk. It was where a patron would have requested access to their deposit box.

Ramone had said that when the bank closed they lost all of the keys to the vault. The last person to see them probably worked right there. She leaned over the counter. The drawers had locks, and there was a small safe. Every door was flung open, and everything was picked clean. There was no nameplate on the counter and only one chair behind the desk.

Brad would be returning any moment, and she'd hate for him to catch her snooping. She hurried back to the round entrance that led to the vaults. But it wasn't there. There was a crescent moon of light where the doorway should be, and then it went black with a loud thud. Someone had swung the vault door open, blocking the round portal to the lower lobby where she stood. She was locked out.

"Hey! Ramone! Open up!" she shouted, banging on the steel vault door blocking her way. There was no response. "Seriously?"

The way back into the vault room from the lower lobby where she stood was through the round portal. The only other option was to go up the marble stairs to the main lobby above, walk down the hall to the rear of the building, and take the service stairs back down. Iris ran the entire way, determined to give Ramone a piece of her mind. She'd left half her notes and field bag on the other side of the damned round door.

She slammed through the service stairwell door into the vault room, yelling, "Hey, Ramone!"

A flash of a blue shirt turned a corner at the end of the vault corridor and was gone.

"Ramone!"

She stormed past the vault toward Ramone's little bedroom. "Ramone, why did you . . . ?"

The room was empty. The service elevator was whirring loudly to her right. He must have ducked out again. "What the hell?" she asked the empty room.

She staggered back to the vaults to collect her things. "I really need to quit smoking," she panted.

Her lungs felt like two black tea bags after her mad sprint. She bent down to pick up her clipboard when something shiny caught her eye.

A ring of keys was hanging from one of the safe deposit doors.

CHAPTER 44

Iris stepped into the vault and touched one of the keys hanging from the lock of Box 249. She paused and looked back out into the empty corridor. Someone had been in the vault while she and Brad were down in the tunnels. Someone in a blue shirt. It must have been Ramone. He always wore a blue shirt, and after her freak-out the night before he was probably just avoiding her.

A chill ran through her as she tried to turn the key. It didn't move. She tried harder. It wouldn't budge. She yanked the key to pull it out of the lock, but it was stuck. She twisted the key, then jiggled it. Finally, she simply unwound the ring from the one stuck key to release the others. There were twelve identical bronze keys on the ring. Letters were engraved on the heads. She flipped through them—"D," "E," "O." "First Bank of Cleveland" was etched around the perimeter of each face.

A loud banging came from the lower lobby. It was Brad on the other side of the vault door.

"Iris? Iris, open up! This isn't funny!"

Shit. She scrambled to open the doorway. She pressed the red button, and the round steel door began to swing, opening the entrance to the lower lobby. The keys were still in her hand. It was too late to put them back without an explanation. She squeezed them in her fist. Brad would surely confiscate them and turn them over to Mr. Wheeler or the owners. End of story. Or she could ask Ramone about them first and then hand them over herself. It wouldn't make much difference. Besides, what Brad didn't know wouldn't hurt him. The second before he came barreling through the opening she stuffed them into the pocket of her field bag.

"Hey, what gives?"

Iris held up her empty hands. "I have no idea. I had to run up the stairs and back down again to get over here. I just made it back down, and I'm kinda pissed. I think I saw Ramone."

Brad grunted and hoisted his field bag back onto his shoulder. "We should go see how your computer's coming along."

Iris gathered up her notes. "So how were the tunnels?"

"Amazing. They go on for blocks. I think that junction is under Euclid Avenue."

"Did you find Jimmy Hoffa?" Iris asked, trying not to let her bag jingle with stolen keys as they walked down the hall.

"No, but I found some strange stuff—clothes and food wrappers. It looks like somebody's living down there or something."

"Ramone said the homeless sometimes get in the building through the tunnels." She tried to sound casual even though the disembodied breathing still rasped in the back of her head. They stepped onto the elevator and headed back up to the personnel office.

"The homeless? Why didn't you say something before?" He glared at her. "Maybe you shouldn't be working here alone."

"I'm a big girl. Ramone's here."

She didn't want it getting back to Mr. Wheeler or anyone else that she was too scared to do the job. They might send her back to the office. A man would never complain about this sort of safety concern, and she knew it.

"I think that you should keep a radio with you from now on in case you need Ramone, okay?"

"Need Ramone for what?" Ramone stepped out of Linda's office on the third floor to greet them.

"In case I need help . . . like opening a door or something. Brad wants me to have a radio," Iris said, avoiding his eyes. She needed to find a way to get him alone to ask about the keys.

Ramone didn't argue. "I think I have a couple sets. I'll bring one up."

"I've been keeping Ramone pretty busy this morning," Arnie chirped from behind a giant monitor. "We've had trouble getting the power to work. We had to patch into the next office."

"You've both been up here all morning?" Iris turned back to the guard, trying not to sound alarmed.

"Yeah." Ramone rolled his eyes in Arnie's direction.

"But . . ." Iris bit her tongue to keep from saying more, especially after all of that big-girl tough talk. She glanced over at Brad, but he was oblivious to everything but installing AutoCAD on the new computer. Someone had been down in the vault, and it wasn't Ramone. Now she had their keys. She swallowed hard. Ramone would get her a radio. She would put the keys back. It would be fine. They were just keys. Someone from the real estate holding company might have had a set. It was their building after all, but it didn't make sense that they had run off when she surprised them in the vault. Iris mentally wrung her hands while Brad explained the CAD layering system.

The lunch hour came and went without mention. Brad, Arnie, and Ramone finally vacated the third floor around 3:00 p.m., leaving Iris alone with a glowing monitor, a two-way radio, and twenty sheets of hand sketches that needed to be digitized by Monday.

The dead calm in the personnel office was only broken by the soft clicking of the keyboard and mouse. Every fifteen minutes she checked in with Ramone. He was starting to get annoyed. After two hours on the edge of her seat, she couldn't take it anymore. She grabbed her field bag and Ramone's radio and headed back down to the vault.

She pressed the call button and rested her forehead on the service elevator doors. Iris tried to remember what the intruder had looked like. Blue shirt and darkish hair, but she'd only seen him from the back.

This was crazy. The intruder might have come back. She gripped the radio tighter, debating whether or not to buzz Ramone. She had no idea how she would explain what she was doing in the vault. She was lost in thought when she felt a hand on her shoulder.

Iris screamed.

"Jesus, Iris! Take it easy!" It was Nick. He backed away with his arms up to guard his face. He still had a faint black eye from the last time he snuck up on her.

"Nick!" She swatted him in the arm. "You scared the living shit out of me! Stop doing that!"

"Sorry! You're right." He laughed. "One of these days you're liable to kill me."

"What are you doing here?"

"What do you think I'm doing here? I came looking for you." He eyed her up and down.

She looked like shit. Her hair was falling out of its ponytail. Her shirt was covered in black stuff. She hadn't slept in two days and couldn't even remember if she had on clean underwear.

"I—I thought our date was later," she stammered. "I need to go home and shower."

The word "shower" made his eyebrows lift and his eyes wander over her body as if he were sudsing her up right then and there.

She hit him in the arm. "Hey, I thought we were going on a real date!"

"Of course! Do you have beer?"

"Huh?"

"At your house. Do you have beer at your house?"

"Yeah, why?"

"Well, I'll need something to keep me entertained while you get ready."

"I just . . ."

The elevator doors opened. She needed to go back to the vault and return the keys, but she didn't want to explain the whole thing to Nick. Mostly, she didn't want to admit she'd taken the keys at all. Wretched guilt gnawed in the pit of her stomach. If Nick knew, she might get in trouble at work for slacking off and stealing from the building. She had no idea if he could keep a secret or if he would keep one for her. Besides, the whole thing sounded so stupid.

"Okay."

Nick followed Iris home to her new apartment three blocks from his house. She chain-smoked the whole way.

"Don't you have to go home first?" she asked nervously as he got out of the car.

"What for? Hey, nice place. Good location." He winked at her and sauntered up to her front door.

She fumbled with the key, feeling his hot stare all over her. She couldn't believe she was inviting him into her house. Her jaw muscles tightened in determination. She would be damned if he talked her into bed again before at least buying her a steak. It wasn't dignified or ladylike or whatever it was supposed to be.

"Thanks! Well, here it is. Beer's in the fridge. Help yourself," she called over her shoulder and then ran into her bedroom.

"I like what you've done with the place," he called through her closed door. She heard him stumble around the forest of unpacked boxes, fighting his way to the fridge.

This was a terrible idea. She hadn't unpacked. The house was a mess. She was standing there naked and only then realized her bath towel was across the hall in the bathroom. She didn't own a robe. She lived alone, so what was the point? Now she was naked and trapped in her own bedroom.

"I haven't unpacked yet," she replied loudly, and searched the room for something to cover herself. Paper bag? Pillowcase? The room was littered with useless objects. It was only three steps from her door to the bathroom, and the kitchen was around a corner and out of sight. She cracked open her bedroom door and searched for her uninvited houseguest. He was in the kitchen, searching for a bottle opener. She could hear him opening and closing drawers. Perfect. She flung the door open and made a naked dash for the bathroom.

She made it. She slammed the door closed and locked it. Iris had just successfully streaked through her own apartment. She couldn't help but laugh.

"What's so funny?" His voice was way too close to the door.

"Nothing!" she sang out, and turned on the hot water and the ceiling fan so that any further conversation would be drowned out. She proceeded to take the longest shower of her life. She shaved her legs. She deep-conditioned her hair. She was debating scrubbing the shower walls when she heard a pounding on the door.

"Hey! Did you drown in there?"

Iris shut off the water and the fan. She wrapped a towel around herself and cracked open the door. "Sorry. I guess I was pretty dirty." She winced. "I mean, I had a long day."

Nick burst out laughing. "Dirty, huh? Well that little sneak preview was pretty filthy, I have to say."

Iris's eye bulged in their sockets. He'd seen her running to the bathroom. Now he was nearly in hysterics.

"You sneak!" she protested, blushing from head to toe. She swung the bathroom door open and slugged him in the arm.

"You're not even supposed to be here. Why couldn't you just pick me up like a normal person so we could go have a normal date?"

Nick backed away, chuckling, as she smacked at him in protest. Iris didn't realize until it was too late that he had backed into her bedroom. Her hair was dripping from the shower, and she was wrapped in a ratty towel that was barely big enough to cover her ass. It was a trap. She took a step back toward the door.

"Hey. Not so fast." He grabbed her by the arm and pulled her against his warm, soft shirt. He gazed down at her, then kissed her softly on the lips. She couldn't help but kiss him back. His fingertips left a trail of fire down her back. He grazed her neck with his lips, and she gasped involuntarily. Before her head could catch up to his hands, her towel was on the floor.

CHAPTER 45

Iris woke the next morning to an empty apartment. All that was left of Nick was an empty pizza box and a handful of beer bottles. She'd chased him out in the middle of the night. She had to work in the morning and was far too uneasy to actually sleep next to him after he'd seduced her again. And again. She rolled over on the dirty sheets and buried her head under her pillow. The bed would have to be burned.

On the way to her car, she decided to bring coffee and dough-nuts over to Nick as a sort of peace offering after throwing him out so abruptly. He couldn't be too angry with her after their night together. At least she hoped not.

She stopped by the coffee shop across the park and drove the three blocks to Nick's little townhouse. A sweet old couple was out walking a dog. Iris smiled at them before climbing up his stairs. She knocked and waited. She knocked again, trying to balance two cups of coffee and a bag of fried dough. On the third knock, a disheveled Nick answered the door in boxer shorts.

"Hey, there!"

Nick squinted in the morning light and said nothing.

"Sorry I woke you up. I just thought I'd bring you some breakfast."

"You all right? You need something?" He was clearly not happy to be out of bed.

"No, I'm fine. I just wanted to say hi I guess." Iris tried to look dopey and lovable, but she realized she probably just looked dumb.

He just stood there scowling at her.

She handed him the coffee and the doughnut bag. "Here, go back to bed. Sorry for waking you."

She turned and scurried back to her car. Being spontaneously romantic was a huge mistake. She drove away, feeling like an idiot.

It wasn't until she was halfway downtown that she realized she'd given him her breakfast as well. They were supposed to sit and eat together and have their first real conversation. She pounded her hand into the steering wheel.

Where were his bedroom eyes and easy smile that morning, she wondered? Now that he'd taken what he wanted yet again, he was happy to let her just stand there like an idiot—an idiot with breakfast for him no less.

Maybe he wasn't awake yet, she told herself. Maybe she ran away before he could throw his arm around her and give her a good-morning kiss. *Sure, and maybe he'd been up all night writing bad love songs about our torrid night together,* she thought sarcastically. How could she be so stupid?

She heard a loud honk and looked up from the wheel. The light was green. The sky was blue, and nobody in all of Cleveland gave one shit about her pathetic love life. She drove the rest of the way to the old bank puffing on a cigarette.

Iris stormed into the building after Ramone buzzed her through and banged on the elevator button. She banged on it again and kicked the wall.

"Whoa, what's wrong with you?"

Ramone was never in the loading dock, but there he was for no good reason. It just figured that someone would be there to witness her meltdown.

"Ramone, let me ask you a question," Iris blurted out. "If a woman brought you coffee and a doughnut the morning after a wonderful date, what would you do?"

"Change my locks."

"What?" she practically shrieked.

"If she's comin' over to my house the morning after a date, she's either desperate or crazy."

Her eyes widened.

He broke out laughing. "Oh, I get it. This woman is you, right? Well, I didn't mean no offense." He was trying to stifle his laughter, but it kept sneaking out of his mouth. He gave her a friendly slap on the shoulder. "So which is it? You desperate or crazy?"

She attempted a smile. "Maybe both."

Maybe Ramone was right. She wanted to go back home and crawl under her bed. Instead, she pulled out her radio and checked the battery.

"Ah, don't sweat it. If the guy likes you, he'll call. Just don't bug him for a while." Ramone smiled. "Hey, try not to buzz every five damned minutes today, okay?"

She nodded, avoiding his smirk by rushing into the elevator. Tears stung her eyelids. How pathetic. She needed to get over herself. She had bigger problems than Nick, and she needed help.

Iris stuck her head back out into the loading dock. "Hey, Ramone?"

"Yeah?"

"Was that you in the vault yesterday? You know, when Brad and I were down in the tunnels?"

"You went in the tunnels?" He raised his eyebrows, then shook his head. "I wasn't down there. Why you askin'?"

"I just thought I saw somebody. Somebody in a blue shirt. They opened the vault door while we were on the other side." She didn't mention the keys. They were still at the bottom of her field bag.

Ramone stopped smiling. "You sure?"

"Well . . . yeah."

"Might have been one of the owners, but they usually tell me before they come. I'll make a few calls." He turned to leave and added, "If you decide to leave the third floor, give me a buzz, okay?"

Iris nodded and ducked back into the elevator as the doors slid closed.

"Sure, don't worry about me," she muttered to herself. "I'll just be up there by myself while some crazy person runs around breathing and dusting! No problem. I'm sure they won't mind that I have their keys . . . Fuck!" She gripped the radio in her palm and took a deep breath.

Up in the old personnel office, everything was just as she'd left it. She plopped herself in Linda's chair. It would take all that day and the next to transcribe her handwritten notes into a computerized blueprint. If she could even get it done in time. As the computer whirred back to life, she wondered how in the world she was going to work ten hours in that creepy office without going completely insane. What she needed to do was go down to the vault and put the keys back where she found them, but after Nick snuck up on her so easily the day before, she couldn't go alone. If the intruder wasn't some geek from a real estate company but actually was some sort of psycho killer . . . She couldn't even finish the thought.

She grabbed the radio to call Ramone and set it down again. If she called him, she'd have to explain how she got the keys and why she took them. She'd have to admit she thought they were his. He might even suspect she had planned to use them to pry information out of him—or worse. If Ramone actually had plans to rob the vault and found out she had taken the keys, there was no telling what he might do. He seemed like a nice enough guy, but she hardly knew him.

Iris leapt up from the desk and began pacing. She was trapped. Between work and Ramone and the keys and the whispering voices in her goddamned head, there was nowhere to go. No way out without coming clean to Brad or Ramone or somebody.

Her sleep-deprived thoughts spiraled as her eyes welled with tears. The keys in the bottom of her bag. Nick's sour face that morning. Ramone laughing. Desperate or crazy—which was it really? She was crazy for stealing shit from an abandoned building, for taking keys that didn't belong to her, for hearing voices, for not telling Brad what she'd seen in the vault. Most of all, she was crazy for letting Nick into her house in the first place. She was desperate for trying to turn a few sessions of sweaty sex into a meaningful relationship by bringing him breakfast. The empty feeling she'd had waking up alone that morning hollowed her out all over again. She hadn't realized how lonely she'd been all these months. Years even. It had been two years since she'd had a boyfriend, and that had been short lived. But Nick didn't give a shit. He just thought she was easy, and he was right. She was desperate. Tears were streaming down her cheeks, and she wiped them angrily.

"Fuck him!" she shouted, slamming her hand on the desk. She'd rather be crazy.

She threw her calculator against the wall. Its batteries exploded out the back. *Good.* Her eyes fell on the locked door. It was getting knocked down by a contractor in a week. *Fuck it.* She stomped over and gave it a sound kick. It made a loud bang against its jamb but didn't budge. She kicked it harder and let out a low growl. It was a relief to really hit something hard. She kicked it again and again.

"Fuck this fucking place!"

Whack!

She landed a kick right next to the locked knob and recoiled in surprise when the jamb splintered and the door moved. She'd actually broken some part of the frame. Iris examined the jamb where the door had been forced a half an inch open. *Maybe I really am crazy,* she thought with a nervous laugh. She'd just kicked a door in. Maybe her lunacy gave her the strength of ten men. The door wobbled in its frame. *Might as well finish the job,* she thought, and threw her shoulder into it. It took four tries, but the damn thing finally broke open.

"Ha! Take that, you stupid door!" she shouted triumphantly.

She stared at her handiwork for a few moments: the splintered doorjamb, the cracked door panel. *Shit.* How was she going to explain how she got the door open without sounding nuts?

A wave of musty, stale air hit her in the face. "Uck!"

She stepped into the hidden room. It was a bathroom, just as Ramone said. It wasn't that different than the one above it where Nick had had his way with her, except it was filthy. A black crust covered the floor by the toilet. Dark grime coated the fixtures. The light filtering in through the window shimmered with dust and soot.

She took another step. Something metal went ringing across the floor tiles and clinked into the far wall. It was a key. Iris picked it up. Black crust flaked off the bronze as she turned it over in her hand. There were no markings on either face. Maybe it was the door key, she thought, glancing back at the shattered frame.

A cheap white shower curtain hung over the entrance to the shower stall. It was pulled closed. Something about it felt wrong. She didn't remember seeing shower curtains in the other bathrooms.

The creeping feeling that someone was watching her inched up her spine. She cleared her throat loudly, not taking her eyes off the curtain. It didn't move. The stagnant air coated her mouth and throat with an acrid film. Iris ordered herself to get the hell out of there and get back to work.

Instead, she took a step toward the shower and timidly reached out her hand. The plastic crackled in her hand, and she swore she could hear a faint buzzing behind it. Squeezing her eyes half-shut, she ripped the curtain open.

A rope hung from the showerhead inches from her face. It was tied into a noose and crusted black and brown. Then she looked down. A mountain of dead flies were piled at the bottom of the stall. Little corpses stacked one on top of the other in an avalanche of shattered wings and hollow black shells. They were everywhere. Dead flies were scattered behind the toilet and along the window-sill. They littered the floor.

The rope was still hanging from the showerhead. Her eyes darted from the noose to the dead flies piled on the floor of the shower. In between the silvery-black corpses, she could now see fragments of what might have once been a gray pin-striped suit. Something resembling a black leather wing-tip shoe was peeking out at the corner.

It was a shoe. It was a suit. They were under the flies. The flies had been eating. She couldn't breathe. Bile flooded her throat. They'd been eating. Her hand was locked in a death grip on the shower curtain. Her arm was trembling. The shower curtain fluttered in the stall, jostling the empty shells of the dead insects. They tumbled toward her feet, falling weightlessly over the toes of her work boots. Something yellow and hard emerged from underneath the layers of tiny corpses. It was a bone.

Someone was screaming; she was screaming. She tore her hand from the shower curtain violently. Dead flies fluttered into the air. Iris stumbled to the toilet to throw up. The toilet bowl was crowded with insect shells. She turned to the sink. It was littered with broken legs and wings. She staggered back. Her mouth filled with vomit.

Flies seemed to be spilling onto the floor after her. The noose swung from the showerhead. Her heel hit the curb of the shower stall, and flies crunched under her feet. She lurched toward the bathroom door.

She crumpled to her hands and knees and vomited on the carpet. Recoiling, she slammed her back to the wall outside the bathroom, seeing nothing but flies. Hungry flies.

Ramone's voice crackled over the radio. "Iris, you there? Iris?"

The radio was on the desk over her head. She barely registered the noise. Her mouth opened and shut on its own. She couldn't make a sound.

"Iris, I'm coming up," the radio crackled again.

A few moments later, Ramone's hulking shape entered the room in a slow crouch, moving toward the broken door. His gun was drawn. He straightened up when he found her propped against the wall and lowered the gun.

"Iris, what the hell's going on? I heard all this racket." He glared at her for a moment, waiting for an answer. Then he noticed the vomit on the floor.

All Iris could do was shake her head.

He raised his gun again and stormed into the bathroom. "Jesus!" he said under his breath, and walked back out. "You find him like that?"

Iris nodded and clamped her hands over her mouth. Ramone had called the pile of flies "him." Her stomach lurched again, but she fought the bile back down.

"You okay?"

She shook her head violently and tears welled up in the corners of her eyes.

"Here, let's get you off the floor." He helped her stand up and guided her back to Linda's chair. "I've got to go call the police. You stay here a minute. If you can, you might want to gather up the things you gonna need. This whole damn place is a crime scene now. Police are gonna lock it all down."

He left Iris staring blindly at the desk while what was left of a dead person lay in the next room. The body had been there all along. Every minute she'd spent in the room, a pile of death had been rotting not ten feet away. She shuddered in her chair. The shadow of a moth flickered outside the window blinds. She stared at it blankly for what could have been hours, unable to bring her mind back.

Sirens rang out in the distance on the street below. She blinked. The police were coming. Ramone had told her to take what she needed. She numbly took an inventory of the desk. It was all company stuff she couldn't care less about. She grabbed her schematic floor plans. She'd worked hard on those. She grabbed her field bag. She looked for her purse for several minutes, until her addled brain remembered it was down in the loading dock with her car. But where were her car keys? She needed her car keys to get home.

Her field bag was full of keys, but none were the ones she needed. Keys to the vault, keys to the building, they were all wrong. She had to get home. She couldn't stay here—not tonight, not another minute. She had to get home.

Iris sprung up from the chair on the verge of hysterics. She smeared the tears across her face, searching the desk and floor for her car keys. It wasn't until she felt a sore spot on her rear end that she thought to check her pockets. They were there. They clinked together as she gripped them in her hand. The metallic clink she'd heard in the bathroom rang out again in her ears. It had come from a small bronze key. She looked down at her shaking hands. It was gone.

She turned her head toward the open door.

On the far wall inside the dead man's room, she could make out the edge of the metal grille of the air vent next to the toilet. Its iron frame cast an odd shadow against the wall tiles, as if it had been pried open ever so slightly. She inched closer to the broken door. The mounting screws for the grille were missing, leaving two empty holes along its edge. The vent was large enough to crawl through. She could hear a voice from the air shaft whisper, "Iris . . ."

Shut up. Iris tore her eyes from the vent and scanned the ground. *Where did it go?* A dead fly drifted into view. *Oh God.* She nearly threw up again. She pressed her back to the wall and slid down, burying her head in her knees, trying to breathe. Something shiny glinted from the carpet at her feet. Inches from her vomit. She squeezed her eyes shut and reached out with her hand until she felt cold metal.

She sucked in a breath and opened her eyes. It was the key.

CHAPTER 46

Monday, December 11, 1978

It was too late to go back to the bank. Beatrice had no choice but to spend the night in the hospital lobby. The seating area outside Admitting was deserted. She found a bench in the corner and slumped down under the fluorescent lights. She didn't bother closing her eyes. She couldn't possibly sleep after seeing Max. She gazed at the small bronze key in the palm of her hand. There was no writing on either side. It could be the key to anything—a gym locker, a small safe, a motel room. It was a secret, and Max had told her to keep it safe.

Max had dyed her hair and was wearing oversized clothes. She was hiding. She said the hospital was being watched. The signature of R. T. Halloran in the ICU register scrawled itself across Beatrice's mind. An "uncle" had come to visit Doris the week before.

"Doris was different . . ." That's what Max had said. "She had her key."

Beatrice was pulling the safe deposit box key from her purse when she heard an elevator bell ring. At the other end of the lobby, shiny metal doors slid open, and a man in a brown suit stepped out. His gray sideburns and thick waist reminded her of Bill Thompson. She hid her face behind her purse. He turned without looking her way and headed out the hospital doors. She watched him leave and tried to guess from his gait if it was Bill. She couldn't be sure.

Max had said they were watching the room. It then occurred to Beatrice that they might be watching her too. Bill, Teddy, or whoever "they" were could be watching her right then. She was sitting there in the open lobby, surrounded by windows and holding Max's key.

Beatrice stood up with a jolt. She gathered her things and rushed out the front door of the hospital. A taxicab was parked near the hospital entrance with its light on. She jumped in the backseat and slammed the door.

"Wha—?" the cabbie muttered as he was jerked awake. He cleared his throat and looked at her in the rearview mirror. "Uh, sorry. Where to, miss?"

She stared blankly at the dashboard. Its clock read 12:05 a.m. "Um . . . the Theatrical Grille, Ninth and Vincent," she blurted without thinking it through. The bar would be closing soon, and then what?

Christmas lights twinkled from the lampposts as the cab headed downtown. She'd almost forgotten it was nearly Christmas. The lights faded as the car turned down Chester and entered the broken-down Hough neighborhood. Its sidewalks and streets were bleak and empty. A shadow of a person trudged across the snow outside her window, then faded away behind a chain-link fence.

When she arrived at the bar, Carmichael sat alone behind the counter, reading the paper. The rest of the place had cleared out on a Monday night. He looked up at the door and smiled under his thick black mustache.

"Beatrice! How nice to see you," he said, waving her over.

She smiled sheepishly and took a seat at the bar. She was exhausted.

"What in the world is a beautiful girl like you doing down here at this time a night all alone?"

She had no idea. "It's kind of a long story. Could I get a cup of tea?"

"Of course!" He began searching behind the bar for a mug. "A pretty girl like you needs to be more careful."

"You're right. Um . . . I'll be right back." She stood up and walked hastily to the ladies' room in the corner. Once she was alone in a locked stall, she pulled out Max's key from her change purse. Its blank face rested in the palm of her hand like a question mark. Why didn't Max just hide it herself? She could have given it to anyone, but for some reason Max wanted her to have it. Her eyes circled the bathroom stall. Where would she even hide it?

Sighing, Beatrice slid the faceless key onto her own key ring right next to her aunt's bewildering safe deposit box key. Her breath caught as they clinked together. They were nearly identical. Beatrice held them up to the light. They were the same size and shape. Doris's key had a full inscription for the bank and the box number, while Max's key was blank. But they matched. They were both from the bank. She frowned at the blank key, more puzzled than before.

She stuffed them back in her purse and tried to focus on the more pressing question of where she was going to sleep that night. There were no good options.

After what must have been a suspiciously long time in a bathroom, she finally headed back to the bar to drink the warm tea Carmichael had made for her. She nodded in gratitude at him but avoided looking him in the eye. He took the hint and went back to his paper.

If only there was a way to get back into the bank, she mused. It was too late to make up a story about having left something behind. The doors were locked. Then it occurred to her that she probably had the key.

Max's keys were still hiding at the bottom of Beatrice's purse. There were at least thirty keys on the ring. She gulped her tea and left a pile of coins on the counter for Carmichael.

"Thanks, I needed that."

He glanced up from the sports section. "You want for me to call you a cab?"

"Oh, no thanks. I'll be fine."

He frowned, and his eyes followed her as she left the bar.

Icy winds howled down Euclid Avenue. The street was deserted. Even the homeless had found warmer places to huddle for the night. Traffic lights flashed red as she hurried across the empty road. The bank tower where she worked was just a shadow overhead. Its windows were dark, all of them except two on the top floor. She stared at the lonely lights and wondered who could possibly be working at this hour.

She slinked toward the three revolving doors that led to the main lobby of the bank. The front room was dark. There were no signs of a guard at the security desk, but she kept her distance and her face hidden until she was certain the lobby was empty. She looked down both sides of Euclid Avenue. There wasn't a soul or a car in sight, only the blinking Christmas lights. She stepped up to the one side door in the storefront and pulled out Max's keys.

She crouched, trying keys one after the other for what seemed like an eternity. Every rustle of stray newspapers and creak of the streetlights made her heart race faster. Her hot breath fogged the glass door as she struggled with frozen-stiff fingers to find the right one. Glancing up into the lobby, she was terrified someone would hear the rattle of the key ring against the doorframe. It was still deserted.

A key finally slid into the lock. She held her breath and turned it; the dead bolt slid open and the door swung free.

Beatrice gently pushed the door open and waited. Sirens did not sound. Men with guns did not come running. She shut the door behind her and turned the lock. The lobby floor was streaked with long shadows, and she hid in one of them, listening. She slipped out of her boots and ran in stocking feet to the marble stairs behind the elevators. She took them two at a time, carrying her dripping boots in one hand and her jingling purse in the other. She didn't stop running until she was through the second floor and back to the emergency stair tower.

Beatrice silently closed the emergency exit door and sat down on the landing to catch her breath. Her heart was fluttering like a rabbit's, and her legs were quaking. She couldn't believe what she'd just done. She must be crazy. She put her head between her knees to keep from hyperventilating.

Once her head felt steady, she gazed up at the endless spiral of stairs. She took a deep breath and got back on her feet. It was a long way up.

After five flights of climbing, she still had quite a way to go. Her legs burned. She gripped the railing and took a rest.

A door slammed several stories up, sending a shock wave down the stairwell. Beatrice sucked in a yelp and backed against a wall. She could hear faint voices overhead.

"I don't care what Teddy says. We have to think about relocating the accounts now. The boxes aren't secure."

"It's a temporary glitch. Let's not overreact."

"Keys are missing. The mole hunt is a bust, and we've lost our inside man. This is not a glitch. We have got to move the accounts now before the shit hits the fan."

"What shit exactly?"

"The board isn't ruling out dissolution . . ."

The voices faded, and Beatrice heard another door close. She stared up after them, still frozen to the wall. Mr. Halloran had mentioned something about a mole. When he asked her to spy on

Max, he said he was looking for "someone who's trying to sabotage the company from within." But the mole hunt was a bust. The inside man had been lost. What did that mean? She slowly counted to twenty before having the stomach to keep climbing.

She stayed close to the wall as she tiptoed up the rest of the stairs, rushing past every doorway. The winding stairs spun over her head around and around, until she was dizzy. She grabbed the doorknob to the eleventh floor to steady herself. Pulling it open, she poked her head out into the corridor. It was perfectly dark and still. She exhaled a sigh and staggered back to the corner office where she slept, wobbly from the climb. She pushed the door to her hiding place open, ready to collapse.

A security guard was crouched on the floor. He held a flashlight and one of her files. A small cry caught in her throat, and she crumpled to her knees. It was Ramone.

She was caught.

CHAPTER 47

"How do you know Max?" The security guard was holding Max's personnel file. It was the one Beatrice had stolen from the third floor.

Beatrice couldn't find her voice.

He had Max's picture in his hand. "You know you weren't foolin' nobody when you said you was her the other night."

Blood was pumping through her at a dizzying pace. She stayed crouched next to the door, clutching the handle.

"Relax. I've been watching you for days. If I wanted to have you arrested, I would have done it already." He waved his hand at her like they were old friends.

Her brain struggled to process the words. He didn't want her arrested. But they were alone in the middle of the night, she had broken the law, and she was completely at his mercy. She instinctively clutched her coat.

"How do you know Max?" he asked again, showing Beatrice the picture he was holding.

"She was my . . . friend," she said slowly, unsure how to even think of Max now.

"She's my friend too," Ramone said, and tucked the picture back in the file. "We grew up together. She helped me get this job. Or at least she told me about it . . . 'Arrest on sight' . . . She's in some real shit now, boy."

Beatrice nodded in agreement and felt her shoulders relax a little. If Max was friends with Ramone, maybe she could trust him. But then again Max had once trusted Bill. From under her lowered lashes, she eyed Ramone's blue collared shirt, worn-out shoes, and dark brown hands. She knew what her mother would think just looking at his skin, but Beatrice searched Ramone's eyes for a threat and found none. They looked worried. He cared about Max.

"She's missing," Beatrice whispered.

"Yeah." Ramone lit a cigarette. "I told her not to go messin' with this shit. She wouldn't listen to me."

"What was she messing with?"

"Big money, man, big money. You go messin' with people that have that kind of money, there's no way you gonna win. I told her that. These bankers here ain't no different than anybody else. They lie, they cheat, they steal. Difference is, they don't get caught. They got the system tied up." Ramone took a hard drag off his cigarette and blew out a thick cloud of smoke. "Max kept talking about bringing people to justice and going to the police. Man, there's no justice. Not in Cleveland anyway. Probably not anywhere."

He was right. Teddy and Jim's conversation about bribes replayed in her head. Even Tony admitted that the police department might be compromised. The money men had friends on city council, and they would be protected.

"She's worried that they're going to try to blame her."

"How they gonna do that exactly?" Ramone demanded, glaring at her.

Beatrice instinctively shrunk away. He might care about Max, but that didn't mean he was above getting angry or possibly violent. Beatrice breathed the wave of panic out slowly. He'd been watching her for days, and if he had wanted to harm her, he could have easily done it already. She was going to have to trust him.

"There's a safe deposit box with her name on it. I think someone has been stashing stolen money and other things in there. I really don't know how it all works." Beatrice paused. "She's not the only one. It happened to my Aunt Doris too."

Ramone stared at her for a long moment and rubbed his eyes. "Son of a bitch. Well, that explains some things."

"Like what?"

"Like why Max wanted me to make copies of some keys. Like why she was always asking about the vault. Why I caught her red-handed in there at three in the morning the other night." He paused. "She didn't know it was me, so she ran off. I tried to catch up, but I lost her in the tunnels. I haven't seen her since."

Beatrice thought of the huge ring of keys she'd found in the ladies' room. Maybe Max hadn't stolen them. Maybe Ramone had made copies of the keys. "I saw her tonight. She's okay. She was in disguise."

"Disguise?" Relief seemed to wash over him.

"Her hair and clothes were different. She looked awful." She paused, trying to process everything Ramone had said. Max had been in the vault. "Did you say something about tunnels?"

"Yeah, there are old steam tunnels under the building. They connect to all sorts of places downtown." Ramone studied her closely for a moment, his eyes hardening. "If you're gonna keep stayin' here, you need to find a better way to get in and out of the building. I don't know what you was thinkin' using the front door."

Her little mouth fell open. He'd seen her. He'd been watching the door. "Can you help me?"

"Help you do what exactly? Why you here?"

"I didn't have anywhere else to go." She couldn't hold back the tears and hid her face. "I don't know if I can help Max, but my aunt's involved too, and . . . and she's dying, and I can't just leave her. Men from the bank are watching her hospital room. They destroyed her house, and I can't go back."

A huge hand shook her gently by the shoulder. "Okay, okay. I'll help you, but you can't just hang around here forever. You need to figure out a plan. You need to find a way out for good."

She nodded at him, and he helped her stand up.

"First off, what's your real name?"

"Beatrice." She wiped her eyes.

"Okay, Beatrice. I'm Ramone." He shook her hand gently. "I'll help you find your way in and out of the building. I'm not going to ask how you got Max's keys, and I'm not going to tell anyone you're here. But you listen to me."

"Yes?" she asked obediently.

"Stay away from the big money men, okay? You can't win."

CHAPTER 48

Stay away from the money men. Beatrice thought about it the rest of the night and all the next day of typing and filing. That meant leaving Teddy and Jim alone. The next night, she stared at the door from her bed in the dark office, wondering what the money men were up to and what it all had to do with Bill and Aunt Doris.

There was a soft knocking on the other side. Beatrice scrambled into a corner as the brass knob turned and the door slowly swung open. It was Ramone. He couldn't help smiling at her petrified expression, and motioned her into the hall. She followed him to the service elevator and down to the lowest level of the building.

He led her through a large corridor with two huge, round steel doors. "These are the vault doors. They're always locked, and they're rigged with alarms, so don't get any crazy ideas. There's TV cameras too." He pointed to a large gray box with a round, black lens near the ceiling.

"What do you mean cameras?" She'd never noticed cameras in the building before.

"Closed-circuit monitoring. They just installed it in the vault last year. They still workin' the bugs out. If the little red light is on, watch out. Someone might be watching."

Beatrice froze, staring at the camera. "Who?"

"Well, that's one of the bugs. During the day, the guard watches the monitors from out in the lower lobby." He led her through a huge round doorway into a lobby area and pointed to the desk. There was a small TV sitting on the corner of it. "At night they usually turn this shit off."

"What's the bug then?"

"People upstairs can't make up their minds when they want it turned off and when they want people watching."

He was walking too fast to answer any more questions. She ran to catch up around the corner toward a large marble stairway that led up to what must be the main lobby. Ramone stopped at the side of the stairs and pushed on the wall. To Beatrice's amazement, the wall swung open, and she found herself in a room no bigger than a closet, staring at a metal door.

"This door leads to the steam tunnels," he explained, pulling out a key and unlocking it.

The door opened to a dark stairwell. Stale, dank air wafted up to where she was standing.

"The best way in and out is through the Stouffer's Inn. The tunnel will spit you out in the loading dock. Security is pretty lax over there. If anyone sees you, just look lost. They'll pat you on the head and send you down the road."

"You don't think they'll suspect something?" She stared down into the dark well, her stomach crawling up inside her rib cage.

"Little white girl like you?" He laughed and slapped her on the back. He handed her a small flashlight and looked over his shoulder at the room behind them. "Now go down and see if you can find your way there and back. I'll be around even if you don't see me."

Beatrice nodded and gripped the flashlight with white knuckles. Down the steep stairs she went. One shaking step at a time, she sank into the darkness below. Ramone closed the door above her and the light vanished, except for the tiny stream of the flashlight. The beam only stretched a few feet ahead down the tunnel before being devoured by the shadows. Her heart hammered loudly against her ribs. It was the only sound except for the occasional drip from the ceiling. It was like being trapped in a cave or coffin.

She crept along the narrow hall with one hand stretched out in front of her. She whacked her head with a howl on a low-hanging pipe but kept going. The walls got tighter and the ceiling got lower as she went. The urge to run, kicking and screaming, swelled in her brain stem. Beatrice sucked in a breath and began to hum the words she knew so well.

"Hush-a-bye, don't you cry. Go to sleep my little baby. When you wake, you shall have . . . All the pretty little horses . . . Way down yonder, in the meadow . . . lies a poor little baby . . ."

The humming helped, and she began to walk a bit faster. She would no longer be a prisoner in the bank, trapped without food all weekend. She might even be able to visit her aunt one last time.

As if the tunnel shared her renewed optimism, it opened into a large cavern. She could stand up straight and stretch. She looked around with her flashlight at the many tunnels that emptied into the room. One would take her to the loading dock of the hotel. One of the placards said "Terminal." That had to be the one. The Stouffer's Inn was next to the old Terminal Tower building. She took another deep breath and began barreling down the tunnel.

The narrow passage went on for what seemed like miles. There were a few turns and bends, but for the most part it was a long straight line. Every once in a while, the tunnel would split. There would be a small plaque that read something like "May Company," or sometimes nothing at all. The smell of rotting leaves grew

stronger as she went. The air was thick with it, until it felt like wet
sludge moving in and out of her lungs. Beatrice kept humming.

A faint rustling echoed in the dark. Startled, she dropped the
flashlight with a gasp. The rustling sounded louder. She fumbled
for the light. The beam bounced off the tunnel walls as she scrambled past the rustling noise coming from somewhere low to the
ground. She slowed her feet. It was a rat chewing on some paper.
She never thought in her life she'd be relieved to see a rat. She let
out the air behind the shriek she'd been holding and kept moving.
Her feet sloshed through shallow puddles, and cool water seeped
through the seams of her shoes.

Finally, there was a bend in the tunnel with a placard that read
"Hotel Cleveland." She decided that it must be the right path and
turned. After another city block, the passage came to an end at a
steel ladder. It stretched up over fifteen feet. Beatrice tucked the
flashlight in her belt and began to climb. The higher she went, the
more her hands trembled.

"Don't look down, don't look down . . ." She went one cold,
slippery rung at a time until she hit a metal plate hovering above
her. It was a hatch door. She pushed up on it, and it gave just a
little. She tried again, and it moved a little more. Shoving with all
her might, she forced the hatch open with a loud clank. Her head
popped up into a room the size of an outhouse. Freezing-cold air
hit her in the face, and she could hear the wind whistling around
the thin walls of the shed. She scrambled up the ladder and looked
around. There was nothing but the faint outline of a door. The handle turned easily and she pushed it open, not knowing what she'd
find on the other side.

Beatrice was in an alley between two tall buildings. She didn't
recognize either one. The plain brick backsides of the towers
hovered over her head. Metal fire escapes and garage doors surrounded her. She stepped out, staring up at them without thinking,
and the door swung closed. She ran back but was too late. It was

locked. She tried the handle, and it wouldn't budge. She felt her pocket and reassured herself that she still had Max's heavy ring of keys. She was certain one would open the door. In the meantime, she had to find out where she was. She made her way down the narrow driveway between the two buildings and onto the street.

A limestone building stood across the road with the words "United States Post Office" etched across the top in ten-foot letters. She rounded the corner and saw a street sign that read "Superior Avenue." Then she recognized where she was standing. She was in the back of the hotel. The wind whipped through her sweater, and she realized she wasn't wearing a coat. She'd followed Ramone not knowing where they were headed. Her eyes darted around the empty sidewalks. It was quite late. All of the windows were dark.

A half a block away up ahead on the sidewalk, the shadow of a large person caught her eye. Whether they were walking toward her or not, Beatrice couldn't quite tell, but she started running back to the door in the alley. She pulled the keys from her pocket. Glancing over her shoulder, she could still see the shadow. At the door, she fumbled to find the right key and willed her fingers to move faster.

A key slid home on the third try. She yanked the door open and leapt inside. The shadow had moved farther down the street. Beatrice let out a breath and backed into the open hatch and nearly fell fifteen feet down the hole. She caught herself just in time, then scrambled down the ladder.

Her nerves were shot from all of the sleepless nights. She told herself to relax as she scurried back down the tunnels. She passed through the cavernous junction and was nearly back to the stairs to the bank when she slammed right into Ramone's ribs.

She screamed, and Ramone clapped his hand over her mouth. "Shh! It's me. You can't come back up yet."

When she could speak without shrieking, Beatrice whispered, "What do you mean?"

"Someone's in the vault."

He led her back to the large cavern, where they could both stand.

"What do you mean, someone's in the vault?" It was after 10:00 p.m.

"One of the bigwigs. He told me it was official bank business and asked me to leave."

Ramone lit a cigarette.

"Is that normal?"

"It's getting more normal these days. But hey, they're the ones with the keys, right?"

"Did you get his name?"

"It's a younger guy. Reggie or somethin'."

"Randy? Randy Halloran?"

"Yeah, maybe." He exhaled smoke. "Only authorized personnel have the combination to the vaults. The combination changes every week. If he can open it, he's authorized."

Beatrice scowled, then asked, "Who changes the combinations?"

"A tall guy. He comes down every Monday morning. Vice president of something or another."

"What's his name?"

"That's 'Mr. James Stone to you, boy,'" he said in the condescending voice of an old white man.

Beatrice's eyes widened. Maybe James Stone was the Jim she'd heard talking in the middle of the night about bribing officials. Ramone tossed his cigarette onto the cement floor. "So how did your trip down the tunnels go?"

"Okay, I guess."

"Like I told Max, this shit is for emergencies only, got it? These tunnels ain't exactly safe."

Beatrice nodded in agreement and waited for Ramone to give her the all-clear signal before climbing back up the stairs out of the dark.

CHAPTER 49

Saturday, August 22, 1998

A team of five officers in uniform flooded the room, carrying duffel bags of equipment. Iris would have put up her hands if she wasn't so petrified. She sat on the floor next to the bathroom door in a daze as they turned on every light they could find. None of them spoke to her. They filed into the bathroom one by one. She could see the flashes of a camera bouncing off the walls in quick succession as if the pile of dead flies in the shower stall were movie stars on a red carpet.

A man in his midforties wearing a sports jacket and jeans stepped into the room. He had on a Cleveland Indians baseball cap. He could have been a middle-aged dad on his way to a Little League game. He looked right at her.

"You must be Iris."

He walked over and smiled warmly at her. She tried to smile back, but her face was frozen.

"I'm Detective McDonnell. I understand that you were the one that found the remains."

She nodded blankly.

"Let's get you out of here." He held out his hand to help her stand up.

Iris recoiled from his hand as though it might strike her. She shook it off and pushed herself up from the floor. Her arm hoisted her field bag onto her shoulder. The sudden weight shift nearly sent her toppling over. The detective caught her shoulder as she staggered back on her heel.

She followed him out of the room, down the hall, and into the freight elevator without looking back. She never wanted to see the place again. When the elevator door finally closed, she sucked in what felt like her first breath in hours.

Her eyes began to refocus. "Where's Ramone?"

"He's being questioned by Detective Mendoza. Would you like to go get a cup of coffee?"

"I could really use a drink."

After everything she'd seen, she could use about a gallon of vodka. The bones buried under the flies rattled in her mind. She grabbed the wall of the elevator to steady herself. Suzanne had told her several people had disappeared when the bank closed. Beatrice's abandoned suitcase still sat in a closet up on the eleventh floor. But the body she found belonged to a man. The young girl's body might be buried somewhere else in the building. She could still see the metal grate to the cold-air return. It had been loose.

"How about a beer? I know a good place."

Iris raised her eyebrows. She gave a small nod and wondered what kind of cop would take her to a bar for questioning. A good one, she decided.

They stepped out of the elevator into the loading dock, where Iris caught sight of Ramone and a large Latina woman talking. He was smoking a cigarette. Iris stared at the gray plumes hanging in the air. Cigarette. Her purse and cigarettes were waiting inside her parked car.

"Tony, you want me to call the coroner?" the plump woman asked.

"Yeah," Detective McDonnell said. "We're going to need forensics too. I'll be back in an hour."

"Um, excuse me?" Iris pleaded with the detective, not taking her eyes off the cigarette dangling from Ramone's lips. "Do you mind if I drop off this bag? It's kind of heavy."

"Absolutely." The detective nodded, then walked over to Detective Mendoza and Ramone.

Iris ran down the steps from the loading dock to her rusted Mazda and dropped her bag inside. It was then she realized the dead man's key was still in her hand. Iris glanced back at the loading dock, where the detective was standing, and opened her mouth to say something. No words came out. She couldn't explain the key. Why didn't she give it to him right away? He would ask questions. She chewed her lip. He might check her bag. She glanced down at the ring of keys and stolen files sitting at the bottom of it. Guilt washed over her. Then panic. She shook it off. *It doesn't matter,* she told herself. *You are not a suspect.* A key didn't kill whoever was buried under the flies. It was just lying on the floor. She dropped it into her field bag, then grabbed her purse and lighter and joined the detective on the loading dock.

"Okay, Rita. I'll be back. No one else gets in that room until forensics arrives," the detective commanded as he led Iris out of the loading dock and onto the street.

The road behind the bank was clogged with police cruisers and flashing lights. Iris wondered when on earth she'd be able to go home. She expected the detective to lead her to a car, but instead he began walking down the sidewalk.

"Come on," he said. "It's not far."

Iris stopped and lit a cigarette. She sucked in enough smoke to overwhelm the taste of rotting insects and vomit in the back of her throat at least for the moment, then kept walking.

"Some fuckin' day, huh?" he said, watching her drag on the cigarette again.

She startled at the sound of an older man, a policeman no less, cursing. She blew out a lungful. "You have no fucking idea."

They walked three blocks and turned into a door. Iris remembered the bar. It was Ella's Pub. Tony shoved the door open and called out, "Carmichael! We have an alcohol emergency!"

A wrinkled old elf popped up from behind the bar. The sight of him almost made Iris smile.

"Ah, Tony! To what do I owe this pleasure?" He rushed out from behind the bar and shook the detective's hand. He smiled a grandfather's smile, and then his eyes fell on Iris. "Ah, *bella!* I remember you. You are working in the old bank! It has been too long. Please come in. Come and sit. What can I get you?"

Iris ordered a Guinness, and the officer ordered a black coffee. He was still officially on duty, she reminded herself, tamping out her cigarette. Once she'd had a large swig of beer and lit another smoke, the detective took out his notebook. Iris glanced over at Carmichael, perched on a bar stool, watching the game. He looked up and gave her a resigned smile that seemed to say, *I warned you not to disturb the ghosts.*

"Now, Iris. Tell me everything that happened today."

Iris downed half her beer in one swig and began to talk. She told him about her job, about working on a Saturday, about being frustrated and kicking in the door. She left out the details of her pathetic romance with Nick and her anxiety over the ring of keys she'd taken from the vault. She'd have to explain how she got them and so much more—the intruder in the building, her conversation with Suzanne, the files she'd stolen. The voices she'd been hearing. He would think she was crazy, she rationalized. Besides, the detective wouldn't care about missing items in an abandoned building. When her car was broken into the year before, the police officer informed her that there was no way the cops were going to waste time trying to find her missing cassette tapes and radar detector. What would this cop care about missing stuff from twenty years ago? It all sounded good in her head, and she repeated the excuses to herself over again as a cold fear gripped her stomach. She had stolen things from the building. If she told the detective, she'd be caught. She might get fired. A fly crawled up her arm. Iris recoiled violently, swatting at her skin.

"You all right?" The detective looked up from his notepad.

Iris shook her head. There was no fly.

She downed her beer. She itched to order another one, but she had to drive home in front of half of the Cleveland Police Department. She asked Carmichael for water instead and waited patiently for the detective to finish scribbling his notes. When he finally did, he looked troubled. The knots in her stomach tightened, and beer rose up in her throat. Were the lies written all over her face?

"You know, I never thought I'd have to go back into that building again." His temples and beard stubble were gray, but his light blue eyes looked surprisingly young, almost boyish, but sad.

"You've been in there before?" she managed.

"Not since around the time it closed. I was just starting out. They gave me the lead on an investigation . . ." His voice trailed off. He pressed a hand over his mouth and shook his head.

"What sort of investigation?" She avoided his eyes. He obviously didn't want to talk about it, but she was desperate to know. "I'm sorry. I just find the building to be so . . . strange."

"Strange in what way?" He raised an eyebrow.

"Oh, I don't know. Things are still sitting on the desks. The filing cabinets are still filled with files." Talking was like loosening a pressure-relief valve. She wanted to tell him everything, to confess it all—Beatrice's suitcase, her notes, the stealing. She bit her lip hard. "It's like the whole building is a time capsule, like a bomb went off in 1978 and vaporized all the people but left everything else behind."

"Oh, a bomb went off all right. When the bank let the city default, the people down at city hall got angry enough to finally let us open an investigation into the board of directors. Within two weeks the place was shut down, and the bank was gone."

"I don't understand."

"The bank holdings were sold off to an out-of-town company, Columbus Trust, and the feds locked the building down to protect deposits. I'm just glad we got a few indictments first. We brought down one crooked family, but the rest got away. Some people disappeared. I think you just found one of them."

The devoured body on the shower floor. She swallowed hard and tried to distract herself from the smell of vomit still lingering in her hair and clothes. She kept her cigarette close to her nose. *Two weeks*, she thought to herself. The city defaulted on December 15, and the bank was sold on December 29. Didn't Suzanne say that Beatrice had disappeared before the bank was sold? She couldn't remember.

"Did you know anyone who disappeared?"

"My sister for one," the detective said, his eyes trained on his mug. He put up a stony facade, but Iris could tell it still pained him.

"I'm so sorry."

He waved his hand at her apology. "It was a long time ago. I just always thought she would turn up by now, you know? Max was like that."

The name Max hit Iris like a lightning bolt. She'd seen the name before in a book, in Beatrice's book. There were still stacks of scribbled shorthand somewhere in her apartment in folders she'd stolen from the file room. And there was the mysterious suitcase. The suitcase had belonged to a woman.

Iris buried her face in her hands. "I think I need to go home."

CHAPTER 50

"Iris, this is Charles Wheeler. We've heard about what happened. Take the next week off to do whatever you need to do to recover from this shock . . ."

Iris walked to the kitchen as the message played and downed three shots of vodka. Apparently a week off from work was the going rate for discovering a dead body at the job site. She wasn't sure how her boss had found out so fast, and she really didn't care.

". . . the project has been put on hold temporarily. WRE intends to cooperate with the police and their investigation; however, all drawings and notes regarding the building and all of its contents remain the sole property of the owner. We expect you to keep the details of your survey work confidential. We'll touch base when you get back."

Liquor warmed her stomach as she staggered to her bedroom. She peeled off her clothes and threw them into an overflowing trash can. Sitting on the floor of her bathtub, she let the hot water run down her face until it ran cold. Every time she closed her eyes, all she could see were flies.

Three hours later, Iris still couldn't relax, even after three more shots, fifteen cigarettes, and four sitcom reruns. Her hands twitched. Her thoughts swayed unsteadily from the flies to the detective's voice to the stolen keys in her field bag. Detective McDonnell had said his sister had gone missing. His sister was Max.

She set the bottle of vodka down and stumbled out of her kitchen. Unpacked boxes still littered her living room floor. The cupboards and drawers and closets of her new apartment were empty. All she'd managed to unpack so far was a coffee mug, a spoon, and a shot glass. *Pathetic.*

She plopped herself down in front of the closest box and tore off the tape. Plates, glasses, silverware, cleaning supplies, and books spilled out as she opened box after box. She couldn't see the floor between the piles of this and that, but there was no sign of it anywhere. Beatrice's folder was gone. She tried to remember packing it, but her thoughts spun out of her reach. The mess around her seemed to spin too. She had to get away from it. She hauled herself up from the floor and held on to the wall all the way back to her bedroom.

TV reruns, couch, vodka, crackers, sleep, and nightmares. The next few days were a blur. The only calls were from her mother, and Iris didn't pick up the phone. She knew if she did she would cry, and her mother would come running. Ellie didn't call, but Ellie never did. She wasn't a phone-call kind of friend. Nick didn't call—not even after Monday morning came and went and he'd no doubt heard about what happened. Iris didn't leave the house. She stayed in her pajamas and only got up to use the bathroom. Her guts coiled in knots as nagging thoughts kept clawing through her drunken haze. She still had the keys. Someone might still be looking for her. She'd lied by omission to a police detective. The only way she was able to sleep at night was by passing out cold.

Tuesday morning she opened her eyes to an overflowing ashtray and an empty bottle. A rustling sound had woken her. She heard it again—scratching and crinkling papers. She sat up from the couch with a start. The room wobbled, and she grabbed the armrest to make it stop. The sound was coming from the kitchen. She swallowed the acid in her throat and picked her way toward the noise.

"Hello?" she croaked.

The sound stopped abruptly. Her heart thumped against her weak stomach as she rounded the corner and peeked into the kitchen. No one was there. *Jesus.* She had to stop drinking; her imagination was running amok. She pressed her forehead to the wall. As she did, she caught sight of a tiny brown mouse scurrying across the kitchen floor toward her. She leapt away from the wall with a shriek and fell over a box.

The kitchen counter was strewn with paper plates and garbage. It was no wonder. The floor was still covered with her unpacked shit. The Friday night sex sheets were still on her bed. Her clothes were piled in disorganized heaps all over her bedroom floor. The walls began to sway. She felt her way into the bathroom and threw up.

An hour later, Iris staggered into her bedroom, stripped the sheets off of the bed, and laid them on the floor. She piled all of her dirty laundry into the middle and wrapped up the whole mess and threw it over her shoulder. She grabbed a fistful of quarters and marched off to the corner coin laundry in her sweatpants.

The Wash N Rinse was deserted. She filled up three washers. As she slammed quarters in each one, a small bit of the weight lifted off her shoulders. She'd finally done something right. She plopped down onto a plastic chair and watched her clothes spin around in soapy water. If only she could throw her whole body in as well and come out clean and ready to start over. She dropped her throbbing head into her hands and shut her eyes.

A fly buzzed past her ear and settled onto the arm of the chair next to her. It rubbed its greedy little hands together, watching her.

She lurched away from it. No one in the world could possibly want her used underwear anyway, she told herself as she backed out of the Laundromat, leaving her clothes unattended.

She flung open the door to her apartment and surveyed the mess she'd made of a once-sparkling new home. It was supposed to be her first grown-up apartment for her new grown-up life. It looked like a vagrant had moved in. It didn't look that different from the homeless hovel on the eleventh floor of the old bank tower.

Four hefty bags of garbage, some bleach, and an entire roll of paper towels later, Iris was ready to finally unpack. One by one the moving boxes were broken down and thrown onto the curb. Dishes stacked in cupboards, books piled on shelves, silverware shoved in drawers, and her carpet slowly reemerged from the chaos. The apartment was starting to look as if a functional adult lived there.

She pulled out the last box she'd stashed in the hall closet and ripped it open. It was the junk box that held everything that didn't have a proper place in her life. She pulled out a flashlight, a pack of batteries, a screwdriver, chewing gum, bandages, a box cutter, and a book.

It was Beatrice's guide to shorthand. Under it she found Beatrice's missing notes, along with the files from the lonely suitcase and the key she'd taken from Suzanne's desk. Key 547. She ran a finger over the number. It couldn't really be the reason Beatrice vanished, she told herself, and tried to believe it. She sat down in the middle of the room and turned to the back page of the shorthand manual, where Max had left a note. She traced Max's pen strokes with her fingertip. Max was a cop's sister. She had disappeared when the bank closed. Just like Beatrice. From the look on his face, the detective was still searching for Max. The old bank haunted him the way it haunted Iris.

That's it. Detective McDonnell still didn't know what had happened to his sister. If Iris could find some clue to her whereabouts somewhere in these notes, maybe he would forgive her for not telling him the whole truth. Maybe he would believe her when she explained she'd taken a few things from the building but she wasn't a thief. She wasn't after whatever was buried in the vault or anywhere else in the bank. She never meant for any of this to happen. It might be her way out of this mess.

Iris picked up the manual, determined to decipher the bird scratch that passed for writing in the 1970s. The first sheet of paper from Beatrice's file was filled top to bottom with scribbling. She grabbed a pencil from her field bag and began decoding the words.

After five minutes the thrill of unraveling the mystery wore off as she stared down a page of nonsense. "Mole hunt bust." "Inside man lost?" Iris decided she must be doing something wrong.

She grabbed the other file, the one from the suitcase. Translating the first sheet, she came up with a jumble of letters and numbers and "D is for three hundred, E is for four hundred . . ." She scanned down, until she finally found something that seemed to make sense. "In God We Trust."

She read the words again and then tossed the shorthand manual aside. *In God We Trust?* Was Beatrice some sort of religious nut or something? It was getting dark outside. It was way past dinnertime. *Crap.* She'd forgotten her laundry.

Iris stumbled out into the evening to collect her clothes. A gray sedan parked across the street pulled out and headed the same direction. She only noticed because it was driving behind her a bit slow. She turned to look at it, and it sped away.

CHAPTER 51

Iris spent half the night trying to find some clue to the disappearance of Beatrice or the detective's sister, with no luck. What she had produced was a disjointed collection of words—"In God We Trust is the key . . . Inside man lost? . . . Mole hunt bust . . . Fuck the mayor . . . Move the accounts . . . Teddy and Jim . . . Tell Max to stay on vacation . . . A bank's only as good as its records . . . the meek shall inherit the earth."

Eventually, she dozed off on the floor and drifted back into the building. It was late. Iris was working overtime again. She was in the old HR office, sitting in Linda's chair, clicking away at her keyboard. The plans were coming together well. She picked up her hand-drawn sketch and squinted, trying to decipher her own sloppy writing. Something dropped next to her keyboard with a metallic clank.

It was a key. A skull and crossbones was etched into its bronze face. She picked it up and stared, mesmerized. A key marked for death. She turned it over and shrieked. There was blood on her fingertips. The key was bleeding.

Iris sat bolt upright on the floor. Heart racing, covered in sweat, she swore she could hear flies buzzing. She clawed at her arms and neck, checking for phantom bugs, and then leapt up from the carpet, itching with them.

"Jesus fucking Christ!" she hissed.

Iris stumbled into the kitchen for something soothing. No more booze; her liver couldn't take it. She opened the fridge and settled for a glass of warm milk. She'd never actually tried warm milk but figured it might help. As the glass spun in the microwave, she rubbed her forehead. For days she'd been too drunk to remember her nightmares. The image of the key from her dream turned in her head. It had been covered in blood. There was a skull on it or something. She suddenly had to check the key she'd taken from the dead man's room to be sure it wasn't there.

She rushed to her field bag and fished the lone key out from the front pocket. Remembering where she'd found it, she took it to the kitchen sink and washed it under the hot water until her hands burned. After the suds rinsed away, she studied the key carefully. The face on each side was blank. There was no skull, but there were no marks for the type of lock it opened or of any kind. It seemed wrong.

Iris went to her purse and pulled out her key rings. She checked her house key, her car key, and her key to the office. Each one had an inscription of some kind. "Schlage," "Mazda," and "Larson" the keys read. Her eyes wandered across the counter. Even Suzanne's mysterious key had the name of the bank and the box number on it.

The keys Brad had given her for the old bank were of all shapes and sizes, but none were blank. She pulled the key ring someone had left in the vault from the bottom of her field bag. Someone who had been trying to open a safe deposit box, she reminded herself. Someone who was not Ramone, or at least he claimed it wasn't him. The keys were all marked with letters and the name of the bank. She still had the dead man's key in her other hand. She looked from the vault keys to the blank key and realized they were very similar. They were all bronze with round heads. She pressed the blank key against one marked "D." The blank key was shorter. They didn't match.

The microwave dinged. Iris set the keys on the counter and went to get her warm milk. She looked into the glass skeptically. It didn't smell appetizing, but she took a sip anyway. The sickly warm liquid slid down her throat, leaving a scummy film behind.

"Uck!" She grimaced and dumped the milk in the sink. She grabbed a beer from the fridge and gulped it down until the taste of thick, sweet milk had rinsed away.

Head now buzzing, she turned back and faced the keys scattered around the counter. The dead man's key sat next to Suzanne's safe deposit box key. Iris narrowed her eyes. She picked them both up and sandwiched them together. They were exactly the same shape and size, and the teeth almost matched. It wasn't a door key that had been left in the room with the body. It was a key to the vault. A nagging feeling crept back into her gut . . . It shouldn't be blank. She paced the kitchen, trying to shake the feeling that the key was somehow the reason the man was dead. She never should have taken it.

Iris finally fell back to sleep around five in the morning with the two keys lying on the table in front of her next to her open phone book.

First thing the next morning, Iris staggered to her car. She had spent an hour the night before searching the yellow pages for a locksmith or key shop. A pimple-faced teenager working the key station at the hardware store wouldn't be much help. She needed an expert.

She had settled on the Lock and Key in Garfield Heights. Its yellow pages ad featured old-timey lettering and a cartoon of an old man carving a key. He was the one she needed to see.

On Turney Road she found the hole-in-the-wall shop. She pushed through the door into a tiny room where the walls were covered in doorknobs—old-fashioned ones, high-tech ones, fancy long-handled ones. She walked straight back to the service counter, where a worn stool sat empty by the cash register. An open door led to a storage room in the back. Iris hit the little silver bell on the counter and waited. There was a hand-painted sign on the back wall that read, "Lost Your Key? We Pick Locks."

She waited for a full minute and was about to ring the bell again when a pretty young woman popped through the doorway. Iris's face fell in disappointment. She couldn't have been more than thirty years old. The little old man who carved keys was nowhere to be found.

"Can I help you?"

Iris doubted it. But she decided she'd driven all this way so she might as well ask.

"I'm not sure . . . I found these keys, and I don't know what they're for." She placed Suzanne's key and the dead man's key on the counter.

"Huh," the woman grunted, and picked each one up. She turned them over in her hands and asked, "Where'd you find them?"

"In my grandpa's old desk," she lied. To make it seem less like she stole them, she added, "He died last year."

The woman nodded, seeming to buy the story. She pointed to Suzanne's key. "Well, this one is for a safe deposit box."

"Really? How can you tell?"

"The name of the bank is here, and this would be the box number."

Thanks for nothing, Iris thought wryly, straightening herself up to leave.

Then the woman scowled. "Did your grandfather work at the bank?"

"Uh, I don't know." Iris suddenly felt nervous. "He was retired for years. Why do you ask?"

"Well, this key would only belong to someone at the bank." She eyed Iris carefully.

"Really? Why?"

"It's a master key." The woman set it back on the counter. "It matches the lock pins for this key and any others like it."

"I don't understand." Iris swore she could feel a fly crawling up her neck. She swatted it away.

"Well, they're illegal now, but years ago banks kept master keys for safe deposit boxes so they wouldn't have to ruin the housings by drilling them open—you know, if the other keys were lost. They were obviously very tightly guarded. I'm shocked you found one in your grandpa's old desk."

"How do you know that this is that kind of key?" Iris asked defensively. The pretty woman behind the counter couldn't have been more than ten years old when the bank closed.

"Keys are my business. I might not look like I know much, but I was trained by the best." She pointed to a small photograph of an old man by the register. "What was your grandfather's name, hon?"

Iris felt her stomach tighten. This was a key shop. They probably got odd requests all of the time, maybe even illegal requests. Cleveland was no stranger to larceny. The lady behind the counter might even have a legal obligation to report her to the police.

"I . . . I'm sorry. This is all so confusing, I just . . . need to go." She quickly grabbed the keys and stuffed them back into her pocket. "Thank you," she muttered, and nearly ran out the door.

CHAPTER 52

Wednesday, December 13, 1978

"Coffee, black!" Randy Halloran slammed his coat and scarf onto Beatrice's desk.

Not a minute later, she could hear him yelling into the phone through his closed door as she scrambled to hang up his things in the executive coatroom. She fetched the coffee and then stood outside the frosted glass, watching his shadow pace back and forth as he ranted, afraid to knock.

"Jesus! I don't care what you have to do, call a goddamn locksmith! I don't give a damn what Stone says. We have a business to run!"

She heard him slam the phone onto its cradle.

Beatrice lifted her small fist to knock, but an older man in a tweed suit thundered down the aisle to Randy's door. He opened it without knocking and slammed it behind him. Muffled voices argued behind the frosted glass. She scurried back to her desk, knowing better than to interrupt.

"I don't give a good goddamn what you think it is your duty to do," a voice bellowed. "You will stick to your job description, or you're fired!"

The door opened, and the old man stormed out. His steel-gray hair framed his blazing face. Beatrice glanced back at Mr. Halloran's office. The door was closed.

She waited a full five minutes and freshened the coffee before gently rapping on the door. "Excuse me, Mr. Halloran."

She heard footsteps thundering toward her and took a step back. The door swung open. He glowered down at her. "I would very much like not to be disturbed this morning."

She lifted the coffee mug in his direction without a word. He yanked it from her hand, spilling coffee on his shoe and pant leg.

"Oh, I'm so sorry, sir!"

"Goddammit, Beatrice!" he thundered, making her jump. "Get my coat."

He shoved the mug back to her, splashing her wrist with scalding coffee.

She scurried away, eyes watering, certain the entire office was staring after her. She dumped the offending coffee in the sink and rinsed her red skin with cold water. She ran back to his office carrying a mountain of cashmere and leather. Her feet halted at the threshold, and she peeked over the top of the pile for Randy.

"Mr. Halloran? I have your coat."

"Bring it here." His voice came from the private washroom behind his desk.

She hesitated and then cautiously walked toward it. She wouldn't set foot inside the bathroom. She remembered too well what had happened the last time.

He straightened himself in front of the gold mirror, running a hand through his thick, coiffed hair. He turned to her with a tight-lipped smile. Something erratic behind his eyes made her shrink from the door. He pulled the coat from her hands.

"Don't think I don't know what you're up to."

"Sir?"

He grabbed her by the wrist. "Don't play dumb with me. You and that friend of yours, Maxine. You two are up to something. Keys don't just go missing. I'm going to find out what it is, and when I do . . ." He squeezed her wrist until she winced. She cowered under him, not daring to even whimper. He dropped her arm and stormed out of the room, leaving her trembling in the doorway.

She drew in a deep breath. He was right that Max had been up to something. She had lots of keys. She had been in the vault. Beatrice walked her shaking legs back to her desk. She tried to reassure herself that he didn't know any more about what Max was up to than she did. He was just acting like a bully. Randy had been in the vault the other night. Maybe he was angry he couldn't find the keys.

She pulled out her writing pad and began making more notes in shorthand. Randy liked to drink. He took long lunches. He yelled at people on the phone. He was in the vault. He was born rich and got a job where his father worked. His father was Teddy. He and his father were big money men, and making money was a dirty business. The argument she'd overheard between Randy and the older man was replaying in her head when the phone rang.

"Hello. First Bank of Cleveland, Auditing Department."

"Beatrice? Is that you?" It was Tony.

"Yes. Can I help you?" she replied as if he were a bank customer. The feeling she was being watched crept up her back, and she quickly slid her notes down into her desk drawer.

"I need to see you. Tonight."

"Tonight?" she whispered. Francine or someone else might be listening. She cleared her throat and spoke up. "Um, of course."

"I'll see you at six. Theatrical Grille." Then he hung up.

"Have a nice day," she sang into the phone, and set it down. She swallowed hard, thinking of the tunnels that ran under the city. Checking her pocketbook, she found her wallet was empty. She needed money for a cab ride from the pub to the alley behind the Stouffer's Inn.

When the lunch hour came, Beatrice headed down to the banking floor to make a withdrawal. She walked through the towering lobby to the long room where pretty ladies waited behind the bars for customers. She scanned the booths until she found a familiar face.

"Hi, Pam!" Beatrice smiled at the woman who had helped her open an employee checking account when Max had insisted on taking Beatrice shopping.

"Hiya!" she said, looking bewildered for a moment. "Oh, you're Max's friend, right?"

"That's right." She forced a smile.

"How is old Maxie? I haven't seen her around lately."

"I think she's on vacation in Mexico." It was the lie Max had designed.

"Vacation? How'd she finagle that?" Pam laughed and then lowered her voice. "I heard she was advanced on her pay for months."

Beatrice tried to keep her surprise from registering on her face.

"That's Max for ya!" Pam waved her hand. "She's always been a wild one. I could tell you stories that would curl your eyelashes . . . So how can I help ya?"

"I need to make a withdrawal. Fifty dollars." Beatrice slid a piece of paper with her account number under the bars. Pam scratched a few notes on the slip and pulled cash from a drawer. As she pulled out her wallet, Beatrice eyed the ring of keys at the bottom of her purse.

"Say, Pam? Do you know anything about the safe deposit boxes here?"

"They're downstairs. Go out past the elevators and down the steps." She slid the cash under the barred windows. "You tell Max she still owes me a favor next time you see her, okay?"

"Okay. Thanks."

Max had money troubles. The thought raised lines on her forehead as Beatrice made her way back to the lobby. She found the staircase that led to the lower level. Down the marble steps, she began to recognize the room from her trip to the hidden door that led down into the tunnels. In the light of day, it was a grand hall almost as nice as the lobby above. There was a large reception desk and a row of red velvet curtains. Crystal and brass chandeliers hung overhead, and the red carpet swirled with flowers and ribbons.

A woman with jet-black hair pulled into a severe bun sat at the reception desk. Cat-eyed glasses perched at the end of her prim nose. She didn't notice Beatrice standing there until she cleared her throat.

"Can I help you, miss?" She studied Beatrice through her thick lenses the way a scientist might examine a germ.

"I'm not sure. My aunt is very ill. She's in the hospital, and she asked me to get something for her."

Beatrice reached into her purse and pulled out Doris's safe deposit box key. She handed it to the woman.

"Are you an authorized agent?" The woman slid the glasses down her slender nose.

"Excuse me?"

"An authorized agent. Did your aunt sign a release allowing you access to the box in the presence of a bank employee?"

"Uh. No." Beatrice lowered her voice. "She had a stroke and I'm . . . I'm the only family she's got."

It was the sad truth, but the woman behind the desk didn't appear moved.

"Unless you have a police warrant or a death certificate with the power of attorney, I cannot legally grant you access to the box."

She set the key on the counter with a firm click.

"I don't understand." Beatrice sniffed. "Aunt Doris just wanted me to get her . . . rosary for her."

It was a small white lie, but she had nothing left. The tears began to pool without prompting, and the key blurred on the counter.

"The best I can do is check the records. What's your aunt's name?"

The woman examined the number on the key and pulled out a file drawer below the counter.

"Doris. Doris Davis," Beatrice answered flatly.

It was a dead end and she knew it; she didn't have power of attorney or whatever it was she needed. The prolonged silence on the other side of the counter made her look up. The woman was staring at her.

"You're Doris's niece?"

"I'm sorry?" Beatrice felt anxiety grip her skin.

"Doris Davis used to work here."

"Yes, I know." Beatrice quickly picked up the key. Investigating the box was a huge mistake.

"No, she used to work here." The woman pointed to the counter. The woman's stony face began to soften. "She trained me years ago. Did you say she had a stroke?"

"Yes, on Thanksgiving . . . You two were friends?"

"Yes, we were." The woman gave a small nod. Her eyes were pained. "I'm so sorry to hear she's not well. Which hospital is she at?"

"University. She's in the intensive care unit."

"I knew something was wrong. I should have called her. She came in every week." The woman pressed a thin hand over her mouth. She shook her head and then regained her composure. "I shouldn't be doing this, but come with me."

The deposits clerk walked around the desk and led Beatrice through the round doorway back to the vaults. An armed guard stood at attention.

"Hello, Charles. The S_1 key please."

The armed guard unlocked a drawer in a wood stand and poked around for a few minutes before pulling out the correct key.

"Thank you." She motioned for Beatrice to follow her and muttered under her breath, "These new security measures are driving me crazy!"

Deep in the metal room, the woman searched the rows and rows of little doors for the right one. Hundreds of metal rectangles lined the walls floor to ceiling. Each one had a number.

"What do you mean?"

The woman found the right box and slid the key the security guard gave her into a hole.

"The security guard . . . They gave him the keys—my keys. I've had the key ring for ten years, and last week they took them and said they needed to be more secure. It's ridiculous." She turned to Beatrice. "You need to insert your key, dear."

Beatrice slid Doris's key next to the first key where the woman was pointing and gaped in amazement as the door swung open. The clerk removed her key, and Beatrice did the same; then she pulled what looked like a long metal shoe box out of the cubbyhole behind the door.

"Follow me." The woman carried the box out of the vault and back into the lower lobby.

"Uh, Shirley, I think you're forgetting something," the guard said.

"Of course," Shirley responded curtly, and handed the guard the key.

Beatrice followed her through the round doorway to a red curtain. Shirley pulled it aside, and Beatrice could see it hid a tiny room. The booth contained nothing but a table, a chair, and a small desk lamp. She placed the box on the table.

"I'll give you some privacy." With that, she pulled the curtain closed.

Alone with the metal box, Beatrice sat staring at the lid.

CHAPTER 53

Beatrice returned to the reception desk with the closed box in her hands. It was heavy. She placed it on the counter, and Shirley looked up.

"Did you find what you needed, dear?"

Beatrice nodded, afraid to trust her voice. She hadn't known what to expect and didn't know what to make of what she'd found. There were more questions than answers, and the weight of them bore down on her shoulders. Shirley must have noticed.

"I hope your aunt feels better soon." Then she leaned in and lowered her voice. "Whatever you do, don't lose that key."

"Pardon me?"

"The key—don't lose it. There's no other way into the box without a police warrant and escort. We used to have ways to open the box discreetly with the right paperwork, but not anymore." Shirley began sorting through papers on the counter as if she was trying to look busy.

"Discreetly," Beatrice repeated, not quite sure what Shirley was getting at.

"Privately. With a master key. Sometimes things get lost, especially when people die . . ."

Beatrice lowered her eyes out of respect for Doris.

Shirley cleared her throat. "Sometimes boxes contain sensitive materials."

"Money," Beatrice said flatly. She'd seen the rolls and rolls of quarters and bundled dollar bills in the back of her aunt's box.

"Sometimes." Shirley leaned in closer. "Your aunt worked her fingers to the bone. I'd hate to see the IRS get ahold of what she worked so hard to save."

The IRS, police, money—Beatrice began to understand. Her aunt came in every week; that's what Shirley had said. Her aunt came in every week with her tips and deposited them into a box for safekeeping. Beatrice had no idea why she didn't just use a coffee can or a cookie jar like everybody else. Either way, Aunt Doris was hiding her tips from the IRS. But that was the least of her concerns.

Shirley seemed content to leave it at that. She lifted the box and carried it from behind the counter and toward the vault entrance. Beatrice followed her and watched her slide the steel container through the open door in the vault. The door snapped closed, and the clerk locked it with Doris's key. Shirley's leather pumps padded swiftly back to her counter.

"You and Doris will be in my prayers."

Beatrice knew this was her cue to leave, but she paused and studied Shirley. "What happened to the master key?"

Shirley looked up and pressed her lips together. "I heard it disappeared." She glanced toward the security guard in the corner and then back to her papers.

"When?"

"Oh, before I started. I'm not sure. Doris is the one who told me about it. Please send her my best. I'll be praying for her. I've got to get back to my work now, dear."

Beatrice nodded apologetically. "Thank you for your help."

Doris and Shirley occupied her thoughts all the way back to her desk. Shirley had broken the rules to help her—well, to help Doris. She may have even broken the law by giving her access to the box. Doris must have been a dear friend indeed.

The master key went missing years ago. Mr. Thompson was raiding safe deposit boxes, but he couldn't possibly have the keys to boxes owned by complete strangers. He must have it. It was the only logical explanation. But a nagging voice in her head told her there was more to the story. There was Jim and Teddy and their late-night conferences about bribing officials. There was Randy in the vault last night. Then there was what she found in Box 547. She rubbed her forehead.

"Headache?" a voice next to her asked. It was Francine.

Beatrice blinked in surprise and turned to look at the neighboring desk for the first time in days. Francine was like a piece of office equipment the way she kept her head down hour after hour. Then she remembered Francine and the rest of the secretarial pool had heard Randy's outburst that morning. Her face reddened.

"It's been a rough day," she admitted.

"Don't mind Mr. Halloran. No one pays any attention to him."

Beatrice smiled weakly, surprised at her candor. She opened her mouth to respond, but Francine had already returned to her typewriter. The moment had passed, but they were the first kind words Beatrice had heard at work in days.

CHAPTER 54

At 5:00 p.m. Beatrice filed out of the building like everyone else. She headed straight to the Theatrical Grille for her meeting with Tony. The bar was nearly full with the happy-hour crowd when she ducked through the door. She scanned the room anxiously for familiar faces. Seeing none, she found the only empty booth and sat down.

A four-piece band was setting up its instruments at the far end of the bar. Beatrice welcomed the distraction and watched the young men polish their brass horns and tune a humungous bass. She didn't notice Carmichael until he was at her side.

"*Bella!* How are you today?" He was carrying a tray of drinks for another table. "I'll be right back."

He returned shortly with a glass of water for Beatrice. "You hungry tonight?"

She nodded eagerly.

"Excellent! I recommend the meatloaf. You need something to stick to those ribs! You are wasting away!"

She blushed in embarrassment but couldn't argue with him. Her clothes were hanging off of her after weeks of inconsistent meals. "Okay."

"Say, how's my Maxie? Haven't seen her in such a long time!"

"I think she's still on vacation. I'll tell her to come by next time I see her." The story seemed to satisfy him for the time being, and he disappeared with her order.

Beatrice went back to watching the musicians and tried to clear her head before Detective McDonnell arrived. There was so much to tell, and she had to sort the secrets and lies from the truth. She was reaching into her bag of notes when she heard a woman muttering in the booth behind her.

"Figures he's lookin'. That Carmichael always was a sucker for Maxie."

Beatrice was too startled to turn around. Some strange woman had been listening to her conversation with the bartender.

"Used to get on my nerves." The voice coughed, then lowered to a near whisper. "Don't be fooled by his jive. If she's really on vacation, she better stay there. Lots of people lookin'. You tell her that!"

Beatrice scowled and snapped her head toward the voice, but the seat behind hers was empty. There was a finished drink and two dollars on the table. She stood up and searched the room for a woman with a husky voice. A crush of people were laughing at the bar while the ice in their glasses tinkled merrily. But there was no sign of a woman who wasn't already wrapped up in conversation. She surveyed the room again and caught a flash of gold lamé, bronze skin, and a puff of black hair slipping out the door.

Not two minutes later, Carmichael came, grinning, with the meatloaf and mashed potatoes. "Anything else? Wine?"

Still speechless, Beatrice nodded.

He was back with the wine before she'd even considered what she'd ordered. She sipped the red liquid anyway, hoping it might settle her nerves. The food calmed her stomach, and once she'd finished both, her brain began to catch up. The voice of the dark woman replayed in her mind. People were looking for Max, and complete strangers seemed to know more about it than she did.

Tony finally swung through the door, looking haggard. He had grown a full beard since she'd seen him, and heavy bags hung under his eyes. He sank into the red vinyl booth and waved at Carmichael. The barkeep brought him a cup of coffee and didn't stop to chat. One look at Tony was enough to know he wasn't interested in small talk.

Tony turned to Beatrice. "So, did you find anything?"

"I think so," she said in a low voice. The bar was crowded, and even though the band was playing, she wasn't sure who else was listening. "Jim may be James Stone. He's a vice president and apparently changes the combinations to the vaults every Monday morning."

Tony nodded and pulled out a small wire-bound pad.

"Theodore Halloran might be Teddy. He's also a vice president of something."

"What else?"

She paused, still unsure what to divulge. Max had told her to keep their meeting at the hospital a secret. "There used to be a master key to the safe deposit boxes that the bank would use if the owner lost their key or died. The key officially went missing over ten years ago."

Tony looked up at this. "So that's how someone is accessing the boxes."

Beatrice nodded.

"Safe deposit boxes are tough for law enforcement. You need a bench warrant and probable cause to drill one open. People can stash all kinds of stuff in there—stolen goods, incriminating evidence, cash." The detective paused and sipped his coffee.

Beatrice felt a twinge of guilt. Her aunt had been hiding her tips.

The detective kept talking. "If someone had a master key, they could even move these items around to boxes that couldn't be traced back to them."

"Boxes in someone else's name," Beatrice thought out loud.

"It's risky. If the mark checks the box, the jig is up. But I doubt people open them very often. So if the perp does it right, they could safely hide a fortune for years. No taxes. No questions. The world's safest piggy bank."

Beatrice remained silent. Suzanne, Max, Doris, and five other women in Bill's filing drawer all had boxes in their names filled with God knows what. A nagging voice reminded her Doris was different. Doris had her key. It was Max's voice.

Tony looked up at her worried face. "Max is wrapped up in this thing, isn't she?"

Beatrice nodded, not wanting to betray more. "Did you find out anything?"

"I made a few calls. It was weird. The mere mention of the bank, and people had to get off the phone. I had to resort to some desperate measures, but I finally found someone who'd talk over at the bureau. Turns out the feds have been quietly investigating the bank for five years but keep running into roadblocks."

"Investigating it for what?"

"Fraud, racketeering, embezzlement, money laundering, you name it." Tony flipped open his notepad and skimmed through his notes, then snapped it closed again. "Money has been disappearing in Cleveland for decades. Urban renewal funds, planning initiatives, school programs. The county, state, and even the federal government have been throwing money at the city's problems for years, and millions are unaccounted for."

"And the feds think the bank is involved?" She strained to recall all the conversations she'd overheard—the lost inside man, missing keys, accounts needing to be moved, police needing to be bribed.

"The board of the bank is made up of every old money man in town. No project gets built in Cleveland without someone from the bank being involved. Every project that lost money had a board member of First Bank of Cleveland at the helm, but the feds can't put a case together. City council won't provide corroborating witnesses. Judges won't grant search warrants." He shook his head, exasperated.

Beatrice repeated Ramone's words out loud: "They've got the system tied up."

Tony agreed with a glance. "Max went to the bureau with some new evidence but got laughed out of the building from the way I heard it. No one wants to take the word of a secretary. Besides, one quick background check, and she was discredited as a witness."

Beatrice stiffened at this revelation. "I don't understand. Max worked at the bank for years, in the Auditing Department no less. If anyone would know, it would be her!"

"Well, juries don't look too kindly at unwed mothers with a criminal record."

Beatrice sucked in air. "Criminal record?"

"It's not what you think. There were race riots in Hough. She was on the wrong side as far as the police were concerned. My father was so angry, he let them bring charges. She pleaded them down, but she still has a misdemeanor for criminal mischief on her record." He waved his hands. "The family went to war over it for a couple of years. It's in the past now."

"What happened to the baby?" she whispered.

Tony frowned, as if the story pained him. "She was just a kid when it happened. Us being poor and Catholic, there was really only one choice. She put it up for adoption."

Beatrice nodded, assuming that was the end of the sad story.

"When the baby came out the wrong color, well, that fell through. My parents made her give it up to an orphanage. I don't think she ever forgave them for that."

Beatrice was stunned. "But, but everyone seemed so happy at Thanksgiving!" Nothing in Max's mother's kind smile even hinted of such a horrible betrayal.

"Max ran away. She was gone for over a year. When she came back, she refused to talk about it. My parents took her back into the house and pretended like nothing happened. That was almost eight years ago. And now she's gone again." Tony kept talking, as if it were confession. "She asked me once to track her baby down, you know, a couple years ago. She made me swear to keep it a secret from the folks."

"Did you find anything?"

"It was a baby girl. I told her she'd been adopted a couple years before. The records were sealed. That's all I could do. It broke my heart to tell her. She was always so sure of herself. She had real spunk, you know."

There was water in his eyes. The easygoing ladies' man she'd met a few weeks earlier was gone. She couldn't bear to see him so pained.

"I . . . I saw her."

"What?" His face went slack.

"She came to see me at the hospital a few days ago. She made me swear not to tell you, but I don't want you to worry."

"Why the hell would she tell you not to tell me? I'm over here busting my ass trying to find her!" He raised his voice to a roar, and Beatrice shrank into the booth.

"She said she didn't think you could help," Beatrice said in a tiny voice, regretting every word. "She's okay. I think she's hiding."

"Did she say where?"

"No." Beatrice stared at her hands, defeated. At least she hadn't broken her word about the key. The key Max gave her was still a secret. She hadn't betrayed everything. The image of its blank face spun slowly in her head.

"If you see her again, tell her to call me, all right?" He stood up and muttered to himself, "I can't believe this shit is happening."

"Okay."

He stopped and looked her hard in the eye. "If things at the bank are as bad as I think they are, you need to get out, Beatrice. You need to get out now. You know too much . . . and no one is going to believe you either."

CHAPTER 55

Wednesday, August 26, 1998

Iris pulled to the side of the road and pried her white knuckles from the steering wheel. She hadn't left her name with the locksmith. There was no way the key lady could report her to the police for what she'd taken from the old bank. Iris rubbed her eyes with stiff fingers. It wasn't just any key. She opened her lids, and there it was, dangling from the ignition.

Out her windshield, she saw that in her blind flight from the key shop she had made it all the way down to Akron. She must have gone the wrong way on I-77. *Jesus.* She had to stop driving and think. Iris pulled off the highway at Route 59 and managed to navigate her way to an open parking meter somewhere downtown.

The tallest building as far as the eye could see was an art deco, brick-and-stone high-rise not unlike the abandoned bank that was driving her to the brink of insanity. The letters at the top of the tower read "Capital Bank." The sign gave her an idea. Iris got out of the car.

The bronze-and-glass revolving doors were almost identical to the First Bank of Cleveland's. She pushed through them into a small lobby. There was a security desk in the corner.

"Um, excuse me?" she asked a rotund guard sitting on an absurdly tiny stool. "Who do I see about opening a safe deposit box?"

"Down the stairs, to your right." The guard pointed to a narrow set of stairs off the lobby.

At the bottom of the stairs on the right was a door marked "Deposits." Inside she found a small room and a large woman stuffed behind a crowded desk. The clerk looked a bit like Iris's mother, with her ruddy cheeks and tight-permed hair.

"Can I help you, dear?" The woman smiled up at her.

"I'm thinking about renting a safe deposit box." Iris took the seat in front of the woman's cramped workstation.

"Wonderful. You'll need to fill out this form."

She handed Iris a clipboard and went back to typing something onto her huge computer monitor. Iris skimmed the sheet. It wanted to know her name, address, social security number, and other typical information.

"Could I ask a few questions first?"

"Sure, honey." The woman pulled her reading glasses off of her nose and let them dangle from a neon-pink cord around her neck.

"Where are the boxes kept?"

"In the vault. It's through that door." She pointed to a solid wood door opposite the one Iris had walked through.

"How do I know that my things will be safe?"

"Would you like to see inside the vault, dear?"

Iris nodded eagerly.

The woman sighed ever so faintly and hoisted her girth off her ergonomic chair. She selected a key from the stretched spiral band on her plump wrist, then led Iris down a narrow hallway, through a round steel opening, and into a room full of locked cubbies.

"This is where the boxes are kept." She pointed to the rows and rows of steel doors. "The vault is locked all hours except business hours. It's monitored twenty-four hours a day with security cameras. Your valuables will be more than safe here."

Iris searched the corners for the security cameras until she saw three little red lights blinking along the ceiling.

"How are the boxes opened?"

"The bank will issue you two keys. You put one here." She pointed to one of two keyholes in a door. "And then I put the bank's key here. The two keys must be turned at the same time to open the box."

Iris stared at the two keyholes. "What happens if someone steals my key?"

"Don't worry. No one is allowed in the vault without presenting identification and signing a log. The thief would have to look exactly like you, have your photo ID, and forge your signature. It hasn't happened once in the twenty-five years I've worked here," she said with a reassuring smile. She led Iris back to her office and slid behind her computer screen.

Iris picked up the clipboard again and sat down. "What happens if I lose my keys?"

"If you lose both keys, the bank will have to drill the box open at your expense."

"How much does that cost?"

"Oh, several hundred dollars."

Iris nodded, then at the risk of sounding morbid asked, "What if I die?"

"You'll find a section on the form where you can authorize next of kin to open the box with proper documentation. I suggest you keep a copy of your will outside the box to avoid a loss."

"What if I forget to pay the rent on the box?"

Annoyance began to register on the woman's face. "By law, we are required to retain the box for five years. At that time, your possessions will be transferred to the State of Ohio. Valuable objects will be auctioned, and the proceeds will be kept in the state treasury under your name."

Still Iris pressed on. "What if someone at the bank wanted to steal something in my box. Can the box be opened by someone here without me knowing?"

The woman gaped at Iris like she'd just suggested the bank was molesting small children. "The keys are kept secure by bank employees."

"Right. But how many bank keys are there?" Iris eyed the elastic key ring strangling the woman's wrist.

"Every vault has a slightly different system. At our bank, we have fifteen keys that open the safe deposit boxes. I assure you that only the people with the proper training and security clearance have access to the keys." The woman announced her irritation as she straightened a stack of forms by loudly pounding them on the desktop.

"Well, what if a janitor or someone found your keys, like, in the bathroom? Wouldn't he be able to open the boxes?"

"Miss, the keys are encoded to only open certain boxes. A janitor wouldn't know which to use. Besides, no one can open your box without your key." She sighed. "Obviously, you have some serious reservations about banking with us. I suggest you do some more research on your own before opening an account."

"Perhaps you're right." Iris pulled the form off the clipboard and placed it into her purse, then stood to leave. "I'll give it some more thought and come back another day."

The clerk nodded and began clicking her keyboard loudly.

Iris paused before finally asking the question that led her down to the Safe Deposits Office in the first place. "Isn't there like a master key somewhere? I heard sometimes the banks keep a master key."

"Where on earth did you hear that?" the woman asked, dropping her hand onto the desk with a thud. "We don't keep dead keys anymore. They're a violation of FDIC policy."

"Dead keys?"

"I'm sorry, but this is really not appropriate." The woman shook her head.

"Why do they call them dead keys?" Iris pressed.

"When a box goes dormant for many years, we say it died. When a box dies it needs to be cleaned out and repurposed for someone else. We used to open it with a dead key and then switch out the lock. Now we have to drill the casing open and replace the entire thing. It's a huge waste of money if you ask me."

"Do boxes die often?"

"You'd be shocked."

CHAPTER 56

The boxes are dead. Iris repeated the phrase in her head, driving home from Akron. It had been twenty years since the First Bank of Cleveland closed. Anyone desperate for their belongings would have filed the paperwork and had their boxes drilled open by now. It had happened several times. She'd seen ten boxes that had been drilled open her first time in the vault. Ramone had said the last one was over ten years ago. The keys were lost. The vault was nothing but a tomb.

According to the Capital Bank clerk, people's deposits were held for five years, but after that they were up for auction. Iris drove up I-77 and wondered whatever would possess someone to put their valuables in a strange vault in the first place. Whatever was deposited would have to be something someone needed to hide, she decided. She pulled off the highway and turned into her neighborhood. Maybe people wanted to leave their secrets buried. Maybe that was why so many boxes died.

But someone wanted back in. Perhaps the county's plan to buy the building had leaked out, and someone figured this was their last chance. In the back of her mind, a dark figure in a blue shirt rushed away from the vault. Someone had been there that day. She pulled to the curb in front of her duplex. She reached into her purse and felt for the ring of keys she had found hanging from a safe deposit box door. There were twelve. These must be the bank keys to the deposit boxes, she figured, as she flipped through them one by one. The woman in Akron said there was a code to them—a trick to make it difficult. Each was marked with a letter that must mean something—"N," "D," "E," "O." They went in no discernible order, but a thief could just try each one until he found a match. There were only twelve. It would still take some time—maybe enough time to get caught. There were over a thousand boxes to open.

Iris shut off the engine and slid the keys from the ignition to examine the one she had found in a room full of dead flies. In her nightmares it had been covered in blood. Marked for death. Its blank face swung from her key ring. Then everything she'd learned that day hit her. The keys dropped from her hands.

She had taken the dead key.

She covered her mouth and stared down at the keys in her lap as if they were murder weapons. There, in broad daylight, were the bank keys and the dead key. Together they would open every safe deposit box in the vault.

Her hands frantically gathered them up and threw them back into her bag. She'd taken evidence from a crime scene. She had even been stupid enough to flash the master key at a locksmith in Garfield Heights. The police knew where she lived. She could just see the headlines—"Disgruntled Engineer Caught Red-Handed." TV psychologists would speculate that the pressures of working alone for weeks in the abandoned bank had bent her already-unstable mind. Ramone would tell them she'd been hearing voices. Ellie would reluctantly testify to her binge-drinking habits. Nick would be called as a character witness to prove she was without morals and emotionally deranged. Her father's recent layoff would be the icing on the cake.

Her chest tightened. She would be the scapegoat if the police discovered anything missing. A media storm might be brewing over the dead body she'd found. Camera flashbulbs would shine light into every dusty corner of the building and the dead vault. People might come looking for forgotten heirlooms. She was breathing much too fast. She'd broken things in the building. She'd tooled around town investigating safe deposit boxes. The keys lay in her purse, beating like the Tell-Tale Heart. She had to get rid of them.

A hard knock on the window next to her sent a thousand volts through her chest. She screamed at the top of her lungs as her head hit the roof. It was Nick. He was standing outside her car door, smiling through the window.

"Shit. Sorry I scared you!" His eyes crinkled.

She collapsed against the backrest and willed her heart to keep pumping. When she could breathe again, she choked out the words "Can I help you?"

"I've been looking for you all afternoon."

"What?" She clutched her purse to her chest and climbed out of the car. "Why aren't you at work?"

"I took a vacation day to help with the workload shortage—a lot of us did." Nick shrugged.

Iris blinked at him, confused. "What workload shortage?"

"A couple of projects fell through. Things are kinda slow. Hey, I heard what happened, by the way. Are you okay?" The tender look in his eye was almost convincing. Almost. If he really gave a shit, he would have called.

"I'll live. What do you want?"

He raised an eyebrow at her.

"Are you fucking kidding me? Forget it!" She pushed past him and climbed the steps to her apartment. After everything she'd been through, he just wanted to screw her again.

"Iris. Iris, I was just messing with you. It's not like that. I want to talk."

"Sure you do."

He climbed the stairs after her and grabbed her by the elbow. "Hey, what's your problem these days? We can't talk?"

"If you were so interested in talking, you would call me." She dropped the keys onto the doormat and slapped her hand against the door in frustration.

"I came over. Isn't that better?" He bent down and retrieved her keys. He handed them to her and lifted her chin with his finger. His brown eyes were tender and sympathetic and disappointed all at once. "Iris, I thought . . . I thought we were having fun."

"Fun," she repeated. The word hung in the air. She dropped her eyes and pushed her door open. He wasn't looking for love or a relationship. He just wanted to have fun with her. It was her worst fear spoken out loud, but somehow she was the one who felt like a liar. She gazed at his rumpled hair and slightly crooked teeth. He had never made promises or proclaimed true love. *Shit, he'd never even called.* She was the one who'd led him on by falling into bed.

"Sure, Nick. It was fun. I just . . . I really can't talk right now."

He held the door she was trying to close. "Okay. Sure. I just wanted to let you know that things at the office haven't been the same—"

"Well, that's sweet," she interrupted, and tried to shut the door again.

"No, I mean they haven't been the same since you found the body. They've been worse. They've let a few people go. Mr. Wheeler has been asking strange questions about the bank. I guess I'm just worried about you."

The expression in his eyes left no doubt. She was in trouble. She was getting fired or worse. The fact that he actually gave a crap about her, at least enough to come over and tell her to her face, hardly mattered.

Her eyes dropped to the ground, and she squeezed the strap of her purse. "Uh, thanks. I'm kinda worried about me too."

CHAPTER 57

Iris closed the door in Nick's face and pressed her back to it, still gripping her bag and all the keys inside it.

"Iris?" he called from the other side. "Ah, what the hell. You know where to find me if you want to talk."

She dropped her purse and put her head in her hands until she was sure he was gone. Mr. Wheeler was asking questions. There had been layoffs. She hadn't spoken to anyone else from the office since last week. She rushed to the phone and called Brad.

"Hi, Brad? It's Iris."

"Iris, hi! How are you holding up, sport?" There was an audible note of concern, which reminded her that she hadn't talked to him since she'd found the body.

"Oh, I'm still a little shaken up, but I'll live." She tried to sound casual. "I'm getting sort of anxious to get back to work. What's happening with the project?"

"Not much, unfortunately. The police have it barricaded. I'm hearing the county is getting cold feet on the deal, and the renovation plans have been put on hold. If the media gets wind of the story, this thing could drag on for months." He lowered his voice. "Things are getting pretty tense around here. Mr. Wheeler wants you to come in Friday to talk about some things."

It could only mean one thing. "I'm getting laid off."

"I can't say for certain, but they've already let two people go." He hesitated and added, "I put in a good word for you."

"Thanks. If the police release the building soon, is there a chance I can get back to work?"

"If we can get the building back on Monday, yeah. I'd say there's a good chance they'll put you back to finish the job, but Iris, I wouldn't count on it. If this ends up on the evening news, the county will probably wash their hands of the whole thing."

Her fresh Berber carpeting, new appliances, and track lighting mocked her as she listened. She wondered how long she could hold on to her new place once she was fired. She had $2,000 in the bank and a big fat student loan.

"Thanks for the heads-up. I'll see you Friday."

Iris hung up the phone with a stifled sob choking her throat. She was getting fired. The fact that she hated the job didn't really matter as she contemplated what it all meant. She wasn't exceptional, or smart, or special, or invaluable. She was expendable. Five years of engineering school and four months of endless grunt work had amounted to exactly nothing. Fired. Failed. Failure. She could already hear her mother's cloying voice trying to make the best of it. Her father wouldn't say anything, but she knew he'd be disappointed. She'd once shown so much promise.

She sank onto her filthy couch and lit a cigarette. All those late hours, all those shop drawings—she sucked on the filter until it burned her lips. Her life wasn't supposed to turn out this way. She'd graduated summa cum laude. She'd perfected her résumé. She'd worn ugly, ill-fitting business casual clothes. She'd learned to give the perfect strong-but-not-bitchy woman handshake. She was supposed to be this "successful engineer," even though she wasn't even sure what that meant anymore. Money? Security? Responsibility? Prestige? All she'd wanted was to make a difference in the world. Now she'd be lucky to stay out of jail. A twenty-year-old pile of dead bugs was going to ruin her life. She stubbed out her cigarette and stormed over to her purse. She dumped its contents onto the counter and searched until she found what she was looking for— Detective Anthony McDonnell's card.

The phone rang and rang. Iris tapped her foot as she waited. She had to get back in the building Monday morning. She'd put all the keys back and act like none of this happened.

He finally picked up: "Detective McDonnell."

"Hello, Detective? This is Iris Latch. I'm the engineer who found the body."

"Iris, how are you?" His voiced warmed on the other end of the line.

"I'm okay. I was just wondering when I could get back to work in the old bank building."

"It's still a crime scene, Iris. The coroner and the forensics team are working hard, but it takes time."

"I don't understand. Isn't this just a suicide case? I mean . . ." Hundreds of hungry flies began to circle. She squeezed her eyes shut. "There was a noose, right?"

"Well, it's a little more complicated than that."

"It is?"

"Well, for one thing the deceased didn't shove a bookcase in front of the bathroom door and change the lock. Someone was trying to hide what happened."

"But hundreds of people worked there, and this happened, like, twenty years ago, right?" She felt herself beginning to whine but couldn't stop. "Isn't there a statute of limitations or something?"

"Not for murder."

Iris felt her stomach tighten. "Now you're saying the man was murdered?"

"I'm not saying anything." He cleared his throat. "It's important to keep the details confidential in an ongoing investigation. We don't want anything leaking to the press. If this is indeed a homicide, the murderer may still be out there."

A blue shirt ran through her thoughts. She swallowed hard. "Is there any chance I'll be able to get back to work by Monday?"

"I'm sorry, but I sincerely doubt it. There are mountains of evidence to collect in that building. The clue to whoever may have done this could still be hiding inside. It might be months before we're done cataloging it all."

"You sound thrilled." Iris sighed heavily into the phone. Fear gripped her stomach. She still had the keys.

"I've been wanting to get my hands on this building for years," he admitted. "We may finally have the political will to complete investigations we began decades ago. You can't just brush a homicide under the carpet, you know."

"Well, then it looks like I'm out of a job." Her voice cracked.

"Iris, I'm sorry to hear that, I really am."

She had to find a way to put the keys back in the building. Her palms began to sweat. She should tell him. She should tell the detective what she'd found. The headline "Disgruntled Engineer Caught Red-Handed" flashed in her head again. She couldn't tell him. She'd just admitted she was getting fired. Nothing filled the void in conversation as she debated with herself.

"Iris, is there anything else I can help you with?"

"What? Um . . . no . . . I just," she stammered. "Maybe I should tell you more about the building. Would that help?"

"Sure. What do you got?"

"Well, let's see . . ." She stalled for time. She should tell him something. She should let him know she was on his side.

"Check John Smith's office on the fourth floor. It's filled with strange files. There's some weird notes in Joseph Rothstein's office on the ninth floor. I think he may have called the FBI about some

things. The personnel files on the third floor are still full of information. I found this suitcase up in a broom closet on the eleventh
floor. It belonged to . . . a woman." She almost said "Beatrice," but
she didn't know that for sure. Besides, it would raise other questions. "Oh, and the tunnels. Don't forget to look into the tunnels
and . . ."

The keys. She should tell him about the keys too. This was the
moment, but a voice in her head reasoned it away. He was a police
officer. He didn't need keys. He had battering rams and lock picks
and drills. The police would find another way into the vault. She
should just get rid of them and never speak of them again. She
could throw them in the river or something. Beatrice would be
found without them. The police would find her. Like the detective
said, the building was full of evidence.

"Tunnels?" he said, interrupting her scrambling thoughts.

"Yeah. Old steam tunnels. The entrance is under the stairs in
the lower lobby."

"Iris, this is very helpful. I may call you again to ask a few more
questions. Is that all right?"

"Sure." She still had a chance to confess. "Detective?"

"Yes, Iris."

Silence vibrated across the line. She wanted to tell him but
couldn't do it. She pictured herself being taken into the station for
further questioning. *No.* She would get rid of the keys on her own.
"Um, do you know who I found in that bathroom?"

"According to his wallet, it was a man named William
Thompson. Now that's confidential. I need you to keep that
between us."

The name rang a distant bell in Iris's head. She strained to hear
it for several moments before it came to her. "'Best Dad on Earth'
coffee mug! I've seen his office! He was up on the ninth floor. His
office was trashed."

"What do you mean trashed?"

"Like someone had torn it apart." She breathed out the air she'd been holding in her chest. Maybe she'd helped the detective enough to make up for what she didn't say.

"Iris, if you can't find another engineering job, you call me, okay?" he said with a laugh. "I might have work for you."

CHAPTER 58

Wednesday, December 13, 1978

Get out. Tony's words repeated in her head as the cab drove Beatrice around the city. She didn't give the driver a destination when she climbed in after her meeting with the detective. She didn't know where she was going. The thought of braving the tunnels and the long, dark walk to the eleventh floor was too much to bear. "Get out," he'd said, but all she had were dead ends. Someone had ransacked her aunt's apartment, and they could be sitting at the kitchen table at that very moment waiting for her. She couldn't go back to the hospital. According to Max, the room was being watched.

The cabdriver passed the First Bank of Cleveland as they cruised down the dark, empty street. She gazed up at the tower looming over her head. Lights were glowing in two windows on the top floor. Whoever it was up in those offices didn't sleep.

Who was it? she wondered. Who turned her aunt's apartment upside down? Who was watching her aunt's hospital room? Bill Thompson was a liar, a womanizer, and a robber of widows. He may have even visited Aunt Doris in the hospital, parading as her uncle. But he didn't work on the top floor. Max had told her the trouble at the bank was bigger than Bill.

Then there was Randy Halloran. He'd been at the hospital—she felt sure of it now. He had signed the visitor's book. Remembering his wild eyes that morning made her shudder all over again. She could still feel his hand squeezing her wrist.

It didn't matter. She should just forget the whole sordid business and leave town tonight. Her aunt would never recover; she knew in her heart there was no point in waiting. Beatrice could just disappear. They probably wouldn't even bother to look for her. She would be just another girl who up and vanished in the night. Max's haunted eyes and faded smile swam back into focus at the thought. She'd made Max a promise. She needed to find her before she left.

The Gothic terminal building pierced the sky up ahead. The front of the building was a fairy-tale castle, but she'd seen the ugly back of the tower in the loading dock alley, where a blank door led underground. Thinking of the tunnels gave her an idea.

"Stouffer's Inn," she called to the cabbie. It was the hotel next to the tower. She counted the cash in her purse and crossed her fingers it would be enough.

The taxi dropped her off under the heat lamps of the hotel awning. A bellman in a gold-studded uniform tipped his hat and opened the door. Inside the vestibule a winding stone staircase led up to the lobby. Its plush red carpet was worn thin at the treads. Dusty crystal chandeliers hung over her head as she climbed the monumental stairs up to the check-in desk. A marble fountain was spraying dyed-blue water at the far end of the giant corridor. Beatrice stepped to the counter and asked for a room.

The tall, thin brunette behind the counter handed Beatrice a card. "These are the rates."

She scanned the list and her heart sank. She was ten dollars short.

"Um, you don't have anything more affordable, do you?" Beatrice remembered the ugly view from the back of the hotel. "Is there anything facing the alley?"

Before the receptionist could answer, the doors to the smoky hotel bar opened across the lobby, and a rather drunk couple stumbled up to the reception desk.

"We need a room pronto!" the man bellowed, slamming his palm on the counter.

Iris glanced over at them and immediately shielded her face with her hand. She recognized the man. She'd seen him before at the bank.

"Get me my usual suite."

"Yes, Mr. Halloran." The receptionist nodded and shot Beatrice an apologetic smile. "Just sign here."

Beatrice kept her hand at her face to hide her stunned expression at the name "Halloran." She snuck a glance at him through her fingertips. His hand was fondling the backside of his companion. She immediately looked away, but not before she caught sight of a shiny, gold hem.

"Teddy Bear, you're insatiable." The woman chuckled in a low, husky voice.

Beatrice was certain she'd heard it before. It was the woman who had a warning for Max. The familiar voice drew Beatrice's eyes back across the floor to where the couple was standing. The woman was wearing six-inch platform heels that laced up her bare, dark legs to her thighs. Her lamé dress barely covered her bottom, and Mr. Halloran's hand had slithered under the fabric.

"There you are, sir. Enjoy your stay," the receptionist said brightly.

With that, Mr. Halloran and the woman in gold stumbled toward the elevators. Beatrice lowered her hand from her temple to her lips when they stepped out of the lobby. The man's familiar steely-gray hair and suit left no doubt. He was the one who had yelled at Randy in his office. He was Randy's father. Teddy Halloran had been standing three feet away with a woman who knew Max.

"I'm so sorry about that. Some of our guests . . ." The pretty receptionist waved toward the elevators with her hand, at a loss for an explanation. "Well, I'm not supposed to do this, but it's late. That'll be thirty-five dollars. Okay?" The woman winked at Beatrice and handed her a key.

"Oh gosh. Thanks." Beatrice clutched it in her palm as relief washed over her. "I . . . I can't tell you what this means to me."

Head bowed, Beatrice rushed into the elevator. Three floors up, she scurried down the hallway until she reached the room. She threw the dead bolt and pressed her forehead to the door. The economy room was hardly bigger than a closet and featured a view of a trash bin, but there was a bed. Beatrice fell onto it and shut her eyes. It had been months since she'd slept on an actual bed. The soft sheets and the plump pillows cradled her. As she sank deeper and deeper into the tufted mattress, she felt the strangling tension in her neck and shoulders recede bit by bit. The tight knots in her stomach loosened one by one as her body slowly went limp.

Inexplicably, her eyes began to water. She blinked furiously, but there was no stopping the tears. She'd spent too many nights lying scared and alone on a cold, hard floor. She finally gave in and just let herself cry. She cried for her aunt, betrayed by the man she loved. She cried for Max and her lost baby. She cried for Tony and his defeated scowl. But mostly she cried for herself. She'd been searching for a new home and a new life, and it almost happened for her. She had teetered on the brink of happiness, until it all went wrong.

Beatrice sobbed until she was wrung dry and her mind was blissfully empty. With swollen eyes, she watched the long, flowing shadows from the window sheers wave across the ceiling for what could have been hours. Her hair, her skin, her bones were worn thin from the grating stress of sneaking around, trying to find answers to impossible questions. She was finally safe, if only for one night, in a place where no one could find her. She'd left her mother's name with the woman at the desk. For one peaceful moment, she dreamt of never leaving the room and staying hidden forever. The thought made her smile. She stretched and sat up in the bed. She would leave town, she decided; as soon as she found Max and returned the key, she would leave.

Leaving town would mean leaving her dying aunt behind. The thought of Doris being lowered into the ground without a witness, without a tear, hollowed out her heart. Doris had no one else. Before Beatrice came along, her aunt's days were consumed by the diner and memories of Bill—that and weekly trips to the bank's vault to deposit her tips into Box 547.

Beatrice eyed her purse. She had taken only one thing from the box. It was the one thing that didn't belong. She pulled it out and looked at it again. It was a book. Back at the bank in the velvet booth, she'd struggled to make sense of the markings before giving up and putting it in her purse. She cracked open the leather binding again and studied the first page.

It was a list with dates and strange symbols and numbers. The first date was September 5, 1962. Two numbers were written next to the date: 545 and 10,000. Beatrice skimmed the rows of figures. The dates ticked by one after the other. At first the entries were sporadic and sparse, as 1962 turned into 1963, then 1964. On the next page something new caught her eye. It was a note that read "15 diamonds." More objects followed—"gold necklace, Tiffany watch, diamond ring." Beatrice flipped faster, looking for something else, something to explain the ledger. As the dates grew more recent, Beatrice noticed the entries were more frequent.

Then something odd in the margins caught her eye. It was a note and a large star in red ink. It was written in a different hand. The note read "Rhonda Whitmore!" The writing looked familiar.

Beatrice scanned across to the date—May 22, 1974—and realized she knew the name. It belonged to the woman who had filed a complaint with the bank over a lost safe deposit box. It was the woman Max demanded her brother Tony investigate. It was the woman who'd been hit by a car days after confronting Bill Thompson. She read the line again.

"5/22/74, 855, 50,000 (b)."

Mrs. Whitmore had lost $50,000 in bond certificates, according to the detective.

Beatrice slammed the book closed and threw it across the bed. Her hands covered her mouth. She'd just been reading a complete record of the safe deposit box robberies. The journal belonged to the thief. It belonged to Bill.

Max had told Tony she'd found some new evidence. It must be the journal. Max had found this book detailing the safe deposit box robberies. Beatrice looked at the note in the margin again. The red ink looked like Max's handwriting. Beatrice had seen it plenty of times, transcribing handwritten notes. Max must have taken the book from Bill somehow. Then she deposited it in Doris's box. *Why?* It was a risk. What if Bill had checked there? He knew Doris.

Max's voice came back to her: "Doris was different. She had her key."

Bill didn't have the key to Box 547. Max asked Tony to return the key to Beatrice. It could only mean one thing—Max had wanted her to find the book.

Beatrice paced the room, trying to make sense of it all. Max had put all of the incriminating evidence in Beatrice's hands. Then there was the blank key. Why would Max trust her and not her own brother? Surely Tony would know better what to do with it. Her only instructions were to keep the key hidden and safe, and that Max would find her when it was all over. But it would never be over. Tony made that clear. No one was going to believe Max, and no one was going to allow the bank to be searched. It was a dead end.

Beatrice flopped onto the bed and stared at the closed book.

CHAPTER 59

The sun streamed into the room the next morning, waking Beatrice from a dead sleep. Her fitful nights in the building had taken their toll. She could barely pick her head off of the pillow. She blinked at the blinding sun and then sat up with a jolt. She was late for work. Her clothes were slept in, and she didn't have so much as a toothbrush with her. She ran to the bathroom to rinse her mouth and smooth down her hair. She looked like she'd slept under a bridge, but it would have to do. Running out of the room in her half-buttoned coat, she nearly forgot the incriminating journal hiding under her pillow. She threw it back in her purse and rushed out into the crisp morning.

There were eleven days until Christmas. The streets were decked in red and green, and the sidewalks were filled with smiling, chatting people on their merry walks to work. Beatrice barreled past them, pushing her way through the gray snow. When she finally reached 1010 Euclid Avenue, she was twenty minutes late. She hurried to the elevators, cursing the clocks. She didn't want to draw any attention in the Auditing Department, at least not until she had left for good.

When Beatrice stepped off the elevator, she realized drawing attention to herself was the least of her worries. No one was at their desk. All of the secretaries were standing in a clump in the corner, talking in hushed voices. Beatrice stood nailed to the ground in the office entrance, gaping at the commotion. Something had happened—something big. Her first instinct was to turn around and run out of the building. Get out. But she couldn't leave yet. All of her possessions were still up on the eleventh floor. She just had to make it through one more day. She inched her way toward the clutch of women.

"What's going on?" she whispered to Francine.

The woman looked out of place standing on her feet instead of hunching over her typewriter. "You don't know?" Francine asked, looking down her pointed nose at Beatrice.

Beatrice felt her heart skip a beat. "No."

"It seems that your little friend Maxine has been up to something more sinister than any of us imagined."

The words "guilty by association" were written all over the woman's hard, lined face. Beatrice opened her mouth to protest and ask more questions, but before she could make a squeak, Ms. Cunningham came thundering up to the crowd.

"Ladies! Ladies, please!" the rotund woman bellowed. "Get back to your desks. This is the First Bank of Cleveland, not a sewing circle. I'm going to dock ten minutes from each of your time cards."

"I . . . I don't understand," Beatrice said out loud, feeling more and more hysterical.

"Mr. Thompson will be meeting with each of you individually this morning to discuss the events of the last twenty-four hours." Ms. Cunningham pointed her dagger eyes directly at Beatrice. "The authorities have also been notified, so I suggest you cooperate."

The blood drained from Beatrice's face. She bit her lower lip hard enough to keep her composure. Her meeting with Tony, the book she'd found, the keys in her pocket, her promise to Max—it all amounted to nothing. She was too late. Max had been found out.

Beatrice spent the next agonizing hour waiting to be called into Mr. Thompson's office. One by one the other secretaries' names were announced from the back. They each walked solemnly to his desk to be interviewed. They each returned looking bewildered. They didn't dare talk to each other, but Beatrice caught ladies giving each other knowing looks. One of the Sisters Grim even turned in her seat to steal a glance at Beatrice, then quickly turned away, shaking her head.

She wanted to run, but her instincts told her if she made one move to the door she'd be stopped by armed guards. If they wanted to arrest her, she argued with herself, they could have done it the minute she walked into the building.

Still, she stayed in her seat until Ms. Cunningham called her name. The other secretaries couldn't restrain themselves from turning to look as she stood up numbly and walked to Mr. Thompson's office. She clenched her hands into fists to keep them from trembling. She might as well have been marching to the executioner.

Mr. Thompson was seated at his desk when she approached the door. He looked up at her and smiled warmly. She was amazed that even after everything she'd learned about him—his thieving, his lechery—she had to fight the compulsion to smile back at him.

"Please close the door," he said pleasantly, without a trace of an accusation.

She obeyed.

"Come sit down." He motioned to the chair. "I know this morning has been a bit unusual, but I want to assure you that we still consider you a part of the First Bank of Cleveland family. We simply need your help."

"What is this all about?" She tentatively approached the desk.

"I was hoping you could tell me." His face showed no trace of guilt or regret for the affairs or the robberies or anything he had done.

She had to play along. She lowered herself onto the edge of the seat and folded her hands in her lap, one tightly gripping the other. "I'm sorry, sir, but I have no idea what is going on."

He studied her carefully as if she were the one with something to hide. He had no idea how much she knew. He seemed satisfied that she was thoroughly confused.

"Perhaps you don't. It seems as though your friend Maxine has been breaking into the building at night." He paused to gauge her reaction.

Beatrice gaped at him with shock scribbled over her face while her heart palpitated in her chest.

"We've also found evidence that she's been sleeping here."

"I don't understand. Sleeping here?" Beatrice squeezed her hands together and fought to not look away. Judging from his expression, he was mistaking her panic for shock.

"Yes, in an abandoned office. Have you seen Max lately?" He leaned forward.

"No, sir. I haven't seen her since she left her job. Her brother said she was on a long vacation."

Someone had found her hiding place. Every morning she hid her suitcase in the broom closet. Did a janitor stumble upon it somehow? She searched her mind, cataloging all of the things she might have left on the eleventh floor. She decided it was safe to look down without drawing suspicion. There was nothing in her suitcase that had her name on it. She had made sure of that. The only things in there besides clothes were the files from Max's desk. Her shorthand notes for her meeting with Tony and Max's personnel file were safe in her purse, and so were the keys. Her heart rate slowed slightly when she realized Max's key was still safe.

She looked up at him with the desperation of a deer on a highway. He smiled kindly again, and she knew she'd escaped detection.

"Well, as I say, we have evidence she's been in the building. We believe she's involved in a crime ring to defraud the bank. Now, we've notified the police and the FBI, and we'd like your cooperation in their investigation."

Beatrice nodded. Tony had said the FBI was already investigating the bank but had only found dead ends. Now the feds had Max to blame. Mr. Thompson was going to frame her for the robberies. Max had the keys at one time. Max had been in the vault. Max had been investigating abandoned safe deposit boxes. It would be easy.

"I just can't believe what you're saying!" Beatrice let her eyes water for effect. She'd wanted to cry all morning anyway. "Max doesn't seem like a thief."

"Oh, you'd be surprised what people are capable of." He looked deep into her eyes, and she fought the urge to shiver with revulsion.

She lowered her gaze as if saddened and nodded. Mr. Thompson was capable of terrible things. The words "Rhonda Whitmore!" were scrawled in red ink across her mind. Was he capable of murder? Had he already found Max?

"Have . . . the police found her yet?"

"Not yet, but don't worry, Beatrice. We will."

Hours after her interview with Mr. Thompson, the words "we will" repeated in her head. She sat at her desk under the watchful eyes of the entire office and tried to look as shocked as everyone else. Mr. Thompson had set the scene perfectly. All of the employees were on high alert, anxious to find Max and save the bank. She looked down at the flip calendar on the edge of her desk. The next day was Friday—the day the bank was going to let the City of Cleveland default.

After the other women had seemed to tire of sneaking glances at her, Beatrice carried her purse to the bathroom and locked herself in a stall. She put her head to her knees and rocked for a little while, tracing the floor tiles with vacant eyes. Tony wouldn't let them arrest Max, she told herself, but she didn't believe it. If Tony had enough clout to save her, Max would have given him the key. But Max had given it to her instead.

She finally left the bathroom and took the elevator down to the main lobby and the pay phone in the corner. She deposited her money and dialed. She listened to the hypnotic ring of the telephone and squeezed her eyes shut.

"Hello?" said a voice on the other end of the phone.

"Mother? This is Beatrice," she said. "Don't hang up."

After a long silence, the voice said, "You've got a lot of nerve calling me up like this. After all this time . . . What the hell do you want?"

Beatrice tried to picture the black-and-white photograph of her mother and aunt arm in arm when they were young, before they hated each other. "It's Doris. She's in the hospital."

"So that's where you've been all this time. I guess that figures, don't it?" Ilene breathed cigarette smoke into the receiver.

"What figures?"

"Huh." Her mother chuckled. "I guess Doris never told you why she left town all those years ago."

Doris hadn't told her a thing. Beatrice had been too afraid to pry. None of it mattered now. "She's dying, Mom. I just thought you should know. She's at University Hospitals in Cleveland."

Beatrice hung up the phone before her mother could say another acidic word. There was no tenderness, no concern, no relief her daughter was still alive. She never should have called. Ilene would never come for Doris.

When she returned to her desk, she began to methodically remove every last trace of Beatrice Baker from the Auditing Department. She tried to make it seem as if it were business as usual. Drawer by drawer, she picked her station clean of anything personal. There wasn't much. Several folders were packed in the last drawer. They were her filing assignments for Randy. He had said the files were sensitive, and that he would only trust them to her. She decided to decipher why.

She pulled them out as if to sort them and studied the pages more closely. Each file contained a list of transactions. The only thing that made any of them different from the other accounting records Beatrice had filed was the labeling system. Instead of a client name and account number, there were a bunch of symbols, "$#$," and a jumble of letters, "LRHW." The symbols and letters varied, but none of them made much sense.

"What are you reading, dear?" Ms. Cunningham's voice boomed behind her. Beatrice jumped.

"N-nothing," she stammered, and shoved the sheet in her hand into the nearest folder. "It's some filing for Mr. Halloran. I . . . wanted to make sure I sorted it correctly."

"Of course. Keep up the good work." She then raised her voice to the entire room of women. "Filing is an important responsibility that shouldn't be taken lightly. A bank is only as good as its records."

Then Ms. Cunningham waddled away. It was the closest thing to a secretarial staff meeting Beatrice had ever witnessed at the bank. Maybe her supervisor was trying to calm everyone's nerves, but she also seemed to be pointing her comments directly at Beatrice.

Once she was certain no one else was looking over her shoulder, Beatrice cracked the folder where she had buried the page she'd been holding. The sheet didn't belong there, she realized, checking the label. Beatrice started to refile it correctly but stopped herself. She stared at the accounting record in her hand and silently repeated what old Cunny had said. *A bank is only as good as its records.*

Beatrice squeezed the paper between her fingers. No one was going to believe a thing she had to say about the bank, Bill Thompson, or the money men, but no one would ever be able to piece together what had happened to the accounting record in her hand either. Her mind made up, she proceeded to shuffle pages randomly into the wrong folders, scattering the data across thirteen files. She walked them over to Mr. Halloran's mailbox and shoved the files inside before she changed her mind. It might not make any difference, but it was something.

When the clock struck five, Beatrice Baker left the bank for the last time.

CHAPTER 60

Beatrice didn't realize where she was heading until she got there. She stepped off the bus in Little Italy and walked the three blocks up Murray Hill to her aunt's apartment, looking over her shoulder the whole way. She stood at the bottom of the dark, covered steps that led up to her aunt's door. The lights were out. There weren't any suspicious cars parked along the curb. It all looked exactly the way she'd left it thirteen days earlier.

She climbed the stairs holding her breath and listened again for footsteps. Nothing. She swung the door open and tentatively stepped inside the cold, dark room. With the flick of the wall switch, light poured down the stairwell. The apartment was just as she'd left it—a wreck. The furniture was still strewn about. Loose papers and kitchen utensils were still scattered across the floor. She stepped over the ravaged pieces of Doris's life and headed to the bedroom. She searched the rubble until she found the photograph of her mother and aunt together. She picked it up and slid it into her purse. Someday she would visit Doris's grave, she promised herself.

Her eyes circled the room, looking for anything else she should take with her on her way out of town. The mink coat was in a pile next to the bed. She shook off her own wool coat and slid the mink onto her shoulders. She was amazed the knee-length fur almost fit. She tightened the belt. Her aunt was overweight from years of greasy diner food, but the young woman in the photograph was different. She had been small like Beatrice once. She hugged the soft coat to her chest as if it were Doris herself.

"I wish I didn't have to go," she whispered.

The clock inside her head ticked loudly, reminding her to hurry. She ran to the hall closet and grabbed a small suitcase. She needed more clothes. Her stash of belongings had been discovered deep in the bank while she was hiding in the hotel. The thought of what might have happened if she had returned to the eleventh floor the night before made her shudder.

Beatrice grabbed the few items she'd left at the foot of the radiator. She ran to the bathroom and threw a spare toothbrush and other essentials into the bag. She glanced up at the mirror and shrieked.

There was writing on the glass. At first she thought it was blood, but she looked closer and realized it was lipstick. It looked like nonsense before she realized it was shorthand. It was Max. She must have been there sometime in the last twelve days. Beatrice scanned the smeared, greasy marks slowly, her heart rate speeding up as she read.

"Get out. They know."

There was more, but the markings blurred together. They'd been written quickly. The only other words she could pick out in Max's shorthand looked like "Lancer Motel."

Beatrice backed away from the mirror. She switched off the light and grabbed her bag from the floor. She rushed out of the house without bothering to lock the door behind her. She peeked down the driveway from the shadow of the stair shed, then slipped behind the building. Running between the boarding houses, she avoided the street. When she hit the sidewalk a block down the road, she slowed to a walk to avoid drawing attention. The engine of a car started up several houses back. It was heading her way. She broke into a run toward the shops and restaurants on Mayfield Road.

The sign for her aunt's old diner was the first light she saw. She dashed inside, letting the door slam behind her. She only dared to look back once she was safely behind the glass doors. A black car with tinted windows slowly passed outside the diner. She was hyperventilating.

A voice behind her said, "Beatrice? Is that you?" She spun around and saw Gladys walking toward her, holding her coffeepot. "Are you all right, honey?"

"I'm fine." She forced an awkward smile while gasping for air. "I was just . . . I was running."

"Isn't it a little cold out for that?" The old waitress scowled and looked down at her bag. "You goin' somewhere, hon?"

"Me? Uh, no . . . These are some of Doris's things. I thought she might like them." Beatrice's breathing was almost back to normal.

"Why are you in such a rush?"

"There was a car out there . . . Some guys shouted something. I guess I got scared."

"Can't say I blame you. You shouldn't be wandering around by yourself at night."

"I know. I just wanted to get to the hospital before visiting hours are over." Beatrice glanced back toward the street. She could no longer see the car. "I should really be going."

Gladys looked down at Beatrice's suitcase again. "You know, that reminds me. I hate to bother you, honey, but Mick asked me to clean out Doris's locker a few days ago on account of the fact that—bless her heart—she's probably not coming back to work. Do you have a second?"

Beatrice nodded reflexively and followed Gladys back to the service area, where Doris must have clocked in every day.

"I know this is terribly awkward, but can I give you her things?"

"Uh, sure. Of course. I'll make sure Doris gets them." Beatrice hadn't planned on ever going back to the hospital, but there was nothing else she could say.

"There wasn't much. She just kept a few emergency items." She handed Beatrice a zippered bag the size of a medium purse. She patted Beatrice's gaunt cheek gently. "If I don't see you again, good luck to you, honey."

CHAPTER 61

Friday, August 28, 1998

"Iris."

She was hiding in the bathroom on the fifteenth floor. The handle of a brown leather suitcase was heavy in her hand. The lights were out, and all she could hear was her own breathing.

Until the voice whispered again, "Iris!"

"What!" Iris hissed back.

The voice was coming from the air shaft. Iris reached out and touched the iron grate. It was loose and it teetered a bit. She jerked her hand back, but it was too late. The metal fell from the wall with a crash that seemed to echo forever. Flashlights slashed through the dark. She could hear hard footsteps in the hall. Iris had no choice. She dropped the suitcase and reached inside the black cavern, feeling blindly until her hand fell on the rung of a ladder. She gripped it hard and pulled her torso and legs into the duct. Voices were coming from the office next door. She began climbing up the ladder one iron rung at a time.

A flashlight bounced off the sheet-metal walls of the mechanical chase. She hugged the ladder and tried to disappear in a shadow.

There was a slatted louver overhead. Thin slices of the muted night sky floated just beyond her reach. Something tickled her neck. It was buzzing. She brushed it off. Then there was another and another, until hundreds of flies were crawling up her neck and in her ears. Screaming and clawing at herself, she let go of the ladder. She fell into the blackness.

Iris screamed herself awake. She sat up, clutching her sheets until the falling feeling in her stomach had passed. She shuddered and buried her face in her hands. She could still see slats of night sky racing away from her as she plummeted down the air shaft.

The clock on the floor read "5:30" and the a.m. button was lit. Perfect. She was up before dawn on the day she was getting fired. She considered going back to sleep, but thoughts of flies forced her out of bed and into the kitchen.

A cigarette and cup of day-old coffee later, it was still only 6:00 a.m. She curled up on the couch and watched the sky grow paler, until the sodium streetlights flickered and then went dead. She was getting fired in two hours and had no idea what she would do with herself. Maybe she would just disappear. No one would care if she did—not really. Nick and Ellie might feel a slight twinge, but their lives would go on without their missing so much as a beer. There was only one person who would really give a shit.

Iris lit another cigarette and picked up the phone.

Her mother answered on the first ring. "Hello?"

"Hi, Mom, it's Iris." Tears flooded her eyes at the sound of her mother's voice.

"Iris? Honey, are you all right? It's so early."

"I knew you'd be up. I had a bad dream."

"Oh, sweetie. No. I wish I could give you a big hug. What's wrong?"

"I . . ." Iris wanted to confess it all—the dead body, the keys, the voices, getting fired, her bad drinking habits, her pathetic love life, her loneliness. She wanted to climb onto her mother's lap and be rocked and held like when she was a girl. Her mother would hold her until she felt better. But Iris knew that woman had her own loneliness and would never let go. She would insist Iris come back home, where her life would be filled up with her mother's nagging complaints about her father, gossip about the neighbors, thoughts on the latest TV show, overbearing advice, and endless chatter, chatter, chatter about nothing. Iris couldn't breathe. She swallowed a sob.

"I don't know. Just nerves, I guess. Is Dad around?"

"I think he's asleep." Her mother's voice fell with disappointment. "I'll go check."

One minute later she heard another receiver get picked up. It was still her mother. "Can he call you back, honey?"

"Uh, sure."

Iris knew he wasn't calling back. He never did. He expected her to stand on her own two feet and didn't want to hear her sniveling on the phone. She knew what he would say anyway. He would tell her to come clean and go to the police. There would be other jobs. She should call the detective once her last day at work was done. Iris stiffened her chin, mind made up.

"That's fine. Everything's fine, Mom. Don't worry about me. Love you."

"I love you too, honey. Call anytime."

Iris climbed into the shower and let the hot water run down her face. When she closed her eyes, she was back in the air shaft. She pressed her forehead against the shower wall. The nightmares had to stop. She had to get rid of those keys.

"Never steal from a graveyard. You might disturb the ghosts," the old man had said.

Iris walked naked and dripping from the bathroom toward her closet. The blinking light of her answering machine stopped her in her tracks. Someone must have called while she was in the shower. She hit the button.

"Iris, this is Detective McDonnell. I'm afraid I'm going to need to ask you a few more questions. Meet me at the bank this afternoon at 2:00 p.m." There was a long pause, and he added, "Don't mention anything about the investigation or the bank to anyone—not even your employer. And Iris, I'm sorry to remind you that withholding evidence from a police officer is a felony."

The detective's last words were like bullets. She stood frozen, listening to the dead air of her machine until it beeped off. He knew she was hiding something. Her eyes darted around her apartment. The police could break in while she was at work if they had a warrant. There was evidence of her thieving everywhere. Scrambling, she gathered up all the artifacts from the bank she'd brought into her home. The keys, her notes from talking with Suzanne, the article about the city's default, her field sketches, Beatrice's file, the files from the suitcase, even the shorthand book. She threw them all into her field bag and zipped it shut.

CHAPTER 62

Iris was going to throw up. Withholding evidence was a felony. She lit a cigarette with shaking hands and told herself that the detective was giving her another chance.

A car horn beeped behind her and she stepped on the gas.

Somehow she was supposed to meet the detective in the middle of a workday without discussing it with anyone. How would she manage that? Maybe she wouldn't have to manage shit. Maybe she would just get fired and walk out. Maybe it wasn't such a big deal. Or maybe the whole meeting was just the detective's way to get her alone and arrest her privately. She pressed her forehead to the steering wheel and waited for a light to turn green.

When she skulked into the office fifteen minutes early, it was as if nothing had changed. The bank and the dead body were all just a bad dream. She found her way back to her cubicle and wished to be a nameless, faceless engineer again. The desk was barren. The computer was turned off. It was as if she had never existed. She settled into her chair and stared at the keyboard, wondering whether she should even bother to turn the machine on. She had no work to do.

She peered out at the sea of desks, searching for a friendly face. Nick was nowhere in sight. She scanned the windows into the offices surrounding her. Mr. Wheeler was lecturing someone seated in front of his desk. It was a female. She was waving her hands. Iris's eyes widened a little when she saw Amanda spring up from the chair and storm out of the office. The rest of the doors were closed.

Brad was sitting at his workstation as usual. She could see only his back, but his head was in his hands. Iris scowled at him for a solid minute. He didn't move. Something was wrong. She walked over to his desk.

"Hey," she said in a low voice to the top of Brad's head.

He glared at her. His hair was rumpled, and his eyes were red. Brad, the perfect proto-engineer who never had a hair out of place, was a mess. He said nothing.

"What's going on?"

"I've been let go," he said, as if he was struggling not to throw his computer across the room.

"You? Are they crazy?" Iris gasped loudly.

He shot her a deadly look.

She lowered her voice. "I don't understand. You work so hard. You've got seniority. What happened?"

Brad stared at his keyboard. "I have no fucking idea."

"What did they say?"

"Nothing. They asked me some questions about the bank and then told me the project was shutting down and they needed to 'reallocate resources.'" He slammed a drawer shut.

"God, Brad, I'm so sorry. That's total bullshit." She kept her eyes on the carpet, not wanting to gawk at him in his agony.

"Iris, we need to have a word," a voice said behind her.

Iris flinched.

It was Mr. Wheeler. Her stomach dropped to the floor. She knew what was coming, but adrenaline came pounding through her veins anyway. She nodded meekly and followed him to his office. She glanced furtively out into the cubes for any sympathetic faces. No one looked up at her.

Once the office door was closed, Mr. Wheeler sat down behind his desk.

"Iris, I'm sure you've heard by now that WRE has been forced to face some harsh realities," he began.

Iris nodded and stared at his polka-dotted necktie as he explained the recent staffing changes. It was corporate crap about maximizing efficiency. She silently wished he would just cut to the chase and fire her already.

"So I'm sorry to inform you that we have eliminated your position for the time being."

There it was. She'd never failed at anything in her life until that moment. She struggled to keep her back stiff and straight so she wouldn't collapse like a dead fish.

"I understand. Thank you for this opportunity," she managed without crying.

"We still have a few more questions if I may. You were involved in a very sensitive project and considering the way it ended . . ." Mr. Wheeler's voice trailed off.

"You want me to keep the police investigation confidential, right?"

Mr. Wheeler smiled with his lips but not his eyes. "It would be terribly embarrassing to the company and our client if the details of the crime scene went public."

Iris nodded. "I understand." She wasn't eager to explain to a reporter how she'd found the dead body anyway. She had enough problems.

"We also must insist that you turn over to us your notes and drawings of the building and anything else you may have taken from the premises." His eyes narrowed. "If we discover that you have retained sensitive materials or any property that rightfully belongs to our client, we will have no choice but to prosecute you to the fullest extent of the law."

His last words hung in the air. The office seemed to shrink around her. She dropped her eyes to the ground so panic wouldn't register all over her face. Iris slowly knit her eyebrows together as if confused. Truthfully, she was. How could Mr. Wheeler, the detective, or anyone else possibly know what she had found in the building?

There was a soft knock on the window next to the door. Iris turned to see the creepy gray-haired partner who had once stopped her in the hallway. He looked right at her and grinned. She could have sworn that he winked at her. Before she could react, he was motioning to Mr. Wheeler through the glass, pointing at his watch. Mr. Wheeler nodded back and waved him away.

It took Iris a moment to re-collect her thoughts. Mr. Wheeler wanted her to return anything she'd taken from the bank. Or else.

"Of course," she said calmly. "I won't need my notes anymore, and I can't think of anything else."

"We're going to need you to clean your desk out by the end of the day. I'm sorry, but it's standard procedure."

"Okay." Iris bit her lip hard and tried to look depressed rather than scared.

Mr. Wheeler stood and extended his hand for a perfunctory handshake, and she took it obediently.

"Thank you, Iris."

Mr. Wheeler held her hand in his a bit too long. He stood uncomfortably close and squeezed her palm hard before letting go. "I know you'll do the right thing."

Iris instinctively took a step backward as soon as she was released. He held the door, and she felt his eyes follow her all the way back to her desk.

CHAPTER 63

Iris had until the end of the day to turn over all of the items she'd taken from the building. She opened her field bag and peered inside. First, she pulled out her field sketches and arranged them neatly in a pile on her desk. There were the keys Brad had given her. There was the skeleton key and the elevator key from Ramone. Those were easy.

Back down in her field bag, several other keys remained, along with Beatrice's file and the files from the brown suitcase. She couldn't give them to both Mr. Wheeler and the detective. She made up her mind then and there to throw the keys and everything else into a random dumpster, where they'd never be traced back to her. Not a random dumpster, she corrected herself, the stinking dumpster in the bank. That was where the keys belonged, and the ghosts wanted them back.

Iris shook her head. She was nuts.

She needed some air. She needed to think. She needed to get the hell out of the cubicle farm. Iris pulled herself out of her chair and strolled as casually as she could to the ladies' room with her giant field bag and purse on her arm.

The bathroom was deserted. Iris caught sight of her hopeless face in the mirror. She was twenty-three years old and officially unemployed. She couldn't afford to be a felon too. She would have to come clean with Detective McDonnell. The keys would have to go to him, and only him.

She bent down to splash cold water on her face. When she looked back up, Amanda was walking in.

"Iris. I just heard the news. I'm sorry."

"Thanks." Iris turned into a bathroom stall to avoid any more small talk and shut the door.

"There are always other jobs," Amanda continued.

"Yep." Iris sank onto the toilet, wishing the busybody would just go away.

"Of course, you'll need a recommendation . . . and to be honest, I'm not sure you're going to get one."

Iris didn't say anything. She was hardly listening.

"Well, it's not like you were a model employee, Iris."

"Excuse me?"

"Do you really think no one noticed that you're constantly late? That you're hungover half the time? That you had an affair with a coworker?"

Iris gasped. "What?" She slammed opened the door to the stall.

"You'd be lucky to get a referral. I suggest you give Mr. Wheeler whatever it is he wants. He has connections all over the country."

"I have no idea what the hell you're talking about," was all Iris could manage. So that was what Amanda was yelling about in Mr. Wheeler's office. He'd put her up to this. Iris wanted to add a big "fuck you" but couldn't muster the breath. The air had been sucked out of the room.

"Have it your way." Amanda turned on her three-inch heels and left.

Iris slammed the door to the stall and sank onto the toilet with her head between her knees. They knew about Nick. They'd noticed her late mornings. Mr. Wheeler could ruin her career if she didn't cooperate, but if she handed the keys and everything else over, she had no assurance he wouldn't just call the police anyway.

She opened her field bag again. A manila folder was sitting next to the vault keys. Maybe the file would be enough to appease Mr. Wheeler, at least for the time being. It wasn't like he could even read the notes. She lifted it out and skimmed her shorthand translations again.

"In God We Trust is the key . . . Inside man lost . . . Mole hunt bust . . . Fuck the mayor . . . Move the accounts . . . Teddy and Jim . . . Tell Max to stay on vacation . . . A bank's only as good as its records . . . The meek shall inherit the earth."

It was all gobbledygook anyway. Iris flipped to the next page, where she'd tried to decipher pages of the other files. "Eleanor Finch: 25,000 . . . Rhonda Whitmore: 50,000."

The words of the last file were in English clear as day but still made no sense. They were letters to safe deposit box owners, explaining that their unclaimed possessions would be handed over to the state if they didn't pay up.

Iris stuffed the papers back in her bag. She would hand the files over with her sketches, she decided. If anyone asked about it, she would just say she grabbed them off a messy desk by mistake. She stood up and straightened her unironed pants. Amanda was right. She had been a terrible employee. She deserved to be fired. What was worse, she had failed to find Beatrice and was about to hand the last traces of her away to save her own ass. Iris was going to be sick.

When she left the bathroom, Nick was standing in the hallway outside as if he'd been waiting for her.

"I heard," he said. The sympathy falling from his face made her want to scream.

"I'll be fine! I just can't believe they fired Brad." If Brad couldn't hold on to an engineering job in this world, she had no chance.

Brad's desk was already collapsed into crisp cardboard boxes. The rest of the office, with its matching desks set in neat little rows, didn't seem to notice. She had never belonged there in the first place. Her chest tightened until she could barely breathe.

"I know." Nick frowned. "If I didn't know better, I'd think it had something to do with the old bank."

"What do you mean?"

"Mr. Wheeler's been grilling everyone that worked on the bank building. The drafters, the junior architect, even me. It seems like the only people being laid off are the ones that were involved in the project."

"But doesn't that make sense? The project has been shut down."

"I'm not sure. They've been asking some pretty weird questions. They also confiscated my camera. And that's not all." He lowered his voice. "I went looking for the photos of the bank I'd uploaded to the server last week. This morning they were gone."

Iris scowled and studied the floor. "Mr. Wheeler threatened to press charges if I don't return any items I might have taken from the premises. I have no idea what he was talking about."

"He said something like that to me too. He said if I didn't divulge all 'pertinent information,' I'd be fired. I'm beginning to wonder if I'm next."

"What did he want to know?"

"He said he knew we were friends and wanted to know if you'd mentioned anything unusual about the bank."

Iris glared at Nick. "He knew we were friends?"

"Yeah. We sometimes go to lunch together. Everyone knows that."

"Everyone seems to know a lot more than that." She stared pointedly at him.

He scowled, catching her meaning. "What? How?"

"I have no idea. I figured you must've told someone about us. 'Cause I sure as shit didn't."

"Hey." He held up his hands in self-defense. "I've got more to lose than you on this type of thing. I could get nailed with sexual harassment in the workplace. I didn't say a word."

She supposed that might be true. "So, what did you tell him?"

"Just the stuff you'd told me about how the building was full of strange files and desks full of paper."

"Did you tell him anything else?" She clutched her field bag a little tighter.

"Just that you were really curious about the safe deposit boxes in the basement." He chuckled, nudging her shoulder. "It was like you were obsessed or something."

"What?"

She almost hit him in the head with her field bag. He'd painted her as a crazed thief. Worse yet, she sort of was a crazed thief.

She headed for the elevators. "I've got to go. Just tell everyone that I had a breakdown and couldn't stop crying, okay? It's not like I have work to do anyway."

"Are you okay?" His eyebrows were furrowed with concern as she stepped into an elevator cab. "Was it something I said?"

"No, it's not you. I just—I just can't be here right now. I'll call you later, okay? Thanks for covering for me."

The doors slid closed. She paced back and forth in the little steel box until the doors opened to the main lobby. It was only 10:00 a.m. She wasn't supposed to meet the detective at the bank for four more hours, but she needed answers now. Across Euclid Avenue, the abandoned bank was waiting.

CHAPTER 64

Thursday, December 14, 1978

Beatrice slipped out the back door of the diner and headed down the alley toward the hospital. Up ahead on the edge of Little Italy was the old Catholic church, where the local Italians attended Mass and sent their children to school. As she approached the rear entrance of Church of the Savior, she heard a faint melody. It grew louder as she walked. The back door was cracked open to the sanctuary. Voices of children singing and candlelight softly beckoned her in. She recognized the song; it was a Christmas carol she hadn't heard since she was a little girl. It pulled her up the stone steps and inside.

The choir was practicing. The sanctuary was empty, except for the children at the altar, the organist, and the conductor. Their small voices rose to the top of the vaulted ceiling, then fell back down to where she stood as though angels from above had joined in the chorus. Beatrice slid into a pew in the back and rubbed her cold hands together. She gazed up at the enormous wood carving of Christ on the cross hanging over the kids. She warmed her hands, not opening the bag Gladys had given her for as long as she could.

It was just a plain bag, but it was the last trace of Doris she would ever see again. Beatrice clutched it on her lap. Nothing inside it would be worth risking another visit to the ICU. Max's warning was still scribbled on a mirror three blocks away. She couldn't go back. With a heavy sigh, she finally pulled the zipper open.

There were cigarettes, a lighter, cold medicine, and a small makeup bag. Beatrice let her hands wander over each item as tears filled the corners of her eyes. It all smelled like Doris. The makeup bag was empty except for a worn tube of ChapStick and dental floss. Down at the bottom, under the makeup and cigarettes, there was something else.

Beatrice squinted at whatever it was, glittering up at her. She grasped it between her fingers and lifted it from the tobacco crumbs in the bottom of the bag. It was a diamond necklace. *What?* She sucked in a gasp, then pulled the necklace, a diamond ring, and diamond earrings out of the bag one by one in disbelief. They sparkled like Christmas lights in the shadow of the pew. The choir started another hymn as she gaped at the gemstones in her hands.

Beatrice dug back into the bag, hoping it might contain an explanation, but there was none. Her mind flew to the journal she had found in her aunt's safe deposit box, and she frantically snatched it out of her purse. Turning to the last page, Beatrice read, "11/22/78, 889, diamond ring, necklace, earrings."

She read the words again and dropped the book onto the bench next to her. Beatrice pictured her aunt in her orthopedic shoes and hairnet chatting with Shirley behind the deposits desk week after week. Shirley would have smiled at Doris sympathetically as she complained about the diner. They had been friends. Shirley said so herself. The guard in the vault, the monitoring of the keys, they were all new security measures that Shirley resented. They had once been Shirley's keys. They had once been Doris's keys. Beatrice stared at the pile of diamonds in her lap.

Doris couldn't have just opened the boxes of strangers. There were procedures. Beatrice remembered them well from the day she'd opened Box 547. Blinking at the jewelry, she also remembered how Shirley had bent the rules once she'd heard her aunt's name. The diamonds in her lap glimmered with the undeniable truth. Somehow Doris had done it. Week after week she had gone into the vault and opened boxes. It still wasn't possible. Even if Shirley did look the other way or go on break or just hand Doris the keys, how did Doris unlock them all?

Oh God. Max's secret key. Blood drained from her face. She grabbed her purse off the floor and rifled through it until she found the key. Shirley had told her that there had once been a master key, and it had been stolen. And there it was in the palm of her hand.

The repossession notices stuffed in Doris's drawer with Bill's sappy love letters began to make sense. They had been mailed to bank customers who were late with their payments. Max had investigated notices just like them and found out that the state had no records of any of the threatened repossessions. Bill hadn't turned the contents of delinquent boxes over to the state at all. That left only one conclusion.

Doris had stolen it all. She was the inside man.

The key fell to her lap. Her hands flew to her mouth to stifle a gasp. Diamonds, cash, savings bonds—she didn't want to believe it, but the records didn't lie. Doris had spent years stealing the precious belongings of complete strangers. Beatrice's eyes flooded.

She grabbed the journal. The first robbery occurred over sixteen years ago. *Why Doris?* She flipped through the handwritten pages. It all must be Doris's writing, she realized. Sheet after sheet went by, until Rhonda Whitmore's name leapt off the page. The woman had come to the bank to protest a repossession. A few days later she was hit by a car.

No. A sob caught in her throat. Her aunt couldn't have had anything to do with Rhonda's death. Doris lived in a gutter apartment in a depressed ghetto. She didn't have money. Her eyes fell down to the mink from her aunt's closet, now wrapped around her shoulders, but it hadn't been worn in years. What had Doris done with the spoils? Was Bill still promising they would run away to the Tropics together? Why hadn't she spent any of it? Was she hoarding it all for the day when she'd leave town for good? The diamonds were heavy in her lap, and down Mayfield Road, Doris lay withering in her hospital bed. A lot of good they would do her now.

Her shaking hands gathered the evidence and stuffed it all back into the zippered bag. Beatrice wiped her tears bitterly. Doris had robbed those poor people. Doris was a thief and a liar. Her mother had warned Beatrice not to trust her aunt years ago, but she hadn't wanted to believe it. She still didn't want to believe it. Doris had taken her in. She'd given her a place to live. She'd helped her get a job.

Her thoughts ground to a halt. Doris had sent her to Bill at the bank. Was she hoping that Beatrice would play some sort of role in their sick game? Had Doris sent her to Max as well? Max had the master key. Did that mean Max knew about the robberies all along? Beatrice squeezed her aunt's bag until her knuckles were white.

Get out. The words repeated in her head as her heart hung heavily in her chest. She was holding a small fortune in her hands. The diamonds would get her at least a thousand dollars, even if they were stolen. It would be enough to leave town and start over.

A hand fell gently onto her shoulder. Beatrice let out a yelp. The choir stopped singing.

"Oh, I'm sorry I startled you, miss." The old priest behind her chuckled. He waved up to the conductor. The children started over, and then he leaned down and spoke softly. "Are you all right?"

Beatrice wiped smeared mascara from her cheeks and nodded.

"The holidays can be a very difficult time of year for many people, I know." He patted her shoulder. "But the sanctuary is closed for rehearsals. You're welcome to come back tomorrow evening."

Beatrice managed a weak smile. "I'm sorry, Father."

She stood up and followed him back to the rear entrance of the church. Shame washed over her. Her aunt had robbed widows and children, and Beatrice had just contemplated doing the same thing. Selling the stolen diamonds would make her no different than Doris.

She paused at the door and noticed a box marked "Donations" on a large table filled with small red candles. "Excuse me, Father?"

"Yes, my child?"

"Why are there so many candles?" She pointed to the red votives.

"They're to remember the ones we've lost and the ones we still pray for." He motioned to a small altar tucked in the back of the sanctuary. Three large candle stands were covered in melted wax like dried red tears. "Feel free to make a donation if you'd like to remember someone tonight."

He left her alone with the candles and the donation box. An old padlock hung open from the latch of the box, its one arm welcoming the world, trusting all, and refusing none. She touched the open lock. *If only this were the way of the world.* Beatrice picked up a candle and held it, then gazed back at the altar and the children. A little slip of paper was glued to the bottom. It was a prayer.

Blessed are the meek, for they shall inherit the earth.

She stared at the words. *How?* she wondered, blinking back her tears. *How will the meek ever inherit a thing?* The men in charge had the system tied up. No matter what she or Max told the authorities, no one would believe them, and the money men would get away with murder. If Max didn't disappear, she was going to end up in jail. Beatrice was going to leave town. Doris was going to die. Were they the meek? Would God save them? Her eyes fell to Doris's zippered bag. *Do we deserve to be saved?*

Beatrice opened the bag.

"I'm sorry," she whispered to a person she'd never met as she pulled the long necklace out and deposited it into the collection box. The earrings were next. Her hand trembled as it lifted the ring from the bag. It was an engagement ring. It had once held someone's dreams for a bright future.

Beatrice held the ring over the open mouth of the donation box and tried to let go. "Forgive me."

Moments later, Beatrice hurried back out into the night. She headed north toward Euclid Avenue, only stopping once to look back at three candles flickering in the window.

CHAPTER 65

The cab dropped Beatrice under a big, blue sign that read "The Lancer Motel." She pulled open the clouded glass door and slipped inside. The lounge was packed from end to end. The swell of the piano, chattering voices, and thick smoke flooded her ears and lungs. She wanted to drown in the sea of faces, but her pale skin and hair were a beacon in the dim light. Head down, she edged her way along the back wall to the bar.

"Have you seen Max?" Beatrice shouted over the din to the man behind the beer taps.

"Who?" he growled, clenching a small cigar between his teeth.

"Maxine McDonnell. Is she here?"

"I don't know what the hell you talkin' about. You want to stand there, you gotta order something."

"Stinger," she shouted, and took the only empty stool.

A strange man in a black leather hat turned toward her and grinned. His bleary eyes wandered up and down her body, lingering on her aunt's mink coat. "You lookin' for somebody, baby?"

"Um, yes. Max? Maxine McDonnell?" she squeaked.

"Heard she left town." He reached out and stroked the fur. Beatrice shrank against the bar. "How you know Maxie?"

"She's a friend." She stood to leave, but the man held on to her coat.

"Where you goin', baby? We ain't done talkin' yet."

"Leave it alone, Sam, she's with me," a gravelly voice said behind her.

It was Ramone. Beatrice gasped in both surprise and utter relief to see the security guard by her side.

"Well, well, Ray-Ray. Looks like you're movin' up in the world." The man in the hat motioned to Beatrice. He blew a cloud of cigar smoke in Ramone's face, then bared a gold tooth.

Ramone squared his shoulders and offered Beatrice his hand. She grabbed it and slid away from the bar. The man in the hat stared Ramone dead in the eye and let go of her coat.

Ramone pulled her out of the lounge and into a blind alley. He threw down her hand and grabbed her by the shoulders. "What the hell were you doin' in there? Do you know who you were talkin' to? Do you know how close you just came to findin' yourself in a new profession?"

She pressed her back against a brick wall in the alley and shook her head slowly. "Ma . . . Max left me a note."

"She did?" Ramone let her go. "What did it say? She all right?"

"I don't know. I found it at my aunt's place. It told me to get out and said something about the Lancer . . ." Beatrice's mind trailed off, still reeling about what might have happened if Ramone hadn't appeared out of nowhere.

"The bitch is crazy!" Ramone shouted up at the starless sky. "I don't know what the hell she's thinkin'! This shit has gone too far!"

"What's gone too far? What has she been doing?" she shouted back. "They say she's been breaking into the building and sleeping there. They must have found my stuff—I don't know how. They say she's been stealing. They've called the FBI! Her brother says he can't help, and no one's going to believe her."

Ramone glared at her without saying a word. It only made Beatrice more hysterical.

"I thought we were friends, but she sent me here to be attacked by what? Pimps? Is that what that man was back there? A pimp? Why did he know Max? Why did he know you? Are you some sort of pimp too?" She didn't care if he was offended. The fact that he had just showed up out of nowhere suddenly seemed too lucky to be a mere coincidence.

"Girl, you don't know shit, do you? It's probably why she picked you."

Beatrice's jaw dropped; then her mouth clamped shut before a stream of questions could escape. She shoved her freezing hands in her pockets and squeezed the master key to the vault. Max had told Beatrice not to go looking for answers. She said that she'd come for the key when it was all over. But then she sent Beatrice into the Lancer with a frantically scribbled note. Either something must have gone wrong, or Max didn't think she was stupid.

"Why are you here?" Beatrice demanded.

He lit a cigarette and motioned back to the lounge. "This was our meeting place back in the day. Whenever things were going bad, she'd turn up and find me here. Max was always in some kind of trouble. Probably 'cause she came to places like this. I keep thinking she'll turn up here again."

"Has she?"

"Not yet. But she sent you in there for some reason. Maybe she thinks we ought to talk. You know, you're more like Max than I ever would've thought. You're the only other white girl I've seen walk in that place alone."

Beatrice couldn't tell if it was an insult or a compliment. "What do you think she'd want us to discuss?"

Ramone stared at the side of the vacant building flanking the alley and sucked his cigarette. "I wish I knew. She stopped talkin' to me about it and disappeared. She just told me to keep my eyes open. So I've been watchin', man, and the shit don't make sense. All these new security measures been put in. They doubled the guards, but ain't no one there at night anymore. They have this new fancy camera system, but the shit is off half the time. The vault's bein' left open at odd hours. It's almost as if they want to be robbed."

"Were they robbed? Has Max been back at the bank?"

"I keep lookin'. If I get my hands on that girl, I don't think I'll ever stop shakin' her. She's gone and got herself in a world of shit. She should have listened to me." He threw his cigarette angrily. "Probably why I ain't seen her . . ."

Max was avoiding Tony and Ramone. She didn't want them getting involved. Beatrice swallowed hard. Between the key, her aunt's apartment being trashed, the hospital being watched, and the FBI, it was too late for her.

"How did they find my suitcase?" She'd been careful to lock it and all traces of herself up in a closet on the eleventh floor.

"Don't think they did."

"But they said they'd found evidence."

"Evidence can mean lots of things, especially when a white man's talkin'. I've been watchin', and they seem desperate."

Ramone had been watching for her too, she realized. Maybe he had followed her back to Little Italy. Maybe he'd followed her to the Lancer. Maybe he was hoping she might lead him to Max. What did she really know about Ramone besides the fact that he knew pimps and gangsters and worked security for the bank? She couldn't trust him or Max. Not anymore.

"I . . . I should go. Thanks for your help back there, Ramone. If you ever see Max again . . . tell her I said good-bye."

"Where do you think you're goin'? You can't just walk home from here, you know. Do you even know where you are?"

Beatrice bit her lip. "Oh, I'm sure there's a bus stop nearby."

"Like hell. Let me call you a cab, okay?" He grabbed her by the arm and led her back toward the lounge.

"I can't go back in there!" She shook her arm free and searched the empty street.

"You're with me."

"No! Just let me stay here. I'll stay in the alley out of sight, I promise."

Ramone dropped her arm and kept walking toward the entrance, shaking his head. "You're gonna freeze to death."

She waited until he vanished around the corner. Heart pounding, she turned and ran to the shadows in the alley away from Ramone and the Lancer Motel.

CHAPTER 66

Eleven blocks later, Beatrice finally stopped to catch her breath. She was on Chester Avenue and twenty-five blocks east of the bank. The freezing air burned her lungs. Her hands and feet stung from the cold, and there wasn't a cab in sight. She hid between the pools of yellow light from the streetlamps, searching the road for a bus, a taxi, anything. Behind her, there was no sign of Ramone or anyone else.

She hoisted her suitcase and kept moving. Chain-link fences and empty buildings flanked the sidewalk. She rushed past a bashed-in storefront. Broken glass was scattered on the floor inside the abandoned store. There were no open stores, no restaurants, no cars in that part of town. Boarded-up buildings lined the street one after the other. Beatrice paused at a bombed-out row of townhouses and shivered.

Making her way closer to Public Square, she hoped to find a cab or someplace warm to thaw out. She fantasized about the lobby of the Stouffer's Inn and the big cushy bed overlooking the alley.

Then it occurred to her. She had no way to pay for it. After the hotel room the night before, she had less than five dollars cash to her name. All of her money was stuck in her checking account at the bank. In her panic to leave the building, she'd forgotten to get it out. How could she be so stupid?

The cold wind cut through her coat as it whipped down the empty street. The suitcase banged against her leg as her feet pounded up Chester toward the tall buildings.

Twenty blocks later, her freezing hands felt as though their skin had been scraped off with a saw blade. Her toes were so numb she could barely walk. The suitcase dangled from the raw meat of her fist until it finally fell to the ground. She doubled over, trying to warm herself. God was punishing her. She shouldn't have run. Behind her, she almost hoped to see Ramone shaking his fist, but she'd run too far and several streets north. He wouldn't find her. There were no cars in sight.

Her dazed eyes circled the street. The buildings had grown taller. The First Bank of Cleveland was only six blocks away. It was the last place she wanted to go, but she had nowhere else. An unlit sign hung over her head. The dead bulbs spelled out "State Theater," and she remembered reading the name on a plaque on the wall in the tunnels.

There was a side alley to the left of the entrance. She dragged her suitcase into the narrow passage between the buildings, searching for a doorway, a manhole cover, anything that might lead her out of the cold. Teeth chattering, she stumbled deeper into the alley between snow-covered dumpsters. She debated climbing inside one to get out of the wind, but then at the back of the alley she saw it. A small shed with a blank door was tucked next to a standpipe. It looked remarkably like the one behind Stouffer's Inn. She reached into her purse and pulled out Max's keys. Her stiff fingers could barely grip the icy metal, and they tumbled into the snow at her feet.

Beatrice crouched down and dug through the razor blades of ice to retrieve the keys from the slush. Out of the corner of her eye, she saw something move. A large shadow in a hooded jacket lurched to a stop on the sidewalk fifty paces behind her. It turned in her direction. Beatrice gasped and snatched the keys from the snowbank. They jingled loudly in her shaking hands as she struggled to slide one into the lock. It didn't fit. The freezing keys stuck to her wet skin as she wrestled another one free. The shadow was moving toward her.

She shrieked in the back of her throat and forced a key into the lock with two raw hands. The door swung open mercifully, and she threw herself inside.

The room was pitch black. She slammed the door shut and leaned against it. The warmth of the room sharpened the stabbing pain of frost in her fingers and toes. She breathed hot air into her hands. Something thudded loudly against the door. She jumped away from it with a yelp. Her purse hit the ground as she fell onto something big and metal. The doorknob rattled back and forth.

"Go away," she whimpered.

Thump. Thump. Then the noise stopped.

Beatrice held her breath, listening until she was certain whoever it was had given up and left. She slowly picked herself up off the metal box she'd landed on and felt around on the clammy ground for her purse. Only then did she realize she had left her suitcase in a pile of snow on the other side of the door.

"Oh no!" she gasped, spinning toward the door. There was no way she was opening it up again. Whoever it was on the other side probably stole the suitcase anyway.

A thin thread of light leaked in through the doorframe. As her eyes adjusted, she could just make out the bulky thing on the floor. She reached down. It was a hatch. She felt her way to a handle. The cover swung up, and she knew what lay beneath it. It was a ladder.

Beatrice felt her way blindly down into the tunnel below. The darkness swallowed her whole. Not even the glimmer of light from the doorframe could reach her at the bottom. She didn't have a flashlight, or a match, or anything. It didn't matter. It was warm, and she was hidden from the world above. She wanted to lie down so badly, she no longer cared where she did it. She crouched to touch the ground below her and cringed. It was wet. A drop of water fell in the distance. Then another. She crept slowly toward the sound with her hands held out in front of her.

The pain in her fingers and toes slowly receded as she inched her way down the tunnel. After five minutes in the dark, she could no longer tell if her eyes were open or closed. Her breathing grew more and more thunderous in the infinite black. The dripping sound led her to a fork in the tunnel. She followed it to the right and down another narrow passageway. She felt her way, searching for a dry place to sleep, until she no longer had any idea how far she had gone.

Hysteria began to take hold in the back of her brain stem. She didn't know where she was. She couldn't see. She was growing more disoriented and convinced she would never be able to find her way out. Her pulse quickened to a dizzying pace. Her throat tightened as her breathing grew more rapid. She sucked in air frantically and stifled a scream. She was drowning in a black sea. She was buried alive. She stumbled forward, no longer even holding up her arms to protect her face. Out. She had to get out.

She was nearly running when her foot caught on something. She yelped as she toppled to her knees. Fetid water seeped into her stockings. The air was close and stale, like rotting leaves. Her hands crawled along the swampy concrete floor, feeling for her purse. Everything was cold and wet, until her fingers grazed something warm and soft. It was a hand.

CHAPTER 67

Friday, August 28, 1998

Iris rushed across the street toward the First Bank of Cleveland, cursing under her breath. Nick had blabbed at work that she was obsessed with the safe deposit boxes. She hadn't told a soul about the keys, but somehow her former boss and a police officer seemed to know she had them. The only person she had showed them to was a locksmith in Garfield Heights, who didn't even know her name, but somehow they found out anyway.

Withholding evidence from a cop was a felony, but if she didn't give Mr. Wheeler what he wanted, he would press charges and ruin her career. Not that a recommendation would even matter if she had a felony on her record. At the moment, getting another engineering job she would probably hate was the least of her worries. She had to find her way back inside the bank and throw the keys into a dark corner for someone else to find. They belonged there.

She ran to the rear entrance behind the building and pressed the call button on the squawk box. Nothing happened. She tried again and waited. *Damn it.* She raced around to the front of the building to see if she could spot Ramone through the windows.

The main lobby was empty. She rested her forehead against the glass. Maybe she could just slide the keys under the door. As she debated what to do next, her empty stare fell on the black velvet sign in the lobby that listed the names of the important men who used to work there. Slowly the letters came into focus. "C. Wheeler, Board Liaison" was at the bottom of the list. Pressing her nose to the glass, she read the name again. Mr. Charles Wheeler had worked at First Bank of Cleveland.

Iris spun to face the building across the street, where WRE's offices sat on the ninth floor. Mr. Wheeler had worked at the bank twenty years ago and now worked a mere two hundred feet away. He could be looking down at her from his corner office windows at that very moment.

"Oh, shit!"

Iris ran from Euclid Avenue. If Mr. Wheeler worked at the bank, he might have known the man who died. He may know who killed him. He may know everything. She rounded the corner. A large, black truck was pulling out of the bank's loading dock. She lurched to a stop and ducked back behind the side of the building. After three harried breaths, she peeked around the corner again and watched the truck pull away. It was unmarked—not even a license plate. It headed east, and the garage door rolled closed.

It made no sense. Where were the police? Where was the crime scene tape? Where was Ramone?

A hand grabbed Iris by the arm. She shrieked.

Detective McDonnell slapped his palm over her mouth. "Come with me," he ordered, and pulled her to his unmarked police car at the curb.

Shit. Iris limply dragged her purse and field bag full of evidence behind her. It was a small relief when he opened the front passenger door and not the back, but she'd never been in a police car in her life. The door slammed shut. The detective slid into the driver's seat and threw the gearshift into drive. Iris wasn't sure if he'd just arrested her but was too terrified to ask.

Without a word, the detective drove across Euclid Avenue and turned down Superior toward the Terminal Tower. Iris forced herself to breathe. She studied the dashboard to keep from descending into hysterics. A photograph of a young woman was taped to the console. Iris had seen her picture before. She focused on the photo as the detective made a few more turns and finally parked in an alley. He turned to look at her for the first time since he'd shoved her into his car.

"That's my sister." He motioned to the faded image. "She was a real beauty."

Iris nodded, not taking her eyes off the photo. "I've seen her before."

"You have?"

Iris scowled, trying to remember where. The colors had been brighter. The photo had been someplace where the sun couldn't reach it. *Ramone.*

"Ramone had her picture in his room next to one of his mom."

"The security guard? . . . I guess that wouldn't surprise me. Max made friends wherever she went." He seemed to brush it off, but Iris could tell by the way he crinkled his brow at the picture that there was more to the story. "Why aren't you at work, Iris?"

"I was fired today. Well, laid off. Things were pretty weird, so I left."

"Weird how?" He studied her intently.

"I don't know. I guess they were asking a lot of questions. I got your message this morning and . . . I got nervous. What's going on? Why aren't the police still in the building?" She couldn't bring herself to directly ask if he was charging her with a felony.

"They've shut the investigation down. The coroner ruled it an open-and-closed suicide."

"What about the bookcase and the lock?" she asked. Mr. Wheeler's name was spelled out in white letters on a kiosk in the back of her mind. It just felt wrong.

"Circumstantial evidence. It wasn't enough to get warrants."

"Oh." Iris frowned and tried not to look at her field bag. "What does this all have to do with me?"

He studied her a moment and said, "You told me some things about the building. I went and looked for the files where you told me to look, and they were gone."

Her mouth fell open. "Gone?"

"Well, at first I thought you might have been pulling my chain, but I could see shadows of what could have been filing cabinets in the carpet. There were also wheel tracks in the dust on the floors. Someone moved them. Recently."

"I saw a black truck."

"I've seen them too. Someone is clearing out the building. I can't get a straight answer from the county, and the building owner isn't taking calls. My boss told me to drop it. They think I'm obsessed with the old bank and finding my sister." He rubbed his eyes. "Shit, I'm surprised they even let me take the call in the first place."

Something was really wrong. None of his words explained why he'd called her, why he'd threatened her about withholding evidence, or why she was in his car. What was worse, he'd just admitted no one was listening to him. "I still don't understand what this has to do with me."

"Someone's been watching your house. I think someone's been following you."

Her blood stopped cold. "What?"

"I'm not sure who it is. I started tailing you last week because you were my only lead, and I'm sorry, but something about your story just didn't seem right."

"My story?" Her voice cracked.

"I don't think you're telling me everything," he said simply. "Now I think you may be in danger. Someone down at the county doesn't want this investigation to move forward. Someone is moving evidence out of the building. Someone is following you. Now, you can either tell me why, or I can drop you off at your house and you can take your chances."

She opened her mouth, but no sound could escape through the knot in her throat. He watched her carefully as she processed what he'd said. Mr. Wheeler knew about her affair with Nick, her drinking habits, and her late mornings. Mr. Wheeler seemed to know about the keys. She could still feel the squeeze of his hand, but this time it was around her neck.

Iris slowly reached down to the floorboards and grabbed her field bag and her purse. She fumbled with trembling hands and lit a cigarette. The detective patiently waited and unrolled her window. She blew a shaky stream of smoke out the window and then pulled out the keys.

CHAPTER 68

Detective McDonnell took notes as Iris told him the whole story. He nodded while she confessed to stealing keys from Suzanne's drawer, the vault, and finally the bathroom floor just inches from the rotting corpse. The last confession made the detective stop writing. His eyes filled with disbelief and then rage.

"You took something from the crime scene? Are you fucking nuts?" He studied her face as if he were actually trying to measure her sanity. "Do you realize that's a felony? You've just destroyed your credibility as a witness. I can't use any evidence you give me! Even if they did let me reopen the case, I got nothing. Goddammit!"

He slammed his hand against the dashboard and turned to the window. Her eyes watered and her cigarette dropped from her shaking lips.

"I was in shock," she protested as she fumbled for the burning ember in her lap. "Can't I plead temporary insanity or something? I'd never seen a dead body before. I walked into the room and picked up this key. Then I found the flies and the bones and I threw up. The next thing I knew, the room was filled with cops.

I didn't realize I even had the key in my hand until I was down by my car and it was . . . too late. I was scared. I thought I was going crazy. I've been hearing voices. Isn't there anything I can do to make this right?"

The detective stared at her hard, and she felt the prison bars slam down around her. She clamped her lips together to keep from wailing.

His glare softened. "So you found some keys. Why would someone be following you, Iris?"

She swallowed hard. "They're not just any keys. I did some checking around. These are the bank's keys to the vault, and this"— she grabbed the blank key with shaky fingers—"this is the master key. They call it a dead key. Together these can open any safe deposit box in the vault."

"You did some checking around?" He rolled his eyes at the ceiling of his car and raised his voice to a roar. "What the hell is it with people wanting to play detective? You sound like my goddamn sister with this crap! Do you know what happened to her when she went poking around that vault? She vanished! For all I know, she's dead and buried somewhere under the city. Is that what you want?"

Iris shrunk into the corner of her seat. He noticed her cowering and ran his fingers through his hair. The toll the bank had taken was written in the creases of his forehead.

He took a deep breath and said calmly, "I'm sorry, Iris. This thing is bigger than you, okay?"

She gave him a small nod.

"So, someone is following you because of these keys. Do you have any idea who it is?"

She took a moment to consider it rationally, though it was hard to think straight with the hysterical shrieking in her head. "Well, I think someone was trying to open a safe deposit box when I surprised him. He left these keys hanging from a lock."

"And you took them?" he asked as though she might just be the dumbest woman on earth.

"I don't know, I thought it was Ramone. I was going to give them back to him. I was hoping he would explain how he got them. They were supposedly lost twenty years ago, and I've sort of been trying to find them myself. But it wasn't him. I was going to put them back. I never meant to keep them . . . It sounds crazy, doesn't it?"

"Yes," he said flatly. "I don't think you realize the kind of people you're dealing with."

"You mean people like Mr. Wheeler?" She searched the detective's face. "I think he threatened me today. Did you know he used to work at the First Bank of Cleveland?"

"Mr. Wheeler?"

"Charles Wheeler is a lead partner at WRE. He used to be a board member or something at the bank. He told me I'd better give back everything I might have taken from the building or he'd press charges, and then he nearly broke my fingers with a handshake."

"Wheeler," the detective repeated, and began flipping through his worn notepad. "He was on the board of the real estate investment company that had bought the property at auction when the building was sold in 1979—Cleveland Real Estate Holdings Corp."

Iris nodded, trying to piece it together. Mr. Wheeler worked for the same company that bought the building at auction. He also worked for the bank. "Do you think he's following me?"

"Wheeler? I doubt it's actually him, but it may be someone who works for him. He's just one of the players in this. The most powerful men in Cleveland have ties to the old bank. Another former bank officer, James Stone, was elected county commissioner a few years back. Now he's running for Congress. Too many important people want to keep the truth buried. If they think you've uncovered something, they'll want to bury you too."

"But I don't know anything!" she protested. Her brain was reeling. Someone working for Mr. Wheeler had been following her. Somehow Amanda and Mr. Wheeler knew about her affair with Nick. *Nick.* Nick was always popping up out of nowhere in the old bank and outside her car window. He had been in her apartment. A chill coursed through her body. Nick was just a guy looking for a good time, she argued. He wouldn't be wrapped up in some weird conspiracy. The detective was studying her as she fought back the panic. She didn't want to have to explain Nick.

"You must know something, Iris."

"What do I know? I've seen strange files and cryptic notes. I found some keys. I found a pile of dead flies, and I'm still having nightmares. It doesn't mean I understand any of it. I even tried. I stayed up late deciphering some weird language, and I couldn't make sense of any of it. All I know is that a secretary disappeared because she knew something about the safe deposits. She left behind these notes for someone to find."

"Notes?"

Her eyes watered as her voice raised an octave. "Yes! Then there was this suitcase I found full of her clothes. She probably died in there, and no one even cared. Now you're telling me someone's following me . . . Am I next?"

"Wait. You found women's clothes? Where?" he asked.

"In a closet. Here I think I'm going crazy. I think I'm being haunted. Someone's been following me around the building messing with me, dusting things, taking things, whispering my name. I don't know shit all right. I wish I did, but I don't."

The detective was staring at the photograph of his sister as if he'd forgotten Iris was there.

"Do you?" She angrily wiped the tears from her eyes. "What really happened when the bank closed?"

"All I can tell you is that when the city defaulted, they were eager to blame somebody. City council opened a full investigation of the First Bank of Cleveland, talking about how the rich had defrauded the public. At first the bank cooperated. They gave us access to files and corrupted accounts. We indicted one big fish."

He read the name from his notepad: "Theodore Halloran, vice president of Finance. He was as dirty as they come. We had him for embezzlement and racketeering. He was on this advisory committee to the city back in the early 1970s to develop an urban planning initiative. They petitioned the government for funds to buy up blighted real estate for redevelopment. 'Urban renewal' they called it. 'Eminent domain.' Millions of dollars disappeared overnight. Technically, I guess you could say they didn't disappear. They were 'mismanaged.'"

"What do you mean?"

"The whole thing was a scam. Halloran and his buddies already owned most of the properties they were buying. They had bought up half of Cleveland through bullshit front operations, like nonprofits, and real estate investment firms, like the New Cleveland League. So Halloran was acting on behalf of the city, buying acres of blighted housing from himself, negotiating with himself, and fixing the prices. He sold properties to the city at an outrageous profit. What did he care? It was federal money. The money went right into the bank's coffers and was never seen again."

A freight truck rolled past the loading dock. Iris thought of the black truck she'd seen leaving the old bank. Cleveland Real Estate Holdings Corp. was a front organization owned and operated by former bank officers. Mr. Wheeler was one of them. They owned the building and were removing evidence. Suzanne had said, "You'd be surprised how many of those fat-cat bankers is still around." She was right.

They might hide behind different company names, but they were the same people.

The detective was still talking. "Target neighborhoods got leveled and then completely abandoned. Neighborhoods like Hough were overrun with displaced families. Rents went through the roof, while the whole place went to hell. When it came time to redevelop all that land the city had bought, none of the real estate developers were interested. And the real crime of it was that they were the ones that lobbied the feds for the whole plan and the grant money in the first place."

The detective chuckled. "Jesus, I sound like Max talking about this stuff."

"So what happened?" Nothing he was saying was calming her nerves.

"When the feds seized Halloran's assets, they found over three hundred thousand dollars in gold brick in a safe deposit box he had rented from the First Bank of Cleveland. He was going to cooperate too. The way I heard it, he was about to roll over on half the board of directors, but he found another way out. He committed suicide. At least that's what the coroner called it."

Iris remembered walking into Mr. Halloran's ransacked office on the top floor of the building. Someone had torn the place apart.

"People started dropping like flies. Old Man Mercer was killed in a car crash. We kept running into dead ends. By the time CPD got a bench warrant to raid the bank, we found out it had been sold. All assets transferred to Columbus Trust in the middle of the night. They were an out-of-town company with no use for the building at 1010 Euclid. It was shuttered and locked up by morning. The building sold at auction a few weeks later. It stopped us cold."

"I don't understand. Why did that matter?"

"The feds were more interested in keeping the bank from failing during the sale than completing the investigation."

The detective noticed the confused expression on Iris's face and tried to explain. "The FDIC insurance on the deposits was over three billion dollars. If a scandal broke during the sale, there could have been a run on the bank. Everyone hears the bank is being sold, people get nervous, and they run to withdraw their money—Great Depression stuff. I tried to work through the red tape for weeks, but I was taken off the case. They said I could no longer be impartial, due to my personal connection to the bank."

"Your sister," Iris whispered, and looked back at the picture of Max taped to the dashboard. She was somehow mixed up in all of it back then just like Iris was now. "I saw a note she wrote. It was in a book I found."

He lifted his downcast eyes. "What?"

"She'd written this note to Beatrice Baker." Iris dug the short-hand manual out of her bag and handed it to the detective. "I found these strange notes in Beatrice's personnel file, and then I saw your sister's name in this book. I guess I thought if I could decipher the notes, I might find a clue to where Max went . . ." Iris didn't complete her thought that she'd hoped the detective would show her leniency in return.

"Did you find anything?" he asked, eyebrows raised.

"Not anything I could make sense of. Just a bunch of odd notes from the Bible and a few names."

The detective gazed at the photograph of his sister and smoothed the tape with his fingertip. "I think she was having an affair with Bill Thompson."

The name struck a nerve. "You don't mean . . . ?"

"The body you found." He nodded. "I haven't told anyone that. According to Max, he was involved in some small-time theft. He was raiding unclaimed deposit boxes, and she got tangled up in it somehow. I couldn't help her. I couldn't help Beatrice either. I just hope she managed to leave town."

"You knew Beatrice?" Iris's eyes grew wide.

"The last time I saw Beatrice, she was in over her head with all of this. She was just a kid."

She reached down and began searching her bag. "Beatrice called a secretary named Suzanne right before the bank closed. She asked her about a safe deposit box that was in her name. I found the key to the box in Suzanne's desk and tracked her down."

The detective did a double take. "What?"

"It's a long story." She sat up when she finally managed to fish the key out her bag. "But this number 547 shows up all over the notes. I think it means something."

"Beatrice called some woman about a deposit box?" He frowned as if remembering an ancient conversation.

He eyed the key in Iris's hand. She gave it to him. He didn't examine it; he just kept looking expectantly at Iris. She squirmed a moment, unsure what he wanted. He finally glanced down to the pile of keys in her lap and back to her face with his eyebrows raised. She nodded awkwardly and handed over all of the bank keys.

He sighed. "It will take me months to get a warrant. I doubt they'll even give me one."

Seeing the keys in the detective's hands instead of her own did nothing to calm her nerves. Iris had finally come clean and confessed, but someone was still following her. Someone thought she knew something. People had disappeared. People had died. A lonely brown suitcase was still filled with clothes and hiding in the building. She felt as though she were right there with it. A tear fell down her cheek.

"Why would Mr. Wheeler and all of those people still care about the bank? Why are they following me?" she pleaded.

"You know what was so unusual about the gold we found in Teddy Halloran's safe deposit box?"

Iris shook her head.

"We only found three hundred thousand bucks. The public records I've researched over the years suggest that, when you adjust for inflation, over fifty million public dollars had been grossly mismanaged between 1960 and 1978, when the bank closed."

"So?"

"We were closing in fast on the case when Teddy offed himself. The feds were involved, and people were starting to get anxious. I think the other members of the board pulled the trigger on the sale to lock up the records and holdings under the FDIC veil, but maybe they messed up. Maybe they didn't have enough time to pull the money out."

"What are you saying? That the money is still in the bank somewhere?"

CHAPTER 69

Iris shook her head in disbelief. How could $50 million just go missing? That kind of money doesn't just get lost in the couch cushions. She hadn't seen any sign of bags of cash lying around, and she'd been snooping. Then it hit her. The vault.

"They lost the keys!" Iris laughed nervously. It was something she would do. "The safe deposit boxes are still full with all of that money, and they lost the fucking keys!"

"Or someone hid them."

She stopped laughing. Keys to $50 million in stolen money had been sitting in her purse. She sucked in a breath. She was a dead woman.

"But it makes no sense," she said, on the verge of hysterics. "Why would they need the keys? They could just drill the boxes, or blow them up for that matter."

"I'm not sure. You're going to have to stick with me until we figure this thing out." He squeezed her hand. "I'm not going to let you disappear too, okay? I'm going to forget where these keys came from as long as you give me your full cooperation, got it?"

Iris was going to be sick.

"Following police protocol for the past twenty years has gotten me nowhere. It may have even cost Max her life. I'm not going to let it happen again."

With that, he climbed out of the car.

Iris sat frozen in her seat until she heard a tap on her window. The detective motioned for her to get out. They were in an alley somewhere downtown. Terminal Tower loomed above them.

"Where are we going?"

"You're going to show me this vault," he said, searching around the alley until he found what he was looking for. "I did some checking on those steam tunnels you mentioned. One of them dead-ends right here."

He walked to a small shed and tried the handle to the door. It was locked. He pulled a pair of metal picks out of his back pocket and knelt down. Iris glanced nervously around the alley. It was broad daylight, but the street was deserted. Everyone was at work except her. She hoisted her field bag onto her shoulder and fought back the urge to run. Within a few seconds the detective had picked the lock, and the door swung open.

He carefully shut it behind them and clicked on a flashlight. There was a giant hatch on the floor between them. It opened with a loud clank. Detective McDonnell followed Iris down a narrow ladder and into a tiny passageway. She pulled her own Magnum flashlight out of her bag and held on to it for dear life as the two of them headed down the dank tunnel.

After what seemed like miles, they reached a brick-lined, vaulted room that served as a junction point. Iris had been there before. She took the lead down the narrow passage that ended at the steep metal staircase. The sign above it read, "First Bank of Cleveland." The first stair creaked loudly, and her heart skipped a beat. She froze and listened, before continuing to climb. At the top, Iris clicked off her flashlight and tried the handle to the access door. It wasn't locked.

Daylight trickled down the stairs above them, giving just enough light to find their way across the lower lobby. The red carpet muffled their footsteps as they snuck across the floor toward the vaults in total silence. Iris dug her fingernails into the palm of her hand. This wasn't happening, she told herself. It was just another bad dream. A police officer would not break into a bank. But that's exactly what they seemed to be doing.

This was a terrible idea, but she had no choice. She was in danger. Someone knew about the keys. Someone had been watching her. The detective needed her help, and she needed his. There wasn't a better plan, but she searched for one anyway. Maybe she could just try to leave town. The image of an abandoned brown suitcase was still hiding in a closet in her mind. Beatrice had tried to leave too.

The round doorway between the lower lobby and the vault corridor stood open. Iris couldn't shake the feeling that they were walking into the open jaws of a beast.

All of the red velvet curtains of the private viewing rooms were pulled open except one. It was the shower curtain all over again as Iris stared at the red fabric from across the room. She stopped and strained her ears for the sound of a madman whispering her name. Detective McDonnell nudged her. They had to keep moving.

Through the round opening, they were greeted by total darkness. Iris felt her way across the marble corridor toward the vault that held over a thousand safe deposit boxes, each with its own little secret.

It felt wrong. Every other time Iris had visited the bank, the fluorescent lights had been buzzing, and Ramone had been wandering the halls. The detective clicked on his flashlight and examined the hundreds of tiny doors. He pulled out the keys he'd taken from her and began searching for Suzanne's box.

The silence was closing in around her. She couldn't shake the feeling of someone watching. Phantom voices whispered in her ears. She tried to tell herself if anyone was there, it would be Ramone. But he didn't answer the ring of the call box. Maybe he was gone.

Detective McDonnell found Box 547. "So, how does this work?"

"Well," Iris said, clearing her throat, "Suzanne's key must go here, and the bank's key goes in this larger hole."

"And these are the bank keys?" He held up the ring of keys she'd found not far from where they stood. "So which one do we use?"

"Why don't you just try them all?" There were only twelve keys, each with its own cryptic letter engraved on its face.

"The lock might break. The pins could be set to snap if the wrong key is forced in."

She raised her eyebrows, and he raised his back.

"What, you think you're the only one who does detective work? These markings don't make sense. The keys are lettered, but the boxes are numbered."

He handed the keys to Iris, and she looked through them. "U," "I," "N," "D," "E_1," "O," "S_1," "P," "E_2," "R," "A," "M" the letters read around the ring. She'd wondered the same thing ever since she found them. There were tiny numbers on a few, but not all of them. Just on the letters that repeated, she realized.

"Oon Day-O Sper-Am." Iris sounded out the letters aloud as she turned the keys over.

"Well, *Deo* is Latin for 'God.'"

"Huh?" Iris scowled at the detective.

"It's Latin. Twelve years of Catholic school," he said with a shrug. "But who cares. I'm sure no one was thinking about God when they rigged this key system."

"In God We Trust is the key!" she nearly shouted, and then clapped a hand over her mouth. In a lowered voice she explained. "That's it! It was written in one of the files. 'In God We Trust' is written all over the dollar bill, isn't it?"

Iris scrambled back to the vault corridor, where she had dropped her bag, and yanked out the file. "See! It says right here 'In God We Trust is the key.' Wait, there's more."

She pulled out another sheet from the file she'd found in the suitcase. "It's a code or something." Iris sat down on the vault floor with the notes and slowly translated.

"What the hell is all of that?" the detective asked, pointing his flashlight at the page of tick marks and bird tracks. "Where did you get those?"

"This stack of notes was in Beatrice's personnel file. I thought it was weird, so I took them. And I found these"—Iris held up the other stack of paper—"in that suitcase up on the eleventh floor. Did you want to see it?"

His face was a stone. "First things first. You can read that?"

"It's shorthand. I found this book, and I've been trying to make sense of it for weeks." She dug out a pencil and wrote in the margins what she deciphered. "'IN DEO SPERAMUS, one hundred at a time.'"

"*In Deo Speramus* means 'In God We Trust,'" the detective confirmed softly.

"What's the first box number?"

He walked deeper into the vault, searching both sides until he found the smallest number. "001," he said, walking back to her. He paused and added, "The last number is 1299."

"Okay, there are thirteen hundred boxes. If there was a key for each hundred of them, there should be thirteen keys, but there are only twelve." Iris lay the keys on the ground and shined her light on them again. She arranged them until they read "I, N, D, E_1, O, S_1, P, E_2, R, A, M, U." Iris trained her light back to where she'd found the keys hanging from a lock. The key still stuck there was labeled "S_2." That was the thirteenth key. The man in the blue shirt must have forced it into the wrong lock. It was stuck.

"So, then, which one do we think goes to Box 547?"

"If I is 000, N is 100, then D, E_1, O . . ." She spun the key ring, counting. "S_1 must be 500, right?"

"Your guess is a hell of a lot better than mine." The detective picked the keys out of her hand. "There's only one way to find out."

He stood up and slid the S_1 key into the lock. He winced ever so slightly and gave it a gentle turn. The key rotated freely. Iris slid Suzanne's key into the other hole, turned it, and the door swung open. Iris couldn't help jumping up and down a little. They had done it.

"I guess they don't let dummies into engineering school, huh?" He grinned.

Iris smiled back triumphantly. She had finally done something right. It was all going to work out now. Somehow.

Detective McDonnell reached in and pulled out a long, silver box. It looked like a miniature coffin to Iris. He carried it carefully to the counter outside the vault. The detective lifted the lid, and they both peered inside.

CHAPTER 70

Thursday, December 14, 1978

A scream tore out of her throat. Beatrice recoiled from the thin fingers she'd felt in the blackness of the tunnel. She lurched backward, right into the body connected to the hand. It was moving.

Beatrice leapt up to run and cracked her skull soundly on a steam pipe. Camera flashbulbs exploded in her head with pain, and she fell to her knees. She let out a sharp cry and doubled over. A flashlight clicked on, flooding the tunnel like a firebomb. Beatrice sucked in a scream and blindly scrambled through the muck away from whoever held the light.

"Beatrice?" a familiar voice croaked behind her. "Is that you? How? How did you . . . ?"

"Max?" Beatrice squinted at the light.

The body lying in a heap on the floor was Max. She looked like she'd been beaten with a lead pipe. Her eye was swollen shut, and half her face seemed crushed in blood.

"Oh my God! Max! What happened?" she gasped, and rushed back to her side.

Beatrice lifted her friend's head off of the filthy concrete floor and held it in her hands. She searched the dirty water pooled around them for anything to stop the bleeding.

"They found me." She coughed. Her lungs rattled with blood.

"Who found you? What happened?"

She just shook her head and smiled. One of her teeth had been knocked out. Beatrice's stomach revolted at the sight. "They were too late. I think . . . I think I got 'em."

As Beatrice's eyes adjusted to the light, she registered the full damage. "We have to get you to a hospital."

Max shook her head. "They'd find me."

"How did you even get down here?" Beatrice asked helplessly. She wouldn't be able to carry her friend out of the tunnel on her back. She wasn't strong enough.

"I got away through the air shaft . . . They were arguing."

"What air shaft? What are you talking about?"

"In the building. I'd been using the air shaft to move around. The grates are loose." She coughed again.

"I've got to go for help. I'll find Ramone or your brother."

"No! . . . No, don't drag them into this. They'd go and get themselves killed. I'll be fine. I don't think much is broken." She struggled to sit and propped herself against the tunnel wall.

"Max, you don't look fine. I need to go get help. You look like you might die or something!"

"Stay out of it, Beatrice. You should just leave. Leave town and forget all of this, okay?"

"Stay out of it? And how am I supposed to do that exactly? I have no clothes, no money . . . You sent me to the Lancer, and I nearly got attacked. If you wanted me to stay out of it, why did you give me this . . . this stupid key?" She wrestled the key out of her purse and brandished it at her.

"Oh thank God you still have it!" Max gasped. "I couldn't risk having it on me. Whatever you do, you can't let them get it. It would ruin everything."

Beatrice slammed it into Max's raw hand. "I don't want it. All I wanted was a job. A normal life. I don't want any part of this—stolen jewelry, missing money, or whatever the hell this is. I'm done! It's none of my business anyway!"

"Isn't it, though?"

"Excuse me?" Beatrice shouted.

"There's a box in your name too." Max flashed a broken grin.

"What?" Beatrice shrieked. "Bill doesn't even know my name!"

"It was opened sixteen years ago. Box 256. You didn't know?"

Beatrice collapsed against the wall next to Max and shook her head. Box 256. What had Doris done?

"Don't worry. I got the keys. I think these are the last ones." Max winced as she pulled handfuls of keys out of her pockets.

There was blood drying on Max's bare legs. Beatrice shuddered. "More keys? How did you . . . ?"

Max coughed. "I have friends."

"Ramone."

"Yeah, Ramone, Ricky, Jamal. Half those guards are from the old neighborhood; the other half are ex-cops. Some even worked with my dad."

"Bill was right? You were sneaking around, stealing things?"

"You're one to talk." Max spat blood onto the ground. "I wasn't the one living there."

"I . . . I had nowhere else to go. Someone broke in . . ."

"I know. I saw what they did. But they didn't find a thing, and they're never going to find these," Max mumbled, and jingled the keys in her hand. Her eyes fell shut.

"Max? Max!" Beatrice jostled her shoulder.

"Hmm?" She didn't open her eyes.

"What's wrong with you? Is this some sort of game? You need a doctor! You're bleeding! How can you just sit there and smile?" Beatrice snatched the keys from Max and threw them down the tunnel.

The sound of the keys hitting wet concrete roused Max back to life. She blinked her swollen eyes back open. "You have no idea what any of this is about, do you? Don't be so naïve, Beatrice! It's about money. Little slips of paper that decide who starves and who doesn't. Who has a roof over their head and who doesn't. Who gets to sleep in a cushy bed and who has to sleep with some filthy old man to survive. It's who owns what and who owns who and who holds the keys to all of it. Well, I got the fucking keys, and they're not getting them back!" Tears were making tracks through the blood on Max's face.

"The keys to all of what?" Beatrice shouted. "Diamond necklaces? Other people's jewelry? Is that what you want?"

"I think you have me confused with your aunt." Max shot her an accusing look.

Beatrice shut her mouth and looked away.

"I want Bill and Teddy and Jim and those bastards to pay for what they did to all those people," Max hissed. "Taking their homes, ruining neighborhoods, tearing down this city to line their pockets. I want to expose them for the crooks that they are."

"How are you going to do that exactly? Stealing keys won't do that. Locks can be changed."

"Ha! They can't change safe deposit locks without informing the customers. There are over seven hundred active accounts that will have to be notified. Seven hundred of the city's wealthiest people will have to be told that the bank somehow lost the keys to their most precious possessions."

Max closed her eyes and smiled. "They're ruined. The bank is finished."

Beatrice frowned. "What about Bill? He has everyone convinced you're to blame for the robberies. For all of it."

"And you believe him?"

"Of course not! I just . . . I don't know what to believe anymore."

"Me neither. I thought you were my friend. Then I'm looking through the files two nights ago, and I find out you have this box. Tell me you knew nothing about it. Tell me you're not going to go running to Bill right now." Saying the words seemed to make her believe it might happen, and Max began crawling after the keys.

"I hate Bill," Beatrice shrieked after her. "I hate Doris too for what she did. But she's . . . she's the only one I had, and she helped me. But it's not right. None of this is right."

"What do you know about right, huh? What, are you some sort of angel, Beatrice? You fly up from the shit hills to save us all?" Max shouted down the tunnel. "You and I aren't so different, are we, Bea? Why did you leave home, huh? Why is your address a diner and your social security number stolen? Who the hell are you to tell me what's right?"

Beatrice sat stricken in the dim glow of the flashlight. She smeared tears with her hand and finally managed, "You gave me the key, and I kept it safe. I could have given it to Bill days ago. What more do you want from me?"

"I want the truth. If you're not helping dear old Doris rob the vault, what the hell are you doing here? Why did you steal my keys? Huh?"

"Your keys?" Beatrice pressed her back to the tunnel wall. She had taken over thirty keys right out of Max's hiding place. "I'm sorry. I was just trying to find the one you took from my aunt."

"Why's it so important to you? Huh? What are you doing down here in a tunnel in the middle of the night?" Max pointed the flashlight into Beatrice's eyes.

"I . . . It was cold. I had to get someplace warm."

"Bullshit. You're honestly telling me you don't have anywhere else to go?" Max motioned to the puddle they were both sitting in.

"No, I don't." There was no point in holding back the tears now. Beatrice let them pour down her face. "I'm . . . I'm only sixteen. I ran away from home, and then Doris got sick and now . . . I can't go back."

Max lowered the flashlight and crawled back to her side. "Why did you leave home, Beatrice?"

"There was this man. He was living with my mother . . . and he used to . . ." Beatrice couldn't utter the words, and she buried her face in her hands. "I got pregnant, and he made me go and . . . lose it."

Max wrapped an arm around her. "Hey, it's okay. It's okay, sweetie. I had no idea. I'm sorry."

"No, it's not okay . . . I'm not okay . . . I'll never be able to get married or have a . . ." She was crying too hard to say "family."

Beatrice hadn't spoken of it to anyone, not even her aunt. For all of her faults, Doris had taken her in without asking questions, despite the fact that they had never met. The only way Beatrice even knew how to find the woman was from the return address on the birthday card she'd received that year. Doris had always sent her a card on her birthday.

Beatrice shook with sobs.

"We're more alike than I thought." Max kissed the top of her head.

Beatrice struggled to regain her composure. She couldn't bring herself to look Max in the eye.

"I lost a baby too." Max wiped blood from her chin.

"Tony told me. I'm so sorry, Max."

"Tony." Max shook her head, then cleared her throat. "I had nowhere to go. I slept under bridges and in bus stops. And then I met this guy. At first I thought I was getting a real leg up. He got me off the street. He gave me a job. I could go home and face my parents. He even talked about helping me get my daughter back. Just a few nights at the hotel, a few nights in the office, a few nights with his buddy. It was never enough. After a while, he stopped talking to me about Mary. Eventually he stopped talking to me at all. After a couple years, he even stopped sleeping with me."

"Bill?"

"No, Teddy Halloran." Max grimaced with pain and stifled a cough. "I met him back when I was hustling. He was always at the Theatrical Grille. I thought he was a gangster at first. All those Covelli boys would come out to hear the music and meet the girls. He seemed to know everybody. Then he told me he worked at this big, fancy bank. He took me to his big, fancy house. God, he was a sick bastard. But he got me the job."

Beatrice stared at the far wall. Max had been a prostitute. That's what she had done when she ran away from home. That's why that strange woman in gold lamé knew her.

"After Teddy was through with me a few years ago, I took Bill out for a drink. I thought with his money and connections he could help me with Mary, that sleazy son of bitch. It was just more of the same. I hired lawyers. I spent all my money." Max wiped a bloody tear angrily.

"I thought Mary was adopted," Beatrice whispered.

"That's what they said. But I didn't believe it. After six years I found her down at St. Vincent's. The birth records were sealed, and the legal fees were a mile high. With my record and now all of this mess, it's going to take a fortune to get her back."

They sat in silence with their backs against the brick wall. The only sound was the dripping of water somewhere down the tunnel. It was like the ticking of a clock. They were running out of time. They were both in a world of trouble. Max had taken the keys. The boxes would stay shut unless there was a warrant to drill them open—that's what Tony had told her. Without Doris's journal, no one would be able to sort out what had happened or which boxes contained what anyway. It would be all right, Beatrice tried to tell herself. But she didn't believe it. Bill still had his files incriminating Max, Doris, and a number of other women. There were still safe deposit boxes rented in their names.

"What's the blank key for?" Beatrice finally asked, already knowing the answer.

"It's the master. It opens every box in the vault."

"Where did you find it?"

"Where do you think?" Max turned a black eye toward Beatrice.

"It was in Doris's box, wasn't it?" Beatrice didn't have to have Max confirm it. Doris was the inside man. The blank key was how she had opened the boxes of strangers. "Did you go to the FBI?"

"Yeah, I tried. I even brought them a solid-gold brick to prove Teddy was up to something big. They wouldn't listen. They held me for twenty-four hours instead, as if I were the thief, then they kept the gold. Just figures, doesn't it? You can't even trust the goddamned FBI."

Beatrice knew no one would believe her either. "Why did you give me the key? That night? Why did you give it to me?"

"I knew you'd help me. You're my friend. Besides, no one would ever suspect you had anything to do with this mess. You're practically invisible in that office—a ghost. People always underestimate women like us."

The files in Bill's office still hung in her mind. "Max, are you sure they won't still be able to trace the boxes back to any of Bill's girlfriends? Or you? Or me?"

Max looked down at the keys she had picked back up from the tunnel floor. "I'm sure they'll pin it on me, but it doesn't matter. Not really. It'll break my mom's heart, and Tony . . . poor Tony."

Beatrice reached down and grabbed her friend's hand. There had to be a way to get her out of there.

"I have to find a way to get Mary and just disappear. They'll never stop looking for me, not after what I've done. Not after what I've seen. Teddy was going to kill me tonight."

Looking at Max's battered body, Beatrice was seeing her own future. The odds of her landing a job and finding a place to live at her age were slim. The police would send her back home. She pictured herself turning to petty theft or prostitution, just like Max. There was no hope for a girl like her, or Max, or maybe Doris even.

The meek shall inherit the earth, Beatrice thought to herself. Another tear fell down her cheek, and she wiped it away. Maybe someday, but she couldn't afford to wait. She would not be meek. Not ever again.

"We have to get whatever is in your box and mine out. It's not enough that the keys are gone. They could make up some story about modernizing the vault and issue new keys," Beatrice thought out loud.

She wasn't going to let Teddy or Bill blame Max or anyone else for what they'd been doing. There had to be a way to make sure. Then something that Ms. Cunningham had said came back to her. "'A bank is only as good as its records.' That's it!" Her voice echoed down the tunnel. "If they lost the safe deposit records, the investors would be furious. The bank would be ruined."

Beatrice reached into her pocket and pulled out the three-karat diamond ring Doris had stolen. She couldn't bring herself to drop it in the collection box back at the church. It was her last hope of getting out and starting over.

"In case I don't make it back here, take this. I hope it helps you get Mary out, I really do." She put the ring in Max's swollen hand. "Now you need tell me how to open the boxes, Max. Give me the keys."

CHAPTER 71

Beatrice tiptoed across the red carpet in the lower lobby toward the vault. Her eyes scanned the security station. The monitors were off. No one was watching, not tonight. She clutched the large handbag on her shoulder and the heavy key ring in her fist. The keys were tinged with Max's blood; they'd left angry red marks on her hand. Beatrice almost lost her nerve.

Voices were coming from the vault corridor. She froze in her tracks.

"I don't give a fuck, Teddy!" one man bellowed. "She got away."

The voices were getting louder. Beatrice spun and scurried silently across the carpet away from the sound.

"We'll find her. She couldn't have gone far. Just stay focused, all right?"

Beatrice brushed past a red velvet curtain. The voices moved into the lower lobby as she ducked behind it into a booth.

"Do you have any idea the mess you've gotten us into? City hall is already breathing down my neck, and the feds are petitioning for warrants. As of three hours ago, the city is bankrupt, and we're public enemy number one. We need to get the deposits out now before the morning papers hit the street!"

"Let's not be hasty."

Beatrice shrank into the folds of the curtain and took only the shallowest of breaths as she listened.

"I'm done playing around, Teddy. Give me the keys."

"Don't be absurd! I don't have them."

"What do you mean, you don't have them?"

"What do you think, I walk around with them in my pockets? What do you take me for?"

"I don't care if you keep them up your ass. We need to move the money tonight. We're under investigation, for crying out loud! The vault is going to be on lockdown. What are we supposed to tell the investors? That we've come up with a new ingenious holding strategy? That's not going to fly. Where is the master key?"

"These transfers haven't been authorized."

"You're out of the loop, Ted. The board wants out."

"Out? Out to where? Where are they going to go? Where else are they going to keep their assets secure and tax-free? Their mattresses?"

"It no longer concerns you."

"Like hell it doesn't! You won't even be able to sort the accounts without me. You really think I just deposited tens of millions in Mr. Wackerly's name or yours or mine, where any cop with a warrant might find it? The deposits have been dispersed."

"You mean, you put them under false names? Do you really think that's going to throw the feds for a loop? A bunch of fake names?"

"Who said the names were fake?"

"They belong to active customers? Jesus, you have balls, Teddy! What's to stop the dummies from making withdrawals, huh? One old lady wants to come admire her coin collection and we're fucked!"

"Keep your skirt on! Most of 'em are dead or don't even know they have a box. That meathead Thompson's been feeding me dead boxes for years. It's part of our little arrangement for me ignoring his indiscretions."

"Indiscretions? Is that what you call homicide these days?"

"Don't you read the papers? That was a hit-and-run, and it was four goddamned years ago. Water under the bridge."

Beatrice's eyes widened. Homicide. Rhonda Whitmore was murdered.

There was a loud sigh. "This whole scheme is just like you, Teddy—too risky. You said it would be easy. You sold the finest families in town on a legitimate, high-yield investment. Sure, they turned a blind eye to the fact it was too good to be true, to be legal, but do you really think they're going to let you drag them through the mud now? The money's not worth the risk."

"What money comes without a little risk? It's a dirty business, Jim!"

"Well, it's simply gotten too dirty. Now that bimbo of yours Maxine is causing trouble. Your drunk son was caught red-handed in the vault just last week. The money isn't secure."

"Leave Randy out of this. I'll handle him."

"Like you handled the investments?"

"We needed to protect our interests, damn it! When the feds moved in, we had to start making adjustments."

"Who authorized those adjustments?"

"When the gold market opened up, we had to get in. Nixon fucked us all when he started printing money, and you know it. Our cash assets would have dwindled down to kindling with this inflation. We had to get in commodities." Teddy's voice was growing louder and more erratic.

"You really thought you could start stockpiling gold and no one would notice?" Jim asked. "My sources downtown tell me the feds still have someone embedded at the bank."

"They'll never make a case! This thing is so tight, they can't even pull a warrant."

"They're watching Bill. He's going to cut a deal."

"Bill can be dealt with," Teddy said dismissively.

"What, you think the river's got room for one more? You should be the one worrying about that, Ted. I'm losing my patience here. Now you're going to give me the keys I need."

"Or what are you going to do? Beat me to death with your fountain pen? I'm telling you, I don't have them."

"If you don't have them, who does?"

Beatrice swallowed hard, not twenty feet away.

"Yes, please tell us, Teddy. Who has them?" It was a different voice now. It was strangely familiar.

"Carmichael, what took you so long?"

Beatrice sucked in a breath. She recognized the voice from the Theatrical Grille. It was the friendly bartender with a soft spot for Max. She peeked through the curtain in disbelief.

"Don't tell me you dragged the Covellis into this, Jim. We have it under control." Teddy laughed uncomfortably.

Tony had said the Covellis were still connected to Sicily. Max had called them gangsters. Carmichael was a member of the Mob, Beatrice realized, and covered a gasp with her hand.

"They hold one of the largest interests in the bank, Teddy, and you know it," Jim said with a sigh. "You're in over your head. We know you've been talking to the feds. I suggest you cooperate."

Carmichael drew out a gun. Beatrice heard an iron click as he cocked it at Teddy.

"Hey, take it easy, Carmichael! Jim, we've been friends for twenty years. You can't be serious! The transfer records are encoded. You wouldn't know where to begin without me!"

"It's out of my hands now. If you cooperate, I'll do my best to protect your family."

"Instead of wasting your time with me," Teddy shouted, "we need to be tracking down that bitch!"

"What does she matter now?"

"She's the only one left that knows how to work the damn keys for one thing. There's some sort of system to it."

"And whose fault is that exactly?" Jim demanded. "That desk clerk, Sherry or whatever her name was, would have cooperated if your drunk son hadn't decided to take matters into his own hands."

"You can't prove Randy had anything to do with that," Teddy protested. "Shirley might have just left town. She might be back to work on Monday."

Beatrice's stomach dropped to her feet. Shirley, the safe deposits clerk and Doris's friend, was missing or dead. Randy might have killed her. She stepped back from the curtain and sank to her knees.

"Let me see if I got this straight. Are you telling me you stashed over fifty million dollars in that vault, and you don't even know how to open it?" Carmichael chuckled. "You fuckin' bankers. Never want to do nothin' yourself. Did it ever occur to you the help might get wise?"

"That's enough, Carmichael," Jim said, and put his hand up toward the bartender. "If some secretary can figure it out, we'll manage. What else can you tell us, Teddy?"

"If I talk, what's to stop you from pulling that trigger, huh? I want to speak to Alistair."

"Who do you think sent us?" Jim sighed. "Carmichael, will you please?"

There was a muffled yell and several thumping sounds. Then nothing.

Beatrice stayed crouched behind the curtain, staring into the dark. The bankers were hiding gold in the safe deposit vault for the richest families in town. Teddy said Bill had been feeding him dead boxes for years. Boxes Doris and Bill had raided, no doubt.

After Rhonda Whitmore's name showed up in Doris's journal, the withdrawals became more frequent. Bill had looked like he'd seen a ghost the day Rhonda showed up at the bank—that's what Max had said. He was finally caught in the act, but instead of handing him and Doris over to the authorities, Teddy saw an opportunity.

The bizarre codes on the pages she'd sorted for Randy suddenly made sense. They must have been the files that kept track of where the bank had stashed millions of dollars. Jim wanted the money out, and so did the Covellis. The Mob was somehow involved with the bank's dealings, and Carmichael worked for them. Being a bartender was just a facade. Beatrice hadn't known him at all. But Tony and Max had known him, she realized. Tony was a police detective; he was the one who told her about the Covellis in the first place. He must have known. Every word Carmichael might have overheard at the bar replayed in her mind—her conversations with Tony about snooping around the bank, the missing safe deposits, the missing master key. Maybe Tony had wanted Carmichael to hear. The old man pointed the gun at Teddy in her head. Maybe the Covellis would bring down the bank if law enforcement failed.

No one, not even Tony, suspected that she and Max had the power to do anything but run. Max was right. They all underestimated women like them.

Beatrice stepped out from behind the curtain with the keys in her hand and crept toward the vault.

CHAPTER 72

Friday, August 28, 1998

A black-and-white photograph of two women looked up from Box 547 in the yellow glow of the detective's flashlight. They were smiling. The glass in the silver picture frame was cracked. Iris picked it up and handed it to Detective McDonnell. Underneath it she found a brown leather book and a candle. That was it.

"What the hell is this?" Iris said out loud.

She couldn't believe Beatrice had called Suzanne Peplinski in 1978 over a photograph. She couldn't believe she'd just broken into the bank for one. It wouldn't solve any of her problems.

"What's in the book?" the detective whispered, placing the photograph back in the box.

Iris flipped it open. It was filled with numbers. She flipped and flipped but found nothing but more numbers in blue and black ink, until something red caught her eye.

"Who is Rhonda Whitmore?" She tilted the page toward the detective.

"You've got to be kidding me! She was the woman Max claimed was murdered in 1974." He grabbed the book and began thumbing through the pages. "All these numbers read like transactions."

"Transactions?" Iris picked up the candle. It was just a cheap red votive that had never been burned.

"I think this may be a record of the deposit box robberies. See here, this must be Rhonda's box number, 855, and here's what was inside—fifty thousand dollars." The detective pointed to the line he was reading, but Iris was hardly paying attention.

A piece of paper had fallen from the bottom of the votive. She picked it up and read aloud, "May the souls of the faithful departed, through the mercy of God, rest in peace. Amen."

The detective looked up from the book and shined the flashlight at Iris. "What?"

"It was on the bottom of the candle." She handed him the little piece of paper.

He studied it, then turned it over. "It's from the Church of the Savior in Little Italy."

"I don't get it."

"It's a prayer candle. My church has them too. You light them for someone that died or needs a prayer."

"But why would someone put it in this box?"

"That's a damn good question," a deep voice said from behind them.

Detective McDonnell spun around, reaching inside his coat. A loud blast fired next to Iris's ear, and the detective's flashlight went flying through the air. It smashed onto the floor. The light flickered and then went out.

Iris could smell smoke. She heard a thump as something heavy hit the ground next to her. Her ears were ringing. Her mind went blank. She felt herself begin to fall.

"Oh, no you don't," the voice said, catching Iris and tilting her back upright.

Without the detective's flashlight, it was too dark to see who was talking. Iris didn't want to see anything. All she could hear was her heart pumping blood in and out of her throbbing ears. Her lungs refused to breathe. The world swam out of focus.

The overhead lights switched on abruptly, making her blink. The red candle was still sitting in the deposit box. She kept her eyes on it, refusing to acknowledge the man behind her, until he touched her shoulder. She jerked away, but her foot bumped into something big and still on the ground. It was Detective McDonnell. She felt her stomach heave and vomited into the open box.

The man behind her chuckled. It sounded muted and far away.

"Well, that's fitting, isn't it? That's exactly how I feel about the whole thing."

The calm laughter made her heave again. The voice wasn't completely unfamiliar.

"Turn around, Iris," he commanded.

The sound of her name made the ringing in her ears go quiet. She shook her head. She didn't want to see his face.

"Turn around!" he barked.

A large hand grabbed her shoulder and twisted her until she could see the gunman. She couldn't make out his face, just features. A jutting jaw, hard eyes, and glistening teeth pulsed in and out of focus.

"Sorry to make such a dramatic entrance, but he was reaching for his gun. I really had no choice. It was self-defense. You'll back me up on that, won't you?" He pressed his gun between her eyes. The barrel was still hot.

Iris stopped breathing and nodded.

"You don't have any idea who I am, do you?"

She shook her head, although she was now certain she'd seen him before.

"Well, I know you, Iris. I know all about you—your late mornings, your drinking, your boredom. I've been watching you from my desk for months. Still nothing?" He chuckled again. "My office is three doors down from Charles Wheeler's. A true professional would know that. But you're not a true professional, are you, Iris? You and your little rebellions, your rifling through file drawers, your sneaking around." He paused and brushed her cheek with the back of his hand.

Iris recoiled but was backed against the counter.

He kept talking. "I was once a lot like you. Stuck in a dead-end life, looking for something better. Looking for a way out. Well, you certainly found one, didn't you?"

She had to say something if only to make him stop touching her. "Ha . . . have you been following me?" she whispered, not daring to look in his eyes.

"I'm not the only one. You've managed to piss off a lot of people, Iris. Nobody wanted that dead bastard to ever see the light of day."

"You knew h-him?"

"You could say that, but the last time I saw Bill he didn't look so . . . chewed up." He grinned at her viciously, and her stomach lurched.

"What do you want?" she whimpered.

"What does any man want?" he demanded. "I'm guessing you haven't the first clue. You probably think it's money, right?"

She stared into the vault behind him, too scared to speak.

"Wrong, Iris! Wrong!" He slammed his hand on the counter and made the metal box jump.

Iris felt it like a slap.

"Money is just a means to an end. I want something far more valuable than money. Respect. I've always wanted respect. And after all these years, I'm finally taking it. I recommend you try it sometime. Getting laid off was no picnic, right?"

Iris shook her head, watching the gun.

"Well, here's your big chance to stick it to old Wheeler but good. Chuck'll just love it. Twenty years working across the street from his retirement fund, and then in the blink of an eye it's gone." He waved the gun to the side for emphasis, then swung it back into her face.

She held up her hands reflexively. She recognized him now. He was the creepy gray-haired guy who'd winked at her getting fired earlier that day. He'd stopped her in the hall a few weeks back when she was running late. Something about the odd look in his eye had made her uncomfortable. With the gun in his hand, it was suddenly clear. He was crazy.

"Who . . . who are you?"

"Me? Oh, I'm nobody now. Chief financial officer of some third-rate architectural firm. That's where they stuck me to keep me quiet. You don't even know my name." He sighed. "I used to be somebody. I was practically royalty in this pathetic town. Then it all came crashing down. It all came crashing down because of two little sluts just like you sneaking around, stealing keys. We lost everything! My father was too busy screwing his brains out to keep his eyes on the prize. He trusted the family business to a bumbling idiot like Bill Thompson. But not to me! Some two-bit waitress was good enough to work the vault, to handle millions of dollars, but not me!"

The smell of sour whiskey burned her nose as he yelled in her face. She grimaced.

He stopped and grinned. "What, have I offended you? You don't think you're a slut? Ha! I've seen what you do with your little friend."

He'd seen her with Nick. His teeth glinted in the fluorescent light. They were coffee stained around the edges. Seeing her shudder seemed to please him.

"'Oh God, Nick! Oh, God! Oh God!'" he called out, mimicking her voice. "You know, you really should try to play a little hard to get, Iris."

Her whole body trembled as the blood drained down to her feet. The room began to sway, and she gripped the counter. "It was you. You were following me."

"Come on, Iris, certainly you of all people know how dull work can be." He winked at her. "Besides, little valedictorian, something about the pathetic, bored look in your eye every morning you scuttled in late for work told me you were just desperate enough to go poking around this dump. And I was right. Mr. Wheeler thought you'd just keep your head down and do what you were told, like a good little engineer. That would have been smarter, Iris, admit it."

Iris felt herself nod, while she tried to focus on anything but screaming. Maybe this man was the one who told everyone at the office about her sleeping around. Maybe Nick had nothing to do with it. Her mind scrambled for something to say.

"It was you in the vault that day. Why did you leave the keys?" she asked.

"Leave the keys? Do you really think I'm that stupid? Do you?" He pressed the barrel of the gun into her chest.

"No," she whimpered.

"You just got lucky. And now you probably think you're clever because you cracked the code, right? Don't think for a minute that I couldn't have figured it out. He couldn't have, but I could, damn it."

His finger seemed to twitch on the trigger. She had to keep him talking. "He? Who? You . . . your father? Who was he?"

"Vice president of Who the Fuck Cares? He's dead. They killed him." The man stopped and picked up the brown leather book Detective McDonnell had been holding. Iris's eyes followed the gun down and caught a glimpse of the blood pooled on the floor. She sucked in a sob and shut her eyes. *God help me.*

"You know, he thought he was so smart. King of the board-room! Guess he didn't realize that when he lost the keys to all that money, his golfing buddies weren't going to take it so well." He pointed the gun toward the vault. "Get in there."

Iris obeyed and scrambled away from the blood. He followed her in.

"You know, they called it a suicide, but how many suicides go to the trouble of breaking all of their own fingers before blowing their brains out, I ask you? They needed a scapegoat, someone to feed to the feds . . . They froze our assets. They auctioned off our estate. They left me with nothing and stuck me in a two-bit firm under Wheeler's thumb. They all counted me out, the bumbling son, but they had no idea who they were dealing with."

He was growing more and more agitated as he talked, and Iris inched her way to the back of the vault. He stepped even closer. "Every filthy dollar they stashed in this place, I heard about it. Bill couldn't keep track of the paperwork between banging secretaries. I read the files. I was getting the old man right where I wanted him, and then those two bitches came along."

"Who?" Iris breathed.

"Shut up." He pointed the gun in her face and backed her against the far wall. "Nosy bitches like you are always asking ques-tions you shouldn't and taking things you shouldn't."

He slapped her hard across the face. The force knocked her into the side wall in a white flash of pain.

"You came along and found Bill's chewed-up corpse. That nearly ruined everything. The feds almost blew the doors off this place, but Dad's old friends weren't going to let that happen. As it turns out, you did me a favor, didn't you?"

He stormed out of the vault and back to the detective's still body. He rolled him over with his foot. The detective's eyes stared upward lifelessly. Iris sank to her knees with a sob. He was really dead. There was no saving her now. The loud clank of a gun, a flashlight, a pair of handcuffs, and a key being slapped onto the counter echoed down the metal vault where she was trapped.

"I'm finally going to make one of you cunts useful." He threw the dead key at her head. It hit her in the neck and clinked to the ground. "Get to work."

CHAPTER 73

For the next hour, the man barked box numbers from the little brown book that had been hidden in Box 547, and Iris opened doors at gunpoint. The first box she pulled out sent her crashing to the ground with one hundred pounds on her chest. The gunman leapt into the vault and yanked it off of her. He threw back the lid and laughed softly. Four gleaming gold bricks lay inside it.

He picked one up and kissed it. "Here's to commodity trading, Dad."

Giddy, he carried it out and crossed the corridor to the other vault door. "Do you have any idea what a Good Delivery bar is worth these days?"

Iris stared dumbly as he pulled a huge metal cart over from across the hall. There were three large filing cabinets stacked on its flatbed. *Run,* a voice in her head screamed. But by the time she'd managed to get back to her feet, the cart was blocking the vault entrance.

"Every single one of these babies can fetch over a hundred seventeen thousand dollars if you can move them."

He motioned for her to bring the other bricks over. They each weighed over twenty pounds. She carried them one at a time and deposited them into a file drawer, not saying a word.

"I see you thinking over there, Iris. You want to know why they didn't just drill the boxes open years ago. Why did they let it sit through the gold boom of the '80s, right?" He pointed the gun at her. "Right?"

She stiffened and nodded obediently.

"Why don't piranhas just devour each other in a fish tank? Huh? They're cannibals too. The answer, you twit, is politics." He grinned, pleased with himself. "The records were scrambled. If any of the families touched a drill, the others would have eaten them alive. It was a twenty-year détente. They've been waiting for each other to die. I wish I could be there to see their faces when they realize that they've been had."

Her arms went slack as he talked. She only comprehended a fraction of what he said.

Then he pointed the gun at her again. "Box 357."

The stack of gold bricks grew four at a time as she opened the doors. He seemed to enjoy watching one hundred pounds of gold fall on her. After the third box nearly broke her foot, he was howling. Iris started yanking the boxes out and dodging them as they banged to the floor as loud as gunshots, making her flinch. A few boxes were filled with cash and jewels, but most were filled with the god-awful weight of gold. Her arms grew rubbery from lifting the bars up from their containers and walking them to her captor.

The man grabbed her field bag from the corner and dumped its contents out. Her tape measure and clipboard crashed to the marble, along with Beatrice's notes. He didn't give any of it a second glance, and ordered her to dump the cash and jewelry inside the bag.

The ninth box was empty except for another red votive candle. He motioned for her to hand it over. She cringed when his hand brushed hers.

"'Though I walk through the valley of the shadow of death, I will fear no evil,'" he read, and then smirked. "That's good advice for you, Iris. Now where were we . . . ? 885."

Iris lost track of how much money, how many diamonds, and how much gold went through her hands. Her eyes wandered down the endless row of doors. There was no way that they could open them all before someone found them there, but that wasn't the plan. The man called another number from the book. He was only checking boxes listed in the ledger.

To keep her mind from cracking, she did the numbers in her head. If each gold brick was worth $117,000, how many bricks would it take to make a million? She could barely keep track of the keys as the gun traced her steps, but she forced her brain to keep churning.

After opening two more boxes of gold brick, she'd figured it out. It would take about eight and a half bricks to make a million dollars. There were at least forty bricks stacked inside the filing cabinets already, but the detective had said over $50 million had gone missing. That was over four hundred bricks. It could be even more. She had no idea what the price of gold was back in the 1970s.

"How? How are you going to get these out of here?" she asked, rubbing her aching arms. The cart would weigh a ton.

"Always the engineer, huh, Iris? Don't worry, the truck won't be here for at least an hour. But we'd better get moving if we're going to get these files packed up." He grinned at her.

That was how he would escape detection, she realized. Hiding the gold in file cabinets and hauling them away in another black truck. He had ordered her to lock each box back up once it was emptied. No one would know they'd even been there.

When he called Box 256, the case clipped her shoulder as she yanked it to the ground. Iris fell to her shaking knees.

The man chuckled. "Get off your ass and open it!"

Inside was another red candle, along with hundreds of keys. These were the missing keys, she realized, running her hands over them. They weren't lost. Someone had hid them, just as the detective said. A slip of paper fell from the bottom of the votive as she picked it up. It was another prayer.

The man tapped his gun against the wall of the vault until she looked up. "What does it say?"

"'Blessed are the meek, for they shall inherit the earth,'" she whispered.

"Ha! I wouldn't count on it. Anything else in there?"

There were two complete sets of bank keys for the deposit boxes, along with rings and rings of others. Under them she found a yellowed piece of parchment. It was part of a birth certificate. It had been ripped in half. The other half lay facedown underneath. Iris's eyes locked on the name "Beatrice Ma—" typed at the top. *Beatrice?* She risked a second look and saw the birth date was June 12, 1962. It was issued by Cuyahoga County.

"What do you got?" he demanded.

"Nothing. Just some junk."

Beatrice. Seeing the name gave Iris a jolt of adrenaline. It was a message.

"Hey, you're not on break. Box 933!" he barked.

Iris pulled herself back to her feet, her mind racing. "The meek shall inherit the earth" had been scrawled in Beatrice's file. Beatrice must have put it there. She had left the red candle. Beatrice had been in the vault. It was her birth certificate in Box 256. She had locked away all those keys in the same box. She had left Key 547 in Suzanne's desk. Beatrice called Suzanne to tell her about the box. Beatrice wanted it to be found.

"Beatrice," she whispered.

"What did you say?" the man demanded.

"N-nothing. I was just . . . praying."

"This isn't fucking church! We have a job to do, Miss Latch! Now get back to work." He threw a red candle at her.

It hit her hard in the arm, but Iris hardly noticed. Beatrice was the reason the vault had stayed locked. She had hid the keys. Somehow a lowly secretary had beaten the most powerful men in town. Beatrice had brought down the bank.

Iris dumped the pieces of birth certificate and the keys into the trash can he'd thrown next to her, unable to tear her eyes from the yellow paper. Beatrice was born in 1962. The petite clothes in the lost suitcase flashed in her mind. Beatrice had only been sixteen when she disappeared. Or was killed.

Killed. The thought snapped Iris out of her trance. When the filing cabinets on the cart blocking the entrance were full of gold, she would be killed. Just like the detective. The thought hit her like a bullet.

"Goddammit, Iris! We're on a schedule. Box 933."

No, thought Iris. She slid Box 256 back and closed its door. Her jaw tightened as she staggered to the next lock. She wouldn't just let it happen. She stole a glance at him as he impatiently tapped his foot. He might have killed Beatrice.

Then she saw it. A key was still stuck in a hole six doors down. Detective McDonnell had said the pins might be set to break if the wrong key was forced in. That must have happened when the man in the blue shirt lost his keys. It had been him, she realized, looking at the gunman. He was that stupid.

She clicked past the correct key for Box 933 and grabbed a different one. She slid it into the lock and heard something tiny snap. Then the cylinder wouldn't budge. She rattled and wrenched it until she was sure the key was bent and then banged on the door.

"Damn it!"

"What? What's wrong?"

"It's stuck!" She wiggled and bent it some more. She gave it a gentle tug and bit the inside of her lip as her pulse quickened.

"*Un*stick it!" he yelled.

"I can't!" she yelled back, and made a show of trying.

"Goddammit! I do not have time for this shit!" He slammed the gun onto the counter and shoved the cart of gold out of the way. Iris shrank against the wall of the vault as he pushed past her and yanked at the small piece of metal. As he wrestled with the key ring, she silently slipped out of the vault.

Iris raced through the lower lobby toward the daylight streaming down from behind the elevators. The marble staircase emerged as she rounded the corner, and she scrambled up the steps two at a time to the main entrance. She could see the street through the glass down the hall and sprinted toward the light.

She only remembered the chains on the doors when it was too late. She crashed into them and pulled at the handles frantically, screaming and banging on the glass, hoping someone might hear. The midday sun glared brightly off cars as they passed in front of the old bank. A man was strolling across Euclid Avenue with a coffee in his hand not forty feet away.

"Help me!" she shrieked, banging on the glass. The man didn't flinch.

"There's nowhere to go, Iris!" the gunman bellowed from the stairs.

She turned and ran through another set of doors.

CHAPTER 74

Thursday, December 14, 1978

Beatrice lowered Box 544 onto the floor of the vault with a soft thunk. It was the box in Max's name, and it contained all the damning evidence against her—diamonds and thousands of dollars in cash. *Money for Mary,* Beatrice thought as she emptied her large handbag to make room. All of the keys Max had stolen, her files, a leather book, a cracked photograph, and three red candles tumbled out onto the bronze floor. She'd taken the candles from the church as a reminder that above all else, she had to do the right thing.

As she stuffed the stolen jewels and money into her bag, her heart filled with doubt. With the box empty, no one would be able to blame Max for the robberies. Max would get her daughter back. But taking the fortune made her a thief, just like Doris. Beatrice picked up a red candle and set it in the box before locking it back in the vault. *Please, God, forgive me if this isn't right.*

She moved on to Box 547. If the police raided the vault, surely they would check Doris's box. Tony knew her aunt was involved in the robberies and had given Key 547 back to Beatrice when they'd met at the diner. He would lead them there. Lifting the lid, she found the same rolls of dollar bills and bags of quarters she'd discovered days earlier. The waitressing tips were her aunt's excuse for going into the vault week after week while her buddy Shirley looked the other way. The money wasn't stolen, and Beatrice would need it to buy a bus ticket out of town. Doris would understand, she told herself. She took the cash and then placed the brown leather book, the written record of all of her aunt's sins, inside the box for the detective to find.

"I'm sorry, Doris," she whispered.

She laid the picture of her aunt and mother smiling into the box. It would be the last time she saw any trace of Doris. Beatrice said a silent prayer and set a candle inside with the photograph, then snapped the door shut.

Box 256 was the one in Beatrice's name. She opened it last, not knowing what might lie inside and not sure she wanted to know. Her heart sank when she saw that the box was filled to the top with stolen jewelry. Beatrice would surely go to prison if Tony or anyone else found it. *Damn it, Doris,* she thought, lifting handful after handful out of the box and into her bag. *How am I ever going to make this right?*

A yellow piece of paper emerged from under the pile. Beatrice picked it up and stopped breathing when she saw the name typed at the top—"Beatrice Marie Davis. Born: June 12, 1962. Mother: Doris Estelle Davis. Father: Unknown."

She sat there stunned as precious minutes ticked by. According to the parchment in her shaking hands, everything she knew about her life was a lie. Ilene wasn't her mother. Her father hadn't run off when she was three. Doris was not her estranged aunt who'd sent her birthday cards but had never bothered to visit. Doris was something worse.

At the bottom of the deposit box lay a picture of a baby. Pink cheeks, blue eyes, and a little yellow bow—a tiny face looked out from the cold, gray metal. *Is this . . . me?* Beatrice had never seen a baby picture of herself—not in Ilene's house, not in Doris's apartment. She picked the photo up and turned it over. "Beatrice" was scrawled on the back along with some other writing that blurred together through her tears. Doris had left the picture in the vault. She'd left her alone.

Hatred for Doris, Bill, and the bank boiled over. Beatrice ripped the birth certificate in half and threw it back into the box. She didn't want any part of Doris Davis. Not her name, nothing. *Better to be locked away forever,* she thought. Her whole life was a mistake. A lie.

There wasn't time for tears. The money men would be back. She gathered all of the vault keys Max had stolen and threw them in on top of the torn paper. The bastards would have to drill every box. She grabbed the last candle off the ground and squeezed it until her palm hurt.

"God help me," she whispered, holding the baby picture to her chest. There was no way to make any of it right. *It doesn't matter anymore,* she thought, and let the candle drop onto the piles of keys. Beatrice Baker was dead. She'd never existed in the first place. She slammed the lid shut and shoved the box back into its hole.

As she pulled two keys from the door to Box 256, she heard footsteps in the corridor. She dropped the last ring of keys into her purse, grabbed her files, and hurried out of the vault.

"Bethany? What are you doing in here?" It was Bill. He stopped her in the doorway.

"Oh! Mr. Thompson!" Beatrice tucked her heavy purse under her arm and quickly wiped her face with her shirt sleeve. She could barely stand to look at him and dropped her eyes to the floor. "You frightened me."

"You shouldn't be in here. Who put you up to this? Randy?" His eyes darted around nervously as if Randy might be there too.

"Um, yes. Mr. Halloran thought I might be able to help with the key problem."

"Key problem?" He narrowed his eyes at her.

"I guess he thought I might . . . be able to interpret Shirley's notes on the key system. I understand that she recently quit."

Beatrice crossed her fingers and prayed her knowledge about Shirley's disappearance would convince him. She motioned to her files so he might not notice her overstuffed handbag. "I . . . I stayed late trying to read her shorthand, but it's really . . . messy."

"But what the hell are you doing in here?" He grabbed her by the arm and dragged her out of the vault and into the corridor.

She struggled to keep talking. "It was foolish really."

"It was. I don't think you have any idea what you've done."

"I . . . I guess I just wanted to try. I didn't want to tell Mr. Halloran I couldn't do it . . . It was silly."

"Silly? Bethany, you have just committed a crime! You're not authorized to be in here. I'll hand you over to the police if you don't give me those keys and tell me everything."

Beatrice let her jaw drop and her eyes bulge fearfully as her mind raced. He didn't even know her name—after everything he'd done to Doris, after everything he'd done to her. The words "Father: Unknown" were still burning in the back of her eyes. She could picture Doris pregnant, getting fired from her job. How the rest of the story fell into place, Beatrice couldn't be sure, but she knew Bill was largely to blame. With his lies and schemes, he'd tricked Doris into doing his dirty work for him.

She squeezed the master key, still hidden in the palm of her hand, and thought about Carmichael and Jim somewhere in the building. Whoever had the key surely had a death warrant on their head. It was worthless without the others, and they were all locked in Box 256—all but the last set in her purse. She gazed into Bill's beady eyes. He didn't even know her name.

With a bewildered frown, she held out the key in her hand. "Keys? All I have is this one. Mr. Halloran said it would open every box in the vault, but as far as I can tell it doesn't do a thing."

Bill's eyes grew wide, and he snatched the key from her hand. "Randy gave this to you?"

Beatrice nodded meekly.

"That son of a bitch," he muttered under his breath. "Bethany, you're coming with me."

He began pulling her through the lower lobby toward the elevators. She glanced at the tunnel door but realized she wouldn't make it. She had to do something.

"Oh, Mr. Thompson, my other file! I really shouldn't leave it." She pulled her arm free and spun back toward the vault, trying to keep her bag from jingling.

"What file?" Mr. Thompson was thrown off balance but quickly recovered and began following her. "Bethany! Get back here."

"It will just take a second," Beatrice called over her shoulder, and began running. She dashed through the dark vault corridor to the service stairs, with Bill lumbering far behind her.

"Bethany! Stop!"

Beatrice raced up the stairs in her stocking feet. The border of the door behind her lit up as the lights in the vault switched on. She burst into the loading dock. Her eyes circled the concrete walls, and the sound of the dock entrance rumbling open sent her sprinting to a blank door five feet away. She closed it behind her and pressed her back to the metal. Her heavy bag swung and hit it with a silvery clank. She was in the emergency stair tower.

The stairwell wound up into the high-rise. She began to run. Her scrambling thoughts searched for an exit as she climbed. In a few hours, workers would file in to the lobby. It would be Friday morning. If she could just hide until dawn, she'd be safe.

The door at the bottom of the stair tower slammed open three flights below her. Beatrice squeaked and hit the wall. She inched up the last three steps to the third-floor entrance. The hinges whined in protest as she cracked the door open and slipped out. The door clicked shut behind her. Her heart fluttered in her chest. She stood frozen, listening. The third floor was silent.

Beatrice turned and fled down the hall, trying doorknobs. They were all locked. She rounded the corner, and panic swelled inside her as she dug through her bag for Max's door keys. She couldn't hide in the hallway, not for long. She turned another corner and finally managed to pull the keys from her purse. The door to the personnel office was straight ahead. The light was out. There were no footsteps or voices. Beatrice fumbled for the right key, glancing down the empty corridor. The correct one slid home, and she slipped inside, locking the door behind her. Out of breath, she crumpled to her knees.

CHAPTER 75

Friday, August 28, 1998

"Goddammit, Iris!" The man's voice echoed from the doorway to the back of the banking room. "I wasn't going to kill you."

His wing-tip shoes thundered down the aisle between teller stalls. Iris silently crawled along the service side of the counter back toward the entrance. His feet clacked all the way to the end of the room, and for a fleeting moment Iris dared hope that they might just keep going out the service exit and give her a chance to escape. But instead they turned. She slipped into a stall and underneath the narrow counter.

"I was going to make a deal an easy bitch like you couldn't resist—fifty grand to go back home to Mom and forget all this. No one would have believed you anyway, Iris—a disgruntled employee, a thief, an alcoholic. But now . . . now I'm going to kill you."

The sound of teller doors being slammed open one after the other thundered off the walls. He was on the service side of the teller booths and was getting closer to where she hid. The door of the stall next to hers slammed open. She was trapped. Pressing her back into the narrow corner, she squeezed her eyes shut.

"That's enough, Randy," a familiar voice commanded from the entrance.

Iris's eyes snapped open. It was Mr. Wheeler.

"Charles! What? What are you doing here?" Randy stopped just outside the booth where Iris hid. She could see the shadow of his wing-tip shoes under the stall door.

"I'd like to ask you the same thing."

Randy cleared his throat. "It seems that one of our junior engineers has been grossly misusing company time. I caught her red-handed down in the vault helping herself to a little severance pay. I was just about to call you."

"Of course you were."

Through the gap of the teller door, Iris could see Randy gripping his gun. His footsteps fell softer than before as he made his way back to the open floor where Mr. Wheeler stood.

"You doubt my company loyalty, Charles. After all these years?"

"You've never been part of the company, Randy. We've tolerated you all these years out of respect for your father. That debt is now paid in full. You're finished."

"Like hell I am! The Halloran family still holds a majority share in the First Bank of Cleveland. Paid for in blood. Damn it!"

Iris had to move. This might be her only chance. On numb hands and knees, she crept out of the teller booth and began inching her way toward the back exit.

"Your stock's been bought up," Mr. Wheeler said flatly.

"What do you mean, bought? By who?"

"When the vault was compromised, the board had to exercise options, leverage its assets. You know how it goes."

"What the hell are you talking about?"

Iris was nearly at the rear exit when the door cracked opened. She scrambled into the last teller booth as a set of black orthopedic shoes stepped into the room.

"Our assets were too locked up, if you know what I mean," Mr. Wheeler said with a cold laugh. "Between the feds monitoring the gold market and our commitment to the privacy of our valued customers, we couldn't just drill open boxes. Not for at least ten years. We had to get out of commodities, Randy. Fortunately, we found an investor with a long-term holding strategy we could live with."

"Hello, Randy," said a voice in a thick Italian accent.

"Carmichael. What the hell are you doing here?"

"I own this place as of today. Me and the family have been investing in the old bank for years. How could we refuse? No taxes. No questions. We're getting gold for pennies on the dollar."

Iris peeked around the corner. It was the bartender from Ella's Pub who'd been so friendly to her. He was holding a large gun in his hand. It was pointed at Randy.

"What?" Randy laughed uncomfortably. His gun fell to the ground with a metal thunk. He took a step backward with his hands up. "Carmichael, I had no idea . . ."

"You know, I told Jim we should have taken care of you years ago, but he thought you might be useful. Who was right, huh?" The old man chuckled like an uncle. "Ah, I remember when you were just a chubby teenager lagging after your papa on the golf course. At least you had some manners back then. I think you had more brains back then."

"Carmichael, I . . . I meant no disrespect."

"Disrespect? Oh no. Certainly not."

"It's not what it looks like," Randy protested. "That girl. She stole the keys. She led that pig cop right in here."

"That was unfortunate," Carmichael said. Then a thunderclap shook the walls as he fired the gun into Randy's chest.

Iris recoiled and smothered a scream in her hands.

Randy's body hit the ground with a thump.

"You see, Randy, the brave detective stopped you in the middle of a robbery with his gun here, but not before you fired a fatal shot." Mr. Wheeler spoke from across the room as though he were at a board meeting.

Randy responded with a wet gurgling sound as he choked on his own blood.

Mr. Wheeler's footsteps came closer. "The City of Cleveland will finally recover some of those mismanaged funds the Halloran family hoarded all those years ago. Detective McDonnell will get a Medal of Honor for his tireless work to uncover the truth. He'll be a hero. So will our dear commissioner, Jim Stone, just in time for the election cycle. You see, Randy, it will all work out for the best."

Iris curled into a trembling ball as Randy released his last breath. The booth was shrinking around her. She couldn't breathe.

The leather clack of expensive shoes came closer, until it stopped just on the other side of the partition where she hid. "You got this under control?" Mr. Wheeler asked Carmichael.

"Not a problem. Bruno is on his way. We'll clean this up and make it right. Give us fifteen minutes before the sirens."

Iris clamped a hand over her mouth to keep from whimpering aloud. The sweet old man was going to shoot her next.

"Be sure to leave a few million on the cart. We'll sort the rest later. What are you going to do with her?" Mr. Wheeler tapped the wood partition next to Iris's head.

A small sob choked out of her throat.

"There's too much blood on the scene," Carmichael said. "We don't want anything to tarnish Detective McDonnell's act of heroism, do we? It will only lead to more questions. She'll disappear, okay? I make sure."

"Just be sure to finish the job. She's not as dumb as she looks," Mr. Wheeler said, then strode out of the room.

Less than a minute after the door slammed closed, the back entrance opened. Two sets of heavy shoes walked into the room. Iris squeezed her eyes shut and shrunk into a corner. They were there to drag her away.

"Bruno, we need to clean the scene. Get our thief here back down to the vault so our detective can shoot him," Carmichael instructed. "Ramone, did you get what I requested?"

A gravelly voice answered, "I got the bag, but I'm not sure what you want me to do with it."

"Do what you like with it." Carmichael paused and there was the sound of a back being patted. "Consider it payment for twenty years of service and you being my eyes and ears in this place."

"I didn't stay here for you," Ramone muttered.

"I know. You stayed here for my Maxie. This is for her too. It's for all the girls that brought those goddamned bankers down. Even Iris here. If she hadn't found that body, those bastards would have sold the building off to their friends at the county and found some way to cheat us out of what was owed. She kept 'em honest, and I always pay my debts."

Something hit the ground with a silvery clink.

"I'll see what I can do," Ramone said.

"You both need to disappear. For good. This warning will only come once. I'm sure you understand. Tell Iris I'm sorry, but I warned her not to disturb the ghosts."

Two minutes later, Ramone pushed Iris, dazed and stumbling, through the loading dock and out onto the sidewalk.

"We gotta move. Keep your head down, Iris."

Iris didn't look up for several blocks. Scenes from the last two hours flashed by with each seam in the concrete—Detective McDonnell's dead eyes, red candles, gold bricks, keys, prayers, jewels, the cracked photograph, the birth certificate, the sound of Randy's body hitting the ground.

Iris's field bag swung heavily from Ramone's shoulder. Back in the vault, she had filled it with cash and jewelry at gunpoint. It was all stolen from the safe deposit boxes. It was Carmichael's reward to them both. It was hush money.

Ramone stopped at Prospect Avenue and waited for the light. Iris looked back over her shoulder. Four blocks behind her, the abandoned First Bank of Cleveland loomed darkly in the sky. For a split second, Iris swore she could see a girl in a window looking back at her.

"Beatrice," Iris whispered.

"Come on." Ramone pulled her forward.

When Iris turned back, the girl was gone.

CHAPTER 76

Thursday, December 14, 1978

Beatrice pressed her face to the windowpane and gazed down at Euclid Avenue. The street below her was empty, except for the dull glow of the sodium lamps and the factory smog. The muted light barely reached the dark room where she stood. The last time she'd been in the personnel office, she'd been trapped in the file room while Bill had his way with Suzanne. Beatrice reluctantly walked over to Suzanne's desk and sat down with her heavy bag.

Beatrice pulled the baby picture out of the bag and studied it again in the faint light. She hadn't been able to leave it in the vault. Seeing her own blue eyes staring out from the photograph broke her heart all over again. On the back "Beatrice" was written in a scrawling hand. Under it was a note she could barely make out in the dark:

Hush-a-bye, don't you cry
Go to sleep my little baby
When you wake, you shall have
All the pretty little horses

A tear fell as Beatrice hummed the lullaby she'd known her whole life. Doris must have sung it to her before her memory had formed, before she had left Beatrice behind in Marietta. *All the pretty little horses,* she thought, looking down at the jewelry in her bag.

Her mind retraced the lines in Doris's ledger. Safe deposit boxes began disappearing the year she was born. Her birth certificate read, "Father: Unknown."

She could still feel Bill's fingernails scraping her palm as he greedily snatched the key. *What a bastard.* He might have been one of the men who had beaten Max. Her throat tightened as she thought of her friend down in the tunnel, bleeding. She picked up the phone and dialed.

"Nine-one-one. What's your emergency?" a faraway voice asked.

Beatrice hung up the phone. Max had told her not to call anyone. Beatrice stared at the receiver. One of the buttons on Suzanne's call director had a word scrawled under a piece of tape. "Home." She touched it sadly. It was too late to call, but she picked up the receiver anyway.

"Hello?"

"Hi. Is this Suzanne?" Beatrice whispered into the phone.

"This is."

"I'm sorry to call so late, but . . ." There were so many things she needed to know. "Did you once know a clerk at the bank named Doris Davis?"

"Who is this?"

"Me? I'm . . . Beatrice." It was too late to lie. "I work up on the ninth floor, and think I found something of hers. Someone thought . . . you might know her."

"God, I haven't heard from Doris in years. At least ten. She was up in Auditing when I started. Nice enough gal, I guess, but she got into some trouble."

"Trouble?" Beatrice's voice cracked.

"I don't like to gossip, but the way I heard it, she was in the family way and got herself fired. It happens all the time. These poor girls fall for the wrong sort of man and then don't have a soul to turn to. So what did you find, hon?"

"Oh, just an old file. Probably nothing."

Doris had been fired. She'd dumped Beatrice in Marietta and started robbing the vault. Or maybe it was the other way around. Either way, she had stashed all of the stolen jewelry in Box 256 and registered the box in her daughter's name. *Was she saving the money for me, or was she just covering her tracks?*

Beatrice cleared her throat. "The department's been auditing the safe deposit boxes. I understand you have one."

"Me? No."

"That's strange. It says here there's one in your name. You might want to look into it. Have a good evening." Beatrice hung up, pulse racing.

She hadn't meant to call or give Suzanne her name, but she needed to talk to someone. Everything had gone wrong, and she didn't know what to do anymore. She reached into her pocket and pulled out Doris's key. The number 547 gleamed in the dim yellow light from the window. Maybe there were reasons Doris did what she did, but Beatrice didn't care. It didn't make it right. She'd abandoned her in Marietta to Ilene and all of the terrible things that had happened there.

Beatrice Baker should never have been born. She slammed the key down and stormed into the file room, snapping on the light. She pulled open the drawer with her personnel file and ripped it out. Her picture, her application, her pay stubs—she stuffed them all into her bag next to the cash and jewelry. She pulled out her shorthand notes describing Jim and Teddy's conversations and her notes on the missing safe deposits and stuffed them into the file drawer, happy to be rid of them. Maybe someone else would make sense of it. She could only hope Tony would find them.

She turned back to Suzanne's desk and slumped down in the chair again. Suzanne and God knows how many other poor women were still tangled up with Bill. Suzanne had a right to know the truth.

Beatrice rifled through her bag. She set Max's last ring of keys aside and searched through the jewelry until she found the right thing. She opened the center drawer of Suzanne's desk and placed a bracelet inside, then frowned. Suzanne wouldn't know what to make of the diamonds. She might even think Bill had left the bracelet there as another gift. Doris's key was still sitting on the desktop. Beatrice picked it up and set it in the drawer next to the bracelet. Between the key and the phone call, it might be enough for Suzanne to start asking questions.

The clock on the wall ticked loudly. Beatrice still had work to do. If she wanted to stop Bill and the bank for good, she had to get to the files and find out where Teddy's encrypted records were kept.

She was just sliding Suzanne's drawer closed when voices came echoing down the hall. Beatrice sucked in a breath. They were approaching fast as she ran to Linda's corner office. The department door flung open.

"I cannot fucking believe you let her get away," a man's voice boomed.

It was Randy Halloran. Beatrice scurried around the desk in the dark and into the washroom. She eased the bathroom door shut.

"What makes you think she'll be in here?" The other voice was Bill's.

"The phone bank lit up on this floor, and look. Someone's been in the filing room. Get your fat ass in there and see if anything's missing."

"That's enough, Randy. I'm still your superior."

"All evidence to the contrary, Bill. Don't you realize what's happening here? The bank is finished! There is no Auditing Department anymore! Now move!"

Beatrice backed up farther. She bumped into something sharp, and stifled a grunt.

"Jesus! Are you out of your mind?"

"Out of my mind? Out of my mind! Yes, a little bit," Randy barked. "The city's going to default in less than an hour, the feds are launching a raid, and you've managed to lose all the fucking keys to the vault. If we don't come up with something quick, we're both going to end up fish food. Now check the fucking files!"

Feeling along the wall, she found the metal point she'd backed into was a corner of the vent grille. It was sticking out of the wall. The smell of fresh air drew her closer, and she realized the large grate was loose. Max had said something about an air shaft, Beatrice realized, as she reached out and pulled on the edge.

"There are hundreds of files, Randy. Nothing seems out of place in here. Besides, Bethany gave me the master key."

"What?"

Beatrice wiggled the grate gently. It inched away from the wall with a faint squeak that made her wince, but she kept willing it open, until it clanked softly against the toilet.

"She said she got it from you," Bill said accusingly.

"Bethany? I don't know anyone named Bethany, and I certainly didn't give her a fucking key. Give me that thing!"

"You know that little blond that works for you? She said you gave it to her."

The door to Linda's office slammed open, shaking the wall.

"And you believed her? What are you, some sort of idiot? The key's worthless. There isn't a mark on it. It probably just opens her gym locker or her goddamn diary."

A metallic clink rang out as a key hit the door to the bathroom where she was hiding. Beatrice let out a tiny gasp, then reached into the air shaft. Feeling blindly, she inched her body into the darkness until she grasped a cold steel rung. She pulled herself onto a ladder, carefully balancing her heavy bag on her arm. Then it struck her. She'd left the ring of keys on Suzanne's desk right where the two men were arguing. Her heart dropped. She almost crawled back into the bathroom. Another office door slammed open. Then another.

"Now that's enough," Bill said, clearly shaken. "I'm sure that girl is in here somewhere."

His voice grew louder. Reaching out from the ladder with a shaking hand, Beatrice pulled the grate closed. The door to the bathroom burst open, and the air shaft flooded with light. Beatrice shrank into a shadow.

"Well, where is she?" Randy demanded, ripping back the shower curtain.

"Don't worry. She couldn't have gone far. We'll find her." Bill picked the blank key up off the ground where it had landed and studied it again.

"We'll find her? What if we don't, huh?" Randy yelled, and whacked Bill hard across the face. The unexpected blow knocked Bill to his knees. "Who's going to find us? I saw Carmichael Covelli waltz in here an hour ago. We're fucked, Bill!"

"Hey, goddammit!" Bill bellowed into the floor. "I thought we had a deal."

"Yeah, it was a nice little scam while it lasted, Bill. But everyone knows you've been talking to the feds. Who you gonna sell out? Huh? Not me!" Randy kicked him in the ribs. "I'm not letting you drag me down with you. Fifteen percent isn't fucking worth it!"

Bill lunged at Randy, knocking him into the sink with a growl. "Everybody's looking to cut a deal, Randy. I've had it with your fucking blackmail and your bullshit! You fucking parasite!"

"I'm the parasite?" Randy shouted, pushing Bill off of him. He punched Bill squarely in the gut and hit the back of his neck as the older man doubled over. On his way to the ground, Bill knocked his head against the toilet with a loud clank and then fell limply to the floor.

Beatrice gaped at Bill's motionless body lying not four feet from where she hid in the air shaft. Blood was pooling onto the marble tiles.

Randy nudged the body with his foot and muttered, "Fuck."

He stood next to Bill's still body for twenty heartbeats, occasionally rubbing his face with his hand. Finally, he turned on his heel and left the room, slamming the door behind him.

The bang of it vibrated in the air shaft, and Beatrice scrambled up the ladder away from the sight of Bill on the ground. The sound of the door crashing back open made her foot slip. The rusted steel scraped her palm as she caught herself with a gasp.

"Sorry this couldn't have ended better, old friend," Randy grunted five feet below her, and there was a faint dragging sound. "Don't worry. They'll all understand. Investments go bad. Deals go bad. Sometimes there just isn't any other way out."

Beatrice covered her mouth and willed herself to not imagine what was happening below her as labored breathing and scraping sounds filtered up to where her feet teetered on a thin steel rail.

"Hang in there, okay?" Randy chuckled uneasily. "It's all going to work out now. You'll see. I'll find a way to get our investment back . . . and then some."

The rattling sound of a ring of keys being waved in the air dragged Beatrice's eyes back down to the square of light below her. Randy had found the key ring.

A second later, the light under her feet went out. Then silence. Beatrice let out a tiny wail and hugged the ladder in the blackness of the air shaft. Her arms trembled against the cold steel as she fought the urge to just let go.

She didn't want to feel anything or hear anything or know anything anymore. There was nothing below her but dead black. Outside the building she had no name, no home, no mother, no father, no life. The heavy bag dug into her shoulder as the weight of it pulled her downward. Randy had found the keys. She'd failed. She'd failed Max and Doris and herself. Her fingers began to slip.

Beatrice clamped her arm around the ladder rung and squeezed her eyes shut. She pictured Randy with the keys, heading into the vault. *No.* She couldn't let him get away with it. She couldn't let the money men have the keys to everything. There was still time.

Slowly, she climbed back down the ladder, balancing everything Doris had taken from the vault on her shoulder. A burr in the steel dug into her palm, and she jerked her hand away. The sudden movement sent her careening to one side of the ladder, with the heavy bag swinging from her arm. In an instant, it dropped to her wrist, and her feet slipped from the rail.

She cried out, dangling from one hand. The bag fell away from her arm as she reached for the ladder. It plummeted four stories, sending a shock wave through the air shaft, and landed with a faint crash far below her.

"What the hell was that?" a distant voice demanded.

Beatrice found her footing and bit her lip to keep from making another sound. A flashlight slashed through the air shaft twenty feet above her.

"It was probably just the wind. We shouldn't even be in here, Cunningham. We don't have the proper warrants."

Beatrice steadied herself on the ladder and stared up at the beam of the flashlight. *Cunningham?*

"I know she's still here," Ms. Cunningham protested. It was her supervisor talking.

"Let CPD worry about it. The bureau doesn't care about some secretary. We need to focus on the investigation."

"What investigation? My star witness is comatose in a hospital bed," Cunningham yelled. She was talking about Doris. Beatrice had overheard conversations about the feds having someone embedded at the bank just that evening. *Ms. Cunningham was the mole?* Beatrice tightened her grip on the ladder.

"What about Bill? I doubt he'll last the night if we don't find him."

He's dead, Beatrice wanted to scream, but she couldn't find her voice.

The probing flashlight clicked off. "I made a promise to Doris that I'd look out for her daughter. From the moment Beatrice walked into that office, I was responsible. That woman risked her life talking to me, and I owe her that."

"You couldn't help what happened."

"That girl doesn't have a chance. CPD will detain her indefinitely, or worse."

"Could we do much better? She's a goddamn juvenile. Our hands are tied."

"The police are compromised. She needs a safe house," Cunningham bellowed.

"Sure. Are you going to take her in? They'll have your ass, and you know it. If she's smart, she'll just disappear."

The voices trailed off.

Tears ran down Beatrice's face in the dark. Doris had turned herself in to the feds. She'd tried to come clean and make things right. She hadn't just sent her to the wolves when she'd suggested Beatrice go work at the bank. Doris had sent her to Ms. Cunningham. She had tried to keep her safe. Her mother wanted her safe. The thought made her hug the metal rail and cry.

She had to get out of there. As her swollen eyes adjusted to the dark, she realized she was still next to the room where Bill had died. She could just make out the bathroom floor in the dim light filtering through the far window. There was no sign of his body but a dark trail of blood on the floor tiles. Blinking the tears away, she noticed something small on the ground not far from the vent grate. It was a key. It had no markings on its face, but she knew what it was.

The key belonged there, laying in a dark pool of blood. No one would know what it could do. No one would even notice it lying on the floor. If anything, it would become police evidence. It was safe.

Somewhere in the building the bankers were scrambling to find the keys and cover their tracks, but it wouldn't be enough. Ms. Cunningham and the feds were putting a case together. The police would come and raid the vault. Tony would find the records of the robberies in Box 547. He would find the gold. The bankers would be brought to justice. It would be all right, she told herself. It had to be.

Beatrice peered down into the darkness below her. The ladder must lead all the way to the lower level and the tunnels. It was how Max had escaped. Beatrice said a silent prayer that her friend was still down there waiting for her. All of the jewels Doris had stolen were down there too. She had saved it all for Beatrice. Doris had done monstrous things, but maybe she had tried to make it right. Maybe her mother had loved her. Maybe.

As she craned her neck up toward the open louver high overhead, she could just barely see a glimmer of light.

EPILOGUE

Ramone pushed Iris through the door of the Greyhound station. It was a haze of stale smoke and day-old coffee. Stained yellow ceiling tiles hung overhead. Plastic benches with torn vinyl cushions lined the walls opposite the front desk. Nothing had been updated in the station since the 1970s. It was like stepping back into one of the abandoned rooms of the bank. The cracked linoleum shifted under her feet. Iris staggered to one of the benches and sat down.

Ramone lit a cigarette and studied the schedule posted on the board above the cashier. Names of cities and departure times jumbled together on the wall.

Cincinnati 6:00 p.m.
Charleston 6:30 p.m.
Chicago 8:00 p.m.

They would be on their way to some random place in mere minutes. A lump swelled in her throat. What about her car? Her clothes? Her apartment? The grim look in Ramone's eye told her everything she didn't want to know. It was gone. All of it.

Her purse was sitting in an abandoned police cruiser in the alley behind a hotel. A police officer was dead. Her apartment would be swarming with cops within the next few hours, unless Carmichael and Bruno stepped in. Either way, she was now a missing person. Carmichael hadn't minced words. They had to disappear.

"So, where you think you're headed?" Ramone offered her a filterless cigarette from his crinkled pack. He wasn't coming with her.

She took the smoke with shaking fingers. He lit a paper match, and she sucked the flame through the tobacco until it burned all the way down her throat. She wished it hurt more. At least pain made sense.

He set the heavy duffel bag down on the seat next to her. It jingled like a sack of quarters, but it wasn't. Iris's eyes flew up to the clerk behind the desk reading a magazine. The woman didn't blink at the sound.

Iris took another long drag and picked at the scratches on her knee. Her pant leg was ripped. Her shirt was covered in soot and tiny dark spots. Blood. It was Detective McDonnell's blood. She could barely hear Ramone talking as blood stared back at her.

"Charleston's nice this time a year."

Iris forced a weak smile. "Where will you go?"

"It don't matter. Nobody's gonna look for me."

"What about this?" Iris motioned to the bag.

"That's gonna be in Charleston or someplace with you."

"Don't you want it?" She figured all of the jewels and cash Randy stole from the deposit boxes were worth a fortune.

"I'll be fine. I've grabbed a few things here or there. I ain't gonna be poor." He winked at her. "Besides, from what I seen of rich people, it don't pay to be one of 'em. Too much money ain't good for you."

Iris nodded. "I can't take it."

"The hell you can't. You gonna need to get set up somewhere. That takes money."

"But none of this belongs to me. It's . . . stealing," she whispered with her eye on the clerk.

"Stealing from who? Do you really think anyone is ever going to be able to sort it out now?"

"But shouldn't we turn all of this over to the authorities?" It was what the detective would want, she thought, eyeing the blood. He would want justice.

"And who do you think those authorities are exactly? Did it ever occur to you that the people who stashed all that gold are the same people sitting at city hall right now? Do you really think they are gonna let you walk into a police station, talkin' about what you've seen? Gonna let you testify?" Ramone looked at her dead in the eye, and she knew he was right.

The detective would want her to live, she told herself. Then he shouldn't have dragged her into the vault, she argued back, but that wasn't fair. She was the one who had gone looking for something in that bank. She had stolen keys. She had disturbed the ghosts. She had found the body. What had she really hoped to find? she wondered. It wasn't money. She didn't want Randy's blood money. It was something else. Tears welled up in her eyes. The girl she'd seen peering out a window of the bank tower might still be trapped inside somewhere. Beatrice.

Beatrice had opened safe deposit boxes and left behind keys and odd clues, cryptic notes and candles. Not just candles. Prayers. Maybe she had felt guilty too. Iris looked down at the torn seat next to hers and tried to imagine how it had looked twenty years earlier when it was new. Beatrice might have sat on that very bench. If she'd made it out of the building alive at all.

"What happened to Beatrice, Ramone? Did she manage to get out?"

"We're runnin' out of time, Iris." He motioned to the clock over the clerk's head.

"Tell me. I need to know."

"Why you chasin' ghosts? Haven't you had enough of this?"

"Please. I need to know she's okay." Iris wiped a stray tear from her cheek.

"Why?" He glared at her, then gave up. "Truth is, I don't know. Nobody kicked up much fuss when she went missing, except me and Max's brother, Tony. Guess he thought if he found Beatrice, he'd find Max. We checked all the places we could figure and then some. The detective even sat up in Lakeview Cemetery every day for a month."

"Cemetery? But if Beatrice was dead, shouldn't he have been checking the . . . ?" Iris's voice trailed off before she uttered the word "morgue."

Ramone nodded, catching her meaning. "We checked there too. No, the cemetery was a long shot, but Tony seemed to think the girls would show up there. I think he still checks there from time to time . . . At least, he did."

"Why?"

"Someone they knew died a few weeks after the bank shut down. Family or something. It didn't pan out."

"They never came?"

"Tony said he might've seen one of 'em hiding in the woods during the funeral. Chased after 'em for a while. I thought he might've lost his mind. He was really on the edge back then. Every girl on the street looked like Max." Ramone paused, staring off into space. "I like to think he was right, though."

Iris realized the photograph of the detective's sister was probably still tucked in the corner of Ramone's picture frame. "Did you ever find out what happened to her? To Max? Is she . . . dead?"

"I thought so for a long time. Some days I even wished she was, runnin' out on me like that. But then a couple years back I got this thing in the mail. No note, no return address, just this. The postmark was Mexico City." Ramone pulled a small photograph out of his wallet. It was a picture of a teenage girl with brown skin and blue eyes.

"Who's that?"

"Never met her. But I know that smile."

He stared at it for a few moments before tucking the photo away and standing up. Iris let him pull her to her feet.

"I gotta go, Iris. You do too. You got your whole life to figure this shit out. Take care of yourself."

He was really going to just leave her there. She bit her lip to keep from crying. "You too."

He patted her shoulder, then headed toward the door.

"Hey, Ramone?"

He turned to look at her.

"Who was it? The one buried in the cemetery."

"Don't go lookin', Iris. That way's a dead end."

"I won't. I just . . . need to know."

He hesitated for a few moments, but finally just shook his head. "Doris . . . Doris Davis."

Ten minutes later, Iris was chewing her fingernail at the back of a bus behind the station. The Greyhound to Charleston sat idling with its doors open as passengers trickled on board. Iris watched the cars go by out the open door, her entire life flashing by with the traffic. It was all over.

Ramone was gone. Ellie, Nick, Brad—she'd never see them again. Her mother would get a phone call that day or the next. *Have you heard from your daughter? Your daughter is missing. Contact so-and-so the minute you hear anything.* The poor woman would have a stroke. She would go running to her father. *Iris is gone! What should we do?* As if the man had the answers. For some reason, both Iris and her mother had always assumed that he did. He wouldn't say a word, and for the first time Iris wouldn't blame him. What could he possibly say or do about any of it? He would just sit in his brown leather chair and be a sad, old man who had lost his only daughter. It wouldn't matter if she had been a success-ful engineer or not. She was gone. Iris stifled a sob. She had lost him too. She'd lost everything.

The bus wouldn't leave for five more minutes. She stepped off with her bag and lit a cigarette. Iris Latch was dead. Maybe she'd wanted to die. She'd been bored, aimless . . . miserable. Maybe that's why she went looking for ghosts in the old bank. Beatrice was forever trapped somewhere in the building, and now so was Iris.

"Fuck it," she whispered. She had to know if Beatrice escaped.

She hoisted the bag on her shoulder and walked away from the bus. Ramone would say she'd gone crazy. He was probably right.

Iris left the taxi at Euclid and East 123rd Street and followed the entrance drive into Lakeview Cemetery. It was a labyrinth of statues, mausoleums, and winding roads that went on for several square miles.

She followed the main road deep into the graveyard. A statue of a warrior woman on horseback brandished her sword over the trail as Iris passed underneath it. It was oddly fitting to be there, walking alone among the dead. Her eyes circled the carved angels and praying mothers streaked with soot and acid rain.

Most of the crypts and obelisks were nearly a century old, but Iris could tell where the newer plots were laid out. The graves dug in the last twenty years were easy to spot. Soaring monuments had shrunk down over the years to tiny slabs laid flat on the ground.

Iris walked along the narrow paths between the grave markers, looking for the right date. The bank closed in December 1978. If Doris died a few weeks later, it would have been 1979. There were no cars trolling or buildings looming or eyes watching as Iris walked through the soft grass. The warm sun filtered through the trees, and for the first time in days she could breathe. The tension in her back and shoulders began to melt. Somehow, despite everything that had happened, the world hadn't ended. The sun on her shoulders reassured her that life would go on with or without her, regardless of the heavy bag in her hand.

Beatrice wouldn't be at the cemetery that day, she told herself. The grave was twenty years old. But Iris kept walking. There were so many questions she needed to ask that only Beatrice could answer. *Where did you go? What did you do? Did you ever find Max? Did you escape with a stolen fortune? Did you try to give it back? Did the ghosts of the bank ever stop haunting you? Will they ever stop haunting me?*

The dates on the graves had reached 1979. Iris slowed her pace and began reading each name. As she walked, Iris felt more and more foolish. Even if Beatrice were there to answer her questions, would it even matter? The answers wouldn't bring back Detective McDonnell, or overthrow corrupt governments, or return stolen treasures to their rightful owners. Finding Beatrice wouldn't really solve anything.

Turning down another row, Iris stopped dead. Something small and red sat between the blades of grass under a large oak tree. Her heart leapt in her chest. Iris dropped the bag and ran over to it.

A red votive candle sat on top of a granite slab. Iris snatched it from the stone. The engraving beneath was marred with several layers of melted wax, but Iris could make out the words "Doris Estelle Davis, 1934–1979."

Turning the candle over and over in her trembling hands, Iris could tell by its bruised surface it had been out in the rain and sun for weeks. Maybe longer. But it was there. Tears spilled down her face. Beatrice had been there. She'd found a way out. Iris fell to her knees. Beatrice was okay. Maybe she would be too.

On the bottom of the candle, a faded label read:

Guide and protect us, O Lord, from our setting out until our journey's end. Guide us to our heavenly home.

ACKNOWLEDGMENTS

The Dead Key might have gotten lost among the thousands of books written each year if it weren't for the 2014 Amazon Breakthrough Novel Award. Thank you to Amazon for giving an unpublished author a chance. Thank you to everyone that took the time to review the novel and vote for it during the contest. Thank you to all of the other contestants for having the audacity to dream big and enter.

I did not magically transform from a structural engineer into an author overnight. Many wonderful people supported me through the trials and errors of this five-year journey. The fabulous ladies of my book club bravely read and critiqued the second draft of *The Dead Key*. My mother, mother-in-law, sisters, and best friends read drafts and encouraged me to keep writing. Cara Kissling made the first attempt to edit the manuscript and help me find my way. Adam Katz provided a thorough and insightful critique that put my writing and the book on the right path. Doris Michaels provided sage advice and guidance. My editors at Thomas

& Mercer, especially Andrea Hurst, shined a light into every dimly lit corner of my novel and helped bring the fuzzy edges into focus.

The Dead Key would not have been possible without my family. My two little boys gave me the courage to quit my day job. They played together as nicely as two brothers could manage while Mommy holed up in her office, writing. My amazing husband read every draft, every edit, every stinking word I wrote and somehow remained my biggest fan. There are no words to express my gratitude.

ABOUT THE AUTHOR

D. M. Pulley's first novel, *The Dead Key*, was inspired by her work as a structural engineer in Cleveland, Ohio. During a survey of an abandoned building, she discovered a basement vault full of unclaimed safe deposit boxes. The mystery behind the vault haunted her for years, until she put down her calculator and started writing. *The Dead Key* was the 2014 Amazon Breakthrough Novel Award grand prize winner. Pulley continues to work as a private consultant and forensic engineer, investigating building failures and designing renovations. She lives in northeast Ohio with her husband and two children, and she is currently at work on her second novel. Visit her website at www.dmpulley.com.